BARONS OF DECAY

ROYALS OF FORSYTH U

ANGEL LAWSON

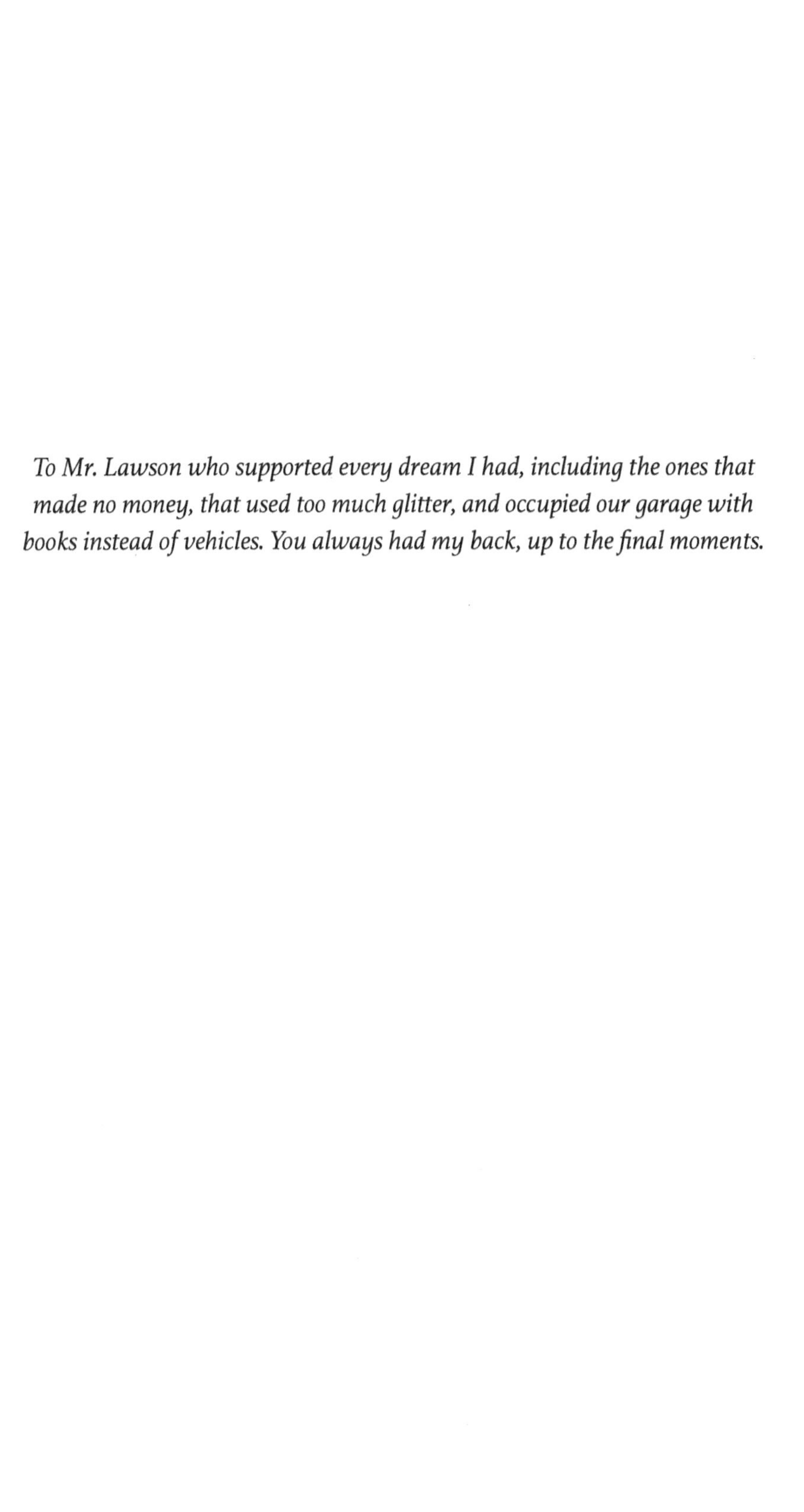

To Mr. Lawson who supported every dream I had, including the ones that made no money, that used too much glitter, and occupied our garage with books instead of vehicles. You always had my back, up to the final moments.

FOREWORD

Monarchs,

This book marks a turning point for me. I've written many books, dozens, but this is the first Forsyth novel I've written on my own.

While I can't speak on the past, I want to be clear about the present: I've poured my heart into *The Barons of Decay*. It's a little different, naturally, but I've done everything I can to preserve the spirit, dark depravity, and twisted beauty of Forsyth that so many of us love.

Outside of my family, getting this story written has been my top priority this year. Every word was chosen carefully, every chapter built to honor the world and characters you've come to know, while also pushing deeper into the shadows.

I also want to take a moment to thank the multiple sensitivity readers who helped me shape Arianette's voice with the thoughtfulness and care she deserves. It was incredibly important to me that her character be written with authenticity, depth, and respect, and their feedback helped make her the strongest, most fully realized version of herself. I love her as an addition to our epic royal heroines, and I hope you do too.

Thank you for sticking with me. I hope this installment brings you back into the underbelly of Forsyth in the best, most deliciously haunting way.

Memento Mori,

Angel

Content Warning:

This is the standard reminder that if you're new to this series, stumbled on it from a TikTok post or Facebook ad, you'll need to turn around and start at the beginning with Lords of Pain. Please read all the content warnings and make sure this is the path you want to go down.

Barons of Decay Contains the following:

• Arranged/Contractual Marriage
  • Age Gap
  • Bloodletting
  • Fertility manipulation/forced contraception
  • Dub/Non-con
  • Physical Abuse/Punishment
  • Captivity
  • Occult practices, ritualistic violence, and dark spiritual themes
  • #237

There is an animal in this book, No Harm Shall come to him! Although he's amazing, he does get into a little trouble. I promise you as a mother to two dogs and a cat, plus the grandmom to two cats and a dog, I value all our creatures, even when they eat my third set of AirPods.

FORSYTH universe
LORDS
ΛΔZ
DUKES
ΔΚΣ
PRINCES
ΨΝΖ
BARONS
ΒΡΝ
COUNTS
ΚΝΤ
LORDS
OF PAIN
ANGEL LAWSON
SAMANTHA RUE
DUKES
OF RUIN
ANGEL LAWSON
SAMANTHA RUE
PRINCES
OF CHAOS
ANGEL LAWSON
SAMANTHA RUE
BARONS
OF DECAY
ANGEL LAWSON
LORDS
OF WRATH
ANGEL LAWSON
SAMANTHA RUE
DUKES
OF MADNESS
ANGEL LAWSON
SAMANTHA RUE
PRINCES
OF ASH
ANGEL LAWSON
SAMANTHA RUE
F
11
F
13
F
14
LORDS
OF MERCY
ANGEL LAWSON
SAMANTHA RUE
DUKES
OF PERIL
ANGEL LAWSON
SAMANTHA RUE
PRINCES
OF LEGACY
ANGEL LAWSON
SAMANTHA RUE
F
12
F
15

PREFACE

Barons of Decay

The events in Barons of Decay go back several months in the Forsyth timeline to the period before the end of Princes of Legacy. A few points that happen before this primary part of the book begins. With that in consideration, please note that some minor things in any of the bonus works do not always align with the overall canon of the books. Timeline math is hard, yo.

- Killian, Dimitri, Tristian, Sy, Lex, & Whitaker graduated from Forsyth U the prior spring.
- Story, Nick, Remy, Lavinia, Verity and Pace have not graduated.
- Rufus Ashby is dead.
- Verity has Justice James in early October
- Story is not pregnant.
- The Barons traditions begin in the fall with a new semester.
- The events in Baroness of Dusk take place the following year, but feel free to go back and refresh yourself with that bonus content: HERE

PROLOGUE

 rianette

September

They say I was dead for three minutes.

Three whole minutes where my heart forgot me.

Where I drifted, weightless, under the water, lungs full of ghosts and river rot.

When I started to decay.

I remember none of it, not the cold or the pull of the river or the boys when they found me washed up against the stones like a bloated bride.

But my skin remembers. My wrists do too. The raw bite of the ropes, the way they burned when I twisted and screamed inside my head, waiting for the rules to change. I don't break rules. Not that one. Never that one.

But someone did.

There's a man. Or a shape. Or a mask.

A *beast.*

Sometimes it looks like an animal, only wrong. Bigger. Wetter. Hungrier.

Other times, it's faceless–just breath and commands and hands that don't feel human.

I hear it in dreams I can't wake from.

I hear him now, whispering from the fluorescent buzz of the hospital lights overhead.

'Chosen,' he says. '*You were already chosen.*'

They ask me questions. A woman with soft hands and a man who doesn't know how to hide his rage. They say he's with the Bureau. I don't know them. I don't trust them. I want to.

I just want someone to be real.

My feet ache from the run. The forest shredded me. My body, my memory, my name. I pick at the scab on my knee until I see red.

They stop me.

They call me *Arianette*. Like it's a spell. Like if they say it enough, I'll return to myself. But I don't know who *Arianette* is anymore. She drowned. She bled. She saw too much. She heard the rules–and obeyed. But that didn't stop the Beast from finding me. Catching me. Hurting me...

So I nod and I shake and I say what I must. I give them nothing, because if I speak, I'll start to remember. And if I remember, he'll come back.

He always does.

Even now, I smell the iron. The salt.

I feel the dirt closing in around me.

And I wonder if I ever really made it out.

1

rianette

October

One, two, three, four.
One, two, three, four.
Tendu
Plié
Arabesque
Sauté
"Ow!" The ottoman flips over, clattering on the stone floor. I grab my toes, hopping on one foot. "Fuck!"

That hurt.

Dropping to the floor, I cross one leg over the other. Wiggling each toe, I inspect the damage. After the last few weeks of my life I've learned my body is tougher than I thought, but breaking my toes? That's something I'm not sure I'd survive.

I can't sleep. Not since I came here. Not for long at least. It's too loud. The sound of the other girls is a faint hum, etched on the inside of my skull. The *crying*. The whispering. The hurt.

The beast.

Instead, I push the heavy pieces of furniture out of the way and create a little space. If I keep moving, I won't fall asleep. If I keep moving, no one can hurt me. If I dance, the noises in my head, in my heart, will fall still.

Awake, I barely remember what happened out in the woods, even less what happened before. The doctor in the hospital said he thought I'd been drugged. Maybe.

Or maybe that's just how my brain works.

The only thing that's ever locked firmly in my mind is what I learned in dance class and *the rules*. My uncle had a fondness for them, even pinning them to the Manor wall so no one could forget. But the rules don't seem to matter here. Not in this cold, barren place. Or if they do, they're a different set of rules I haven't been told.

I think I'm just waiting.

Satisfied my toes are still in one piece, I look up, catching myself in the huge floor-to-ceiling mirror propped against the wall. My hair is down now, no longer twisted into the tight, organized braids I used to wear. Instead, it spills loose, dark strands brushing over the slope of my clavicle.

I twist, checking to see if the bruises I woke up with in the hospital have faded. They're ghosting along my ribs, still visible under my brown skin. They bloom like violets across warm-toned skin. The scars at my wrists are raised, ridged, stubborn. I lift my hair and find the healing mark behind my ear, the skin there slightly lighter, tight with new memory. Every mark tells a truth, even the ones I can't remember. They don't vanish–only settle deeper, like stories etched beneath the surface.

Shadows.

That's what the Baron King's loyal followers are called, Shadows.

Is that what I am now too?

I don't think so. I'm destined to be a bride. A king's bride. The Black Wedding must be soon, although I've lost track of days. There are no windows in this room. Even at the Manor daylight streamed in. We had time outside–mandatory. No one likes a sickly child. Here, the heavy, wooden door only opens when one of the men brings me a meal. They're cloaked in darkness too. Silent, only their eyes and foreheads visible, the bottom half of their face obscured. I know they are one of the shadows, a Beta Rho. They leave the food on the end of the bed, taking the prior tray, eaten or not, and then leave, as silent as they came.

The only person I've seen, or spoken to, since arriving is the doctor from the hospital, Dr. Stallworth. He comes in to check on my injuries. To make sure I'm healing. He's nice, but men often pretend to be. Right before they take.

The rest of the room is similarly utilitarian. The bathroom is spare, with basic toiletries. Nothing sharp. Nothing poisonous.

They know better.

The unused bed is small, but not uncomfortable–which is why I stay clear. An armchair with carved arms and legs, the match to the ottoman, sits in the corner. A closet, securely locked. The walls are bare other than one shelf filled with books. I pulled one out and the spine cracked, the brittle, musty pages turning to dust.

I stand, flexing my toes, straightening my spine.

This isn't a place of life.

It's nothing more than a chamber of death.

~

Tendu

   Plié

   Arabesque

   Sauté

   Tap, tap, tap.

I stare at the door. No one has ever knocked before. Normally, there's just the sound of the metal key, scraping against the lock.

I blink, unsure if I made it up. That happens sometimes.

Another knock follows, louder this time. Knuckles rapping against the wood.

"Hello?" I call out, my voice cracking, dry from disuse.

"Arianette," I hear, the voice muffled but distinct. Female. "May I come in?"

I look around, wondering if I'm being watched. If this is a test. Heart pounding, I step to the door and press my ear to the wood.

"Who..." I swallow, trying to make my voice stronger. "Who is this?"

"Regina. The Baroness."

The Baroness.

"Oh." Butterflies come alive in my gut. "Yes. Please."

When the door swings open, she's not alone, one of the shadows holds the key, but I'm not interested in him. I'm focused on the woman; her straight spine, full lips, and painted eyes. Her dress is black. Sheer. The sleeves drape gently over her shoulders, like spiderwebs. The neckline plunges, exposing the soft curve of her breasts.

She's gorgeous. Elegant. *Royal.*

"You can leave," she tells the man, taking the key from him and sliding it into her pocket. He nods, her directive unchallenged. She shuts the door behind her, then appraises me. "How are you feeling?"

Well, that... that is a loaded question.

Are my bones broken? No. My bruises are healing. The wounds are no longer infected. But the nightmares, the day-mares. They seep in at the edges–a cacophony of voices. Some here. Some there. Some buried deep inside my chest. The home. *The beast.* The sensation of mud between my toes.

I give the answer I've learned is the only one people want. "I'm fine."

Her dark eyes sweep over the room, at the pushed-aside furniture. Instantly, I'm jealous of her smooth, ebony skin. There are no scars around her wrists. No bruises refusing to fade. "It feels like ages since I was in this room."

"You've been here?" I ask, trying to imagine her on the little bed. In the stark bathroom. How could someone so beautiful, so gorgeous, come from this dull place?

She nods. "Before the Hunt."

"The Hunt?" I repeat, the words drawing out a flicker of a memory. Forsyth is filled with ceremonies, and there is nothing rich people love to talk about more at parties than the royals and their traditions. I've never been a part of one. Never seen the spectacle, but on the nights I danced for these people I heard things, the retellings, the awe. "You mean the Barons' Hunt."

"I mean, the *Baroness* Hunt." She runs her hand over the wooden finial on the corner of the bed. A gold ring with an onyx stone glints on her finger. "I had the barons give you my room. For luck."

"But," I start, trying to organize my words. My understanding, which, frankly, is limited. "I'm arranged to marry the King. My uncle set it up. We'll have the wedding. I'll be his wife. I can't also be Baroness."

Regina cuts her eyes at me. "You can, and *will,* be anything the King wants you to be."

"What are you saying?" I ask, but the room has become muted, my heartbeat thudding heavily in my ears. I've been hunted before. Wasn't once enough?

"The King is prepared for you to fill both roles. That of his wife and the Baroness to his men. First, you have to prove your worth and that happens in the hunt."

"Will there be other girls?"

"No," she says, lips curved down in a frown. "Not this year."

She crosses the room and stands before the closet door, taking out a flat metal key and unlocking it. Inside, a single outfit hangs. Regina leans in and pulls out the hanger, turning to show me a dress with narrow straps that cross over the shoulder. "This was also mine." Her fingers run down the fabric, pausing on a tear. "You're to put it on and wait. At midnight you'll be taken from the crypt to the starting point."

My mind spins. Whirling fast, like a pirouette.

After placing the dress on the bed, she turns to me and takes my face in her hands, thumbs smoothing down my cheeks. "Despite contracts and deals inked in blood, you have to prove yourself, Arianette. In years past, there have been four others. One for each point in the star. North, south, east, west, and the undeclared. This year, there is only you, which means the hunt will be vicious. The Hunters will be more ruthless. You aren't just proving that you're worthy to be Baroness but to be the King's Bride." Her long, lacquered nails drag along my skin. "You've survived one hunt. You can do it again."

"How?" I ask. "How did you do it?"

"In the past, you needed to last the longest, beat out the other girls. This time, it is you and only you. Time is your only weapon. Keep quiet. Hide when you can, for as *long* as you can. The hunt only lasts until dawn, which means the longer it takes for the Barons to find you, the less time they'll have..." She swallows, hand fluttering to her chest. "The less time they'll have to claim you."

I don't know what that means. What any of this means. "I'm supposed to be a bride. I'm supposed to serve the King."

"There is room for only one female in the Baron King's crypt, but like him, you have to earn it."

There's one more question that I have. One I'm afraid to even speak aloud.

"Will it hurt?"

I see the pity flicker in her eyes.

"Pain is the gatekeeper to destiny." She takes a step toward the door. "And that's what this is, Arianette, for all of you. A night of claiming destiny."

2

———

D amon

THE PASSAGE LOOMS AHEAD, long and dank, our boots heavy on the stone floor. The walls are the same, one rock built on top of the other. The ceilings are low, so much at times that I have to duck my head.

There's only one question that circles through my mind as I follow the lit torches mounted on the wall: *How the fuck did I get here?*

There's something about the way the shadows creep in, the flickering light making the walls and ceiling seem to narrow and tighten. My shoulders tense. Like I'm carrying a weight. I don't know if it's the dead buried in these walls. Or maybe it's just the secrets wedged in between every rock, every grain of mortar.

Or if it's why we're here tonight.

We reach the end of the hall, coming to a metal grate covering the exit. A cool breeze wafts through the gaps. The smell of the forest on the other side. My sense of direction is shit, but I know we're on

Baron land, in the forest that splays out between the crypt and the river.

"These tunnels run all over the city." It's the first time Hunter has spoken all night. Bending, he reties the laces on his boot. "They're part of an elaborate system of catacombs, evacuation routes, facility management, and secret passages that have been overtaken and expanded by the territories in Forsyth to assist in the drug, gun, flesh, and death trade."

When he straightens, I get a better view of the tattoos creeping up his neck, rising above the collar like they're trying to escape. His pale eyes, the light blue even more translucent in the torch light. It's hard to tell in the dark clothing, but he's fit. Lean but strong.

"Any idea how long this is going to take?" he asks.

Armand tilts his head, trying to get a look out the bars. "No fucking clue, but I'm going to be pissed if we're in here for too long." He sniffs, then waves a hand across his face. The movement draws my eyes to the onyx cufflinks securing the cuffs of his button-down shirt. "It stinks in here. Thank god you didn't bring your stupid mutt with you."

Although I agree about the dog, I don't say anything. Ares, Hunter's dog, goes everywhere with him. He's a cool dog. Smart, although a little skittish, with a brindle reddish-brown and black striped coat, and a goofy underbite. I figured he'd bring him with us tonight, but when the time came for us to leave, he gave the dog a chew toy and left him in the room.

I fight the urge to tug at my collar and take a shaky breath. Armand's gaze flicks to my throat, to the jagged scar. He wants to ask. It's visibly killing him not to. But judging from the cufflinks and aristocratic slant of his nose, he's been raised too polite to ask. Probably beaten into him on some shiny, polished, living room floor.

Instead, he says, "I've heard about you."

"Yeah?" It's the distraction I need. "How so?"

He touches his eyebrow, then lip. "That if you want to get something pierced in Forsyth you're the man to go to."

I shrug, tongue touching the labret piercing on my lip. "I work a few hours a week. Mostly house calls."

Personal houses, frat houses, the whorehouse. I'm not picky, but he's right, I'm good.

"I've been thinking about getting one of those, you know," he grins, cocky and sure, and grabs the front of his pressed pants. "Prince Albert."

"That would fit." Hunter snorts. "With you being East End and everything."

"My mother is East End," he sneers with the cocky arrogance of privilege. "I'm a free agent."

Armand is the kind of guy that rumors and gossip follow around like a fan chasing a teen heartthrob. Being a piercer is akin to being a bartender or hairstylist. People get nervous around needles and then get chatty as fuck. They love to talk while we're working and the wayward Prince has been brought up more than once.

Hunter's right. Armand's East End all right. Born and raised. But he vanished for a bit, sent out of the country or something by his rich parents, presumably to cover up something. That's the detail no one is sure about. Drugs? Assault? Something worse?

Honestly, I don't give a shit. Not about him, or Hunter, or the dog. Well, the dog is okay. Right now I'm just reminding myself that there's enough air. Enough room. It's temporary. This isn't the first time I've been caged up in a room with other men that I don't know, but the circumstances are very fucking different.

I lean against the wall, stone cold and wet behind me, and try not to think about how deep underground we are. How long it might be. How the fuck I got here in the first place.

Not *here*-here–not just the tomb vibes and damp socks. I mean *here*. Forsyth. This tunnel. These freaks. This... second chance.

Because none of this was supposed to happen.

Back when I was a freshman, I was normal. Or trying to be after years of trouble. Forsyth U, class of god-knows-what. I lived in a dorm like everyone else. My roommate? Remy fucking Maddox. Son of one of the richest men in Forsyth. He talked in riddles and painted like he was haunted. We got along, sort of. He'd zone out with charcoal under his fingernails, I'd make grilled cheese on an illegal hot plate. We bonded over late-night noise and the fact neither of us really fit in.

He's the one that pulled me toward DKS. Not on purpose. I don't think Remy pulls anyone. He just drifts, and you either get caught in his wake or you don't.

I got close. Rushed. Went to the Fury. Saw some shit.

But something about it–it didn't sit right. Not the way Saul Cartwright watched me like I was dirt under his fingernails. I wasn't legacy. I had no royal connection. To him I would be nothing but a gunrunner–expendable. So I backed out. Dipped before I got the brand or whatever it was they were planning.

Then I got locked up.

It wasn't even a glamorous charge. Dumb mistake, second offense. They gave me twenty-four months. A long time to be nobody.

But inside, I did what I was supposed to. Kept my head down. Took classes. Punched through credits like they were drywall. They had this weird program–some partnership with Forsyth, some rehab-through-education shit. I passed every test.

I didn't think it'd matter. I figured I'd ride it out, maybe knock a few months off if I stayed clean.

Then outta nowhere, a guard pulls me aside and says, "You've got a benefactor."

I thought it was a joke. Or a setup. But the paperwork was real. Someone *anonymous* was willing to cut my sentence down to 72 days. Not months. *Days*. On one condition: I had to re-enroll full time at Forsyth U.

I didn't ask questions. I signed whatever they put in front of me. What the fuck else was I gonna do? There's no pussy in prison.

The black envelope showed up on my doorstep–the shitty efficiency I lived in just off the Avenue. It was late summer, the week before classes started. The handwriting on the envelope was in bronze, my name handwritten in fancy script:

Damon Anthony Kemp

On the back, a thick glob of bronze-colored wax, a raised penta-gram, announcing the sender.

The Barons.

I'd glanced over my shoulders, making sure that no one was watching. There was someone, but it was just Old Lady McAfee chain-smoking on the steps while she played a game on her phone.

Still, I didn't open it until I was inside, using a knife to loosen the wax seal. I'd be a fucking liar if I pretended like the contents didn't shock me.

Damon Anthony Kemp,

You have been invited to rush Beta Rho Zeta for the fall semester.

August 30th, Midnight

Forsyth Cemetery

Plot #112

Memento Mori

I'd considered bailing. Was this really something I needed? Outside of protection in the Pen, I wasn't much of a joiner. That's pretty much why I bailed on DKS. But this invitation... it didn't seem like a request. More of a command. Plus, I was curious. Who wouldn't be? An invite to the most exclusive frat in Forsyth? The most dangerous?

Hell, I kind of just wanted to see where the bodies were buried.

I'd shown up, one of a couple dozen, including the two with me right now, who seemed just as surprised to find that it was an inter-view under the guise of being a party. We ate, drank, and bullshitted one another until the sun came up. I'd woken up, face down in the dew-covered grass, lying next to a hundred-year-old gravestone. I was nursing one hell of a hangover and ready to swear off frat life for good. That day another envelope was on my doorstep instructing me to come back again that night. Same for the next day, then the next. It wasn't just parties, although there was plenty of debauchery in the form of free-flowing booze and sexy crypt chasers dressed in black, all wanting the first crack at the new recruits.

But there was something else just under the surface. Individually, we'd been tested. Academically. Physically. Mentally. We'd been asked to prove our skills, our prowess. To challenge our fears.

After seven days, I received the final envelope.

An official invitation to join BRN.

I went from living alone in my shitty apartment to being surrounded by an entire fraternity of men who are now my brothers. Men who have all taken the same oath, sworn our fealty to the Baron King.

Except, we are not all equal. Three of us have been chosen for attributes that only he understands. To wear the mark. To deliver it.

I've wondered about this a million times over the last few weeks. What did he see in me during the recruitment phase that made me different? Some kind of excellence that I don't see myself?

What is it about this kid, Hunter, that caught the Baron King's eye? I don't know much about him, myself. Just that he works the night shift at WXFU and has a stack of engineering books on his desk. There must be something else, right?

And then there's Armand. By the way, what kind of fucking name is Armand?

A rich kid's name, that's what. His clothes. His posture. His entitled, snobby attitude. The air of contempt at anyone who crosses his path. Privilege. That's the word I'd like to tattoo on his forehead. Privileged Fuck Boy. Is that what bought him the golden ticket or is there something else lurking under all that entitlement?

The three of us arrived at the Baron's house on the same day. Suitcases, backpacks, and in Hunter's case, a cardboard box, and a dog at his feet. We went to classes during the day, studied our pledge books, and fulfilled our personal obligations. Hunter left several nights a week for the radio station, where his smooth voice carried over the airways. Armand woke up early in the morning to work out with the rowing crew. I continued hustling on the side, taking on piercing clients.

During all of this, we never saw the Baron King. Our pledge period was overseen by the two former Barons. *Two*, not three, the third's whereabouts were unmentioned. These men are smart, loyal, trusted to slowly hand over tasks, or really, what I see now they really were–*tests*.

Tonight we find out if we passed or failed. Will we be given the role of leadership? Be the hands of the King? Or will we be cut loose and banished, a failure to Forsyth?

That is what waits on the other side of the metal bars, and if we succeed, we'll participate in the Barons' most coveted event:

The Hunt.

SHADOWS DON'T SPEAK.

"Finally," Hunter says when the gate finally opens.

I lift my chin, allowing Hunter to go out of the tunnel first. He steps into the night and pauses, taking a long look at the man releasing us. He's wearing a long black cloak with a hood shadowing his face. Well, not his face, it seems. The mask, black like the rest of his clothes–gloves and boots included. Unfeatured other than slits for the eyes and nose.

Flickering torchlight guides the five of us to a clearing, a circle made of stone. Our brothers stand around the edge, dressed identically to the two that brought us here. Faceless. Nameless. The only color is a bronze circular clasp at the neck, a pentagram holding their cloak in place.

It strikes me how different the Barons are from the other fraternities. The Lords are chosen by points, a game played amongst one another, against everyone. The Dukes take it to the ring, in front of a crowd. To the victor and all that shit. And for fuck's sake, the Princes. It's just one giant spectacle for everyone to see and most of all, talk about.

But the Barons? We're initiated under the cloak of night. In the shadows *by* Shadows. It's isolated, secretive, and now that I'm here, I wonder if I've made a terrible mistake.

"The King awaits," a faceless Shadow finally speaks. "You may approach the throne."

Throne?

Across the circle, the Shadows part, revealing an extension of the circle, and the massive throne on the other side of an obsidian altar. The firelight shifts across the throne and the material it's made of, welded pieces of jagged iron. I see them for what they are: instruments of death, or really, the tools of power. It's impressive, but all eyes are on the man sitting in the seat.

The Baron King.

Even though we've been initiated into BRN, this is the first time we've been in his presence. He's dressed in a thick black cloak with a hood that covers his head. Underneath is a black suit. The firelight shines over the toes of his oil-colored wingtips. His hand rests casually on the arm of the throne, a gold ring glinting on his finger. But it's his mask that draws every bit of my attention. It bears none of the non-descript markings of the Shadows' masks. Cast in bronze, the sides mimic sharp cheekbones and the hard line of his jaw. The forehead splits into two pointed horns while the mouth is curved into a permanent line, giving away nothing, yet holding all the cards.

It's then that I realize we're the only ones without a mask. Everyone knows who we are. They'll know exactly who succeeded and failed.

The King stands and the men around me kneel. I do the same, as do Armand and Hunter.

"Welcome, my Shadows, new and old." His voice is loud–strong–carrying over the small gathering. "Tonight is a night of tradition. Of declaration and fealty. If you doubt, state it now, because once the clock strikes twelve, there is no turning back."

The air falls quiet. Nothing but crickets and the rustle of leaves.

I'm enraptured, unable to leave even if I wanted to. This man–this *King*–the power that drips from his very presence is intoxicating.

His gaze falls to the three of us kneeling in the center of the pentagram. "A traitor worked his way into my kingdom last year and the consequences... were unfortunate. I can not allow disloyalty, not just for my safety, but for yours. For all of Forsyth, because the city, the entire royal system, is under attack. We are in a time of upheaval and rebellion, and while the Royals fight their petty battles, skirmishes over territory, narcotics, and guns, the bodies continue to fall. Women, our most prized, continue to go missing. Fingers are pointed," he clasps his hands behind his back, "at the guilty *and* innocent."

"Because of those trials, I have a mission. One that influenced my choices for leadership. Each year I comb through the population of Forsyth for the most capable men to serve me and to lead Beta Rho." He gestures and two of his Shadows step forward. One holding a cup. The other a sheathed knife. "Forsyth is ripe with history and tradition. These ceremonial objects go back to the beginning of our organization. To our very foundation."

The Shadows set the cup and knife on the altar and step back. The cup–really a chalice, is grayish white, with ornate designs, carved elegantly on the surface. The stem is thick, the bottom is rounded where it meets the base. I stare at it a moment longer than I need to, the time it takes for me to realize it's made of bone.

"The three of you have been chosen for your specific attributes, for the needs of my kingdom. For the needs of Forsyth. We will put an end to the decay rotting in the soil, infecting every seedling, poisoning our very existence. As Barons, we embrace death, but we respect life. Someone, something, out there is threatening our people and it must end."

He grabs the knife and slowly removes the sheath. The handle, revealed in the light of the torches, is also made of the same substance as the chalice–carved bone. The blade is sharp, with a jagged edge, and just below the blade an ornate carving flares out before curving downward, as if to protect the thumb.

Sweat rises like pin pricks on my neck.

The scar on my throat itches, like it's been set on fire.

In a swift move, he holds the point against his scarred palm. "From blood to blood, a Baron is born. We live in the shadows, listening, waiting, observing, until we become one with the darkness. We do not fear death. We do not take life. We usher the fallen through the veil."

My breath hitches when he slices the tip of the blade down the thick, scarred flesh, a signal he's done this over and over again, sacrificing himself for Beta Rho. For Forsyth. Blood comes to the surface and then slowly slides down his hand. The chalice is placed beneath it, a vessel to hold the blood.

We're silent as the blood fills the cup, and as he holds his hand up, another Shadow steps forward to wrap his hand in a strip of black cloth. Otherwise, it's quiet as a tomb, nothing but the flickering lights and sounds of the forest. I take it all in, every last moment, including when he steps in front of Armand and demands, "Repeat the oath."

Armand swallows, and for a second I worry he didn't do his studies. He fucked around and failed to memorize the details in the pledge book. Memorization comes easy to me: words, facts, history. But he takes a deep breath and begins, "I, Armand Joseph Stein, give my fealty and oath to you, the Baron King, to my brothers, the Shadows, and to the souls of Forsyth." The King hands him the blade. Armand takes the point and presses it into his smooth flesh. He doesn't disguise the wince, but there's no hesitation as he pulls the blade across until blood rises. "From blood to blood, a Baron is born. Tonight, I am born anew, at your service, loyal to your command." The cup is lowered under Armand's clenched fist. Blood flows into the cup. "If my oath is broken, my loyalty compromised, I will suffer the consequences."

The process continues, the blade is cleaned, and Armand's wound is wrapped in a strip of black. The King moves before Hunter, who quickly repeats the oath in that low, raspy voice that has lulled many of us to sleep after a late night. I watch Hunter move quickly–decisively–stabbing in the point of the knife and slicing it across his palm. I try to loosen the tight muscle at the back of my jaw, and take a breath, but I can't take my eyes off the blade.

Licking the ring at the corner of my mouth, I catch the scent of sweat, metal, and copper. Steel and blood. It's as familiar as my own skin.

When the King stands before me, it's like everything else vanishes. The Shadows in my peripheral. The torchlight dims. Armand and Hunter no longer exist. It's me, the King, and this blade.

"Repeat the Oath."

"I, Damon Anthony Kemp, give my fealty and oath to you, the Baron King, to my brothers, the Shadows, and to the souls of Forsyth." My blood hums as I reach for the bone handle, surprised and impressed by the weight. The handle is smooth, like a hundred hands have worn it down over time. I feel the surge pulsing through me. The compulsion and want. I don't want to rush. I like to savor it. Make it my own.

Parting my lips, I press the tip of the blade just under the base of my index finger, applying the right amount of pressure. A bead of blood surfaces and I drag down, from one end to the other, peeling away the skin. It stings. Sharp, like a bite.

"From blood to blood, a Baron is born. Tonight, I am born anew, at your service, loyal to your command." I make a fist, feel the warm slick blood coat my palm, and watch my blood drip into the cup, mixing with the others. I notice that the inside is stained from other years, other oaths. I lift my chin and look the King in his dark green eyes. It's the only part of his body that is visible. When our gazes meet I feel a connection in the moment. "If my oath is broken, my loyalty compromised, I will suffer the consequences."

The Baron King takes the knife from me and stands before us. "From blood to blood," he repeats, lifting the chalice into the air. He steps toward Armand and dips his fingers into the cup, pulling them out coated in blood. He touches Armand's forehead, wiping a bloody mark on his flesh. The pentagram. He does the same to Hunter, and then to me. The blood is warm. The scent nauseating. I feel as if the blood has been burned into my skin.

"Rise! With this mark, my blood becomes yours, making you worthy of participating in this hunt, the final task to claim the title." He waves forward three men. "Prepare your leaders for the hunt."

I sense someone behind me, moments before he wraps the cloth over my nose and mouth. Glancing sideways, I see Armand and Hunter, their faces covered the same way. There's a design over the mouth, the imprint of teeth and bone. I assume mine is the same.

"Every hunter must be stealthy, but also armed," the King announces. "You will each take one weapon with you."

He steps before Armand and hands him the bone-handled knife.

"I'll use it well," Armand says, running his fingers down the carving.

The King shifts his focus to me, and jerks his chin at one of the Shadows. He walks out with my bow. It's black. Sleek and deadly.

"You aren't being sent to kill, but I assure you this will be a fight."

I wrap my hand around the grip, feeling the comforting weight in my hand. A tickle of excitement flutters in my gut. As I adjust the strings, the King steps toward Hunter.

"You already have your weapon," he says. "One sharper than any blade. One quieter than any arrow."

He taps his temple. Once. Twice. Then points at Hunter. "You listen. You wait. You watch."

A silence drops across the room. Heavy. Intentional. I glance over at Hunter, and yeah–his breath's caught. I don't miss it. He tries to keep his expression flat, but I see the flicker. Whatever this is, it's hitting him somewhere deep.

The King steps in closer, into Hunter's space.

"You'll see the cracks where no one's looking," he says. His voice is lower now, but I hear it all. Every word. "You'll find what they bury. You'll witness what they want to hide. And I have no doubt, you'll find the girl."

There's something about the way Hunter nods–slow, measured, almost reverent. Like he's finally being seen for what he is. Not a kid. Not just a voice behind a mic or a freak with a dog. Something colder. Smarter. Meaner.

And maybe I get it.

He's not like the others, puffed up and swinging weapons around. Armand's over there practically jerking off to the knife in his hand. The others are tense, waiting for orders. But Hunter? He's already writing his own script.

The King steps back, satisfied, and Hunter just stands there. I've seen killers. I've seen manipulators. Whatever he is, he's the kind that waits 'til the lights are out and the locks are off.

And I get it, now more than ever–why he's dangerous.

Why the King chose him.

The moment passes and the King looks over our heads and announces, "Bring in the girl."

My shoulders tense in anticipation. 'The Girl' is the biggest perk of being a Royal in a Forsyth frat. The Lords have their Lady, the Dukes their Duchess, and of course the Princes' and their Princess, who has just given birth to the newest heir. The Baroness belongs to us, and I'm itching to get my hands on her.

The hard click of heels echoes off the stone path, and I turn my head in that direction. I blink in confusion when I see the woman walking into the ring. She's gorgeous. Sexy as hell, in a black dress and five-inch heels. She's bold and strong, and I realize immediately that although she's a Baroness, she's not *our* Baroness.

"Regina, my Sinister Sister," the King says, gesturing for the woman to approach. "Lovely as always. Have you prepared your sister for the ceremony?"

"Yes," she says, climbing the steps to the throne. She bends and presses a kiss against his neck. "She's all ready for you, Daddy."

On the other side of Hunter, I don't miss how Armand's eyebrow arches at the endearment.

He's the only one of us who has seen the new Baroness, apparently sent to pick her up from the hospital. It's known that this girl, Arianette Hexley, was snatched off the streets and held captive for three weeks. Hunter reported on the situation on his show and it's been all over the news. Images of her were locked down, apparently for her safety, or maybe at the King's command. Armand didn't say much about her, just that she was unhinged, and should be 'fun.'

Movement from the path draws my attention and like a shift of fog, she emerges. I soak her in, this girl that will belong to us. She's nothing like the woman that walked in before her with confidence and grace. She's smaller, a little younger, and her eyes catch me off guard, big and brown, *uneasy*. Her straight hair frames her neck—brown skin smooth, soft-looking. Skin I'm itching to touch.

I worry the ring in my lip, checking out her tits. They're full, nipples peaked at the cool night air, and I can already imagine them threaded with my needle, the heavy weight of a piercing at the tips. Her waist tapers before flaring out into curvy hips and my fingers curl, thinking about what she'll feel like.

She steps into the torchlight, and it's impossible not to notice the circles under her cautious eyes or the timidness in her walk.

"Arianette," the King greets her, "welcome."

I watch how he looks at her, trying to see if there's a hint of something there, an attraction or affection. It's known that they are arranged to have a Black Wedding, which makes no sense in the scheme of things. No one has told us how this will work. Isn't he married already? Although I've never seen this wife. How will we share the girl who is married to our King? All I see is formality. A contract among the elders in the community.

Forsyth is weird as fuck, and here I am with a bloody pentagram painted on my forehead, about to dive in head first.

Arianette passes in front of us, her long, thin limbs moving gracefully. She's not shy, her gaze skimming over the three of us. It's hard to tell in the torchlight, but I think she bares her teeth.

I try to get a read on her, but it's hard.

On the outside, she may look easy to break, malnourished, and weak, but prison taught me not to underestimate anyone. This girl was chosen for a reason.

"Come close," the King tells her, and she moves to the bottom step, the hem of her dress swishing against her calves. Regina sits on the arm of his chair, his hand trailing over her thigh as he stands. "These are your Barons, sworn to the brotherhood by blood and oath." His hand lifts, a finger pointing at each of us. "Armand, Hunter, and Damon."

Her gaze flicks down the line, and I feel the oddest sensation build in my chest. Something dark and powerful that doesn't dissipate, even after she's returned her focus to the King.

"And you," he continues, "shall become Baroness, ascending to the place of royalty if you survive the night, replacing the current Daughter of Darkness." The two women, who couldn't be more opposite in demeanor, share a glance. Regina, all precision and poise in her smooth braids and straight spine, a woman who carved her place into the Barons and at the side of the King. Her ebony skin shimmers beneath the firelight, drinking in its warmth like a shield. Arianette, wide-eyed and fidgeting, skin catching the warm glow along her high cheekbones with a soft, untested sheen–less a royal and more a girl playing with the idea of being one.

"At the strike of midnight, the hunt will begin. Only the marked can participate, but my Shadows will be there to keep the game in motion. They know not to touch, not to interfere, but they are loyal to their leaders and will assist them."

He bends, lifting Arianette's chin with his gloved fingertips. "Do you understand, my Daughter of Night?"

She looks up at him, those dark eyes wide, and I wish I knew what was going on in her crazy little head.

When she speaks her voice is low–reverent. "I understand."

"You may start at the first toll." I look around, wondering what clock he's referring to. "A head start, as your Barons will come at the final toll. You start the night an innocent, but you'll end it as part of the fold, one of us. Claimed by darkness."

I hear it, the deep chime echoing across the night. The clock tower. Did that crazy fucker actually get the Dukes to wind it up?

He drops his hand and raises both arms into the air. "Let the hunt begin!"

Arianette seems frozen, her feet glued to the ground, her eyes darting to Regina who hisses, "Run!"

That seems to snap her out of it, and she zig-zags past. Before I can even process it, she's gone, vanished into the dark.

"Whoever captures her first will give her the mark," the King reminds us as the clock counts to twelve. "And the sooner you catch her, the longer you will have to claim the Baroness. There are no limits, except the one."

Each and every one of us has already sworn to this one rule, when we accepted the pledge to BRN.

The Baroness is to survive the night a virgin.

3

rianette

RUN.

The word rattles against my skull as I race into the dark.

It's pitch black, only a pale sliver of moonlight shifting through the canopy of trees overhead. Not enough to avoid the whip-thin branches slicing into my arms and legs. Too dim to expose the uneven ground, the tree roots, and rocks. I take the brunt, the nicks and the cuts, the bruises, to delve deeper, getting far away from the fire.

Away from the men. The masks.

A chill tiptoed up my spine when I stepped into the circle.

The King, grand and bright, commanded the scene, Regina sitting at his side.

Daddy, she'd called him, and he'd stroked her hair, touched her with gentleness.

But we weren't alone. Like their name, they clung to the edges, stealing the air from my lungs. The Shadows stole the oxygen, with their black, blank faces, and cold, lifeless eyes. It's no surprise that they're thieves. Not with the way they steal souls. One innocent at a time.

At least none wear the face of the beast. But three of them wore the face of death, flesh removed, only the bone remaining.

Dangerous. The powerful always are.

But I know my truth. I got away once; I can do it again.

The final chime of the clock reverberates in the distance, the midnight hour. They'll be coming now. Hunting.

Hide, the Baroness said. Stay hidden as long as I can. The more time they have the more damage they'll do.

They. Armand, Hunter, and Damon.

Names but no faces—at least not in full. I did my best to memorize what I could. Burn their images into my mind. All I can conjure is Armand's white knuckles gripping the knife, the glint in Hunter's blue eyes, and the sleek bow slung against Damon's back.

My heart beats like a drum, like the sound of footsteps on the ground. The sound of a dance beat—*One, two, three, four...*

Snap!

They're coming.

Fear ratchets across my nerves and I look back. A mistake. I stumble, toe kicking into a root, arms flailing, striking something big. Something solid but warm.

Something—*someone*—with hands. Panic rises in me, a scream lodged in my throat. I wait for the dark laugh, the sneer of conquest, but in the pale moonlight I see the arc of a full-face mask looking down at me.

A Shadow.

He can't hurt me. The King said so.

Still, I spin, running back the opposite way. I slam into something again, this time rough and biting into my flesh. Pressing my back against the tree, I exhale, allowing my eyes to shut.

Not far away I hear a coy voice call out, "You can run, Sister, you can hide, but I'm going to find you..."

Calm, Arianette. Stay calm.

Nothing can hurt me.

I'm in control.

"You're in a field, right? Sun beating down. Warm breeze. Flowers everywhere."

The reminder comes like a whisper, and I take one breath, then another.

"What color are the flowers?"

"Periwinkle."

The color. Soothing purple. Warm like a blanket. Safe.

Wrapping myself in it, my breath grows steady–sure. Nothing can get me when I'm here. Not the Shadows. Not the dog. Not the beast. It's too bright. Too exposed.

The whistling sound hurtles toward me. *Hurtles,* like it's carried on the wind. Not a whistle. An arrow.

I duck. Inches above my head the bark splits, ripped apart by the tip.

The bark scrapes against my shoulder blades as I inch around it, taking tiny steps to get to the other side. I'm crouched there, feet up on the roots, heartbeat pounding in my ears as the footsteps approach.

"Dammit." The swear raises every hair on the back of my arms. I hear a grunt and the sound of the arrow being pulled from the tree trunk. "Where the fuck did you go?"

Sure he's going to find me, I wait, bracing myself for the moment. I must imagine it when he walks in the opposite direction, his heavy feet stomping over the dead leaves. But after a moment it's just me, my heartbeat, and the darkness. Steadier, I push away from the tree and look up, catching a glimpse of the full moon. It's shifted, night is passing. The minutes eat away at the clock. My eyes adjust, the world a moonlit-soaked gray.

I'm too exposed here, there must be somewhere safer. *Run!* But I know better. Running is loud. It's obvious. Dangerous. I slow. Creeping through the forest, I use my hands as my eyes, running over the rugged trunks, feet careful over the rocky terrain. Ahead there's something dark. Up close I feel thick leaves, bendy branches. Dropping to the ground, I crawl underneath, pushing into a thicket, and pull my knees into my chest, making myself small.

The minutes pass, my heartbeat slowing until all I hear is crickets chirping and night creatures roaming. How many are Shadows, I'll never know. They could be a foot away, an inch, living and breathing, keeping me within the boundaries of this game.

They are both my protectors and enemies.

I'm so lulled into a sense of quiet that when I hear the footsteps crunch on fallen leaves, I think I'm dreaming. I hold my breath, wrapping my arms around my legs to make a tight ball, listening.

One set of footsteps.

He stops and starts. Moving slow. Careful. Meticulous. Then I hear, "You out here, Sister? You close?"

The voice is deep. Amused. To him, this is all a game.

I'm not naive enough to think it's anything but.

"I think you're close..." he muses. "Crouching down. Hiding in the dirt, burrowed in the ground like a rodent. I'm not used to getting my hands dirty, but I'll make an exception for you."

He's close enough that I hear him inhale, taking a deep breath, and for a terrified second I wonder if he can see me, or worse, smell me.

He lingers just outside my hiding place, pacing back and forth. A cramp ebbs through the muscle in my calf, aggravated from being curled up so tight. Pain shoots down my leg to my foot and I bite down on my bottom lip. Closing my eyes, I bring up my safe space again, the periwinkle flowers, the warm sun, and block the pain out–block *him* out.

I fade out, lost in my safe space until it's quiet again. Did he leave? Did I fall asleep? That happens sometimes. Missing time. Lost memories. Tears burn at the corner of my eyes, the pain in my leg sharp. My corner of the forest grows still and I dare an exhale. I know he's just the first of the three. There will be more and next time I won't be so lucky. In the distance, a curse bounces off the tree trunks.

Calls for me to come out carry on the breeze. Whatever happens tonight, I won't make it easy on them. I can't.

For now, the night is still. The hunters far away. I let my muscles loosen, dare to stretch my leg, flexing my foot to get the feeling back–

"Gotcha."

The voice is a dark snarl, connected to fingers clamped around my ankle, locking me to him with an iron grip. He's strong, dragging me from my hiding spot, my skin tearing against the unforgiving ground. He doesn't drag me to my feet. Instead, he shifts his grip to my wrists, pinning me to the forest floor, blocking out the moonlight, his body heavy over mine.

That's when I catch his scent, under the sweat and adrenaline. It's not the scent of a person. It's from a place, and for the first time since all of this began, my blood runs cold.

"Thought you got away," he says, nose next to my cheek. "Or that maybe one of those two would get you first? The pin cushion and the nerd the King thinks is so smart?" He snorts. "No fucking chance, I doubt those two have ever spent time in the wilderness like I have. Do you know that I held my first rifle when I was five years old? Shot my first buck when I was six? From there it was pheasant, boars, alligators, and big game." He works my hands over my head, pushing them together and binding them as one. His eyes glint off the moonlight, making him look every bit of the devil he seems to be. "I've gutted and dressed every animal worthy of catching, but do you know what my favorite game is?"

"No," I whisper, knowing that men like this only play games that hurt.

"Virgins," he says smugly. "Not everywhere places a value on it, but Forsyth? It's like sitting on a pile of gold. There's only one thing that makes it better." His breath is hot on my ear and his teeth press into the lobe, giving a quick bite. "A virgin claimed for a Royal."

His hand pushes up my skirt, hot and clammy against my thigh. "I worked my way through as many potentials as possible, sullying them up when I could. It wasn't hard. Most of the little legacies have a shitload of Daddy issues and there's nothing like giving away your innocence to show them just how valuable you are." His fingers reach my panties, curling into the waistband. "A few got away. I put in a bid to be the one to take Story Austin's in the pit, but her stepdaddy had other ideas. Leticia Lucia went missing before I could get to her and then the Count had Lavinia locked up tight for two years before the Dukes got their hands on her. And Verity Sinclaire? No one saw that coming. She was nothing but a basic cutslut." His laugh is mean, and his fingers twist deeper against my hip. "Although, secret babies are so on brand for the Princes that we should have."

I don't know the people he's talking about, but there's no mistaking the bitterness in his tone. He's angry. Jealous. Vengeful.

"Everyone wants to know why Armand Stein came back to Forsyth," he says, voice even in the darkness. "How did a spoiled East Ender earn the coveted position as Baron? Truthfully, I didn't." His fingers yank hard, dragging the underwear down my legs. I hear them land in the dirt. "I'm not here to just fuck you, Sister. That's just my fee to do the dirty work of others."

His palm flattens on my thigh, pushing them apart. I fight back, squirming underneath him. "Do you know what you did to deserve me?"

I shake my head, even though I don't think he can see me. I catch the scent, *his* scent, it's cloying, dank. Terrifyingly familiar.

"You never should have run, Arianette." His knees rise, holding my legs apart. "And once you did, you never should have stopped." The rip of his zipper cuts through the sounds of the forest. "It's simple really." He kneels before me and his profile catches the moonlight. The mask covers the lower half, the ghoulish skull jeering at me, but his eyes are not human. "You know too much."

I feel something press at the heat of my entrance, hard and unrelenting. I squirm against him, the muscles of my thighs straining to shut, the channel between us shuttering closed. "Don't be a bitch," he growls, lining our bodies up. "This is the best thing that'll happen to you tonight."

His hips thrust and a sharp intrusion pushes into me, eliciting a howl that rips from my throat. It feels like I've been stabbed with a hot poker, my insides on fire. Surging upward, I snap at him with my teeth, catching the corner of his mask. I yank back, fighting against him, inside and out.

"Feisty, huh?" he laughs, face revealed, proving he's as much of a devil covered or not. He drops my wrist to recover the hard line of his jaw. "Go ahead, come at me." He spreads his arms wide. "I like a little violence with my sex." To prove his point, he reaches behind his back. His next move is swift, revealing the glint of a blade. It slices through the moonlight, landing diagonally across my throat. "I have no problem using this, Sister. It's your choice."

I tilt my head and look at him, really see him for the first time, and say, "You used to be a sweet boy. Towheaded with innocent eyes. You're tainted. They tainted you, too."

"Shut up," he hisses, dragging the tip of the blade down my neck. "This is exactly why you have to die."

He leans over, angling himself again. I don't know what it feels like to have the full invasion of an enemy inside. But I've seen it happen. A witness to too many crimes. But this time, I'm on the other end of the weapon.

Footsteps echo against the trees–short, sharp, fast. Someone is coming. His head snaps to the side, distracted. "Jesus Chris–" he starts to shout, pivoting toward the noise. His knife hand jerks. A second figure barrels through the brush, slamming into him. Armand stumbles, caught off guard, twisting hard. The blade lashes out, wild, catching only air. He tumbles over his own feet, scrambling to recover.

"No!" he bellows, weaponless now, eyes darting. "Take her! She's your prey!"

He spins back toward me, like I'm the lesser threat, but everything shifts, slows. The world blurs at the edges, turning still and crystal-clear at the center. I see the knife in the dirt, half-buried in leaves.

I crawl.

Fingers stretch.

Close.

Mine.

The carved handle is familiar in my grip, like it's been waiting. Like it belongs.

Armand lunges, trying to beat me to it, but I'm faster. I rise with the blade in my hand and dancer's grace in my blood. He reaches for me, fingers grazing my arm–but I catch the cuff of his shirt, twist it, hold him just long enough.

Our eyes lock.

Dark.

Malicious.

I drive the blade forward.

Hot blood arcs, splattering my skin. He gasps, a wet gurgle that bubbles and flails. His hands clutch his throat, eyes wide, disbelieving. I tear the blade free, the fabric ripping under my fingers.

He collapses sideways, slumping into the forest floor. My breath comes ragged and deep, like I'll never get enough air again. I'm still holding the knife in one hand. A scrap of his shirt in the other. They're both soaked. Both mine. Both binding me to this moment.

It would be so easy to slip away.

Periwinkle.

But I'm not alone. From the shadows, a voice cuts through the quiet.

"Drop the knife."

I freeze. Turn toward it.

A figure steps forward. Calm. Tall. Watchful.

"You're not going to outrun us," he says, chest rising and falling. Dark ink on his pale skin teases from beneath his shirt collar. Flaxen hair curls at his temples, just above the cut of his mask. "You've already been caught."

Two of them now. One with a bow already drawn–silent, focused. Both with their faces half-covered, jawbone and teeth etched in white.

I shift the blade toward them, even though my arms tremble. The blood on the knife has dried tacky. I've already killed one man tonight.

But he deserved it.

He broke the rules.

Now I'm surrounded. Two against one. There's no more forest to vanish into. No more magic left to summon.

The knife slips from my fingers, lands in the dirt with a dull thud.

The Hunt is over.

I've been caught.

4

H unter

WITH HIS ARROW STILL NOCKED, Damon walks over and picks up the knife. My chest rises and falls with every breath. I didn't know what to expect when I followed the other two men in the forest, but it certainly wasn't this.

I circle around Armand, his blood now one with the forest floor, and nudge him with my boot. The body shifts lifelessly and I squat, fingers searching for a pulse. His skin is warm, but I don't find one. Not a surprise considering the pool of blood that came from the wound on his throat. Whatever happened, we just missed it. "He's dead."

If I expect some kind of reaction from the girl, I don't get it.

"Looks like you've caused some trouble, Sister." Damon's words come out as a taunt, which, to me, feels like a bold choice, considering the circumstances. "Killing a Baron, *your* Baron, seems pretty fucking stupid."

The girl says nothing, just lifts her chin in defiance.

When she'd walked into that ceremonial circle, I hadn't been impressed. She seemed small. Lost. Overwhelmed. But out here, covered in blood and dirt, with that knife steady in her hand, I see something else—something fierce simmering beneath the surface. Her slender neck, the way her hair falls loose and wild around her face, those soft lips pressed into a line—I catch myself watching, looking for what I'd missed between then and now. How I'd missed it.

She's dangerous.

Damon smirks, and glances over at me. He's also coated in sweat, pieces of his dark, slicked-back hair falling onto his pale forehead, covering the bloody pentagram. He's still got the bow tight in his hands, knuckles white with tension. "An act of defiance like this could lead to immediate death."

"Do it," she dares, "and bring my body to the King. Lay me at his feet. *Then* see whose blood will be spilled."

He looks like he's considering it–and it's fair. Killing her would be an act of loyalty, we've just declared our fealty to the King, but something about this whole thing seems off. How did she get the upper hand? Armand is a big guy, twice the size of her, and although I don't believe a fucking word of his hunting stories, she shouldn't have been able to take him down.

"He's right," I say, moving closer. I can breathe easier now, but the adrenaline continues to pump through my veins. "We could kill you for this." My hand shoots out, fingers clenching around the soft column of her throat. She gasps and struggles against me. My palm aches from the cut but I ignore it, tightening my grip. "A sacrifice no one in Forsyth would argue."

"You won't." Her words come out in short gasps. "You're different from him. Both of you." Her blood-soaked and dirty fingers pull against mine. "He wasn't one of you. He wasn't loyal to our King."

"And how the hell do you know that?" I ask, my curiosity more genuine than I'd like to admit.

I'd joked earlier about Armand being from East End, but the kicker is that I'm from there too. Just different ends of the spectrum.

He grew up behind iron gates and private security, a family crest above the fireplace.

Armand's family has power. Mine? The opposite. They take care of the powerful.

That's the food chain in Forsyth. Someone like me, smart but broke, doesn't rise. I get noticed for doing things quietly, not loudly. I'm the kind of person they ask to fix their car, update their computers, be their tutor–then pretend I'm not in the room. And if I'm lucky, they toss me a scholarship and call it charity.

But for some reason, it offends me that this girl notices it right off.

She licks a splatter of blood off her lip. "His blood is wrong. Tastes like sin and treachery."

Christ, this woman isn't just a killer. She's deranged.

Damon walks the perimeter of the area, kicking over leaves and rocks, like he's looking for any other weapons. He bends suddenly and picks up something soft and pliable. Carrying it over, he holds it out and it only takes a second for me to realize what they are; dirty panties.

"He did this?" I ask.

She nods.

He tried to rape her.

Damon, who has said nothing about me having the girl by the throat, walks toward me slowly, unwrapping the black cloth from around his hand. I release her, pushing her toward him, and watch as she sags and takes a gulp of air. He reveals the cut the King gave him on his palm. It's dark, but still fresh, and he holds it up to her face and asks, "You said his blood tasted wrong. What about mine?"

She grabs his wrist and pulls his hand close to her face, tongue darting out and laving the wound. I watch them in both horror and fascination, a clench deep in my belly. "Salty," she says, "like the earth." She drops his wrist, unimpressed. "But none of you are him."

"Him?" Damon asks, curling his fist.

"My King," she breathes. "Even if he gives me to you, I will only belong to him."

"Is that what you really think?" Damon asks, his voice slightly muffled under the bandana. "Because *if* you survive the night–which I'm not so sure will happen when the King finds out what you've done–you'll belong to us, too. And right now I see a stupid, crazy bitch who thinks she's better than her Barons. That she's smarter than her King, who, by the way, hand-picked *us* for leadership. Including the one you killed. Who gave *you* to us, not the other way around." He laughs, empty and hollow, the sound reverberating against the dark night. "It seems to me that maybe before we finish out the ceremony, you need to learn a lesson." His hand, the one without the cut, lands hard on her shoulder. "Get on your knees."

Fuck.

"No," she says with an authority she doesn't possess.

He cuts me a look, maybe asking for permission. I shrug, more than willing to see this play out. "I don't give a fuck what you want, you Baron-killing cunt." He shoves her down, her knees scraping against the dirt. "Open your fucking mouth."

She clamps it shut, but his fingers grip the sides of her jaw, forcing it open. He makes a loud noise in the back of this throat and bends over her, their foreheads nearly touching. Lifting the bottom of his mask, his lips part and a glob of spit hangs between them and lands, slimy and warm, against her tongue. She coughs, gagging, but Damon's having none of it.

"Swallow it," he commands, thumb grazing over her throat, forcing the muscles to relax. Her body reacts instinctively and I see the bob of her throat as she swallows. She gags again, but he forces her mouth closed and holds it shut with his dirty fingers. "That's a good girl. I knew you could do it."

The instant his hand is off her jaw, she leans back, gathering her own saliva, and spits in his face. He blinks, momentarily stunned, until he moves so fast that I barely see his hand swing back until the *crack* of his palm slams against her cheek.

"Fuck, it figures," I shake my head, biting back a laugh, "she *is* a crazy bitch."

Damon's hand slips behind her head and he grips Arianette's hair, yanking her face up. "A crazy bitch that's about to know what it feels like to choke on my cock."

His words are definitive, and after what I've witnessed tonight, there's no doubt he'll do it. And fuck no, I'm not going to stop him. I've been wound up all night. First with the ritual, then with the hunt. She hid from us longer than I expected, but I see now that this girl shouldn't be underestimated. The look in her eye is wild and feral, similar to the way Ares looked when I found him in the back alley behind the radio station. Skinny. Dirty. Traumatized. He almost bit my fucking hand off. I have no doubt this girl would do the same if she was given the chance.

Ares needed to learn to obey his handler and she is no different.

Damon has no problem unzipping his pants with his cut hand and releasing his length. It's long and thick, already hard, and she eyes it with horror. "I'm going to give you one last chance to act like a good girl, Baroness," he says, fingers twisted tight against her scalp, "and treat me with some goddamn respect." He pulls out the blood-stained knife and holds it to her throat as if he knows it's an ask too far without some added pressure. "You're going to suck my cock. You're going to swallow every last drop of cum, and then you're going to do the same for my brother over there, understood?"

She glances over at me, eyes pleading. If she's looking for help she's going to the wrong person. Watching her get throat fucked? I've been hard since he spit in her mouth.

"Listen to him, and maybe you'll survive the night." It's like my words pierce through her like Damon's arrow, the hope extinguishing from her eyes. The resistance draining from her body.

It's kind of pathetic.

Damon widens his stance and strokes up and down his cock. "Touch it, Sister. It won't bite." She takes him in her hand, but pulls back suddenly. He shivers and inhales. "Fuck yeah, don't be afraid of the metal."

Of course this guy has his dick pierced too. I shouldn't be surprised. Damon's been cool since recruitment started. A little quiet and moody, but that works for me. I'm not moody, but I prefer to be alone. It was obvious from the jump that neither of us had the pedigree to be in this position. No bloodline. No legacy. Two randoms plucked from Forsyth because the King sees something in us no one else does. We were brought here for a reason–what, I still don't know–but all expectations fell away when we entered the ceremony. The rules of society were replaced with those of the Barons. Hours later I'm sweaty and pumped with adrenaline as I watch my new brother get a handjob.

Again her eyes meet mine and I let her see me run my hand down my thickening cock, then tell her, "Lick it."

I just about shoot my load when her tongue darts out and swipes over his tip.

Fuck.

"That's right. *Jesus*," Damon mutters. "Now open that sexy little mouth and let me fuck those pretty lips."

He guides her by the back of the head, the knife still precariously close. There's no fight when the head of his cock pushes past her lips, and her mouth circles around him. He groans, and I stifle my own quiet moan, shoving my hand down my pants.

"That's right, Sister, take him in–all of it–every fucking inch," I jeer, stroking myself as I move closer. Damon thrusts in and my balls clench. "That'a girl." I look up at him and add, "Fuck, she's doing it."

"Yeah, she is." Damon's hips rock, pounding into her, quick and hard. It's too much, too fast. She tries to catch her breath, but he doesn't stop, doesn't care. He's caught in his rhythm, slamming his cock into her mouth over and over like a dog rutting. She cuts her watering eyes to the side toward me, noticing that I've unbuttoned my fly and have my dick in my hand.

This is even better than at the Sanctum.

I imagine that it's her mouth around me instead, my cock pumping into her, gliding past her teeth to the back of her throat. The image makes me desperate. Hot. Sweaty. Achy, and the last fucking thing I want to do is come before Damon does.

Thankfully, another shudder runs through him, and his thrusts grow jerky, his breath erratic. "Fuck, fuck, fuck," he chants, lost in the motion, until his spine seizes, fingers twisting tight in her hair, and he stutters to a stop. He groans, pumping into that red, open mouth, filling her up. She sputters and gags, choking on his cum.

That's enough to set me loose, my orgasm exploding in a long stream. I grip the base, spilling out on the forest floor. She watches me–*sees me*–and fuck if that doesn't make it even better. Damon pulls out while keeping her jaw open with his strong fingers. "Last squirt," he tells her, leaving a pool of cum on her tongue.

He steps back and exhales under the mask, the tension eased from his shoulders.

"You want her?" he asks, with a little jump and the zip of his pants. "I got her loosened up for you."

"Nah, I'm good." I tuck myself back in and kick dirt over the seed on the ground. I look up at the sky, still dark, but we're running out of time. "We probably need to head back."

Damon turns back to her and grabs her by the arm, jerking her up until she stands on wobbly feet. He studies her, then says, "You've got a little..." he lifts the edge of his mask, and wipes a shiny spot next to her lip with the corner of fabric. "There, all good."

As if that little wipe can clean up the mess we just made.

Damon must know it too because he adds, "I won't tell the King what happened to Armand, as long as you keep your mouth shut about what just happened." His eyes dart between the three of us and something firm passes between us: an understanding.

We walked into this forest as hunters and prey.

Now we're walking out with secrets.

5

───────────

rianette

I'M NOT foolish enough to think I can escape.

Even if I could, where would I go? Back to the Manor? Never. It wouldn't matter anyway. I'm arranged to marry the King and there's no escaping that either.

They don't know that though, and a strong hand grips each of my biceps as we navigate our way back to the ceremonial circle. Half of the Shadows guide us, the swish of their dark robes against the leaves and dirt, a parade through the forest with fire-tipped torches.

The other half trail behind, two carrying the limp body.

The farther we get from the body, the more I wonder if I've done the right thing. The fine piece of cloth I tore from Armand's shirt is still clutched in my fist. I didn't even notice the button until Damon shoved me on my knees. I needed an anchor of some kind. A talisman to connect me to this world.

Disassociating has always been easy for me. A crutch. I've always been told that I'm impulsive. Reckless. Even with all the discipline. The dance classes and structure. I've never been able to control all sides of myself. But a killer?

I wouldn't have thought so, but maybe I'm different than I was before I was taken.

That man... the one whose blood I spilled, he was no ally of my King. I did what was right. What was loyal, but I know not everyone sees what I see.

His death has already led to consequences. I feel them in my aching jaw and scraped knees. If I felt control when the knife was in my hand, I lost it when the Baron invaded my mouth. I can still taste his seed, bitter and salty, hardened like a rock in my belly.

"Were you serious?" I blurt, stopping at a felled tree. The trunk is massive, the bark thick and peeling, like it's been down for a while. Raising my foot to climb over it, I wobble and must take too long, because fingers tighten on my left bicep, and I'm lifted into the air by one pair of strong arms and passed over to another.

On the other side, Hunter asks, "Were we serious about what?"

"That you won't tell the King what I did." I look over my shoulder and see the body swaying like a hammock between the two Shadows. His mask is fully down around his neck, revealing the sharp cut of his cheekbones, hollow and pale. He was handsome, his bone structure similar to the friends of my uncle. The people I entertained. The Shadows navigate the tree trunk and Armand's arm falls off of his chest. No one picks it up and his fingers trail across the dirt.

"I want to say you've paid your price," Damon replies. "But you've also revealed your true nature. You're dangerous, Sister. It's a risk not to tell him."

I rub the button, remembering how the light snuffed out of Armand's eyes. "Please don't. I don't want him to be angry with me."

"You maybe should have thought of that before you murdered one of his hand-picked Barons. A man who took an oath of loyalty three hours ago," Damon points out.

.   .   .

BEING RAISED at the Manor taught me how to be quiet. How to study the men and women that came in the door. Children in my position learn quickly how to assess the people around us. Are they good? Bad? Manipulative? Dangerous?

None of that prepared me for The Hunt. For being chased through the woods by men who have the right to hurt me. I still haven't seen either of their faces, and it plays tricks on my brain. I know them better by their eyes, the piercing darkness that Damon pins on me, sharp as the arrow in his bow. Hunter's are lighter. Blue? Gray? They change with the light. That may be all I know of their faces but I do know them. The weapons between their legs, those are imprinted in my brain. I know that the one I choked on turns a blistering red when it's engorged and is wide enough to split the corners of my mouth. Hunter, the one that watched, his looked thick in his hand, growing longer with each stroke.

In that moment, I know that they both got something they wanted–no–*needed*. And that's the only reason I think I may have a chance to survive the rest of the night. This is confirmed by the look shared by the men over my head, and Damon confirms it saying, "As long as you're a good girl, then we'll keep your secret."

I think he means obedient, because no matter how much he wants me to be good, I'm not. That may be the only truth I know.

"Can you?" he asks, lifting my chin with his dirty finger.

I nod. "I'll be good," I promise, and it's enough that he believes it, even if I don't. Satisfied, he grabs my bicep again and we continue forward. The rest of the walk back is quiet, until the Shadows part, and we're back where it all began.

My attention goes straight to the King, waiting patiently on his throne. Regina sits by his side, her fingers casually combing through the hair on the back of his neck. A drink sits on the arm, a warm amber liquid halfway to the rim. I know from experience that drinks like this can bring out the worst in men. Does it have that effect on the King? Or does he have more control over himself than others?

I track the moment he sees Armand. His lifeless corpse is the end of our little parade. Regina's eyebrow lifts, her dark eyes leveling with mine. Heat runs up my neck and I twist uncomfortably. Exposed by my own impulsivity.

Whatever the King thinks about me, or the blood splatters soaked into my skin, my puffy, swollen lips, or the scent of sex he must be able to smell on my breath, he keeps it to himself. Instead, he looks at the body and says, "I've lived through many initiations, many hunts, and I do my best to stay out of the details of what happens in the dark hours of the night. I've seen many Barons and their Baroness return in a state, often bloody and broken. Traumatized and tormented. It's all part of the process," he leans forward, "but this is the first time one of my Barons has returned dead. Does anyone want to speak to what occured out there?"

"He," Damon starts, then pauses, "*Armand* disobeyed your command." I watch, shocked, when he reaches into one of the deep pockets in his pants and pulls out a scrap of fabric. He holds it in his fist, gray and dirty. "He defiled her, forcing her on her knees and feeding her his cock. He was going to take her virginity next, but we got there before he could defile the Baroness."

His words slither like a snake, both truth and lies.

The King's focus shifts to me. "Is this true?"

I consider the truth, that Damon was the man that violated me. In turn he'd reveal that I was the one that killed Armand. I don't want the King to have a reason to send me back. That's the last thing I want, so I nod, the lie caught in the tangles of my throat.

"Was he successful?"

I shake my head.

"Speak, Daughter. I need to hear your words. Tell me exactly what happened."

"After he forced me to…" I clear my throat, "he tried to do more. He pushed me to the ground and held a knife to my throat." I nod at the ivory-colored knife on Damon's belt. "He tore off my underpants and tossed them in the dirt." I take a deep breath, swallowing the tears. I don't know why I'm crying now when I didn't cry then. They're the first tears I've shed all night. In weeks. "He tore into me, but just a little."

"You're still intact?"

"Yes..." sweat rises on my neck, "...I think so."

He's quiet for a moment, and Regina fails to meet my gaze. I think he may reject me. Consider me spoiled. Rotten. Useless. My uncle will be furious. And I will have nowhere to go. Nowhere to live because I refuse to go back to that house. Never Again.

Finally, he says, "Check her."

The men move as a unit, Hunter holding my arms and Damon bending before me, taking off a glove. Hunter lifts up my skirt, exposing my lower body to the entire circle.

"What are you–" I start, but Damon's warm hands push my thighs apart. Our eyes meet, his the darkest gray, hard and stormy, and without warning he pushes his finger inside. The shock of pain is startling, like rubbing sandpaper over a wound. I scream, fighting to clamp my legs together, "Stop! You're hurting me!" I look over at the King, pleadingly and sob, "Please."

"Enough!"

Damon's rough finger withdraws, leaving me with that same empty ache that I felt before. He holds his finger up and lifts his chin to the King, declaring, "Dry as a bone."

"Perfect." He leans back, tension easing from his shoulders, and for a brief moment I'm pleased that he's pleased, and my own body, tired and achy and exhausted, relaxes. But then I look up to the dark sky and remember the night is far from over. There isn't a streak of sunrise, not yet, and that means one thing.

"Prepare the altar," the King declares, "it's time for The Claiming."

6

———

D^{amon}

IT FEELS like hours since I was back in that tunnel, waiting for the night to begin. Hours since the clock tower struck its twelfth, bone-shaking chime. I've never experienced pitch black like that of the forest, nothing to go on but instinct and desire, but tracking the girl had been a thrill.

The first second I saw the Baroness I knew she was something special. I *understood* why she had been chosen. Those big brown eyes, pupils a pinpoint in the flickering torchlight, felt like looking into a portal to her soul. There was something deep and dark inside of that small frame, and when I heard her scream echo off the forest trees, my instinct was to get to her. Fast.

First.

Hunter and I almost collided as we both ran toward the sound. By the time we reached her, she had the knife clutched in her bloody hand and a dead man at her feet. She looked wild–*deranged*–but fully in control. She'd just slit a man's throat. Her *Baron's* throat and I had a feeling she would've taken us both out as well if I didn't have my bow locked and loaded.

This bitch is brutal.

And it was obvious to me that she needed to be handled immediately. If she killed one Baron she'd have no issue with killing two others. So, I asserted my dominance on her, and got some much needed relief at the same time.

And fuck, she looked gorgeous with my cock buried in her throat.

You would think that would have been enough, but now I can't stop thinking about how tight she felt around my finger when I checked her pussy.

That was a reminder that the Baroness is not for the taking. At least not her pretty, tight, little pussy. The King called dibs. I'm not worried though, I'll keep her secret and she'll keep mine.

"Each Baroness must be claimed and marked by each of her Barons," the King says from his throne. "All the instruments you need will be on the altar. There are no limitations other than the ones set before the hunt." He taps his fingers on the arm of his chair, the ring flashing. "Sunrise is coming, I wouldn't waste any more time."

Arianette's eyes dart to the altar, but the Shadows have already jumped into action. One of my brothers stands before me and gestures for the knife. I hand it to him, the blood dried, and he sets it next to the matching chalice. Then I notice a stainless steel box and it takes everything in me not to respond when I see it.

The box is mine and was in my room when I left.

"What the–" I start, but the King speaks again.

Cloaks billowing, the Shadows swarm around Arianette next, hands grabbing at her wrists and ankles. She kicks out, that wild glint flickering in her eye as she fights back. *Oh fuck.* Hunter must realize it the moment I do, because we push our way in. "Bind her hands," he says, grabbing one of the straps at the corners of the altar. The straps are made of coarse black leather and they're threaded into anchors bolted to the sides of the table. We work quickly, understanding that if we give this girl an inch, she'll take more than a mile. If she gets her hands on that knife again, I have no doubt she'll cut our fucking dicks off.

Once she's secured, I glance around at the men in black masks. "Go. Get away from the table."

There's a hesitation, but they all fall back to the edge of the circle. Even though the King is watching and the Shadows are all around, it's like everyone vanishes but me, Hunter and Arianette, who is now stretched corner-to-corner, arms and legs wide. My cock twitches, thickening at the sight of her like this.

The Claiming is a rite, the final part of our initiation. It's the reward for making it through every step. The markings? Well those are the deepest, darkest parts of the Barons' lore. The details collected and recorded in the thick pages of our pledge books, preserved for generations.

These women have been bitten, burned, and branded. Lashed, inked, and choked. In the past they've been fucked–thoroughly and publicly. It's the choice of the Baron how to leave their mark, but as my eyes land on the silver box, I suspect that the King has more of a hand in these decisions than I realized. He's the one that brought me my tools.

He knows me better than I thought.

Arianette fights against her restraints, a loud scream ripping from her throat followed by the ramblings of a madwoman. "The demons are coming! They're taking my soul. Spoiling my blood!"

I slap a hand over her mouth and bend down, whispering in her ear, "I thought we agreed you were going to be a good girl..." She jerks her face back and forth, but my hand is bigger, and I force her still. "Since you're not, I need to remind you that I don't trust you any more than you trust me, but if you don't shut the fuck up, I'll tell the King what really happened out in those woods tonight."

Our eyes hold and I try to elicit a promise from her. She blinks and I tentatively raise my hand, prepared for the second that I do, she'll let out one of those shrill, bone-curdling screams.

Thank fuck she doesn't.

Even so, I'd love to teach the little witch a lesson, but she's not mine to destroy, although we have been given permission to break. I exhale and step back and try to regain my composure. Hunter slides into my place, his hand reaches out, but he doesn't actually touch her. "Settle down, Sister, tonight is your night." His voice is quiet but strong, how he sounds on the radio. "I know you want this. I can smell it on you, feel it in every vibration in your body. You want to be Baroness, but to get that, you're going to need to submit."

Slowly, the fight leaves her. All the tension and resistance in her arms and legs vanishes. "There," he assures her, voice both chilling and soothing, "now, this is going to hurt. A lot, but like the saying goes, it'll only make you stronger, Arianette. That's what it takes to be a Royal House Girl."

It's like a switch flipped and he's moved from one personality to another and she seems to have fallen straight into it.

I lean over and tuck a wild strand of hair behind her ear, trailing my fingers down her throat. She shivers and I grin down at her. "That's better," I lift the knife, "now, let's get rid of this ratty, dirty dress so I can see you better."

Starting at the bottom, I slice the blade through the fabric, ripping all the way to the neck. It falls away, revealing her body to us for the first time. Her tits are round and perky, the nipples a shade darker than her skin, which looks almost bronze under the flickering torches. Splayed out like this, I can see healing, mottled bruises along her ribs, presumably from her prior escape, and dark, puckered scars around her wrists. I reach out and brush the back of my fingers over the peak, drawing it into a hard point. "Sensitive," I say, moving to do the same to the other. Arianette's breath hitches and I laugh. "You like that, huh?"

Her jaw tightens. Pissed? Horny? Both are fun. "I bet you like them teased. Don't worry, Sister, I'll suck and play with them for so long that you won't even need a cock to come." I tilt my head at Hunter. "What do you think, Brother?"

"I've never seen areolas that big before."

Jesus.

But he's not wrong.

"Hand me that box," I tell him. He lifts the box and passes it over her body. "Thank you."

Setting it down, I flip open the top and take a quick assessment, making sure nothing has been touched or moved. Everything looks in order, and I remove a packet and tear the edge, pulling out a clean cloth. Quickly, I wipe down the edge of the blade, meticulously cleaning off the blood.

"Torch," I call out, and a Shadow emerges, offering his flame. I run the blade under the heat, the metal turning crimson. There's not a sound as I sterilize the knife, even the King watches with interest. Satisfied, I withdraw the blade from the fire and hold the bone handle to Hunter. "You first."

I made my first mark out in those woods.

And my second? It may have to wait.

Hunter looks at the knife like he isn't sure what to do with it. The kid is weird. Quiet, but obviously a goddamn chatterbox on his radio show. Underneath the dichotomy I sense the darkness in him. He looks way too comfortable holding that knife and he sure as hell didn't stop me from throat fucking the Baroness in the woods. Fuck, he encouraged it.

Arianette's chest rises and falls while her eyes keep track of the blade. But he sets it on the side of the altar and reaches for the chalice. There's a long hesitation before he dips two fingers in the bowl and draws them out coated in darkening crimson. The blood drips down his fingers as he sets them on her collarbone and drags a long sweeping mark to the cap of her shoulder.

I step back and watch as he paints her, slashing marks over her rib bones and belly. Her stomach caves, twitching from the gentle touch. Goosebumps rise along her flesh, stimulated from every stroke. The artwork is crude. Elementary. But the way she tries to lift her hips lets me know her body is reacting despite her resistance. Maybe just on instinct, or maybe the ceremony is getting to her. The heat from the fires, the King's watchful eyes, the moon overhead. Every swipe of blood, every touch of his fingertips brings Arianette one step closer to being ours.

He moves to her tits, dabbing the tips of her nipples in red. A growl rumbles in my chest, dark and possessive, loud enough for Hunter to glance up and lift an eyebrow, encouraging me to join in. I'm an artist and my medium is sharp metal, but hell, I can play Picasso for the night.

The blood is lukewarm from sitting out during the hunt. I coat my fingers and step to her forehead. I draw three letters: BRN, claiming her for the house. Fuck, this girl looks good coated in red.

Moving toward her feet, I decorate her legs, climbing up her thighs.

I reach the apex between her legs and her hips make the smallest of movements. She wants me to touch her. To release all the built up tension from the night. Murder. Rituals. Lies. Blood. She may be innocent, but she's still horny. I have no doubt of that.

Does she deserve it?

Probably not, but I want to see her squirm.

I barely process Hunter crudely drawing the star and circle between the valley of her breasts or him wiping off his hands, I'm too busy looking at the sweet pussy I'd had the pleasure of touching at the King's command. The inside of her body belongs to him, but the outside, that's all us.

I graze a sticky thumb between her legs and her body trembles.

"Keep doing that," Hunter tells me, picking up the knife. *That* I do notice. Leaning over her body, the blade glints in the firelight as he lowers it to her chest.

"Please don't," she whispers, eyes wide and pleading.

"Every Baroness receives the mark, sister," he explains, pressing the tip of the blade into her skin. At the same moment I flatten the pad of my thumb over her clit. She groans, teeth bearing down on her bottom lip. The blade curves and starts down the first line of the star, carving deep into her flesh. Her eyes squeeze shut and a scream rips from her mouth. Down between her thighs, I apply more pressure, rubbing a slick little circle over her clit.

"One down," he tells her, before starting on the next.

Her eyes flick to mine. There's conflict in them, fear and want.

The urge to scream and run. Right now she's ours, tied up, blood soaked, panting, and in pain.

"Every time he cuts you, I'm going to give you a little stroke," I explain, holding my fingers a hair's breadth away from her body. "Just a little lesson that pain can also come with pleasure." I grin. "Especially if you're a good girl."

This woman is wicked to the core, there's no doubt about it, but that's what makes this so fun. Hunter continues making his cuts and for every one I tease that hot little nub. Her hands make tight little fists by her side, her chest rising and falling in quick breaths. There's no doubt the pain is severe, the cuts causing a fresh cascade of blood to slide down between her tits and pool on her belly. Her cries become more erratic, less distressed, and more pleading. Hunter starts the curve of the circle to finish out the pentagram and I tell her, "It's time to let go, Sister. Let me feel you come on my fingers."

Picking up my pace, I flick the tiny nub, my cock growing harder with every touch. In the small amount of space she can move, her hips chase my movements, wanting it so fucking bad. I could give it to her and watch her unfurl, but...

Where's the fun in that?

I bring her to the edge, to the place where she wants it more than any of us, more than she wants the pain to stop. On her chest, Hunter finishes the pentagram, the two ends of the circle meeting like a snake eating its tail. Her breath catches, her pussy warm and slick, and then I withdraw my fingers. Her reaction is a strangled cry.

"Good work," I tell Hunter, wiping my fingers off with one of the cloths. I'm impressed. Not many people can handle this level of handiwork. Unless they have experience.

He holds out the knife. "You want in?"

"Hmm," I muse, moving around the altar, well aware that Arianette's breath is still unsteady, her hips chasing my phantom touch. It would be so easy to give her what she wants, but she needs to understand who holds the power here. And it's not her. The pentagram is solid. It'll scar nicely. "No."

He nods, wiping the blood off the knife with the hem of his shirt, unaware that I prefer to do my marking in private and when I have more time.

Looking back at the King, I notice the orange-pink glow rising behind the trees. He lifts his hand. "Bring her to me."

She watches as Hunter and I quickly untie the binds and when she's loose, we help her sit up.

"Can you walk?" Hunter asks.

She winces. "Yes."

"Good." I brace one side of her and Hunter the other. In her ear I whisper, "Stand before the King and accept your role."

She looks like a nightmare. We all do, covered in blood and dirt. It's been a long night, filled with violence and betrayal. Secrets and deceit. All of it, the Hunt, the Claiming. I understand it a little better now. It's not just an initiation. It's a bond that ties us together.

That doesn't mean I trust her though. Fuck no.

"Dawn is breaking," the Baron King says, rising from the throne, "and the hunt, as well as your initiation, are complete." His gaze falls to Arianette, who stands before him naked and blood soaked. "And now my new Daughter of the Night, you must take the Oath of Fealty." He places his hand on her forehead. "From blood to blood, a Baroness is born."

Arianette, trembling from the cold and possible blood loss, repeats him word for word.

"Today, I am risen anew, at your service, loyal to my King and the men who claimed me." She continues, swallowing at the end of the sentence. "If my oath is broken, my loyalty compromised, I will suffer the consequences." He looks out over our heads and adds, "Memento Mori."

A low but strong chorus echoes through the trees. "Memento Mori."

A new season has begun.

7

———

H^{unter}

We carry him by the shoulders and ankles.

Armand's heavier than I expected. All that swagger, boiled down to muscle, blood, and bones. In engineering, we call it dead load–the static weight a structure has to carry no matter what. Permanent. Inescapable. That's what this feels like. Like I'm hauling something the world was never meant to support for long.

DK takes most of the weight without complaining, his jaw tight, brow furrowed like he's not here at all. Somewhere else. Maybe back earlier tonight. Back to the table. To her. I know I can't get it out of my head, either.

Her.

Get *her* out of my mind.

I'm sweating despite the cool morning air, the chill settling in under the cloak now that we're away from the ceremonial ring and its torches. I'd wanted a shower. Sleep. Instead, we got our first real job as Barons. A privilege, the King said.

"Ushering the fallen through the veil."

We don't speak as we follow the Shadow leading us down the path, winding through trees. It eventually gives way to one of the crypt entrances tucked against the side of the hill, half-buried under wisteria.

"Careful," the one holding the iron door open says. "Watch your step."

Inside, it smells of earth and old metal. Damp stone and rust and time. There's a sense of history here, thick and quiet, like the walls remember every name ever laid to rest within them. This place has been hiding bodies for generations. And now, we're part of it.

Servants of Forsyth. Of life and death.

That's what the King said.

But no one tells you what it feels like to carry death in your hands.

We still have blood on our hands from the Claiming. It's caked on my fingertips and I can still feel the warmth of her skin as we painted her, the ripple of goosebumps rising across her velvety brown flesh. Her dark, soulful eyes carried a trace of mania, but she knew we had leverage and that kept her from fighting back. DK took the fall for killing Armand, which means we own her beyond the ceremony. My fingers ache around the memory of the knife, the way it fit in my hand too well. I can still picture her–strapped to the table, body trembling. Was that fear? Or want? From the cuts? From DK's playing with her pussy?

Pain or pleasure?

Maybe both.

Her eyes were wild when he removed his fingers. I know that look. I've seen it. Felt it. Desperate for just a little more. By the time we reach the second door, my arms are screaming, and it's a relief to lower Armand down onto the stone slab. We let him rest flat on his back. It's more definitive like that. More real. His throat is open, the slash deeper than I thought she could manage. Skin split clean, from one side to the other, across his throat. The muscle beneath is jagged and wet.

"Huh," I mutter, shifting his foot so it doesn't fall off the slab.

"What?" DK asks.

"Guess Royal blood looks like the rest of ours after all."

"Seriously." DK rubs his palms on his pants and leans in to study the wound. "Fuck. She got him in one swipe."

I glance at him, then at the line across his throat. That scar of his–it's gnarled and angry, different from the one we're staring at now. But if he doesn't bring it up, I won't either.

"Are you surprised?" I ask. "That she did it?"

"Maybe," he admits. "Although, from what we know about her... she was strong enough to get away from whoever had her. Maybe this isn't her first kill."

I lean back against the wall and breathe through my mouth. The whole crypt hums with silence, like the dead are listening. Listening and waiting.

"She didn't hesitate," I say, nodding at the cut.

"Nope." DK's hand runs through his dark hair, then his teeth worry at the ring in his lip. "She's not like other girls."

"No." I lick my dry lips. "She's smart–hiding from us longer than I thought she would. Calculated. Armand was twice as big as her, and she still got the upper hand." I replay the scene in my head. "She waited for the opening and took it."

"Dangerous smart," he says. No judgment in it. Just fact. Maybe even admiration. Or fear. Or both.

"Do you believe her? That she didn't just kill him because she panicked?"

She'd defended herself fast. Claimed Armand was trying to rape her. There was evidence. Her panties–torn and dirty on the ground. His pants–unzipped. The Shadows had tucked him back in before carrying him out, but we'd all seen.

"I do," DK says, glancing up. "She killed him because he broke the rules."

There's a long silence after that. The crypt seems to hold it, keep it.

I stare at Armand's slack face. Glossy eyes, just barely open. He was the only real Royal among us. A fucking Stein. His family will want him back. Cleaned. Embalmed. Placed in a gilded tomb in the cemetery like a relic. He won't be like the others down here. The ones the Barons tuck into the walls of the catacombs, the ones who hold up Forsyth's foundation for eternity.

But we brought him here. We touched the truth of it.

DK rises, brushing off his palms. "Guess this makes us real Barons now."

He's probably right. More than the oaths or the rites. This is the job.

"What happens next?" I ask, turning to the Shadow by the door.

"Normally, this would be the start of the journey through the veil," he says, frowning down at Armand. "He'd get a Baron ceremony, but honestly? I'm not even sure it counts since he didn't survive the Hunt or make it through the Claiming."

The thought of Armand giving Arianette a mark on the altar is chilling. Not that what I did to her was a picnic, but I have a feeling he would have made her suffer.

"Due to the circumstances," my new frat brother continues, "the King will handle this one directly."

I give Armand one last look. His expensive watch. His polished shoes. None of it mattered. Not in the end.

Life is fleeting.

And it can end in the most unexpected ways. By the most unexpected hands. My stomach twists. I think of the knife. The way her fingers curled around it like it belonged to her.

Like it always had.

The weirdest part?

That's exactly how it felt in *my* hands, too.

THE BARONS' room is located in the old chapel, now called the House of Night. The walls and floors are stone, making the hallways and rooms constantly cool. A fire is already lit in the hearth, low but steady, casting amber light across the room. It's a far cry from the ancient dormitories on campus, where the carpet smelled like stale beer and mold. People roamed the halls all day and night, disrupting my sleep and studies. I couldn't complain since I lived there for free due to my father working for the university, but the House of Night has a quiet serenity I don't take for granted.

The room is big enough for all three of us to share–a requirement, it seems, for the Barons to live in a community. There are three beds and dressers and a big closet divided for us to share. Now, only two of the beds are made up. The third is already stripped bare, nothing but a mattress and silence.

Armand's gone. Not just dead–erased. His things packed up, no sign he ever slept here. The wardrobe doors creak faintly, open now and empty. His shelf on the wall, bare.

We'd only been here a few days, moving in just after they accepted our bids to join BRN. Not really long enough to settle in, but when three men walk into the forest on a hunt, you expect everyone to come back. That didn't happen.

Ares lets out a soft, nasal huff as he trots over to me, tail wagging slow and low. He sniffs my pants, my boots, his nose twitching at the blood I didn't quite wash off down in the tunnel. Dirt. Ash. Death.

"Yeah, I know," I mutter, raking a hand through his brindled fur. "Smells like hell."

He presses his forehead against my shin for a second, then wanders back to curl by the hearth, eyes watching the flames. He's always alert. Never fully relaxed. Not even when I'm here.

I was surprised when the King allowed me to bring him into the House of Night. I figured a pet would be a dealbreaker, but either he's a fan of dogs, or that's how bad he wanted me to join the ranks. Why, though? Why me? Us?

I glance up to ask DK, but he's already stripped off his shirt and disappeared into the bathroom without a word. The pipes groan to life. I hear the sharp hiss of water, the clatter of boots kicked aside.

Alone for the first time in hours, I sit.

The chair by the fire is too stiff to be comfortable, but I don't move. The warmth licks at my shins. My body aches from the weight of Armand, from the weight of what we just became. Real Barons. I guess.

I lean forward, elbows on knees, watching Ares stretch and resettle with a huff. His ears flick at every sound–he's always listening. Always bracing.

I wonder if she's bracing too.

Her room is down the hall. The door was shut when we walked by. Is she alone now? Asleep? Still awake with adrenaline coiled tight in her gut? Is she thinking about how we chased her down? What DK did to her? How I watched...

My spine tingles, a warning about getting too close. I'd taken the risk tonight when I painted the blood over her smooth skin. When I held the knife. But there were people around: the Shadows and King.

It was safe.

The door creaks open, and DK steps out, steam trailing behind him. Damp hair, clean shirt clinging to his chest. He smells like soap and something herbal. He catches me looking and shrugs. "You're up."

I nod, using all of my strength to get up. I feel like I haven't stopped moving since last night. As I pass him, he doesn't say anything. Doesn't ask. But I know he's thinking it too.

What comes next?

We've only just stepped into our roles. Just caught our first real whiff of rot and truth. And Arianette–she's in the thick of it. Closer to it than either of us, and more dangerous than we realized.

The shower is hot, I step in, water beating down on my neck and shoulders like it can burn off everything that's happened.

The knife. The blood. Her breath hitching under me. The way Armand's body felt in my hands.

Dead weight.

We may have left Armand in the crypt, but that weight: heavy, wet–*inescapable*–has already settled into my bones.

And no amount of scrubbing will ever get it out.

8

rianette

PAIN.

That's all I feel as the weight of a cloak is thrown over my shoulders and I'm led back through the cold underground tunnel. The damp scent is overpowered by the coppery blood that has seeped into every one of my pores.

It aches in my chest, like that knife had carved all the way into the bone. It throbs in my pussy, a pulsing reminder of the invasion–the *denial*–I'd survived, of the overwhelming current brought on by fingertips. And then my skin. It's cold and raw, the bloody marks tightening as they dry. Their hands had been all over me. *In me.*

I didn't understand what the King meant when he said I would be claimed. I didn't know that it meant more than being caught and carried back before being anointed Baroness. I didn't know that it meant my soul would be taken too.

Or maybe I didn't know I had that much left to be stolen.

The night is a blur. This always happens. My memory is short. Flawed. *Periwinkle*. When I look down at my hands I can't remember everything that they've done. If they've hurt or helped. Or if those things are the same.

I'm led through the maze of passageways, twisting and turning under the earth. I try to count turns, gain my bearings, thinking we've walked far enough to get back to my room. It's not until we reach a stone staircase that I pause, sure that this isn't the route we came before.

"Where are we going?" I ask, unsure if I can go any farther. The adrenaline of the night has slipped away and exhaustion is creeping in.

To my shock, the Shadow speaks. "You're moving to the House of Night, Baroness."

"Oh." I frown. "Where was I before?"

"The catacombs, beneath the cemetery."

He starts up the stairs and I follow until we reach a thick wooden door at the top. Another Shadow waits there and we exit into a hallway. The temperature rises immediately and a shiver creeps across my skin from the difference. The floors are hardwood, and lights made of iron hang from the vaulted ceilings. I'm taken to another wooden door and let inside.

Regina waits for me.

She must be able to tell that I'm on the verge of collapse, because she doesn't speak, just takes my hand and leads me across the room. I barely process the soft carpet or the large, iron bed tucked against the wall. My body and mind are both numb as she gently pries the button from my palm.

She holds up the hard black circle, her eyes narrowed. "Is this his?"

His.

An unspoken name for an unspoken act. I nod, and I feel numb as she pushes me into the steaming shower, adjusting the nozzle away from the wound on my chest. The water is a reprieve, an excuse to finally let the hot, angry tears fall.

I let her wash me, scouring the dirt and blood off my body. She gently works soap down the lengths of my hair, but all I can feel is the pounding heat burning into my scalp. It's the kind of pain that is welcome, that reminds me I'm still alive. I'm no help, letting her lift my hands and feet. The hard bristles of a brush run under my nails, against my heels. I want to tell her it's no use, nothing will remove the sins.

"Sins don't wash off." The voice is stern. Male. *"They're imprinted on your soul."*

"What did you say?" Regina asks.

I blink at her, and then around the shower stall. It's just the two of us.

"Nothing," I mumble, trying to draw myself back to the surface. Regina shuts off the water and grabs a large gray towel, wrapping me in the soft fabric. "Thank you."

She pats me down, carefully drying off every inch of skin and my hair, wrapping the same color robe around my body. She points to a small vanity chair and I sit, watching as she rummages through the drawers with those long, manicured nails. She squeezes the water from my hair and removes the towel, letting the damp strands fall down my back. Gently, she massages jojoba oil onto my scalp. Her touch is the opposite of what I experienced during the Hunt.

From the bottom drawer, she removes a first aid kit, along with a clean towel.

"Can I check your wound?"

Modesty left me hours ago, and I let the sides of the robe fall away. The pain radiates from the center of my chest.

"This is going to sting," she warns me, unscrewing a jar. The scent of alcohol hits me, and she dabs a cotton ball over the top. "Ready?"

I nod and close my eyes. The first touch is cold, the second a flash of burning pain. I bite down on my bottom lip and hold back a cry. *Periwinkle.* I search for that place, the fields and flowers, but it's harder and harder to get to.

"Take a deep breath," she says. I in-and-exhale, trying to fight the panic. The smell of alcohol fades and I catch a hint of her spicy perfume. It's sexy and dark, just like her. Her next touch is more gentle, the smooth swipe of ointment covering the jagged flesh.

Opening my eyes, I ask, "Why are you doing this?"

She shrugs and unwraps a flat, square bandage. "I'm not sure."

"Did someone help you after your hunt?"

She shakes her head, her long braids falling over her shoulder. "No. I came back here and crawled in the bed in the other room." She swallows, like she's trying to hold something back. "I was alone. Scared. I thought about ending it all." I try to meet her eyes, but her gaze is focused on my wounds and her lashes are so thick I can't. "But I also knew I was chosen and that's an honor. An honor I needed to accept."

Her words hit home, more of a salve than the one spread across my chest. A question nudges the back of my mind and I summon the courage to ask. "You called him 'Daddy' out there."

"I'm his Daughter of Darkness." She looks up at me with a small smile. "Or I was, until tonight."

"He called me Daughter too, but..."

There's going to be a wedding, and I'll be his wife. I can't be both. Also, I don't know what it's like to have a father. I was raised at Strong Manor, by nannies hired by my uncle.

"You have a different path, Arianette," she tears off a strip of tape and adheres it over the bandage, "one that I don't envy for you. But you were chosen for a reason. We all are. The King is wise. He will take care of you and in return you will take care of him. Your Barons will become your world. Whatever demons were chasing you on the outside... you don't have to fight them alone anymore."

It's simple, too simple, and from the expression on her face, it's clear she knows it.

"And in return?"

She gently touches the gauze on my chest. "That mark means something in Forsyth and it means something in this house. That oath you repeated? The blood spilled? That's a contract between you and the men in this house." She takes my hand and squeezes it. "You belong to them, Baroness, body and soul. By serving them, you are serving your King."

We share a long look and a feeling that I didn't have when we first met burrows in my chest. Before, Regina was this graceful Royal who knew all the answers. Now, I see her for what she truly is, a warrior.

Me? I'm not sure that's the right word. I feel on edge. *Raw.* Ready to explode.

What she's saying is that I have to trust these men–trust the King–but if they showed me anything tonight it's that that isn't possible. Everything that transpired was out of deceit and fear. Distrust. And worse, Armand showed me there's something dark in this house–a threat to the very man he swore an oath to. He may not have worn the beast's mask, but he *was* a demon that had to be slayed.

How can I be sure there aren't more?

$$\sim$$

"THIS IS EXACTLY *why you have to die.*"

I'm flattened on my back, a hand clamped over my mouth, keeping the scream locked in my throat. My hand raises, fingers curled, prepared to lash out.

"Jesus, Baroness. Do you ever just quit?"

Not until he's dead for good.

My fingers tighten–to nothing. No knife. I blink, and the hazy form of the man in front of me solidifies. It isn't Armand, even though he does have a puckered wound at the neck.

A ghost?

No. *This* man is alive, dark eyed and breathing. He no longer smells like the dirt and decay of the forest. He's clean. Soapy. I wonder if the fingers splayed across my mouth are the same ones that touched me *down there.*

Damon.

"Dreaming about the Hunt?" he asks, keeping his hand over my mouth. He thinks I'll scream if he removes it. He's right.

I nod, listening to my heartbeat pulse in my ears.

"Remembering what it was like to kill a man?"

Again, I nod. The memory floods over me every time I close my eyes.

He's so close, his body straddling mine. It's still daylight outside, probably just a few hours since Regina helped me into bed. Before she left, she tucked my hair into a silk bonnet, and I pull it off now, letting my hair cascade down my shoulders.

I take him in, that dark hair pushed away from his forehead. I get the sense his color is off. His cheeks are still a ruddy pink from the heat of the fire, but underneath his tan skin, he's pale. For the first time, I can see the rest of his face, the various metal pierced and poked through his skin. His jaw clean, freshly shaved, revealing the hard lines of his features.

"I've never killed anyone," he confesses. "But I have been killed." He lifts his chin, showing me the scar. "My heart stopped–at least that's what they say." I watch him. Watch those piercings in his cheeks that look like dimples. "But don't worry, Baroness, I'm not going to tell anyone what you did. Especially the King. Not as long as you behave."

With his eyebrow arched, he slowly removes his hand from over my mouth. I swallow back the scream, understanding this game. Secrets. I'm good at secrets, even when they claw at my insides trying to escape.

"I didn't get a chance to give you my mark, but I wanted to do it before the day of the Claiming is over."

Under his weight my mind flashes back to him between my legs when I was on the altar. To the way he teased me, drawing me close to the edge of a cliff, before pulling away and leaving me squirming.

"The cut..." I start, drawing my hand to my chest. It pulses like its own heartbeat.

"Hunter gave you that," he says, eyes shifting, and for the first time I see the stainless steel box on the bedside table. "But I wanted to give you one of my own."

He leans over me, reaching for the box. His shirt shifts, giving me a view of the hard muscles lining his abdomen. Settling back on my hips, he lifts the lid and shows me the contents. They confuse me, until he says, "I'm going to pierce you."

"Oh." Well, that couldn't be so bad. I'd never had a piercing before. My uncle didn't allow it and any girls that came into the Manor wearing them had them removed.

"This requires a delicate touch, and you have to be very still." He eyes my wrists, they're red from where they'd bound me to the altar, and beneath that scarred from before. "I don't want to tie you up again, but you have to promise me you won't move and I'll promise to do my best not to hurt you."

I don't want to be tied up again. Ever. "I promise."

He smiles, one corner quirked up. "Sit up."

Moving to a sitting position, I wince at the pain in my chest. Damon stares down at me, the look in his eyes indiscernible. His pupils are dilated and his tongue worries the hoop in his lip. I'm not prepared when he reaches for the hem of my gown and lifts it over my head.

Once again, I'm exposed to this man. His gaze roams over the bandage between my breasts. A dot of dark red blood seeps through the padding. "I knew the minute I saw them that this is how I wanted to mark you," he says, brushing his fingers over one nipple and then the other. They tighten into hard pebbles, sending that warm zing down my belly. Seemingly unaware of how my body is reacting, his forehead furrows in concentration. "A captive bead would look perfect here…" He lifts a stiff peak in assessment. "But we'll start with the barbell for faster healing."

"You're piercing my nipple?" I ask.

"Both of them." He directs his attention to the box and starts removing items. There's a bottle of alcohol, a tool that looks like scissors but the ends are flat with an opening on each side. Everything is neat and packaged carefully. My belly flutters nervously as he removes a package of latex gloves and pulls them on one at a time. Next he eases a needle out and holds up the pointed tip. That urge to fight, to *scream* bubbles in my chest, but I know that if I do he'll tell the King about Armand. I don't want to upset him. I want to be a good girl. I never want to be sent back.

"Will it hurt?" I ask.

"Probably," he admits, then lifts his shirt showing off his abs and chest. The peek I got earlier didn't do him justice. I knew he was strong, but now I see the muscles behind the power I've experienced first hand. Under the swath of tan skin are hard-packed muscles, with a thick line of brown hair traveling between his belly button and jeans. He's not showing me that, but up higher the silver hoops pierced through the soft flesh of his pinkish-brown nipples. "The left hurt more than the right, but now it's just more sensitive." He grabs my hand and flattens my fingers over the metal ring. "The pain can be worth the pleasure, Baroness. I tried to teach you that on the altar."

I know he's talking about his fingers flicking and rubbing against my pussy. How it felt combined with the sharp tip of the knife. I gently tug against the bar and he hisses, licking his bottom lip. "Christ," he mutters, and I feel the hard swell between our bodies. He pushes my hand away and drops his shirt before reaching for me again. He thumbs the peaks back to attention. "Yours are already really fucking sensitive. This is going to make it more intense."

Having his hands on me feels both right and wrong. Good but bad. Just like him, I realize. This man is nothing but ambiguous, even without the mask. I squirm under his touch, but it only seems to encourage him even more. Tugging and pinching the nipples until I squeak, "That hurts."

"Mmhm." He releases me and I close my hands over my aching breasts. Damon busies himself with tearing open an antiseptic wipe. "Let's clean you up."

The alcohol is cool on my inflamed nipples, raw from his touch. I exhale, trying to settle my nerves, until I see him pick up the tool that looks like scissors. I slump to my back, as much to get away from him as anything else, but before I can blink, he's got my right nipple in a death pinch.

"Hold still," he murmurs, spreading the tool.

"Wait–" The clamp snaps around the peak of skin, followed by the sharp pinch of pain shooting along my nerves, eliciting a body-quaking shudder. A scream loosens in my throat, but he looks down at me with a hard gaze and I exhale a quiet shudder instead.

"That's right, Baroness," he encourages while picking up the needle with a delicate touch, "deep breaths, one after the other."

I want to fade away, slip back into the dark recesses of my mind, but for once in my life, I'm fully alert. The sharp pain searing through my tit lights every nerve, every neuron on fire, including my brain. I'm very aware that everything about this moment is the opposite of the earlier ceremony. Daylight streams through the stained glass windows and there are no lurking Shadows or the intimidating presence of the King. We're both clean, our flesh scrubbed raw, the blood and dirt washed away. This time there are no masks between us. I can see the demon in front of me.

I take another deep breath and watch as he presses the needle against the tender flesh. I can't feel it, the clamps already too painful.

"Be still," he murmurs, and then pushes the needle through. My fingers twist in the bedsheet and a bright, white light flashes in front of my eyes. The scream throttles inside, but I puncture my bottom lip and he quickly pushes the bar though the fresh hole. Pierced. "Great job," he tells me, releasing the clamp. "When I first saw you, I thought you were too weak to handle this, but I was wrong." He looks up at me, lips curved. "You're different than you seem."

The praise rolls over my skin like a salve and I take a deep breath and tell him, "Do the other one. I'm ready."

"Yeah?" The piercing in his eyebrow quirks in surprise. "You're used to this, aren't you?" The rough pads of his fingers run over the scars on my wrists. "You're familiar with pain."

The question throws me off and I don't know how to answer. Pain is subjective. I know that. What others go through is nothing compared to my life, but pain is familiar. It's in the way my feet hurt in my pointe shoes, the way my muscles burn after a performance, the way my heart pounds every time I step across the Manor's threshold.

That's the thing about pain; it can always be worse.

The man in front of me, he's my Baron. My King chose him and that is all that matters.

"The King could have kept you for himself," he tells me, wiping antiseptic over the other nipple, "but he gave you to us. That's not what men do when they value something."

My worst fear. Not that he's given me to his men, but that he doesn't need me. I've seen what happens when people are no longer needed–wanted. "How do I become that?" I ask. "Valuable?"

"I've already told you," he lifts the clamps, "you just have to be a good girl."

Damon turns back to his work and I'm glad there's no time to recover, no acclimating, before he snaps the clamp over my left tit and the pain starts all over again.

As the sensation ripples through my body, and Damon marks me–*claims me*–I know it in my core.

There is no rest. There is no escape.

There is only pain.

9

Timothy

THE OLDER I get the more grateful I am to survive another day.

With the sun rising and another Hunt behind me, I exit the tunnel into my personal quarters. My bed, imposing and made of solid black oak but with the most comfortable mattress money can buy, taunts me after the long night. In the past I would have succumbed, sleeping off the revelry. I'm older now. More disciplined.

Graves, my assistant, is already in my room, waiting for my arrival.

"Congratulations on a new class of Barons," he says, taking my cloak and mask.

"I'm not sure congratulations are in order." I run my hand through my hair, loosening it from the weight of the mask. The entire night had been on the verge of disaster. Sure, everything looked to standard. Tradition makes that easy. Follow the rules, adhere to the rites, and the pieces fall into place. But after the last two years, I'm finding it challenging to pretend things are *normal* in Forsyth. If that's even a possibility. The old Kings are gone, picked off one by one, and a new crop of leadership has risen. I'm the last one standing, and if I can't get a handle on what's happening in this city, I have no doubt I'll be next. "We'll need to notify Trudie Stein and let her know her son is coming home."

"Today?"

I shrug out of my suit jacket and rest it over the end of the bed before removing my tie and shirt. "Maybe tomorrow. Let's analyze the body first."

"I'll contact Shepherd and have her come out to the morgue."

It's good to have the coroner on call. "Perfect."

Graves places the mask in a bronze case and folds the cloak, securing them both in a cabinet by the door. I finish undressing and he opens the glass doors that lead to the patio off my room. I'm not the only one with discipline. It's one reason we work so well together.

Gibson Graves is a former BRN, class of '98. Back then, we'd been fraternity brothers and good friends, enjoying the spoils of being rich and entitled. Pussy, psychedelics, power... it was all at our fingertips and we took it by the handful. We'd drifted a bit after graduation, but when I became King, I needed a confidant. Someone smart and capable but most of all, someone I could trust. Graves was the first person I contacted after my cousin Benji killed Clive Kayes and left me with no choice but to claim the throne. For many years he was the only one who knew the truth behind the Baron mask–a secret he's never revealed.

"You're sure about these two?" he asks, and I know he's referring to Kemp and Sorrin. "They're different from your regular picks."

"Times have changed. The last thing we need is entitled brats stoking the flames of chaos right now. And beyond that, I don't want to keep one eye over my shoulder, looking for a blade in my back. I need loyalty and commitment. I need hard workers. Smart men."

"So you want a guy who dropped out of high school and has a prison record?" he asks.

"If prison records kept men from leadership in Forsyth we'd all be screwed," I point out. "Kemp has a GED and a tested IQ of 155. He could have graduated from high school with honors if he'd been included or had a stable living situation. Academics aren't his problem–the chip on his shoulder is his downfall–that's why I arranged his early release and scholarship to make him eligible."

"And Sorrin?" he asks. "What does he bring to the table?"

I'll admit that from the outside, Hunter Sorrin seems like an unlikely pick. Quiet. Academically driven. Lacking in adequate social skills, but after reviewing his background I noticed some trends. "He has an attention to detail that is unparalleled. Give him a task, a challenge, a subject of interest, and he'll master it quickly. He's obsessive, and right now I need someone that can bring that kind of focus to the work I'm trying to accomplish."

"They're outcasts, Timothy."

"And that may be exactly what makes them so useful!" I snap. His eyebrow lifts at the loss of my temper. Taking a deep breath I add, "I appreciate your concern and I understand you're looking out for me and the fraternity, but I assure you that my moves are in the best interest of all of us."

"I trust your decision." He nods toward the porch. "The bath is ready."

"You're a lifesaver."

Shucking my pants, I walk outside in my shorts, and dip my fingers in the galvanized steel tub.

"Fifty-two degrees," Graves notes, nodding at the thermometer.

"Jesus," I mutter, wondering why I put myself through this. "One of these days my balls are going to shrivel up and fall off." Not that I have much use for them. Abstinence has also become part of my process. Learning to channel my urges into something more productive. Denial can be good for the soul. I push my shorts down and sling a leg into the tub, feeling the icy water. There's no time to fuck around, not when it's this cold, and I quickly submerge myself. "Fuck."

Graves starts the timer. The amount varies. After a workout I'll shoot for ten or more minutes. After a long, stressful day or night? Five will do the trick.

"Any idea what really happened out there?" he asks, leaning his hip against the tub. He's wearing a light gray button-down and dark gray slacks. A thick gold watch wraps around his wrist. His eye for fashion is impeccable, which has been a help over the years.

"I have my speculations." The girl looked wild when she came back from the hunt. Blood all over her hands, dirt on her knees and feet. Predator or prey? Maybe both, if I'm to believe Kemp. Someone tore her panties off, a clear indicator that an attempt was made to break my single rule. "I'm sure the Shadows bore witness, but as you know, the details of the hunt are never revealed to those not participating." It protects us all. Dangerous things go on during the hunt. This isn't even the first death. Those had been considered accidental. Hazing gone wrong. But this? This was no accident.

But what was it?

"I assume everyone made it back from the ceremony?" I ask, body shuddering. Every nerve pleads to get out and get warm. I mentally tell them to suck it up. This is good for us.

"Kemp and Sorrin are in their rooms cleaning up. The Baroness is also in her room." I nod, pleased everyone is finally under one roof. "Regina opted to stay behind and see to her wounds."

That's a bit of a surprise. Regina has always had an aloof nature, but after tonight's events, it's probably best to have someone check on the new Baroness. "Thank her for me."

"I will."

Just like the other Baronesses that have come through during my reign, I've set her up with a trust fund. Like all Royal women, the sacrifices and secrets my daughters carry with them are substantial. Unlike Ashby, I don't poison them and leave them to rot in the soil. Or Payne, who put them to work in his whorehouse. Cartwright discarded his Duchesses like trash, too focused on an unattainable purity that left him alone and heirless. And Lucia? Good riddance. He was nothing but a glorified pill pusher, hellbent on destroying Forsyth for his own gain.

No, I've always viewed my Baronesses and Barons like my own

children. They need security, nurturing, and guidance. All the things my own son, Remington, rejected.

My teeth start to chatter as Graves reaches for a towel and clicks the button on the side of the watch. "Time."

"Thank god." My muscles scream as I grip the sides of the tub and pull myself up. Water rushes down my body and my cold skin meets the warmer air with relief. I waste no time getting out. As I wrap the towel around my waist, Graves places a robe over my shoulders. Warming up gradually is the key.

"For what it's worth," he says, handing me a cup of freshly poured tea, "I think it's likely that Stein had it coming. Whoever eliminated him probably did you a favor."

I can't argue with that–and I don't. He was killed by his own weapon. A humiliating defeat. Armand was here for a reason, hand selected like every other Baron during my reign, but Graves is correct. Anyone who can't survive The Hunt is a liability–especially this year when the stakes are so high. There's no room for error.

"What does my calendar look like today?"

He smirks. "Is that your way of asking if there's time for a nap?"

"Is that your way of saying I'm getting too old for this bullshit?" I snap back. "Because if it is, fuck you."

"Not a chance," he smirks. "You're in better shape than you were when we were in college."

He's right. Back then, youth and genetics were all I needed to get through the day. I lived the hard, partying life that comes with being a royal and never woke up with a single hangover. A random crypt chaser and a dash of regret maybe, but a hangover? Never. After I became King, I realized I needed to take care of myself. Not just for me, but for the men I lead. For my daughters. Our motto may be, *'Remember you must die,'* but that doesn't mean today. I don't fear death, but I sure as hell do everything I can to stave it off. I lift weights, practice Jiu-jitsu, meditation, and yoga. Twice a year I commit to a spiritual journey on ayahuasca. I eat well, foregoing sugar and supplementing when and where I can. My body fat is under ten percent. And yeah, I shrink my balls in ice water every goddamn morning. Whatever it takes.

"I'm not saying you need a nap," Graves continues, "*but* there is time for you to get some rest before Dean Hexley arrives."

Fuck. I'd forgotten–*no*–blocked out the meeting with Arianette's uncle. Insufferable bastard. "What time?"

"Two PM." He walks over with the teapot. I wave off a refill. "While you're dealing with him, are there any special instructions for the girl?"

"No." I shake my head. "She's to be treated like any other Baroness." I'm not sure what to make of Arianette. She's not the kind of girl I'd normally pick for The Hunt, but the choice wasn't mine. That arrangement had been made years before. There's an edge of unpredictability about her that I don't understand, or like. She's obviously a fighter–she managed to escape her kidnapper when none of the other girls missing have been seen or heard from again. Well, at least alive. But there's also a fragility about her that makes me wary that she's up to the task of being a House Girl and even more so, my bride. "From what I witnessed tonight, I suspect the men will have their hands full."

"Excluding..." he prompts.

"Yes, her virginity." I fight an eye roll. The price of virtue in Forsyth is overinflated. Personally, I don't give a shit, but under the circumstances of our contractual agreement, Arianette must stay pure until our wedding night. "Other than that... she's theirs to break in as they see fit."

The Baronesses, or my Daughters of Darkness, are under my purview as King, but the Barons will see to her training. Technically, I'm still married to Amber. And despite her betrayal and descent into madness that has kept us apart for decades now, I've remained faithful to the spirit of our vows, by never divorcing her or taking on a new partner. The Baroness allows me the appearance of companionship without the obligation–although things will change with the Black Wedding. If things had gone differently, Remington would be marrying the Hexley girl. He'd be a Baron and in line for the throne, unfortunately his allegiance is not with his blood family, but with the Bruin-Perilini clans.

It even would have been possible to rearrange the agreement for Whitaker Ashby to take his place. His Baron blood is more pure than my own. But the Ashbys have circled around the Princess–their Princess–and he is as unlikely to return to BRN as my own son.

No, there are burdens of being King that fall to me and no one else. Not my son, Ashby, or the newly chosen leaders of DKS. That decision was made when I killed my cousin and banished my wife for her sins.

I am the one that wears the mantle, *the mask,* even when it requires me to do things I'd rather not.

And marrying Arianette Hexley is one of those things.

THE DEAN IS NOTORIOUSLY PUNCTUAL, arriving exactly at two on the dot. I'm masked and waiting in the library when he's ushered in by one of the senior members of the fraternity.

"Dean," I gesture to one of the chairs by the fire, "it's always a pleasure."

Arianette's uncle, Owen Hexley, is anything but a pleasure. The man in front of me is well dressed, his shoes Italian and his watch Swiss. He has no royal ties, no bloodline that grants him privilege in the city. His obligations are to the university and the well-being of the students. Academia is competitive. To get to the position of Dean, or more accurately, Provost, at a university like Forsyth takes a particular skill set, one more in line with a politician than the duties held by the Kings of Forsyth. He'd wash his hands of all of us if he could, but the frats and the university are interconnected. One doesn't exist without the other. We need him for our continued recruitment and he needs us to keep his doors open and pockets lined.

I've known Owen Hexley for a long time, but today I see him in a different light. He's no longer the slim, studious, man that I knew in college, having bulked up over the years. But his eyes... they're a deep brown and carry a haunting intensity.

Arianette has her uncle's eyes, and a flash of her gazing up at me from the altar, ready to sacrifice herself to me and her Barons, strikes me like a bolt of lightning.

"I received the announcement that my niece was initiated as Baroness last night."

Five letters went out this morning, hand delivered by my men. Four to the separate territories, and one to Strong Manor, to the man sitting in front of me.

"She achieved her status at sunrise," I tell him. "It was a moving ceremony."

"I'm sure," he says, giving me a wary look. The mask makes people nervous, a benefit I thoroughly enjoy. In addition to hiding my true identity, it allows me the freedom to speak the truth more freely, in a way I couldn't as Timothy Maddox. "My niece isn't supposed to be a mere House Girl," he reminds me, crossing one leg over the other. "She's to be your bride."

"I'm well aware." I try not to bristle. A man with this much power over me should be strapped to the teeth. Instead his weapon is a piece of paper more powerful than any gun hustled down on the Avenue. "The wedding is still on," I tell him, "but you and I both know this arrangement is in name more than reality."

"I know nothing of the sort–"

"She's barely a woman, for Christ's sake!" A mentally distressed one at that. "She should be with her peers. She should get an education. Further her interests. As Baroness she will be able to achieve that, while also being under strict supervision and protection."

"That was not our deal."

"No. The deal was that when your niece came of age she would have a black wedding with a male blood relative to the throne. As I am heirless," or at least Clive Kayes is, after I killed his son, Benji, "I am the only option and I will fulfill the obligation. But the girl I picked up at the hospital is ill-prepared for the duties of a King's wife. She's barely capable of taking care of herself."

"Are you implying that my niece is defective in some way?"

"She's young and vulnerable," I reply with sympathy. "You should be thankful I've taken her off your hands, not making demands."

"She was fine before she was taken," he begins. "It's not my fault those monsters traumatized her." His eyes meet mine. "At least they left her intact. The doctor at the hospital confirmed it."

I scowl beneath my mask. Hexley doesn't know it, but I'm well familiar with the signs of mental disorder. The inability to focus, mood swings, heightened emotions, the vacant, faraway looks, the fear that vibrates off their body. Both my wife and son are afflicted, and their illness has destroyed our family. This girl... well, I'm not one to armchair diagnose, but her distress goes deeper than her kidnapping. It permeates her very being. No, she's been afflicted for some time.

But a deal is a deal, and I'm not walking away from this empty-handed. "How I manage my recruits, my Barons, and the Baroness in my house, will be my decision." I feel my temper rising and I take a deep breath. "There is only room for one woman in the House of Night, and that woman will fulfill both the roles of Baroness and my wife."

He's quiet for a long moment, but I see the wheels turning in his head. "As long as she is your responsibility and is treated as a royal."

Because that is what this is all about. He wants access. A link to royalty. To our power.

But a lingering vision of Arianette keeps surfacing in my mind. Those wild, scared brown eyes watching her men as they painted her in sacred Baron blood. The way she took our symbol being marked between her breasts, swallowing the pain. I watched her body tremble as DK stroked her sensitive flesh, drawing her to the edge and then retreating.

I may not experience the Hunt and Claiming directly, but these men are an extension of myself. Their hands do my work and the work they did on Arianette was enlightening.

I've experienced many BRN ceremonies over the years, but even with my annoyance over this arrangement, I felt a difference with this girl. My reply is low and firm, "She became *my* responsibility during the initiation last night."

"You say that," he glances down to inspect his nails, "but I'll need proof of consummation."

"Are you asking for a front row seat? Or for me to hang a bloody sheet off the Kayes Crypt for all of Forsyth to see?" I sneer, disgusted by his presence. By the fact I'm lowered to this position with a man of no royal standing. No power to make such a demand. But that's the thing. Hexley has something I want, and this arrangement is what gives it to me.

"I'm aware that it's a Baron's way to be dramatic, but cut the theatrics. A medical exam will do."

"And when you get that, I'll get what I want?" I tap my ring on the wooden arm of my chair, my impatience growing. "As promised?"

"You'll receive the keys once the ceremony is performed and I receive my proof."

I nod curtly, ready for this man to leave my sanctuary. I figure the best way for that to happen is to give him exactly what he wants. "The Black Wedding will take place in two weeks."

He perks up. "So soon?"

"On Halloween," I affirm, ignoring the way his lips turn down with his distaste for our rituals. "You'll receive an invitation shortly."

"Then I consider the matter settled," he stands, as ready as I am for him to leave. "Give my niece my regards and let her know I'll see her at the ceremony, where it'll be my honor to unite our families."

There's something about this man I don't trust, and it's not the false pretension that oozes out of his every pore. Not once has he asked to see Arianette. Not when she was found on the riverbank, not when she was recovering in the hospital, and not while she's been in my possession.

He may not have royal blood, but he sure fucking acts like it.

10

H unter

"...BEFORE I go, I want to discuss something that has been on my mind. Rebirth. I know that's usually a spring theme; hatching eggs, baby bunnies, and hungry little caterpillars eating their ways through everything they run across." I lean back, one hand scratching Ares' ears and the other holding a tightly wrapped cigarette, a curl of smoke rising from the tip. "In Forsyth, fall is the catalyst. It's not just the start of a new year, with new roommates and classes starting all over campus with the opportunity for each of us to fill our still evolving brains with knowledge. There's a fresh round of Greek recruitment, new tribes of Royals have been selected, their House Girls chosen for whatever the year plans to throw at them, which," I move my mouth close to the microphone and add quietly, "for the lucky won't be getting snatched off the street in broad daylight..." I take another drag, this one slower than before. I only allow myself one for every hour of the show and my shift is winding down. "I digress... *rebirth* is in the air. Quite literally for the Princess who just dropped a new princeling, and certainly for the BRN who just initiated their new Barons and claimed a new Baroness under the full moon."

I suck the very last of the tobacco out of the cigarette, then let the paper burn to the end before stubbing it out. "It's a new year, new opportunities, new loyalties, new lies." I set up the next song, the first strains of music hitting the air. "As always, I leave you on this fine fall morning with the most sincere of blessings from WXFU: Wake up, Forsyth. Wake up, and smell that sweet decay..."

I turn the music all the way up and slide the chair away from the desk. The next DJ, a girl named Everly, waits outside. She's a journalism major and treats her morning shift like she's an investigative reporter at fucking CNN.

She enters as I pack up my bag and sling it over my shoulder. "Do you really have to smoke in here?" she asks, dramatically waving her hand in front of her face. "It's like walking into my grandfather's house."

"It's part of my process." It's an argument we have every time she follows my shift. "And your grandfather sounds cool."

"Trust me, he wasn't." She hangs her coat on the hook behind the door. "He was a recluse with no friends, rotten teeth, and black lungs." She looks down. "Morning, Ares."

Ares sits patiently and I grunt, giving him the approval to greet her. He pops up with excitement and nudges her with his nose. She strokes the soft black fur on his head. "My first news update is in fifteen," she says, looking up at me, "but I saved room for any juicy tidbits you wanted to add?"

It's barely been a day but word has already traveled about the new Barons. I know the King made an announcement, notifying the other Royals about our appointment. Despite the fact the Forsyth Greek system is formed of well-organized criminal enteprises ranging from the sex trade to running guns to torture, each house excels at one particular skill: gossip.

"No comment."

"Including the fact that there were only two Barons listed instead of the traditional three?"

Armand. Fuck, I have no idea how that's going to be handled, but until I'm told directly... "Like I said, no comment."

"Be that way," she grumbles, before clamping the headphones over her ears. I slip out the door, Ares at my feet, and head to my truck parked in the empty lot. It's still dark outside, the sweet spot where the world is still asleep but a new day has begun. The Chevy's heavy door opens with a creak, and I tap on the seat. "*Hop.*"

He jumps in, settling himself on the cherry red, leather passenger seat. Besides Ares, the truck is the most important thing in my life. I'd bought her from a musty old garage near Northridge. At the time it was a piece of shit, more rust than metal, but I could see the value in the old girl, and paid five hundred cash. Over the past two summers, I'd painstakingly restored her, inside and out. She's a fucking beaut.

Pulling out on the Avenue, I spot the sun starting to rise over the east and the reality of the last thirty-six hours hits home. At this point yesterday, I'd seen a new brother die, watched a girl suck another man's cock, and had just finished carving a pentagram into that same woman's chest.

A woman, who for all intents and purposes, *belongs to me.*

It had been wild, no, exhilarating, I think, navigating the truck to the parking lot exit. Two blocks away is the highway that heads away from town. The House of Night is on the outskirts, an old stone castle transformed into a home. *My home*, at least for the next year.

I'd crashed most of the prior day, sleeping off the intensity of the night before. I woke up, ate, and came into the station for my Sunday night shift. Class starts in a couple of hours and I want to at least change and check in before heading to campus on my first day as Baron.

Baron.

Fuck. That still blows my mind.

On impulse, I turn right instead of left, away from the highway, towards town, not ready to go back yet.

The whole experience, from finding the envelope tucked into the door at my dorm to going through recruitment, then being singled out as a leader... it doesn't make sense. Not for a guy like me. I've got no royal ties. In fact, I've been pretty publicly dismissive of them on my show.

But then again... the Shadows? Nameless. Faceless. *That* I get.

I feel like I've already lived most of my life in the shadows. Invisible in a town that runs on prestige and elitism. We may not have had power or money but my parents doted on me, excused my strangeness as quirkiness or on some days, genius. Despite their encouragement, I knew I didn't do much to help my cause. I was weird. Nerdy. Too focused on my hobbies and shunning the status quo. I was unathletic, and my feet were too big for my body–at least until I hit nineteen–when everything evened out and I saw the benefit in taking care of myself.

It's not like I didn't try to make friends, but if you didn't have a certain last name and it wasn't emblazoned on a building or the back of a jersey, much less stamped on a credit card at the age of twelve, then no one was interested. Not the guys and *definitely* not the girls. Not when there were guys in the school with last names like Payne. Or Bruin. Or the worst... Ashby.

Now, by some twist of Forsyth fate, I'm one of them.

The truck engine rumbles as I roll past campus, which is as quiet as the cemetery at this time of day. I try to reconcile that newfound fate. It's illogical for a kid who spent his lifetime alone, entertaining myself and finding projects that I could do on my own. '*Hyperfocus*' my school counselor called it. Fuck, the better word is *obsession*. I never had any control over the topic. Whatever it was at the time, came to me, and latched on tight, like I never had a choice. Trains. Puzzles. Bitcoin. Forging. Modifying cars. Experimenting with chemistry.

My dad often took me to work with him, I guess hoping that being on campus, around the non-stop energy of college life, would rub off on me. It didn't. If anything it proved I was just as invisible there as I was in other places in my life. Even more so when I found the crawlspace.

I wasn't just invisible. I was *hidden.*

It ran behind the Forsyth dorms–low ceilings, pipe-bent corridors, ducts fat with dust and the smell of rusted copper. My dad was doing maintenance. Swapping out something in the boiler room. Told me to "stay near," which for me meant "go explore." I didn't think much when I saw the warped vent cover. Or how the screws were already half-stripped, basically an invitation.

The space opened easily–tight and dark and humming with mystery. I crawled on elbows and knees, drawn by the faintest light bleeding through the slats ahead. And then I saw them.

A girl. College-aged, wrapped in a fuzzy towel, fresh out of the shower. I held my breath and watched her towel drop, revealing her soft, damp body. Tits small but perfect. Pussy bare. My pulse quickened in my veins, in my ears. A drumbeat of warning that I fully ignored.

There were vents to every room on the hall, a window into a world I'd never be allowed in on my own. I should've looked away. Should've been sick or ashamed or scared.

But I wasn't.

I was *hard.*

Not because of the bodies. Not exactly. It was the *access.* The control. The way they had no idea I was there; breathing, sweating, devouring them through the slats.

I went back the next night. And the next. I started to memorize their names. Their schedules. The times when they were alone with their boyfriends or girlfriends. I witnessed it all, virginities lost, head being given, pussies eaten like a buffet.

I brought tools to adjust the vent angle, a little sound recorder for the moans I'd hear. For their laughter. My skin prickled every time I slipped into the dark and rubbed myself raw.

I told myself I wasn't hurting anyone. That watching wasn't the same as doing. Watching was better.

Which is where I find myself now, rolling the truck to a stop in the back lot of the Maddox Hotel. The eight-story building is just outside of campus and acts as the primary hotel for visitors of the university.

It's upscale, the complete opposite of the shitty places down on the Avenue, with a coffee shop in the lobby and a rooftop bar that overlooks the city. Those are of no interest to me, which is why I park the truck in the quiet lot, cracking the window and leaving Ares with a blanket, a travel bowl of water, and a new rawhide bone. I rub my forehead against his, saying, *"Braver hund,"* and exit the vehicle.

There are two places I tend to go after my shift at the station: to get new ink, or to get off. Today I'm feeling like the latter, and cross the empty parking lot towards the non-descript dark gray door leading to the basement of the hotel.

I knock twice, and the peephole hatch slides open.

"Nocturne," I say, glancing over my shoulder until I hear the locks unlatch, sliding out of place, and the door opens to a faceless keeper. He's wearing a mask, and hands me one to put on: this one is the opposite of the one from the Hunt, which covered the lower half of my face. This one obscures the nose and eyes, leaving the mouth available for use. I slide the elastic band around the back of my head and start down the dimly lit staircase that leads to Noir Sanctum.

Everyone is masked in the club. It's a rule. No names. No faces. It's Baron territory after all, but no one here knows I'm an actual Baron. This isn't a place for the frat–more for civilians–interested in anonymity mixed with a little depravity. The owner of the hotel and club, Timothy Maddox, is well known to be DKS down to his roots. He made a place for his people.

I'd stumbled on the club by accident–the way any red-blooded teenager does: porn. *Voyeurism* porn, to be specific. At first I thought it was a joke. Why the hell would Forsyth need an underground sex club? We already have a brothel and a strip club. But sure as fuck, it exists, and it's not easy to get in. Maddox, unlike the Lords' Velvet Hideaway and Princes' Gentlemen's Chamber, has standards. This place doesn't require ID, but you do have to have a password, which can only be acquired through a rigorous application process. It took me four months to find someone willing to even share the application. Well, four months and a few pictures of my cousin Alisha's feet.

I didn't really expect to get in, an engineering major from the university with no money or connections, but one day an encrypted message came through my phone. When I opened it: the password. I get a new one every other day.

Downstairs, I'm met by the sound of laughter. A blonde in a corset perches at the bar, leaned in close to a man in a simple domino mask. Her top's so tight her breasts swell high with every breath, a leather choker snug at her throat–black with a gold ring. An open ring. *Invitation.*

Her eyes flick up to mine as I ease into a seat at the other end of the bar–my safe spot.

"Whiskey. No ice," I tell the bartender, eyes skimming the room. I'm not here to drink. I'm here to watch.

The walls are lined with burgundy velvet, rich enough to drink. Three dim chandeliers drip low from a black ceiling, casting pools of golden light that don't quite reach the corners. In one of them, a woman sprawls on a chaise while a man kisses up her thighs. Another corner holds a trio–two men and a woman, laughing between slow, exploratory touches. They make it look so easy. So natural.

I sip. Small. Needing something to occupy my hands and distract me from the stiffening between my legs.

Over in a booth, a woman sits in the middle of two men. All three are making out, sharing long kisses. She runs her hands down the front of their pants, working both of them at once.

The first time I came to the Sanctum, I felt like a voyeur. Like a ghost. But somehow, the distance made sense. I don't do touch. I don't trust myself with it. But here, I can participate in the silence. In *observation.* Here, it's all rules, signals, structure.

The blonde at the bar stands, trailing her fingers down the masked man's arm. She glances back at me once more before they disappear into the hallway. She knows I'll follow. Not to join, but to witness.

I wait. Count to twenty. Set my drink down with a quiet clink, and step after them.

The hallway branches into private and semi-private rooms. If the door's open, you're welcome to watch. It's early still–some rooms are dark, but others flicker with candlelight and movement.

I find them three doors in. The man is unlacing her corset with careful fingers. She faces the mirror above the bed, watching herself come undone.

She sees me. Doesn't flinch. Just smiles.

He frees her tits–full, flushed, already peaked. He palms them, rough but reverent. Her body leans into it, hips swaying slightly as he trails his mouth down her sternum. She adjusts her choker with a teasing touch.

"Want to come play with us?" she asks, lips parted, eyes sultry.

"No." I step inside and drop into the corner chair. "I want to watch you play with each other."

She pouts, but it's theatrical. The man's already unzipping. Confident. He knows his role, just like I know mine.

"Bend her over," I say, clearly and calmly, expecting no obedience but inviting it all the same.

The man hesitates for a beat, our masked eyes meeting for a brief second. He doesn't have to obey my directives, but his tongue darts out and he roughly spins his partner, sending her sprawling forward. Her tits sway, nipples brushing against the sheet. He lifts her skirt and tugs off her panties, tossing them to the side.

A memory of dirty gray panties on a forest floor pops into my mind. I imagine the Baroness like this, bent over and submissive. The erection I'd managed to keep under control thickens into a hard rod.

The woman looks back at me, breath warm, expectant.

"Here," I command, getting her attention. I gesture between us. "Eyes right here. Watch *me* while he fucks *you*."

The dude is into it, as much as she is, his cock hard and straining against the latex. She keeps her hazel eyes focused on mine. Behind her, he wraps his hand around the base of his cock and angles himself toward her entrance.

She nods, her pink tongue darting out to wet her lips.

He strokes himself once, steady. "She ready?" I ask.

He checks, slick fingers gleaming in the low light.

She's moaning before he even enters. He fills her slowly, deliberately. No frenzy, no rush. Just pressure and rhythm and a shared, building pace.

Her eyes stay locked on mine, even as her mouth falls open. Her cheeks flush deeper when I shift forward, elbows on my knees, watching them like a slow-burning ritual.

"Grip her hair," I murmur. "Let her feel it."

He does, twining the strands around his fingers, and yanks. *Hard.* Her moan deepens.

This is the Sanctum at its best. Control, performance, reverence, and release. It's what I crave out there, in the real world, but can't seem to grasp.

Her eyes flutter shut, and I call out a reminder, "Look at me."

This moment is not about intimacy. It's about control. Can I get these people to do what I want? When her eyes blink open, obeying, my cock thickens again.

Leaning forward, I get closer to her. Strands of her hair have fallen from the clasp, and lipstick and eye makeup are smudged. Her eyes dart to my mouth, like she thinks I'm going to join in, maybe kiss her, maybe unbutton my pants and thrust my cock between her parted lips.

"He's going to take you to the next level," I explain, looking from her to him. "Wrap your hands around her throat."

"My–" her words are cut off by his fingers clenching around her neck. The man doesn't skip a beat, thrusting into her erratically, his orgasm close. I can't get enough of the push-pull between them as she struggles to breathe and he edges himself, wanting this to last longer.

The throbbing in my cock intensifies. "Fuck, that's good."

Her eyes are wide, changing from sex to fear. A tremble builds in her limbs. She may be scared but she's also turned on. The energy between us, the three of us, is electric, and the urge to reach out to pinch, to bite, to throttle the very essence out of her is fucking consuming.

No touching.

That's the rule.

I tilt my head. "You scared?"

She nods.

"Of me or him?" I ask.

Over her shoulder he groans, the orgasm ripping through him. His fingers tighten, hard enough that her eyes flutter shut. Her body convulses, not just from the lack of air, but from her body finally getting release.

The man drops her and she flops forward, life and pleasure wrung from her body.

I lean forward and ask again. "Who are you scared of? Me or him?"

The sound of heavy breathing cloaks her voice but there's no mistaking it when she says, "You."

TURNING INTO THE LONG DRIVEWAY, I park the car by the standalone garage behind the house. It's still early and there are only a few lights in the stained glass windows. When I get to the back entry I'm surprised to see Graves waiting by the door.

I'd left Blondie and her man in a sweaty pile at Noir Sanctum, barely making it to the bathroom before cumming in the sink. When I got to the truck, I felt the urge lessened, my body purged, and found a happy Ares napping with his bone.

"Good morning," Graves says as I walk up. Curiosity nags at me, wondering if he knows where I've been. I release the worry quickly. It was only a few nights ago that the King not only watched but encouraged me to carve a mark in a girl's chest. "I know you're just getting off a shift at the station, but the King has requested to see you and Damon before the day starts." He steps aside, allowing me to enter the house. "He's in the library. Shall I take Ares back to your room until you're finished?"

"Thanks," I say, giving the dog a pat and sending him on his way. The House of Night is larger than it looks, the word 'chapel' deceiving. It was formerly a large campus, including a separate dormitory used to house monks. Currently the members of BRN live there. The Barons and Baroness live in the main building, now organized into a large home. From what I've seen there is a kitchen, living areas, and multiple other bedrooms, including the one DK and I share. The King's living quarters are in the former rectory, attached to the back of the building. I follow the long hallway to the library and see DK standing outside. "Any idea what this is about?"

"No fucking clue." He tugs at the ring in his eyebrow. "Could be just about anything."

DK lifts his hand and knocks on the heavy door. A low voice calls for us to enter and we step inside the King's private office for the first time. The room has a rich warmth to it, thick carpets on the floor and heavy floor-to-ceiling drapery. Smooth leather chairs are arranged in front of the massive stone fireplace, and his dark mahogany desk, covered in neatly stacked piles of books and papers, takes up the east-facing wall. Behind it, the wall is covered with a black curtain.

Otherwise there are books everywhere. Shelves lining all available wall space. I glance at the spines as we walk toward the King, who is sitting at a small round table under one of the windows, the early morning light streaming through the colored glass. The titles reach out to me, tugging on my curiosity. Mythology, religion, paganism, atheism–all the -isms, actually. There are rows about history, others stacked end-to-end with biographies. Then the sciences.

It would take a lifetime to read all of these, I consider, approaching the table, where the King has a plate of food in front of him, his knife and fork already in hand. He's masked, still bronze with the horns curved upward, but overall this one is less formal. He's covered from his forehead to just under his nose, leaving his mouth unobscured.

"Sit," he directs, pointing to the empty chairs across from him. We've barely settled into our seats when two plates appear, delivered by one of the servants in the house. It's similar to the food in front of him. A bowl of oatmeal, eggs and bacon. A dish of berries sits on the side. "We all have busy days, so I figured we do this over breakfast."

"Do what?" DK pulls the black cloth napkin into his lap, adding quickly, "If you don't mind me asking."

"BRN business," he replies, "along with some other details about your positions I'd like to discuss."

I take a tentative bite of oatmeal. It's lightly sweetened, maybe with honey?

"Typically this is a meeting held with all three of my new Barons. Obviously, we're down one."

DK takes a deep breath and then starts, "Armand–"

"There's no need to discuss. I'm not here to ask for details. That truth will reside in the forest, but murder in our house is unacceptable. We clean up death, we don't cause it. We tend to take care of the destruction caused in other territories, but this is just another sign of how things have shifted." His lips purse with thought. "The difficulty with Armand is that he comes from a powerful family. His mother is well-connected and a vocal member of the community. She will be devastated at the loss of a son she believed had no flaws."

"So she won't believe he tried to rape the Baroness?" I ask.

"No. She will believe he was entitled to take what he wants, even if it belongs to me."

"Fucker," DK mutters.

"Indeed." He laughs. "For now keep quiet about it and if anyone asks, the official answer will be that he declined to take the oath and we haven't seen him since. It wouldn't be the first time someone didn't live up to expectations. I'll handle Trudie."

"Are you going to replace him?" I think back to Everly's questions at the station. "Initiate another Baron?"

He shakes his head. "No. We'll move forward as is."

He finishes his breakfast and reaches into his pocket, removing a small silver container. He opens it up and dumps a dozen or more pills into his hand. They're capsules, various colors of compounded powder. DK's eyebrow raises. "I don't believe in pharmaceuticals," the King says. "Everything we need, body and mind, can be found in nature."

The man sitting in front of us is strong and healthy, his shirt-sleeves tight against his biceps. Whatever this man consumes, it seems to be working.

"Now, the other matter at hand, the Baroness."

Shit. Did he find out about what we did to her in those woods? The lies DK told to cover for her? I force myself to breathe normally.

"Normally, the Barons and House Girl have their own relationship. She's there to support you within BRN and among the other houses. I've never interfered in this dynamic. She belongs to her Barons body, mind, and soul." The muscle at the back of his jaw tenses. "Unfortunately, as with everything in Forsyth right now, things are not normal."

I'm tempted to ask what is 'normal' for a man who oversaw a blood oath and ritual this weekend, but I hold back.

"As you know," he continues, "the Baroness and I will have a Black Wedding on the thirty-first of October."

"That's only a couple of weeks away," DK notes.

"Yes, and during that time it will be your responsibility to make sure Arianette is protected from outside threats, attending to her classes and obligations, and trained for her role moving forward." The words are spoken without a hint of flexibility. If I've been wondering why I was chosen as one of the Barons, something tells me this is part of it. "Whoever kidnapped the girl is still out there. I've kept her under tight security since she was released from the hospital, but the Baroness, just like all of the House Girls, must have a public-facing persona. Starting today, she'll return to campus as a full-time student and perform the duties of Baroness, like all the girls before her, under your supervision."

DK and I exchange a look, the same thought running through our heads. He's the one that actually says it. "Do you think she's actually capable of these things? She seems a little..."

"Erratic," I blurt, recalling the way she looked moments after killing Armand.

"*Fragile*," DK stresses. "From our interactions... I'm not convinced she can behave like the other House Girls."

The King takes his time before answering, ultimately saying, "I agree she is unique. Naive. Raised in an isolated and controlled environment that should have prepared her for the day she would marry a King. I do not know if her behavior is the result of her upbringing or the kidnapping–maybe both. In an ideal world we would have more time, but that isn't the case. We have weeks, not months, before Samhain." He looks between us. "Because of that, your job will be to train her for the duties required as both Baroness and my bride."

"Train," I repeat.

"On the outside this means her dress, her behavior, her attitude and acclimation to Forsyth society, but I know what's on your mind, and rightly so. The Baroness should be yours to break-in, to fuck and screw, and to suck your dicks in the stacks at the library. I'm not taking that away from you, not exactly, but there are things that are off limits."

"I'm guessing her virginity," I say.

"You guess correct." He reaches for his tea and takes a sip. "Also, no kissing."

DK shoots me an agitated look, but neither of those are a concern of mine.

"Is there anything in particular you'd like for us to focus on?" DK asks, his gray eyes darkening. "You know, in respect to training."

He waves off the question as if it's an annoyance, not discussing the ways we can defile a woman. "I want her compliant, both at home and in public. I want her to behave like a Royal, even if she isn't one, and for the females, that includes a certain acceptance of their role within our system. So, whatever it is that you need to do to make her that way–do it."

My mind goes right back to her on her knees, lips circled around DK's dick, and instantly I go hard, cock twitching under the table. It took the threat of telling the King about Armand to get her to comply. Threats will only go so far in a situation like this. Ares didn't know a single command when I found him. If I can train a dog to fetch, sit, and stay, there's no reason I can't train a female to submit.

"I think we can handle this," I tell him. "Or rather, handle her."

DK is quiet next to me, his hands clasped under his chin. He doesn't explicitly say he agrees, but he gives the King a nod.

"Good. With that settled, I have a meeting to attend." He stands, stepping away from the table, and checks his watch. "She's had breakfast in her room and should be ready for her first day of classes. Graves said she'll meet you by the garage."

It's a clear dismissal and I grab the last piece of bacon from my plate and pop into my mouth as DK and I head back into the hall. I'm not great with non-verbal cues, but it's obvious that he's pissed.

"You're angry," I point out, less of a question than a statement.

"I'm sure as fuck angry." The hand pushing through his hair tugs at the ends. "One of the perks of being a Baron is the free use of the Baroness."

"Free use?"

"However and whenever, bro." He gives me an incredulous look. "She can't refuse."

"He just said that we could–"

"Teach her to behave like a Royal? How? Neither of us have a fucking clue." He storms down the hall, getting us farther away from the library. "But it also makes sense, because no real Royal would put up with a batshit crazy girl like Arianette. He picked two random outcasts to be his Barons. Not because we have something he wants, but because we don't have the bloodlines, the money, or the power to push back on the fact he didn't make us Barons," he seethes. "He made us fucking babysitters."

11

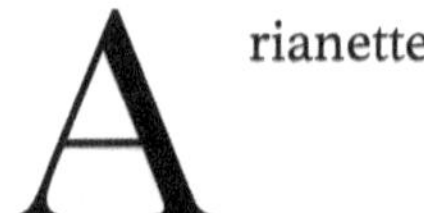

A rianette

I'M NOT sure how long I've been sitting on the edge of the bed waiting for the knock on my bedroom door. I've been up for hours, stomach twisting and turning with nerves.

Today is the first day of school.

Getting ready was a challenge. Every movement seemed to aggravate the pain in my chest and nipples. I spent an hour holding a cold washcloth over each breast, taking deep breaths as I acclimated to the piercings. I'd dug through the full closet and dresser for something to wear, finally settling on an outfit that seemed appropriate and comfortable.

I spent time on my hair and experimented with the makeup I found in the vanity drawer. The only time I've worn makeup was during my dance performances, where the other girls and I would take turns painting each other's faces before going on stage.

Today, I go for something different, mimicking Regina's style. I applied a smoky shadow and dark eyeliner. I stopped short of the bold lipstick, opting for a shiny gloss instead. Standing in front of the mirror, I tugged down the sleeves of my black cardigan in an attempt to hide the fresh wounds and old scars on my wrists. The skirt exposes my scabby, bruised knees, but I found a pair of thick black socks in my dresser drawer that pull high enough to cover them.

I don't think anyone can see the metal bars pierced through my nipples.

At least if they don't look too hard.

I jolt at the heavy knock on the door, rushing over to open it. The man on the other side of the door isn't one of my Barons or a Shadow. For a split second I wonder if he's my King, but there's no ring on his finger and he's unmasked.

The Baron King is never seen without his mask.

"Good morning, Baroness," the man says with a grin. He's around my uncle's age, his blond hair lightly silver around his temples. "We haven't been introduced yet, but I'm Graves. I work for the King."

"Good morning," I reply. "I'm Arianette."

"Your Barons are waiting to take you to the university and I'm here to take you to them," he steps back, giving me room to step into the hall. "I also had a message from the King."

My pulse quickens. "Does he want to see me?"

"No, not today." His expression turns sympathetic. "He's a very busy man–"

"Of course." I pull my sleeves over my thumbs.

"–today is a big day. It will be the first time your peers will see the new Royal leadership of BRN." He gestures for me to take a turn, leading down another hallway. "He also wants you to understand that it's imperative that you stay close to your Barons when you're not at home. It's important to follow their guidance and orders when you're in public."

"I can do that." I have done that–the throbbing pain in my nipples a constant reminder of the control they have over me.

"But most of all," his eyes flick down my body and then back up, "remember you're a representative of BRN and the House of Night. How Forsyth views you is directly related to how they view the King."

There's something heavy behind his easy tone. A threat perhaps. Threats are something I understand. "My future husband shouldn't worry. I am devoted to him and showing Forsyth that loyalty. I won't cause any trouble," I promise. "I'll be a good girl."

He coughs, his fist rising to cover his mouth. When he recovers he smiles gently and says, "I'm sure you will be, Arianette."

I follow him down a hallway that eventually leads to an outside exit. At the door he stops and lifts a leather satchel from a hook on the wall. "Something for you to carry your supplies for school in." The black leather is soft and worn. My fingers run over the stamped pentagram on the flap. I open it up and see a notebook and a case for my pencils and pens. Tucked along the side, I notice a bag with a drawstring at the top.

"Are these..." I ask, heartbeat fluttering. I loosen the string and look inside. The shoes are a rich, warm brown hue, a color that perfectly matches my skin. The satin gleams in the light. "They're beautiful."

"New pointe shoes for your class. You'll find the other items you need as well."

I grin, the sensation strange after so much time. "Thank you."

"You're welcome, Arianette," he replies. "Have a good day."

If the fact that the King made sure I was taken care of isn't enough, I'm equally not prepared for that first step outside the house. Other than the Hunt, this is the first time I've been outside since I was found by the river–not that I remember that. For the weeks I was held in the crypt there were no windows, and even here the glass is muted with color.

Looking up, I shade my eyes from the sun that is already over the trees, bright and glaring in my unaccustomed eyes. I feel off balance, like a baby deer taking its first steps, and it's made worse when I attempt to loop the satchel across my body. A sharp pain spreads over my chest from both the piercings and carving.

"Are you seriously wearing that?" I stop in my tracks, looking for the voice coming from across the driveway where Damon stands next to the open door of a big black truck. His eyes are dark–*angry*–matching the attitude of his all black clothing. A long jacket, shirt, jeans, and boots. Behind him, sitting on the blood red driver's seat, Hunter peers out.

It's the first time I've seen him without a mask and despite his height, and the tattoos visible just under the collar of his button-down shirt, I'm struck by how boyish he looks. His light brown hair is neat, but looks like the slightest breeze could undo the tidiness. Like his body, his face is lean, nose straight. It's his eyes that throw me off. Pale blue but intense, like they're tracking my every move.

"Is this wrong?" I ask, fussing with the hem of my skirt. When I found it crammed in the closet with the other outfits, it seemed perfect. With the way Damon is staring at me... I must have been wrong.

Damon swallows and says, "It's–"

"You look like a fucking schoolgirl." Hunter snorts.

I glance down at the black and gray plaid skirt that hits mid-thigh. It's a little short, but I found thick socks in the dresser drawer, and a cute vintage button-up cardigan with beading around the collar. "I'm *going* to school."

"You're going to *college*," Hunter repeats, like I'm an idiot.

Am I? Am I an idiot?

I'd spent years thinking about what I would do if I was allowed to go to school–*real school*–not the cold basement room at Strong Manor where all of my classes were held. We had a teacher, Mrs. Whipple, who was old and mean, her temper short as a fuse. Our uniform consisted of khaki pants and a blue collared shirt. No variations.

Even after being admitted to Forsyth, my uncle only allowed me to attend online. My only classes outside of the house were for dance. Somehow in my head this was the outfit I'd pictured. I'm not sure where it came from. Maybe a book or a TV show.

"I didn't know," I tell them. "This is my first day and I don't want to screw it up."

"It's not about screwing up," Damon snaps, running his hand

through his hair. "It's about looking like the Baroness. Like the kind of woman the King would marry."

My heart rate skitters, the anxious feeling of doing something to displease him rising in my chest. "Should I change?"

"It's too fucking late." Hunter cranks the engine and the big truck rumbles to life. "I'm giving a presentation in my mechanical engineering class at ten, so get in."

There's a beat where we all look at one another, but the standoff is between the two of them. Finally, Damon grunts and says, "Fine."

He doesn't move as I approach the open door, but he grabs my arm, leans in and asks quietly, "How are your tits?"

"They hurt," I reply, squeezing between him and the truck, "but I think you know that."

I spent most of the night alternating between trying to remain completely still and easing the pain with a cold washcloth. Another reason I'd chosen the cardigan was because I could button it over the top of the new piercings. Tossing my bag onto the floorboard of the truck, I leverage myself onto the running board. Moving slowly, I try not to do anything to irritate the wound on my chest or my healing nipples.

"Pick up the pace, Baroness." Damon's hand flattens under my skirt and boosts me up. His fingers dip between my thighs, brushing over my pussy. His touch sends a jolt of heat through my body and tears well in my eyes. But worse, my nipples tighten, igniting a fresh throb of pain across my breasts. I scramble to the middle of the bench seat next to Hunter, who frowns down at me.

"Are you crying?" His eyes flick to Damon, who has climbed in behind me and slammed the door. "Why is she crying?"

I feel dizzy from the overload of my senses, the pain and humiliation, the confusion my body feels when I'm around these men. Inhaling, the cab smells like a mix of leather, soap, and cigarette smoke. It's warm with the bodies so close. I can't help but think of the things their hands have done to me.

"Show him," Damon says, elbow propped on the car window.

"What?" I lift my arms to cover my chest, but that just hurts more. I wince and shake my head. "I don't want to."

"Can she say that?" Hunter says, those pale eyes looking over my head to Damon. "She can't say no to you, can she?"

"No, she can't," Damon replies, a small smirk on his mouth. "Because here's the thing, sister, the King has given us our orders, and we're here to prepare you for him, and the one thing he doesn't want is a mouthy bride who talks back." He moves his hand behind my head, his thumb grazing my neck. "He wants a good girl that follows directions. Don't you want to be a good girl for him?"

All I want is to serve my King, and make him happy. "Yes."

Damon's thumb dips underneath the collar of my sweater. "Then show your Baron why you were crying."

My hand shakes as I reach for the top button on my cardigan and push it open. With my eyes focused on the shiny knobs of the old-fashioned looking radio, I loosen button after button, until the smooth, black satin camisole is revealed. Damon's finger pulls at the collar, dragging the loose fabric away to expose my breasts.

"Fuck," murmurs Hunter, seeing the piercings for the first time. "When did you do that?"

"Yesterday afternoon. You were crashed out."

Hunter reaches out, his finger flicking the hard knob at the end of one of the bars. I hiss, choking back a sob. His eyebrow arches and he bobs his head. "Nice."

Damon's wide hand slips under my breast and lifts it with a surprisingly gentle touch. "They look good," he says, inspecting it. "It's normal for them to be sore–it could take weeks for the pain to ease. Did you clean them this morning like I told you to?"

"Y-yes." He drops his hand, and the weight of my breast sags, tweaking the piercing. "Are you finished?"

Damon shrugs. "For now."

Hunter steers the truck off of the property, and I quickly cover myself back up, buttoning the cardigan to the very top. The cab feels so tight, my legs cramped over the hump in the middle. Damon's thighs are spread apart, taking up most of the space. I distract myself looking out the windshield, taking in the driveway splitting the forest, different looking in the daylight. The trees are changing colors, the tops filled with bright red, yellow, and orange.

It was summer when I'd walked out of that dance studio–the afternoon air steamy. One minute I was walking home the next–

"Planning an escape?" Damon asks, draping his arm over the back of the seat.

"No." I blink, drawn out of a memory I can't access. "I didn't realize we were so far from town. My uncle's house is basically on campus. I've just never been out here."

Hunter drives over a pothole and the car dips, heaving us up and down. My tits bounce and I whine, clasping my hands over them to keep them steady. "God, that hurts."

Damon's hand lands just below my skirt but above the socks. His fingers run along the skin and he says, "Remember what I told you the other night, sometimes the best way to handle pain is with a little bit of pleasure."

"Is that what that was?" I ask, thinking about how he drew me in, getting my body to respond to him, and then yanked it away. "Don't pretend you want to make me feel good."

Thankfully, Hunter seems determined to get to school as fast as possible, foot pressed down on the gas. I brace myself against the quick turns, thighs clamped tight, fighting Damon's wandering hands. It's a relief when we arrive on campus, and I gawk at the big brick buildings. I've seen them before, obviously, but now it's real. I'm a student at Forsyth U.

That same excited energy rushes back through me as we enter the parking lot, the truck towering over most of the other vehicles. It's crowded but Hunter drives up to a bank of empty spots near the sidewalk. Right before he turns in, I see a design painted on the pavement: the Baron's pentagram.

"You get your own parking spot?" I ask, looking out the window. There are groups of people walking up and down the path that leads toward the biggest of the buildings. Everyone looks so mature and confident. The opposite of how I feel.

"Apparently it's one of the perks." Hunter kills the engine, then mutters, "Or at least one not taken from us."

Damon snaps off his seatbelt and shifts, facing us; the movement draws his coat back and I see the butt of a gun tucked into his jeans. "A few ground rules before we get out of the car." The teasing tone from earlier is gone, replaced by a sternness I can see on his face. "No talking to anyone other than me and Hunter. Ever."

"Not even the other members of BRN?" I ask.

"Not until you've proven yourself," Hunter says, not bothering to follow up on what that entails.

"No wandering off. You stick close at all times," Damon lists off. "Graves gave us a copy of your schedule, which mostly aligns with ours."

"What about my dance class?"

"You'll still go, but one of us will be with you."

The truth is that I'm okay with this arrangement. Whoever kidnapped me is still out there. I don't know if they're watching and waiting for a second chance.

It becomes obvious the moment we step out of the truck that my kidnapper is the least of my problems.

I don't know where they come from, dozens of people swarm like they've been hiding behind cars and bushes, holding cameras and microphones, lights flashing in my eyes.

"Arianette, how did you escape your kidnappers?"

"Did you know who killed Laura Walker?"

"Were you there when Laura Walker was killed?"

"Is it true that your attacker wore a mask?"

"Is the Baron King behind this? Did you see his face?"

"Is there a sex ring in Forsyth?"

The questions come at me like gunfire, rattling off one after the other. The lights hurt my eyes and I hold up a hand, blocking out the blinding light.

"Arianette, do you know anything about the other missing girls?"

I don't know who asks the question, but the voice triggers a wail. Not one from me but one in my head.

"Is there anyone out there?" The voice echoes off stone. "Please, if there's anyone else here, answer me."

The voice ricochets between my ears, leaving me disoriented. I wobble and a strong hand grabs me by the side, jerking me into hard warmth.

Damon.

"Everyone back the fuck off." Hunter steps in front of us, blocking me from the reporters, but it's too much. The panic I've been fighting off for days–*weeks*–surges through me. The pain and the overwhelm.

"Will Miss Hexley comment on her kidnapping?" A brave reporter steps forward, holding a recorder out.

"Fuck no." The voice comes from the side of the crowd. From a massive man, with tattoos covering his hands and arms, all the way to his face. He's handsome, his stride lazy but powerful. He doesn't even pretend to hide his weapon under a coat, the silver-handled pistol tucked visibly in the back of his pants. He's terrifying, and from the expression on every reporter's face, they seem to know it too. "You really think you can come up in here and make demands on Royal leadership like this?" he asks, eyeing the crowd. "Maybe I'll call my brother and see what he thinks. Little Bird," he calls out, "you want to do that?"

"I guess." She flips her pale blue hair over her shoulder before pulling her phone out of her top. "But you know how pissed he gets when his workout is interrupted."

"Don't," the reporter that asked the last question says quickly, taking a step back. "We'll go." There's a soft murmur among the crowd as they scatter, slithering back to whatever cesspool they came from.

Damon doesn't release me from his grip when the man turns, squaring his broad shoulders to the three of us.

"Nick Bruin." His piercing blue eyes pin on me. He crosses his arms over his chest and says, "We need to talk."

12

D^{amon}

"Welcome to my office." Spreading his arms wide, Bruin enters the student center like some kind of god. Or really, a fucking royal.

A few students scurry out of his way as he and the girl stride toward a table on the other side of the open space. At least a couple assess me and Hunter, probably wondering who the fuck we are, but the majority of the attention is on his woman and her tight jeans and low-cut tank and the strappy hot pink bra showing underneath. Spread across her chest is a massive tattoo, intricate wings spread from shoulder to shoulder, a skull for the insect's head. Between that, and her sturdy boots, I have no doubt she'd be fierce in the ring.

But the attention is short-lived, all eyes glued to the Baroness. There's an attempt to be discreet, whispers and subtle glances. More than one of the guys gives her legs a longer than necessary appreciative look, and my hands curl at my sides.

I'd never spent much time in this building for one simple

reason: Royals. They seemed to congregate here during the day, staking out different corners of the room. Even now there are cliques representing every frat. The LDZ linger in a sitting area near the entrance. They carry themselves with the vibe of unwavering popularity, their members having both deep legacies and pockets. A few of the guys are in football letter jackets but most just have that frat boy look that makes me want to punch them in the face. The sorority girls with them are attractive–*respectable*–an irony since it's widely known that their main source of income comes from a brothel.

Hypocrites.

Over by the windows, PNZ occupies a set of tables pushed together. The cluster of men and women look like they should be in a perfume ad. Maybe luxury cars. They look like a bunch of pussies, but the shake up in East End is well known. Recently, their King, Rufus Ashby, was overthrown by his own sons *and* daughter. The bloodlines of this group are so pristine their family tree doesn't branch so much as twist into a single, complicated and perverted vine.

Hunter pulls out the chair for Arianette, who seems like she's not fully with us. Her eyes are wide like a deer in headlights, and before she sits, I slide underneath her, grabbing her by the waist, and pull her into my lap. Her body is warm and soft, and I wrap my arm around her waist, anchoring her down.

"Remember," I murmur in her ear, "be a good girl."

She's stiff in my lap, clearly overwhelmed from what happened outside. That kind of ambush was bullshit, and I have no doubt the King will be pissed when he finds out. That's an issue for later, because across from us, the blue-haired girl gives Arianette a sympathetic look that I don't appreciate. As Bruin takes the final seat, I instinctively tighten my grip.

Mine.

Hunter looks over at a DKS leaning against a column a few feet away and says, "Who's that?"

Without looking, Bruin replies, "That's Kaz, current Duke."

I lift my chin and he nods back, but he makes no effort to move closer.

"You're DK, right?" Bruin asks. "Remy says you're the only guy he recommends for piercings in Forsyth."

I shrug. "Talent recognizes talent, I guess."

"He's opening up a new shop," Nick says, tapping his ink-covered fingers on the table. They've got the letters D. U. K. E. across his hard, worn knuckles. "Down at the old Royal Gazette building."

"Royal Ink," I comment. "I heard Maddox was opening up a spot."

"Guess news travels fast."

"Among our shared clientele, I suppose it does."

"How long is this going to take," Hunter blurts suddenly, checking his watch for the time. "I've got a presentation across campus in–"

"You're a Baron now," Bruin interrupts, "*fuck* presentations."

"But it's my–" Hunter begins, but he's cut off again.

"You tell your professor frat business came up. He'll chill." He smirks. "Or better yet, he'll just give you the fucking A."

Hunter's expression seems to convey both horror at the idea and curiosity. At the very least he stops arguing.

The girl clears her throat and says, "Since no one introduced me," her eyes shift to Bruin, "I'm Lavinia, the Duchess."

"Lavinia Lucia?" Hunter asks, eyebrow lifting.

"*Bruin*-Perilini," Nick corrects.

She rolls her eyes. "We were hoping we could talk to the Baroness about some things."

"She's not answering shit," I reply for her. Everyone knows there's a DKS locked up right now for the kidnappings. And everyone also knows he denies it. It's not a surprise they'd be waiting to pounce. "She's here to go to class and go home. King's orders."

Lavinia nods, gaze shifting to Arianette. "I love those shoes," she says, looking down at the shiny patent leather shoes with a narrow strap and buckle. As much as we ribbed her for dressing like a child, she looks entirely too fuckable in that short skirt and the knee-highs. I got a semi the second she walked out of the chapel door.

If that wasn't bad enough, the semi turned fully hard when she showed me her tits. I can't fucking wait to sink my teeth into that metal bar and give it a pull.

Arianette looks back at me, and I realize she's asking for approval to respond to the Duchess. I don't really give a fuck, but it's probably best not to start off on the wrong foot, so I give her a quick nod.

"Thank you," she says, hands pulling at the edges of her sleeves.

Nick leans to the side and I start to reach for my weapon, when he pulls a roll of cash out of his pocket. Peeling off a few bills, he hands them to Lavinia. "LB, how about you go get something for you and the Baroness from the coffee cart over there. I need to talk business with the new Barons." His eyes flick from me to Hunter. "As long as that's okay with you."

After everything that's gone down today I'm not sure that I am, but the coffee cart is only a few feet away, and when I assess the area, I recognize a few of the guys sitting at the next table.

Shadows.

I guess Bruin isn't the only one with backup.

They're in regular dress, but I recognize them from recruitment. Pale-faced Carson stands just out of earshot, while Mateo, with his dark hair slicked back in a ponytail, sits at an unoccupied table nearby.

"I think that'll be okay." I squeeze her thigh, digging my fingers in a touch too hard. "You go with the Duchess for a few minutes. We'll be right here."

"Come on," Lavinia says, encouraging her to follow, "they've got this incredible chocolate cold foam that's as addictive as Scratch."

Nick stares appreciatively at his Duchess' ass as they walk off. When they're out of earshot, Nick turns back to me and Hunter. "Schoolgirl vibe, huh? Who picked that out," he assesses Hunter and winks. "It was you, wasn't it?"

"What?" Hunter seems shocked. "She did that on her own."

The fuck? Why is he looking at Arianette like that? The flare of anger–*possessiveness*–that surges through me is startling.

Confusing.

"Well it's a bold first day move, especially for the King's future bride, but what the hell, she pulls it off," he continues, unaware of how close he is to losing those pretty blue eyes. "So listen, it would help all of us if she could give us some details on what went down during the time she was missing. Anything would help. Sounds. Smells. Hot or cold. Inside or out..."

Hunter's fist closes on his thigh and I wonder if he feels the same about anyone getting near the Baroness right now. I can tell this needs to be handled diplomatically, saying, "She's not exactly in the state of mind for an inquisition right now."

"Right." Nick nods. "We'd be gentle about it. Lav can even be there if that helps. I know she can be a little crusty, but she's even won the cutsluts, and they're as impenetrable as Fort Knox."

"I don't think it's a good idea," Hunter says. "She's still recovering."

"I'm not asking her to take us on a field trip. Just answer a few questions." His tone is tense. "We've got a man taking the heat for these crimes and he had nothing to do with it."

"Are you sure?" Hunter asks skeptically. "No other girls have gone missing since he was locked up."

Bruin leans forward like he may grab Hunter by the throat. The size of his body is intimidating as fuck, but he inhales deeply and says, "Yes, I'm fucking sure. The goddamn police and that idiot Fed have tunnel vision." He grimaces and his shoulders slump slightly. "But it's not just about Ballsack. It's the fact one of our cutsluts was snatched off of our streets and murdered. Stella St. James was connected to both the Lords and Princes and she's MIA. Someone is cherry picking our women, including *yours*. Four other girls are still out there, and if the police aren't going to do something about it, then we have to do it for them."

I understand what he's saying. It's why the King wants us to keep the Baroness so close. It's why the Shadows are two steps behind, and that guy Kaz has his eyes on the Duchess right now and not Bruin. I glance over at Arianette, who tugs at her sleeve and focuses on the cup of coffee as Lavinia speaks to her.

Hunter leans forward, elbows on the table. "The Baroness is

getting acclimated to her new position. I'm sure you're aware that the initiation process and early days of settling into these roles can be complicated."

"Complicated?" Bruin snorts and relaxes back in his chair. "Try total shitshow. I locked the Duchess in an elevator overnight to keep her from running away." His eyes flick over to his girl, warm and impressed. "That was a fucking terrible night."

"So you know what we're going through," I say, although I doubt it.

His jaw tightens and I get the feeling Bruin isn't used to not getting what he wants. Which means he must really want to talk to Arianette if he's playing nice. "Fine. I just need you to do what you can. We've got to get our man out of lockup."

I bristle at the idea of anyone being in jail, much less unjustly. "We're also going on our King's orders. Things have an extra layer of complication there."

"I bet they do." His eyebrow raises. "You tell your King we need cooperation moving forward."

"Is that something people do," Hunter asks, "just make demands of the King?"

"The Baron King and I go way back." He laughs, and pushes his chair back, clearly finished with the conversation. "While you're at it, ask him what kind of gift he wants for his wedding. I hate buying shit off a registry. Too impersonal."

Lavinia walks back over, Arianette a step behind. The Duchess leans into his side, and he bends down, pressing a kiss just under her ear. "Want some?" she asks, holding up her coffee.

"You know I'm off sugar." He grins at the two of us. "The first fight of the year is next weekend."

Shit. I forgot.

Along with a mentally unstable Baroness we can't fuck, a sweet parking spot, and being hounded by the media, there's one more perk to being a Royal I'd forgotten about:

Friday Night Fury.

"W HAT DID THAT BLUE-HAIRED BITCH WANT?" I ask the minute we step outside.

"Moonlight." She walks quickly between me and Hunter, that little skirt swishing across her thighs.

"What?" Hunter asks, giving me that 'this bitch is crazy' look over her head.

"Her hair looks like strands of moonlight."

Jesus Christ. This day is turning into a clusterfuck. Five minutes after telling her not to speak to *anyone,* I'd sent her off with the Duchess.

At least I can figure out what the snake dressed in a bear suit wanted from Arianette.

"You didn't actually say that to her did you?"

The last thing we need is everyone knowing the new Baroness and King's new bride is... off.

"I told her I liked it, and she said she liked my hair too."

I take a deep breath, doing my best not to lose my temper.

"I need to get to class," Hunter says, hitching his bag over his shoulder.

"Hunt," I snap. "Listen to Bruin. Tell that professor to suck your Baron dick. We've got bigger problems."

Those problems keep staring at us as we walk through campus, word having undoubtedly spread about the media in the parking lot, or worse, that we'd had a public sit down with a Duke. Would Bruin have done that with an established Royal with bloodline and legacy? I think the fuck not. The way he spoke to us, the way he talked about *our* girl. All of it grates my nerves.

But Hunter isn't having it, and he starts off toward the Engineering building. The lit class that Arianette has been signed up for is in the same direction, so we tag along.

"What else?" I prompt, going back to the Duchess. "What did she say?"

"Bears have sharp teeth. Butterflies have wings. She liked my eyeliner."

I run my hand through my hair and try not to panic. On one hand, the Baroness isn't in the state of mind to reveal anything of value. On the other, I'm not sure I'm buying what she's telling me and the farther we get from the student center, away from Bruin and the Duchess, the more pissed I get. We look weak. Disrespected. It's not until the third asshole stares down Arianette that I realize another problem.

All of these fuckheads looking at her, eyeing her long, dark legs and that tiny skirt. Wondering what her tits look like under that goddamn modest sweater. She's mine, I want to scream, ripping off her top to show the whole goddamn student body how she's been marked by her Barons.

Hunter heads inside and on a whim, I grab her by the upper arm and follow.

"Don't we have class?" she asks.

"We're going to support your Baron while he gives his presentation."

Hunter moves ahead of us, opening the door. We step inside the cool brick building, and follow him to the lecture hall. The entrance is at the back of the room, students filing in and then heading down the tiered rows. The room is crowded and the professor is already at the front of the class. Hunter leaves us, heading toward the podium with his laptop already out of his bag.

"I don't like it here," Arianette says.

"Yeah, I'm not a big fan of academic pretension either, but we're staying." I lead Arianette to a quiet corner behind the back row–a wide view of the entire room. I don't speak as I move her body between mine and the half wall, pinning her in. "And we need to talk."

She wiggles against me, aware that she's trapped. Her tight little ass grazes my crotch and fuck, here we go again. Down below the professor, a middle-aged man, skinny with barely half a head of hair left, announces, "Today, Mr. Sorrin will give his presentation on Nanofluids Thermal Applications."

Whatever the fuck that is.

Hunter moves behind the podium, and the overhead lights dim, just leaving the ones directed at the stage. I lean down and whisper in Arianette's ear.

"You're walking around school looking like a sweet, innocent virgin, in that tiny skirt and buttoned-up sweater. Did you see the Duchess? Her tits were on full display. That's what a woman who fucks her men looks like. Not," I drag my hand up her side, "not this, doll baby."

She flinches, probably from pain from the piercings. Good.

"And yes," I continue quietly, as Hunter rambles on about the *'wide range of applications in industries such as energy, electronics, and manufacturing.'* "I know that you're technically a virgin, but you walking around clueless about how fucking hot you are makes me look like a loser. It makes Hunter look like a rookie dumbass. Like we're the King's hired hands and not *your* men."

And I'm pretty fucking tired of it.

"There are consequences for everything, sister, especially in Forsyth." I push my hand under her skirt, reaching for the strip of fabric that covers her pussy. Yanking it aside, my fingers dip underneath, feeling the warm, damp heat. My cock, which had already been throbbing painfully between my legs, is now fully erect, desperate to feel the slick heat of this woman. "And this is the consequence you get for walking around like a teasing slut in front of the entire campus."

She doesn't fight me, but she's not exactly compliant. Her spine is rigid as I yank her panties down to her thighs and then push a knee between her legs to keep them apart. My fingers stroke down her pussy, and there's a gasp as I coat her lips with the slippery fluid that's nothing but her body betraying herself.

Keeping her pinned, I manage to get my zipper down, freeing my cock. I waste no time, sliding down her ass cheeks until the head of my cock eases between her legs. Jesus. My mind nearly blanks just from the sensation and I exhale into her neck.

She cranes her neck to look back at me, but I grab her neck and snap it forward. "Look at your Baron. Think of him holding that knife. The way he looked at you while he was carving into you." Almost like he hears me, Hunter's eyes flick up to where we're standing. If he comprehends what we're doing, he doesn't let on, going on about '*...enabling more sustainable energy solutions...*' "Do you remember that? How fucking wet you were?"

Her nod is small.

"You felt like that because no matter how sweet and innocent you may be, sister, deep down you're like every other woman in Forsyth, a dirty slut." Clasping my hand around her waist, I rock into her painfully slow, covering myself in our building heat. She gasps, hands lifting to cup her tits. "Hands down," I command. "If you don't want them to hurt, stay still."

Leaning back, I lift her skirt to get a better view of my cock sliding in and out of her. The brown swell of her ass is smooth and I thumb apart her crack to dip a finger inside. Instead of squirming to get away, she lifts up and spreads her legs.

Horny bitch.

We're far enough back that no one can see us above the room, only Hunter who is still presenting. I've got no fucking clue what a nanofluid is, but I know her cunt is about to get filled with an entirely different kind of liquid. It's tempting to say fuck it all, to bury myself in her pussy and take the consequences, but the truth is that this is good. Really fucking good. My pulse hammers as my orgasm builds, but just like last time, I want to draw her out as far as I can go, all the way to the very edge.

'*Enhanced heat transfer,*' Hunter continues and for a minute I think he's fucking with me, but I glance up and see the words on the screen. '*Energy storage system...*'

Arianette's knees start to tremble, her hand gripping mine to stay standing. "You're close, aren't you," I whisper in her ear, knowing I'm one second from busting the biggest nut of my life, which is insane because I'm not even inside her. She sucks in a gulp of air, and her fleshy thighs tremble around me.

Yep, so fucking close.

I pull back, gripping the base of my blistering cock in my hand, and withdraw from the heat. Her neck twists, and she faces me with parted lips and a frustrated glare.

"Don't stop," she whispers, and I see the damp sheen on her forehead.

Desperate *and* horny.

Good.

Shoving a hand on her lower back, I bend her forward, hard against the wall, and push up her skirt. I barely get it up before I come, thick hot cum surging from my cock. I paint those pretty brown asscheeks with streaks of white, my cum coming out with a force that surprises me. If I thought I needed to be inside her to come hard, I was mistaken. Seeing my cum drip down her ass is spank material for weeks.

In fact...

I dig my phone out of my pocket and pull up the camera, snapping a pic for later.

I don't miss the anger and frustration screwing up her face as I tuck myself in my jeans, a sure sign that whatever pleasure she was hoping to get from this is over.

Crouching, I slide those panties back up, letting the cotton soak up the semen. "I may not be able to claim you the way I want to, sister, but I can leave my mark in my own ways."

'...nanofluids are emerging as a game-changer in thermal applications, with their enhanced heat transfer capabilities offering significant benefits across a range of industries...'

Down below, Hunter wraps up his presentation, looking like he feels as satisfied with his work as I do with mine.

13

rianette

IF I THOUGHT the scrutiny on me as I walked across campus this morning was intense, it only gets three times worse when I arrive at the performing arts building with a six-foot-three Baron hovering nearby.

I want to feel safe at the university; whoever kidnapped me is still out there, but they're not foolish enough to come after me again with my Barons next to me and the Shadows hovering nearby, are they?

Turns out that wasn't the problem anyway. The media, rushing at us the minute we got out of the truck, their loud voices and cameras flashing. And then the Duke.

Nick Bruin.

I've never seen a man that scary in my life, and the one walking next to me right now used a knife to carve into my chest.

I barely heard a word he said, more aware of the hard press of Damon's body against mine, and the Duchess' cool gaze.

Cloaked in Shadows, we went to the coffee cart and she'd spoken to me. I think. I was distracted by the prickle across my skin, the sharp zing in my nipples, the lingering feel of a hard cock against my ass. I couldn't stop staring at the tattoo on her chest, the dark but delicate lines of the wings.

"It's a death's head moth," she said. I was staring.

"Bears have teeth," I said, snapping my jaw.

"Well, this Duchess has wings."

I look up at the Maddox Performing Arts building, and breathe slowly, remembering the first time I walked into the building. I'd just turned eighteen and it was my first class outside of Strong Manor. Before college, my uncle brought the dance instructors in-house, just like all the other teachers, but a stipulation for the arrangement between him and the Baron King was that I must be enrolled in Forsyth University. Most classes I was able to take online, but dance? Those are required to be in person.

Those two things: the Baron King and the university requiring my attendance... those are the things that finally got me out of the Manor–even if it was just for a little while.

"I've never been in here," Hunter says, following through the front doors. The building itself is gorgeous with big glass windows exposing the first two floors. The downstairs consists of a large lobby filled with student artwork, and an entrance to the theater. A curved staircase cuts through the mezzanine, leading visitors to the upper floor as well as private classrooms, dance studios, music rooms and galleries.

"The dressing room is down this hall," I explain to Hunter. DK left for his calculus class after the presentation was over. I still feel his presence though, the sticky fluid he left on my behind has started to dry into a hard paste. "Do you want to wait for me out here?"

He hesitates. "I'm not supposed to let you out of my sight."

"It's a women's dressing room." Proving my point, two females with dance bags slung over their shoulders skirt past us and enter the swinging door. "It's for women only."

"Yeah, I don't think so," he says decisively, jerking his head for me to follow as he walks away.

"Are we leaving?" I ask, panicking. "Please don't make me miss the class–"

He stops as quickly as he'd started, jerking open the nearest door. The room is empty, dark until Hunter flips on the lights, illuminating the smooth hardwood floors. A barre stretches across the wall. A dance practice room.

"This'll work." He drags the one chair in the corner of the room away from the wall. Sitting, he focuses on his phone, only looking up when he notices I haven't moved. "Go ahead," he says, "change."

I've never had a huge sense of autonomy–that hasn't been a privilege in my life. I shared a room with the children my uncle took in, making privacy impossible. I'd changed among the other performers, I'd been tested, touched, and tracked. I'd been *taken*. And all of this was before I came to the House of Night. But what I've experienced over the last few days has made it perfectly clear: my body isn't my own.

Dropping my bag, I pull out the leotard and tights given to me by Graves this morning. I already know that any exercise will be torture. My nipples ache and the carving feels dry and itchy. I also know that no one cares. Slowly, I unbutton my cardigan and hang it over the barre, then lower the side zipper on my skirt and let it fall to the floor.

Hunter doesn't look up as I undress, as I peel the crusty panties off my body. I'm more humiliated by the white stain in the crotch, the one I know was left there by the build up of my own desire.

"Did he make you come?" The question comes as I'm tugging the footless tights up and over my hips.

Our eyes meet in the floor-to-ceiling mirror.

"What do you mean?"

"During my presentation," he rests his book on his lap, "he was touching you, wasn't he?"

"He–" I swallow, "he didn't enter me."

He nods, those pale eyes sweeping over my body before going back to the phone.

"What are you looking at?" I ask, wondering what makes a man stare at a phone rather than at a naked woman.

"My dog."

"A video?" I grab the black leotard and step into the leg holes.

"No, he's got a tracker that tells me how much activity he gets a day. One of the brothers was assigned to walk him today. I just want to make sure they actually did it."

Instinctively, when he says the word 'tracker' I touch the scar tissue behind my ear. It had been there so long I forgot about it and was removed by my kidnapper. The King hadn't placed another one in me. Why? Does he not care if I'm snatched away again?

No. The Barons are watching me, keeping me safe.

"I've never really been around dogs. My uncle only kept the guard kind. Big. Mean. Trained to hate everything."

He looks up at me then, his gaze softening, the usual wariness slipping from his shoulders. "Ares isn't like that. He's nervous, sure— but not mean."

I catch his eyes in the mirror. "Why's he nervous?"

Hunter pockets his phone, then crosses his arms. "I found him last winter after a shift at the radio station. Looked like he hadn't eaten in days. And his eyes..." He trails off, shaking his head. "They had that thousand-yard stare. Like he wasn't really in his body anymore. Like someone had wrung the soul out of him."

My chest tightens. "Was he... abused?"

Hunter nods once. "I think so. You can tell in the way he reacts to things. Don't ever pick up a stick or broom or anything around him."

I blink. "Will he attack you if you do?"

"No." His mouth twists. "He'll just get scared. Might knock something over, or hide under the bed for hours. It's not anger he remembers. It's fear. It didn't take much for him to trust me: regular food, a calm steady voice, and now he's completely loyal."

"Maybe he'll like me," I say, more to myself than Hunter. Wiggling into the leotard, I get above my waist and then suck in a breath before pulling the compressed fabric over my breasts. "I hate these things," I suck back a sob.

"The outfit?"

"The piercings."

His eyes flick back to my tits. "They hurt?"

"What do you think?" I snap, tugging at the top, and face him. "Tell me the truth, can you see them?"

Sliding his phone into his shirt pocket, Hunter stands and walks over. His eyes are zeroed in on my chest and he says, "Definitely."

"Ugh. My teacher isn't going to like that. She wants clean lines and we're supposed to look professional, not like dancers down at the Gentlemen's Chamber."

His eyebrow lifts. "You know about the Gentlemen's Chamber?"

"Of course." I pull at the fabric near my tits, trying to make some room, but the spandex snaps back and I yelp. Wincing, I add, "My uncle has meetings there. I've heard him talk about it."

Hunter stares at my chest, forehead creased in concentration. Again, he reacts without speaking, going back to the chair–no, the bag by the chair. He opens the primary zipper and digs around, finally locating something. He palms it, and crosses back over to me, tossing it once in the air before catching it.

"What's that?"

"Tape."

"Tape?" I stare at the round object in his fingers.

"Yep." He lifts his chin. "Pull down your top."

It's not a request. I tug down the cap sleeves and push the scoop neck down, revealing both the bandaged cut and the silver piercings. He spreads his fingers, using them to measure the bars, then tears off a strip of tape.

"Getting that off is going to be a problem, right?" I ask, eyeing it warily.

"We'll deal with that later."

Later? "But–"

He slaps the stark white tape over my nipple, covering the bar and everything else.

"There," he says, covering the other nipple. "That should work."

Unsure, I ease the top back up and turn to face the mirror. Sure enough, my tits are almost smooth. Certainly better than before.

"Thank you," I say, still worried about the removal process, "I guess."

"If there's a problem, I just want to find a solution." He strides over to drop the tape back in the bag. "You ready?"

It's not the way I envisioned my first day back to class, not with tape over my nipples and crusty cum glued to my ass, but it's better than dancing in a dark crypt by myself.

"Yeah," I say, grabbing the bag holding my pointe shoes, "I'm ready."

14

———

H_{unter}

I shouldn't be here.

Well, not *here*-here. We'd been told specifically by the King to keep an eye on her and not to let her out of sight, so I'd been with the Baroness since my presentation was over, sticking by her side while she changed for class, then escorting her to the auditorium.

What I mean is, I shouldn't be *here*. Like *this*–up above the auditorium in a place no one's supposed to go, crouched on the catwalk like some creeping shadow.

But that's what I am lately. A shadow more comfortable lurking around the edges than anywhere else.

When I'd dropped Arianette off with the other dancers in the class, they were already up on stage, stretching their limbs and practicing their moves. I'd offered to hold her bag, then eased to the back, watching her carry her shoes in her fingertips. When she got to the stage, she looked awkward, both in and out of place at the same time. It made sense, knowing this is her first day back to class.

I also felt awkward, but for different reasons. I felt too exposed watching her out in the open, so I faded back until I found something familiar, the access point backstage. I'd been here once before with my father while he fixed an electrical problem. The lure of a dark, quiet place to hide and the master key in my pocket made it easy to take the metal stairs up to the rafters.

From here, with her bag at my feet, I can see everything without being seen. It's not just the view that's different from this position. The air is thick with the scent of rosin and sweat, while the muffled music chords echo across the wide, dark auditorium. Peering down, I notice how her shiny, brown satin pointe shoes almost shimmer against the stage floor.

I shift my weight, careful not to creak the metal beneath me. Earlier, I watched her change. She thought I wasn't looking, that I was focused on my phone, but I'm good at that, watching quietly–discreetly.

She peeled off that stupidly sexy schoolgirl sweater and skirt, pretending like DK's cum wasn't still wet between her legs. I'd wanted to ask for her to show it to me, tell me what it felt like to have him take her like that in the back of the classroom. If it made her horny to know that anyone could discover them, or what it was like to know I was watching.

I wanted to kill him for putting me in that position. I had to focus on my presentation, pretending like I didn't know what was going on at the back of the room. The hormone-fueled urge to watch them was only slightly overruled by the logical part of my brain and the awareness of where I was and what I was doing. Still, I was thankful for the podium being in place to block the outrageous boner painfully throbbing against the front of my pants.

I was still hard when she slipped off her panties, which were still damp with DK's cum. She'd wiggled into the leotard and tights–clothing that, for once, wasn't a costume or armor made for the men around her. The spandex fit her like a second skin, hugging her curves. She looked hotter like this, comfortable.

Carefully, quietly, I unzip her bag and feel around, stopping when I feel the silky, lace fabric. It's too hard to see up here in the dark, but I know they're white and stained.

Now, down on the stage, she's at the front of the group, facing the rows of open seats in the empty auditorium.

She stretches first, long limbs folding into themselves and then extending like they've done this a thousand times. There's none of the usual tension in her body, none of the brittleness she carries everywhere else. Her spine curves like a bowstring, arms lifting in a smooth arc overhead before she drops into a deep bend, palms grazing the floor. She rises with an easy, almost arrogant grace, her head high, hair pulled tight, legs long and sure.

It's strange. No, *unsettling*, how different she looks here.

On stage, she isn't the fragile, erratic girl we met in the forest. She's sharp, yes–but different. Purposeful. Every inch of her is dialed in, fluid, and composed.

When the instructor steps forward and sets up the count, she doesn't even wait. Arianette is already moving, predicting the sequence before it's given, responding before the cue. Her body knows it. Even after all the trauma and scars the muscle memory remains, snapping back to the shape of the music before it starts.

The other dancers move with her, echoing her pace. Maybe I'm imagining it, but it's like they're all just orbiting around her. Her timing is intuitive–freakish, even. She doesn't seem to think about anything; she just *is*. No second-guessing. No fear. She transforms out there. Like the stage eats all the noise inside her head and spits her out pure.

I can't look away.

There's a moment when she spins and lands with a perfect pointed foot, and her eyes flick toward the shadows. Not up at me. Not quite. But enough that I wonder if she *knows* I'm here watching. She finishes the turn, spinning smoothly. Keeps dancing. Keeps owning the space.

And all I can think is: *this girl is dangerous.* Not just because of what she's done. Not even because of what she might do. But because when she moves like that, it makes me forget about everything else.

Even the way she held onto that knife in the woods, a dying man at her feet.

Even the way she took my mark at Claiming.

Even with who she *really* is, the King's future wife.

The instructor claps her hands, the music starts again, and I lean over just a little more to watch, enthralled. She's so different when she moves like this. All that feral energy she carries like a second skin–it's still there, but it's reshaped. Channeled. Like she's not running from the dark anymore, but dragging it with her, weaving it into every arch and kick and spin.

There's power in it.

A spirit unleashed.

Wild and in control at the same time.

The music hums in my ears, thumping with the steady count of the teacher's beat: *One, two, three, four...* my throat tightens along with the front of my pants.

She dips low into a plié, the edge of her leotard revealing the smooth curve of her ass, the muscle in her thigh flexing just enough to make me glance down at the panties in my hand.

Lace and cotton, thin and girlish, but stained with DK's cum. I know she was aroused when he was fucking with her in the back of the class. I could see it on her face. I press my nose to the crotch of the panties and inhale. Salty, with the hint of flowers along with something else. Something I shouldn't crave as much as I do.

She twirls again, arching into a backbend, chest heaving, neck bared, sweat catching in the light. Her lips part around a breath I can't hear but feel–deep in my spine, in the ache that crawls down into my cock.

I shift my weight on the catwalk, careful not to creak, and lean against one of the supports, then unzip. The metal teeth part just enough for me to reach in and wrap my hand around the aching heat of my cock. I'm already leaking, just from watching her move, and it makes the slide slick, easy. I wrap the panties around the shaft and stroke.

Fuck.

My head tips back, eyes rolling for a second. I'd been fucking desperate for her all day. From the moment she walked out in that little skirt, then when DK unbuttoned her sweater to show off the new hardware, to the strip down when she changed. It's been a long day of constant teasing and now that I'm alone, I want–no *need*–release. I force my eyes open again. I don't want to miss a second. She lifts her arms, sways her hips, then spins. Like a prayer in motion, a curse made flesh.

My grip tightens, the lace dragging just right, soft and damp and smelling like her, *them,* the two people I'm bound to by oath. I pump slower, drawing it out, matching the tempo of her movements. My hips twitch against the air, with every flick of her wrist, the rise and fall of her tits, and the delicate point of her toes. I imagine that it's all for me. Even if she doesn't look up, even if she never sees me, I pretend she knows.

And that these dirty little panties? She fucking left them for me.

I bite down on my lip to keep from groaning. The pressure builds fast, first in my balls, then climbing my spine. My hand moves faster, rougher, the lace twisting as I fuck into it like I'd fuck into her– desperate and possessive. My cock swells, throbs, pulses between fingers slick with her scent and my own need.

Gripping the railing with my free hand, knuckles white, I come hard into the cotton, body jolting with the force of it. The orgasm tears through me like a live wire, white-hot and explosive, shuddering down every nerve ending until I'm panting, spent, trembling up in the rafters.

Below me, she doesn't stop dancing. Not when I wipe my cock with her panties, or when I stuff them back in her backpack. She may not have known what I was doing up here, but she will.

Arianette will understand that I'm always watching, whether she's aware of it or not.

By the time I make it back down, the music has cut out and the instructor is dismissing them with a round of tired applause. Dancers stretch, laugh, peel sweat-soaked shirts from their bodies. I lean against the doorframe of the corridor and watch her before she notices me.

She's radiant, flushed with exertion, tiny wisps of curls clinging damply to her face. I stick to the side, watching her chest rise and fall as she chats with two girls and one guy. The guy's too close. Tall, good posture, those long dancer's limbs that say he knows what he's doing with a partner. He says something and she laughs. *Actually laughs.* The sound bubbles out of her like something girlish and untouched, and for a split second I want to erase him.

Just a flick of a wrist. Just one whisper in the right ear.

But I don't move. I *watch.*

The jealousy is there–sharp and sudden–but it's not rage. Not yet. It's instinct, possessive and primal. That little flare in my chest reminding me: *she's mine. Even if she's his. Even if she belongs to all of us.*

When she finally notices me, her whole face softens. Her lips part, her eyes dart past her friends, and she crosses the studio with that dreamy sway she has, like her body hasn't caught up to her mind. I like seeing her like this–loose, warm, unguarded.

"Hey," she says, "Where'd you go?"

Huh. She noticed I wasn't in the auditorium.

"Around," I say, letting my voice drop just enough that only she can hear. "I'll always be watching out for you."

A little crease forms between her brows, like she's trying to decipher if there's a double meaning to my words. I hand her her bag and she slings it over one shoulder. I wonder if she'll smell it when she opens it later–feel it in her bones, realize she was part of something without even knowing.

"DK's class should be over soon," I say. "We can meet him at the truck."

She nods and follows me out of the auditorium. I feel calmer now, lighter in my chest, like something toxic finally worked its way loose. I know it's only temporary, because deep down I don't want to live in the shadows. I want her to see me while I touch myself, when I unravel. I want her to know what my cum feels like, *tastes* like. I want to see that moment in her eyes–when she realizes I've been starving for her this whole time.

But I'm not ready.

Not yet.

Not for the look she'll give me when she really *understands* what I am. What I want to do to her. What I've *already* done when she wasn't looking.

Because the truth is, I don't trust myself. Not to be face to face with her, with all the heat and need I've been burying under skin and bone. Not to let her see me fully unmasked, without the shadow to protect us both.

If I'm that close–if she lets me in like that–I might not stop. I might let the thing clawing behind my ribs, the one that doesn't give a fuck about rules, loose.

So I keep my eyes forward. I walk a step behind as I walk out the Fine Arts building door. I'll keep her safe. I'll smile when she smiles, and I'll act like I didn't just come in her panties while watching her move like something out of a goddamn fantasy.

15

rianette

"Where would you like your dinner tonight," Graves asks from my bedroom doorway, "here or in the dining room?"

"The dining room?" I repeat. The question comes as a surprise. Or really, the option. I've never been to the dining room. Or anywhere else in the house that isn't underground. "Will the King be there?"

"Unfortunately, the King will not be attending dinner. He has an important meeting elsewhere."

I inhale, sucking past the pinprick of hurt that comes from the realization my King isn't interested in me. "What about my Barons?"

"They're participating in a BRN meeting tonight, so no, they won't be there either."

That information delivers less of a blow. At least I can hope to get through dinner without being pierced, prodded and covered with bodily fluids.

"I think I'd like to eat in the dining room," I declare.

He nods curtly and says, "Then follow me."

We take the same hallway as I did this morning when I left for school, but instead of turning left when the hallway ends, Graves turns right, deeper into the chapel. He moves quickly, our footsteps echoing off the stone floors. I try to absorb it all. The woven tapestry hanging on an empty wall, embroidered at the top, in thick yellow thread, are the Greek words Beta Rho Zeta. Below that is the pentagram, identical to the mark on my chest. Throughout the house are other symbologies of the Barons. There's a glass case filled with animal skulls, mottled gray and white with age. On the center shelf, spotlit, is the bone chalice and knife from my initiation. I pause, looking for remnants of my blood and flesh on the tip.

"Ahem," Graves says, urging me along. I drag my eyes from it and follow him past a wall decorated with dozens of masks. Horns and fangs, tusks and teeth. I close my eyes and try to remember the beast but the imagery is gone, more of a whisper now than a threat, lost in the trauma between now and then.

"This way," Graves says, taking one quick turn and then another, until he enters a set of arched double doors. He steps aside and gestures for me to come in. There is a plate already on the table, covered by a silver dome. I don't need to see the meal to know it's there, I can smell it. Savory sauces, roasted meat, grilled vegetables. A basket of rolls sits to the side, and a small plate with a flower-shaped pat of butter. To the top right is a small plate with a piece of chocolate cake, a dollop of cream on top as well as a raspberry. My mouth waters and my belly grumbles, signaling how long it's been since I had the coffee in the student union.

There's only one place setting, and Graves pulls out the chair. "Sit, Baroness. Enjoy your meal. If you need anything feel free to ring the bell by the door."

He removes the dome, revealing the plate of food. The instant he's gone, I reach for the rolls, stuffing one in my mouth before grabbing another. The beef is tender–so soft there's no knife supplied other than the short blunt one next to the butter. I taste a bite of bitter asparagus and snatch another roll, this time using the little knife to shave off a curl of butter. As I slather it on, something catches my eye on the wall to my left. It's a floor-to-ceiling mural, at least twelve feet tall, and divided into four panels. When I finally recognize what it depicts, a tremor runs down my spine.

Bread still in hand, I inch closer. The imagery is dark; feral. The first panel displays the vivid imagery of the Baron King on his throne, horned mask covering his face. At his feet are three hooded barons, kneeling to take their oath. I feel the flicker of the torchlight. The scent of the burning fire. My eyes dart to the next panel and instantly I'm taken back to the pitch black of the forest. Crickets chirp, creating a cacophony only drowned out by the beating of my heart. I smell the dirt, the blood. Taste the salt on my tongue. A figure cowers among the trees in fear. I'm her. She's me. While cloaked hunters follow steps behind.

I drag my eyes away from that scene, from that night, to where the Barons make their move, catching the girl, dragging her back through the woods, to the final scene.

The Claiming.

The painting spares no details of the ritual, starting in a series of smaller panels, top to bottom. She's stripped, then splayed on the altar where she's marked, blood oozing down her pale skin into dark red pools. I obsess over where our stories diverge, this woman is taken by each of the masked men. Their members on painted display, phallic and engorged. They don't take their turns, filling the new Baroness in every orifice. Her mouth, her pussy, her ass. Her eyes are half-lidded and lazy.

This... *this* is a claiming.

That dull fire throbs between my legs, the one Damon stokes into a frenzy and so quickly takes away.

I step to the right, centering myself in front of the final panel. Just beyond the trees the streaks of pink and purple indicate the sunrise and the Baroness and Barons kneel before the King. I run my finger down her spine, feeling the ridges of every bone, knowing what it's like to be this woman, to be a part of this ritual, yet also understanding that I am different.

I step back, taking in the entirety of the mural, and can't help but wonder: who am I in this house of darkness and night?

FEELING UNNERVED BY THE MURAL, I pick up the plate holding the cake and the small spoon next to it, and head back to my room. I pass the masks, trying to ignore the feeling that there are eyes behind them watching my every move. I turn at the cabinet filled with bone, fingers twisting at the bronze knob. Locked.

When the hallway splits again, I make a right, plucking the raspberry off the top of the cake. Sweet flavor covers my tongue, and I take a bite of cake.

Ugh. So good.

Sweets were few and far between at Strong Manor. I try not to shovel it in, taking small bites, which is why I think I don't realize until I've taken another turn that there's no tapestry down here, nothing familiar at all, just black frames hanging on the charcoal-colored walls. Each has rows of men, their names underneath. At the bottom it says, Beta Rho Zeta and a year.

Shadows.

Coming to the end of a hallway and another set of double doors, I try the knob. It turns easily, and I peek into the room beyond. The walls are painted a deep green, reminiscent of the forest. I'm drawn inside, looking up to the ceiling, which is still green but almost black. To my right I see a cloak hanging on a hook. I run my hands down the thick fabric, lifting the sleeve to my nose, catching the scent of earth and pine. It's not until I see the mask next to it that I comprehend where I am.

The King's room.

Leaving would be smart, but this is the room of the man I'm arranged to marry. A man I know little about, and the pull is strong. I step in farther and absorb all I can: the windows that overlook the forest with rows of candles perched on the sill, a soft rug under my feet, the stone fireplace set at an angle. Trinkets on top of a dresser catch my eye. A wooden dish holds a few coins and a silver ring. I set the cake plate and spoon on the windowsill and pick up the simple band–slipping the ring easily over my thumb. I touch everything, the bottle of cologne, a melted candle, a pair of cufflinks, until I get to a picture frame. I lift it to look closer and see a woman and a fair-haired little boy.

Setting it back down, I curl my fingers around the handles in the drawer. I'm inching it open slowly when I hear the echo of footsteps down the hall, and a voice.

A man's voice.

My King's voice.

No, no, no, no... he can't find me here. No one can. That much I know for sure. Spinning around, I run forward, slamming into the footboard of the bed. The bed is huge, carved black wood–definitely big enough to hide something underneath. I duck down, shoving my hands under the edge of the comforter, feeling around for space to hide, but it's blocked. Bolting up, my eyes ping between two doors. One has to be a closet. I make a choice, grabbing the knob and stepping into the dark space. I inhale the scent of leather and wool. Definitely a closet. I slowly close the door–almost close the door. Whoever is coming has already entered the room and I don't want to risk the click of the latch falling into place.

"Any idea if Trudie knows what's coming?"

That comes from Graves. Who's Trudie?

"Doubtful or she would have been on the doorstep by now."

My heart skitters at the sound of the King's voice, thrumming so loud I'm terrified he'll hear it.

"The offer to notify her myself is still on the table, Timmy."

I hear the sound of drawers opening, and footsteps near the bed. I line my eye up with the slight gap, but can only see the vague outline of movement.

"Unfortunately," the King says, "telling a mother her son was killed during BRN initiation falls to one person and one person alone."

The context of their conversation snaps into place. He's speaking of Armand, and Trudie must be his mother.

Graves' voice moves closer, too close, and I instinctively take a step back into the folds of the clothing. "What are you planning on telling her? The truth?"

"According to the coroner, Armand died from a slit throat, made by the blade that I gave him for the hunt." Outside the door, I hear the rustle of fabric and quietly shift in an attempt to see. I catch a swath of flesh, the hard lines of his back. "That could be collateral damage," the King moves, pulling on a black shirt, "a stupid mistake or petty squabble between the men as they fight over their prey."

"That could be..." Graves repeats, the sentence left unfinished.

"Yes, it could be, until you explain that the angle of the cut identifies that whoever did it was shorter than him." He pauses. "*Much* shorter and there were zero hesitation marks. A clean cut, through and through."

He knows, I realize. *He knows* I killed Armand.

"That is a problem," Graves notes.

A shadow falls over the closet door, filling the small gap. I wait for the door to open, to be exposed, for all of this to be over once and for all. Instead, the gap vanishes with a hard click, as it latches into place.

Softer now, muffled from the closed door between us, I strain to hear him add, "A problem that could destroy everything I'm working toward."

16

H^{unter}

"*Geschäft.*"

Ares bolts into the dark, grassy area in front of the chapel, happy to be out of the house.

I feel the same, needing a moment of quiet. The frat meeting went well, it's just that forty college-aged men are loud as fuck. The tension building up to the Hunt had eased considerably, the members of the group happy to have the leadership settled. I still feel out of place, like I can't actually believe this has happened to me, but I've spent a fair amount of my life feeling like the odd man out, so really, this is nothing new.

Now I just have power.

I pat the inner pocket of my jacket, a subconscious move from the days when I smoked a lot more than just during my shift at the radio station. It's not even the nicotine I crave. It's the routine–something to do with my hands.

The meeting ran late, meaning Ares had to hold out for a trip outside. Now he's exploring, rustling under the hedges. We're both nocturnal, even on the nights I don't work at the station.

I'd found him last winter, half-dead in the alley behind WXFU. Soaked through, limping, one eye swollen shut, and completely covered in fleas. Just a skinny shadow of a shepherd with more ribs than muscle. No tags. No collar. Just a quiet kind of desperation, like he'd been running from something worse than the cold.

I didn't need a dog. Didn't want one. I was already stretched too thin with class, the station, my projects. But when I crouched down and held out my hand, he didn't flinch–just looked up at me like he'd already decided I was his.

I wrapped him in my jacket, brought him home, and gave him a warm bath. I never said out loud that I'd keep him. Sometimes you find a stray and sometimes the stray finds you, and when you're both a little broken, it makes sense to stick together.

He's smart, protective, and took to training well. But that doesn't mean he's not slow as hell when he's trying to find the perfect spot to piss.

Fuck. I really want a smoke.

"*Hier*," I call, followed by a sharp whistle. In the pitch black that surrounds the house I see his eyes first–the yellow reflected off the light over the doorway. He trots toward me, stopping one last time to lift his leg, before we go back inside.

We head down the hallway that leads back to the room DK and I share. Ares' ears perk up just as I see a shadow cross the far wall. Not a Shadow, but the actual shadow of a person. "*Sitz*," I command quietly. He drops to his haunches with a low growl. A moment later, Arianette tiptoes past, looking over her shoulder.

"Huh," I mutter, looking down at my dog, who has visibly relaxed now he recognizes her, "what do you think she's up to?"

I'd actually planned on seeing the Baroness tonight, but the meeting ran long. "*Komm*." We walk down the hall and turn toward the south wing of the building. There are two bedrooms down here. One for the Barons and a separate one for the Baroness. There's also a den with comfortable couches and an entertainment system. A small kitchenette sits off to the side. I'd explored everything the first night we moved in, wanting to get my bearings. But other than the ride to and from school, this is the first time I've seen her outside her room.

Down the hall, her door closes with a soft click.

I pass by and enter the den. Ares darts ahead, rushing to see DK, who is sprawled out on the couch, playing a video game.

"Hey, bud," he says, rubbing his palm over Ares' head. They get along, which is good. Dogs feel better when they have a pack and it's been just the two of us for a while. He circles around and lies down at DK's feet. I walk over to the cabinet and grab a glass. "You feel good about the meeting?"

"I think so." I shove the glass under the lever for the ice maker and the motor churns. Ice falls in a rush, the cubes clanking loudly against one another. "You okay with the Fury decision?"

That had been the big topic during the meeting: who was going to represent BRN during the next Friday Night Fury. Traditionally, one of the Barons steps up, but neither DK nor I have any interest in the 'traditions' of this place. Mateo fought last year, and was eager to defend his win. Works for both of us.

"Yeah," he says, eyes trained on the game. I notice that when he's concentrating his teeth toy with the hoop in his lip. "There's plenty of time to get our faces smashed in by one of those lunatics."

"Agreed." Getting punched in the face increases the chances of a concussion. I need my brain to be fully functional, not impaired by choice.

He holds up the controller. "You want to play?"

"Nah, I'm good."

I start toward the doorway and Ares lifts his head. "*Bleib,*" I command, then dip into the bedroom. I strip off my shirt and pants, grabbing the worn sweatpants from the edge of the bed and stepping into them quietly. The house creaks in the kind of way that lets you know it's listening. I pause, still barefoot, eyes landing on my backpack slouched against the wall.

Right. The container.

I crouch, unzip the front pouch, and slip my hand inside until my fingers graze the cool glass container. Small, inconspicuous. Not the kind of thing anyone would notice unless they were looking for it. I pull my hoodie over my head, tuck the container in my pocket, and grab the glass of ice. DK is still focused on the game, and I use the distraction to exit quietly, slip into the hallway, and head straight to Arianette's room. I tap lightly on the door.

"Come in," she calls out.

I step inside the room. It's similar in shape to ours, but hers only has one bed instead of three. It's massive and made of iron, with scrollwork not only at the foot and head, but underneath. A stone fireplace sits in the corner with an armchair nearby. She's sitting on the bed, knees pulled up to her chest. "Oh," she says, eyes darting to the door behind me and then back at my chest. "It's you."

"Yes, it's me." I glance over my shoulder. "Were you expecting someone else?"

She shakes her head, but there's an edge when she asks, "What do you want?"

I could ask her where she's been. Why she was creeping around the house, but it's not really any of my business. My job, as instructed by the King, is to keep her safe. To train her for her position of wife. Assessing her, she looks to be in good shape, other than her general wariness. To be fair, the last time a man came into this room, he inserted metal bars into her tits.

"I came to check on the wound, make sure it's healing appropriately." I set the glass and container on the bedside table. "Take off the sweater."

I've already seen her topless once today, so there's not much hesitation as she unbuttons the cardigan and lifts the camisole up and over her head. My mouth dries at the sight of the round fullness of her breasts, and my body predictably reacts, a surge of heat rushing between my legs. I like how big her areolas are, and the urge to run my thumbs over them—to suck them into hard peaks—brings a burning flush to my skin.

Between her tits, the bandage is discolored from the wound underneath, and white tape is still plastered over her nipples. The color is glaring against her brown skin. It should be a turn off, but it's anything but.

I did that.

We did it.

She's ours.

"Any pain?" I sit on the edge of the bed. My erection fights against the cotton front of my sweats.

Her jaw drops. "Are you fucking kidding me?"

I glare at her. "It's just a quest–"

"Yes, Hunter, I'm in pain. Everything hurts. The wound is bad enough, but my tits feel like there are hot needles seared into them. Somewhere between a throbbing ache and firecracker stuffed inside. They're tender. Swollen. Every single move feels like I'm being stabbed." Her hands move to cup them, full and fleshy, and gold flashes on her thumb. A gold band that wasn't there earlier in the day. "Why did he do this to me? You already marked me. The Claiming was over."

My eyes shift to the bandage between her breasts. I don't have to ask DK why he came in here and mutilated Arianette a second and third time. He wanted to leave something permanent on her, just like I had.

"Let me take a look." I'm not a doctor. Zero interest in spending decades in school only to get mired in a pile of bureaucratic paperwork. I've taken a few first aid courses and managed to earn a merit badge in medical emergencies for Scouts before I dropped out. I peel away the bandage slowly, making sure not to rip off any repairing flesh. It's still shiny from the ointment, but the first thing I notice is that the design doesn't look that bad. In fact, I'm pretty goddamn impressed with my work. The cuts are clean, even, and the pentagram is fully legible. The circle isn't perfect, but it's not like I had my compass out there.

"Why are you smiling?" she asks, her brown eyes narrowed into slits.

I cough, peeling off the rest of the tape. "It's healing well," I assure her. "It looks good."

She nods, but then asks, "And the piercings?"

"That's why I brought the ice." I dig out a piece from the cup and hold it up. "It'll help with the pain and remove the adhesive."

Closing her eyes she settles against her pillow and slightly arches her back. I touch the cube to the side of her breast first, and she exhales, "Christ, that's cold." A ripple runs along her flesh, goosebumps rising to the surface. I run the cube up and over the tape, gliding from one nipple to the other.

"Does that help?" I ask, shifting in my seat trying to relieve the pressure of my erection.

"It doesn't feel worse." Her tongue darts out and her body squirms against the sensation, and I don't miss the way her gaze roams over my bare chest, taking in the tattoos. They start over my pecs, spread to my left shoulder and rise up my neck. "It's like when something already hurts so bad, any more pain just starts to feel numb." Her fingers twitch, not quite touching, but close. Then softly, "What do they mean?"

I glance down, running my hand over the black lines and inked symbols like I'm reading them in Braille. "This one," I tap the design over my left collarbone–a precise rendering of a Möbius strip woven with thin lines of circuitry, "reminds me nothing's ever really linear. Time. Learning. Grief. You loop back before you ever move forward."

Her eyes track the motion.

"And this–" I shift slightly, letting the light hit my right pec where a geometric atom breaks apart mid-burst, fragments morphing into stars. "That's the moment I realized physics wasn't just numbers. It's poetry. Everything beautiful explodes before it settles."

She leans in, and I feel her breath before her words. "And your shoulder?"

I turn, letting her see the left one fully–where lines of code form an incomplete ring, a halo broken in two. "That's a segment of the first program I ever wrote that didn't crash. It modeled chaos theory.

Unstable systems." I pause. "I didn't understand it fully then. I just knew it worked. Kind of like me."

She brushes a fingertip near the ink, feather-light. "And the other side?"

"Blank." I meet her gaze. "I haven't earned it yet."

The cube melts, and I pick up another, continuing to run it over the tape until the ends begin to curl. Pinching the edge with my fingertips, I slowly lift, removing the tape.

"It worked," she says in relief.

"Between the wet and cold, the adhesive shrinks up and turns brittle," I explain, moving to her other nipple and pulling its tape off too. The tips are raised, peaked from the stimulation. I don't notice any infection. "I brought you something else."

I reach for the container on the bedside table. It's small with a screw top and I quickly open it. "This is a numbing cream."

Arianette rises up on her elbows. The move makes her tits bounce and jiggle, settling slightly to the side. "What do I do with it?"

"Rub it on." There's an edge to my tone. She notices.

Her fingers dip into the cream and I watch as she glides it over the dark nipples. "Promise me something." Our eyes meet. "The next time he comes to do something like this to you, make sure you call me."

"You'll stop him?"

"No." I shake my head. "I want to watch."

"Oh." I can tell the cream is having the desired effect as she rubs circles around the metal bar, working it into her skin.

Her shoulders loosen and she falls back against the headboard. "It's tingly."

"In a bad way?" I ask.

"No, not bad." She shakes her head. "Can I ask you something?"

I give her a curt nod.

"When DK touches me... why does he stop?"

"What do you mean?"

"On the altar, and today in the class. He touches me, makes my heart beat and my skin feel like it's on fire. I feel... excited, like I'm chasing something instead of being chased. Like I'm on the edge of a tall building, ready to jump off, but then he stops and it's just..."

I push the words through the lump in my throat. "Just what?"

"I want to say gone, but that's not right either. It hurts. I feel desperate. Like I'm out of breath without taking a step."

"Show me."

She frowns but it's lazy, the chemicals in the cream having started to take effect. "What?"

"Show me what he did to you. Today, the other day. What does he do?"

She shakes her head. "I shouldn't."

I pause, letting my response roll about my head for a moment, before asking. "Are you disobeying me, sister?"

"I, I–" She's caught. Her role is to obey her Barons, and I've been nice. Providing her with something to ease her pain. But I also know that she sees me as the man that chased her through the woods, carved her skin with my knife. I'm dangerous, and she just slipped into my trap. "I'm not disobeying you." She couldn't even if she wanted to, the amount of mandrake I used isn't enough to knock her out entirely, but it is enough to make her compliant. I'm not prepared when she adds, "Good girls don't touch themselves."

My eyebrow shoots up. "Says who?"

She shakes her head, teeth bearing down on her bottom lip. She doesn't want to tell me. That's okay, I can find out later. I walk over to the armchair and drag it closer to the bed. "Now," I position the chair near the foot, "move to the edge of the bed."

She slides over, tossing one leg and then the other over the side. Topless, she sits back on her hands, that short little skirt still teasing me. She's so much closer than she was earlier today when I sat up in those rafters and rubbed one out. So very close.

"Show me how DK touches you."

Her knees rise up and then fall to the side, and she lifts up the little plaid skirt, showing off her panties. "He touches me here first," she says lazily, fingers wandering between her thighs. "Teasing me."

"He takes his time?"

"Sort of," her head tilts to the side, "until he gets to the spot."

"What spot?" I ask, digging my nails into my thigh.

"This one." She yanks her panties to the side, giving me a sweet view of her pussy. Her legs spread wider. "Here." She flicks her clitoris, then bites her bottom lip. "Right there, then he rubs it really hard."

Yeah, I bet he does.

"Does that feel good?"

She nods, hair falling over her shoulders, across those pretty nipples. "Yes."

"Then touch it. Just like he did." I lean back, spreading my legs for room. "Make yourself feel good."

Her finger makes a little circle, rolling over her clit. My own fantasy comes to mind, of me pulling out a cigarette and lighting it. Taking a long drag to get the end nice and red. Then I'd bend over and stab it right into her clit, letting the nerves burn.

I blink.

Fuck.

I take a deep, ragged breath.

That's why we look and we don't touch.

"He slid his... you know against me," she says, "pushing it between my legs."

"Say the word."

"What word?" she asks innocently.

"*What* did he slide against you?"

She squirms, more embarrassed to say the words than do the act. "His erection."

I make a face.

"Fine. His penis."

"Do better."

"His dick?"

That earns another expression.

"His cock."

"There you go." I lick my bottom lip. "Was he wet?"

"The tip."

"Were *you* wet?"

She nods. He fucked her from behind. Getting his dick sloppy wet as he rubbed over her cunt. I saw it from down on the stage, only half focused on my presentation because I could see them up there. I could see the expression on her face.

"How about now?" I ask. "How wet are you?"

"A little."

"Show me." She spreads her legs wider, showing me her fingers slipping across her pink folds. "Your fingers."

She holds them up and they're slick and shiny. Coated in her own desire. My chest rises, knowing that that desire comes from looking at me.

"Lick them." She opens her mouth to say something, *to argue,* and I warn in a low voice, "Don't make me tell you twice."

Her tongue darts out, licking over the tips of her fingers.

"Now suck."

The pads vanish, deep in her mouth, and she sucks, sloppy and wet. It's as much as I can stand, and I shove my hand under the elastic band of my pants, grabbing the base of my cock. It's hot and heavy in my hand. Throbbing. Harder than I may have ever been before. Harder than with the girls at the Sanctum or at the Hideaway, who will do any goddamn thing I ask them to do, as long as there's enough cash.

But there's something about seeing Arianette like this, following my every command, not because I'm paying her–but because I *own* her.

Dammit.

A trickle of cum spills from the tip. No. Not yet.

Arianette's fingers dip back between her legs, and her breath turns jagged. Her eyes are hazy, either from the mandrake or maybe just from being so turned on. I let her get through the build up, I won't stop her. Not like DK. That's not my thing.

"You getting close?" I ask her. "You right on that edge?"

She nods, rubbing herself furiously, her tits heaving. I stand, abdomen caved, fisting the base of my dick, fighting the urge to give myself a long stroke. Her eyes are on my body, dragging from the tattoos over my chest down to the cut muscles that create a sharp V. I bend over her, keeping just enough distance not to touch her, and breathe, "Let yourself go, sister. Stop chasing and embrace it."

Her eyes slam shut the second it hits, her nose scrunching up. Her mouth falls slack, that pink tongue taunting just behind her lips. I watch the orgasm take her, her fingers curling against her sex. She moans, the sound caught in her chest.

I slide my hand from my base up, giving myself the freedom to release, to cave, the urge to touch her too much. Just feel her skin. Feel the throbbing pulse beneath my fingertips. I lunge out, wrapping my hand around her throat, pushing her on her back. Arianette's eyes fly open. Her breath is caught under the pressure of my fingers. I want nothing more than to see the vacant lapse in her eyes as I thrust myself inside.

"Hunter," she fights against me. My fingers close, both around her throat and my cock.

I shove a knee between her thighs, barely getting them open before I cum, thick and hot, all over her still quivering pussy.

"Please stop."

I blink, dragging myself out of the fog, looking at the girl with her dark, scared eyes covered in my cum. We share a beat, a long moment, where we both know this could go further. What I can't tell is how much she wants it.

Flinching, I release her, and take a step back, leaving before I'm tempted to find out.

17

T imothy

ADJUSTING MY MASK, I step past the bouncer and into the dark haze of the club. Monroe is behind the bar and I gesture to him as I walk toward the secluded corner booth. Graves called earlier and reserved it for me. I could have gone to Trudie's home to tell her about her son, but some things are better handled in public with society as a witness.

Also, I needed to get out of the house to consider the facts of what I'd learned about the Baroness. She'd been the one to take Armand's life.

Shrugging off my cloak, I hang it on the hook next to the booth, and I've just taken my seat when a waitress appears, placing a napkin and glass on the table in front of me.

"Thank you, sweetheart."

"You're welcome." Her lips quirk up, but falter, obviously a little nervous. Who wouldn't be? She's serving Forsyth Royalty. I lift the glass and take a sip. Club soda. I swallow it back and lament that it's on nights like tonight that I wish I still consumed alcohol.

I look to the stage across the room, where a woman spins on a thick black ribbon. The ribbon covers her most sensitive parts, but even I'm impressed by her performance–it's borderline erotic– evident by the interest from a table of young men near the front. I'm sure they'll be requesting a private show in one of the back rooms before the night is over.

"Drinking alone now, old man?"

I look up and see Pace Ashby standing by the table with a knowing smirk.

The Ashbys are one of the growing members of new Royals that know my true identity. One word from him and the club would know that the man behind the mask isn't Clive Kayes, but Timothy Maddox. But even this one, with all his impulsivity, is aware that some secrets are for a reason. It's better for all of us for mine to remain unknown.

"Is that a crime?" I reply, glancing around the smoky club unable to shake the sense that although nothing is out of place, something is different. The same intimate tables fill most of the floor, and Monroe, of course, is manning the bar. The crowd is a touch younger, but that happens every fall, as men turn twenty-one and are eager to step into the club. Drinks are being served by beautiful young women. The uniform has been altered slightly, with tight short shorts that cling to their firm butts and thighs. The sequined vests are new, too, although seemingly a little more modest, but the V-necks provide a hint of what's below. Their smiles feel a little less forced. Their movements less strained. "It feels different in here."

"Fuck yeah it does," he says, leaning against the edge of the booth and crossing his tattooed arms over his chest. "That's the sensation of what it feels like to get rid of a hundred-and-seventy-five pounds of toxic bullshit."

Ah, yes, Rufus.

"That could be it."

I'd long suspected the girls working at the club were afraid of Rufus, possibly here under some sort of duress. Regina often came with me to my meetings, and she'd sit stiffly next to me, like she knew something I didn't. Pace may be right, the removal of one thing can spark a full transformation.

Trudie arrives in the club, handing her suede coat to one of the servers. She takes no notice of the show on the stage or any of the other attractions in the room. She's a force to be reckoned with, a rarity in Forsyth, a female with power not based on royal status, but rather money and connections. It's how Armand ended up in my initiation, deservedly or not.

Mommy pulled strings.

I lift my hand to get Monroe's attention, but a waitress is already at the table, setting down her drink of choice–a dry martini. Two olives. My club soda is replenished, and soon we're alone.

"I can only assume this is about my son." She picks up her glass and takes a quick swallow. "What's he done now? Groped one of the whores you keep down in your crypt? Snorted an eight-ball of Scratch? Caught skinny dipping in your fountain?" She plucks out the toothpick holding the olives and bites off one with her teeth. "You knew his reputation when you agreed to take him on. What's that saying? No backsies, even for a king."

Her flippant attitude about her son tells me enough about how *and* why he found himself sliced to death on his own weapon. He's impulsive. Entitled and most of all enabled. I'd allowed him in not just as a favor to his mother, but because he had access to corners of Forsyth that I didn't. But the last thing I need among my ranks is someone weak. I'd already been betrayed by one Shadow. I couldn't risk it again.

"This is about Armand," I tell her, "and I hate to report to you that he's dead."

She'd just bitten off the second olive when she gasped in surprise. Eyes wide, she coughs, or attempts to–her airway blocked. Hands flailing at her throat, I give her a long, slow blink, trying to decide if I allow death to take her, or do I intervene?

"Fuck," I mutter, realizing I can't have two Stein's deaths on my hands and I rise, circling the table to drag her from her seat and wrap my arms around her, plunging my fist against her diaphragm... once, then again. The olive ejects, flying across the darkened room. Body shaking, she gasps for air. Pace Ashby takes that moment to pass by with an eyebrow raised at our positioning. "You two need a room?"

"Get her a fucking glass of water!" I roar, releasing Trudie and strengthening my jacket. "Are you okay?"

With a hand to her throat she nods, and the waitress rushes over with a glass of water. Trudie drinks, more liquid spilling from her trembling hand than she swallows. "Sit," I direct, while jerking my chin at the waitress to leave. She leaves. Trudie sits. "Your son is dead. He attempted to betray me during the initiation ceremony. Foolishly, by the way. Taken out by his own weapon." I shoot her a withering look.

"I don't believe it."

"You don't believe that he attempted to betray me? That he intentionally violated my rules?" My hand clenches under the table. "The one *and only* rule, I may add."

"He was young." Tears build at the corners of her eyes. I'm not sure if they're for her son or because she almost choked. "Impulsive."

"There are witnesses," I continue, although the story given to me has inconsistencies. Inconsistencies that I plan to follow up on. "And in light of that act, it's a good thing he was extinguished before I found out, because the consequences would have been far, far worse."

We stare at one another, all the smugness and bravado she carried in with her long gone. The tears have dried up, confirming those were more about a physical reaction than an emotional one. What Armand tried to do was enough to cause a war, and she's a woman without an army. Reaching past the water for her martini, she takes a shaky-handed swallow before adding, "I want his body."

"It's already been delivered." Her jaw sets, and I see the hard lines of age against the sides of her mouth and eyes. "Thirty minutes ago. The official story will be that he died in a tragic accident during the Hunt, beyond that, I expect there to be no discussion outside of this table." I run my fingers over the damp sides of my glass. "That includes the truth about his betrayal."

She nods, wanting to say more but smart enough to keep her mouth shut. Slowly, she collects herself, finishing her drink and standing. She waves for her coat, and a moment later it's around her shoulders. And like that, the grieving mother is gone, and once again, I'm left to pick up the pieces.

"MIND IF I TAKE A SEAT?"

A man steps between me and the woman I've been watching perform on the stage. It's a man I'm familiar with but haven't been personally introduced to. Before I answer, he slides into the seat Trudie occupied.

"Agent Alessio Knight," he says, lifting the lapel of his jacket to reveal the badge clipped to the inside pocket.

"Baron King," I reply, lifting my glass and drinking the last of the liquid. "Unfortunately, I was just on my way out."

"I'm sure you can spare a few minutes of your time," he says casually, "but we can do this down at the station if you'd prefer."

The tactic is old but effective. The only way I'm setting foot in the Forsyth Police station again will be in handcuffs. I inhale and settle back against the seat. "What can I do for you, Agent Knight?"

"Just following up on a conversation we should have had a while back," he notes. "I've managed to interview every other King in Forsyth, although some are more cooperative than others. I just had this nagging feeling that there was one person I needed to speak to about the recent disappearances in town."

I'd been waiting for him to show up on my doorstep, but he's not stupid enough to do that. He has no warrant–nothing other than suspicion. His appearance tonight could have easily been about

Armand, but Trudie is nothing but discreet. Her son's death is a humiliation.

I decide to cut to the chase. "I understand the need to be thorough, but I can assure you no one involved in the BRN fraternity has had anything to do with the missing girls."

"See, that's the problem I'm running into. Everyone says they're not involved, but you're the only one that walks around in a mask that hides your true identity and is rumored to hunt women in the forests."

"Rumors don't hold up in court, Agent Knight." I eye the younger man. He's got the attitude of a man with power, but his suit jacket is cheap, off the rack, and he needs a haircut. I've heard my own rumors about him and the Madam down at the Hideaway–about his lineage. I frown. "It's my understanding you have a person of interest already in custody."

"We do, but that hasn't led us to the four girls we know are still out there."

"And what? You think that I can?" I scoff. "I assure you, Agent Knight, if there was a way to find these young women and return them home safely, I'd do whatever I could. Do you not recall that a female of value to the Barons was harmed as well?"

"Oh yes, I recall." His jaw sets, the hard muscle in the back throbbing in annoyance. He thinks for a moment before saying, "Which is why I'm here to tell you that I'd like to speak to Arianette again, to see if she remembers anything."

"You had access to her in the hospital," I remind him.

"She was still in a state of trauma, drugged, making her information unreliable." He scratches his cheek. "She may be able to tell us more now about who took her, where she was held."

It's reasonable, but from what I learned from the coroner today, Arianette has blood on her hands, making any contact with the authorities a risk. "She's still in a vulnerable state. I don't think it's a good idea."

"So vulnerable you're going to call off your wedding?" When I don't respond he shakes his head with a dark laugh. "Of course not, nothing will get in the way of another Royal sticking his dick in an innocent, *young* girl in order to continue the family line–"

"Enough!" I hiss, blood thundering in my ears. I slam my hand on the table, the King ring front and center. "You shut your mouth about things you do not, and will not, ever understand." I take a deep breath in an attempt to regain my composure, while Knight assesses me. Fuck him. "If you're so worried about bloodlines and lineage, and you want to dig around in the family trees of Royals, I suggest you look at the Purple Palace."

"Due to recent events, Rufus Ashby has been cleared as a suspect."

"I'm not talking about Rufus, although we're all better off with him gone." I lower my voice. "There are other bloodlines in that house that are more tainted than the rest. As the saying goes, the apple doesn't fall far from the tree."

He sits back, wheels turning in his head. I take the opportunity to stand, reaching into my pocket and tossing cash on the table.

"I can assure you, Agent Knight, that no one in Forsyth wants these women found more than I do." I grab my cloak and throw it over my shoulders. "And while you do your job, I'll do mine. We'll see who ends up finding them first."

IT'S LATE when I return and the house is quiet. Even the hallway that leads to Graves' private wing is dark. I step into my room, hang up my cloak and start to remove my mask.

Until I notice it.

There's no delay between me pulling out the switchblade and snapping it open. No hesitation as I jerk open the closet door. Nothing. No one. It's not until I'm sure there's no one else in the room that I take a breath and cross over to the dresser. The framed photo of my wife, Amber, and Remington, is askew. Positioning it back into place, I search for any other intrusion, and see a plate sitting on the windowsill–a slice of half-eaten cake frozen exactly as the trespasser left it.

That's when I look back at the dresser, and rage builds in my chest.

Not only has someone been in my room, touching my things, leaving trash…

Something has been stolen.

And I know exactly who took it.

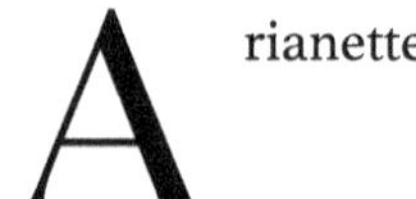rianette

BANG!

"Where is it?"

I jolt upright at the sound–at the voice–fearful of the looming figure at the foot of the bed.

"I said, where the fuck is it?!"

"Don't hurt me," I beg, confused and groggy, wondering how it found me.

The Beast.

"Don't play dumb with me, little girl," he snaps.

Trying to clear the cobwebs in my head, I pull on a thread, remembering that the last thing I did was wash Hunter's cum off my body and crawl into bed.

"You were in my room." He seethes, holding a small plate in front of my face. The cake I'd eaten after dinner–and forgotten–less than an inch from my nose. He slings his arm back, flinging it across the room, where it crashes into the stone fireplace and shatters to the hearth. "So tell me, sister, where the fuck is it?"

"Daddy?" I ask desperately, finally understanding that it's not the Beast. Worse, the King is in my bedroom, angry and upset. Behind his mask his eyes flick to my bare breasts, then back to my face where I'm rubbing my eyes, trying to wake up. Trying to make sense of this. "I don't know–"

"Don't you fucking dare call me Daddy." He lunges at me, clamping his hand around my wrist. "My children don't steal from me. They don't lie."

"I didn't do anything!" I shout, kicking out. "Let go!" But he doesn't, wedging my thumb open with his bigger, stronger fingers. He yanks the ring off my thumb and holds it up.

"I've been lenient with you because of your age and history. Patient out of *obligation*. I was even willing to overlook the fact you eliminated Armand because your Barons covered for you." His voice trembles with barely contained rage. "I figured the story must be true, that he tried to taint you–"

"He did!"

"–But now I see that you're a sneak. A *thief*." His hand thrusts out, circling my neck, and he drags me from the bed, forcing me to stand. "It's no stretch to assume you're also a liar."

"I didn't lie! He shoved me to the ground! Ripped off my panties! He was going to rape me!"

"Maybe so, but you didn't tell the truth did you?" His hand is massive and easily wraps around my throat. "You let them lie for you and take the blame. Well now, you will pay the consequences of your deceit." He steps back, dragging me with him. "Open the cage."

"W-what cage?" I ask, then see the two figures emerge from the dark corners of the room: Damon and Hunter. They look like they both were roused from bed. Hair disheveled, Damon is shirtless, wearing nothing but a pair of shorts. Hunter is in a thin T-shirt that clings to his broad chest, cotton pants cover his legs.

They must have been watching the entire time.

I hear rather than see a lever connect and an ornate door swings out from under the iron bed. Reality slams home. He wants to lock me in there. "Don't–"

"Shut your lying mouth." He steps close until our faces nearly touch. The tips of my nipples graze his chest, making them tighten into hard pebbles and sending a rush of pain-fueled heat through my body. "You will obey the rules of this house, sister. You will *obey* me. And if you don't, I will let my Barons *and* Shadows have you before sending you back to your uncle in disgrace."

Panic claws at my throat and I beg, "Don't send me back. I'll do whatever you want!"

Ignoring me, he gives the guys a quick nod and they descend on me, grabbing me by the arms and shoving me to the ground until I'm on my hands and knees. For once, I don't fight. I can't. Not if I want to stay. It comes as a surprise that the roughness of their touch is familiar now, expected. I crawl into the cage like an animal, knees aching. There's no room to sit up, so I curl onto my side, the hard floor cold and biting against my bare skin.

"She'll stay here until I am sure everything in my room is in order," the King says. I can only see the bottom of their legs and feet. "And since you two decided to cover for her indiscretions, you get to sleep in here and keep watch, understood?"

"Yes."

"Understood."

As if they have a choice.

A moment later, the King's shiny black shoes disappear from view, leaving the three of us alone. I hear a whistle and Ares' soft footsteps enter the room, his wet, black nose sniffing around the edge of the cage. There's no missing the irony that the true animal is outside the cage, while I'm locked inside.

"You want the bed or the chair?" Damon asks, breaking the quiet.

"The chair," Hunter grunts, dropping back into the seat he occupied a few hours before. I can see his ankles, and Ares curled up on my discarded shirt. Above me, the bedsprings creak under Damon's weight.

It's not until the room is fully silent that I let the tears fall. It's not the cold floor or the fact that I'm naked. I deserve this for being stupid, nosy, impulsive.

No, the real reason I'm upset is the knowledge that I've disappointed my King, and I have no idea how to fix it.

"QUIET, ARIANETTE, BE A GOOD GIRL."

I'm standing by the edge of the stage in my leotard and tights. There's an audience tonight. They're enthralled by the boy on stage, how mature he looks in his blue suit, how cleverly his fingers move over the chords. I'm nervous, my stomach aches. I tug at the sleeve of my uncle's jacket.

"Shhh!" he snaps. I haven't even said anything.

There are two different rows of children. One for performers. One for the others. I'm jealous of the girls' dresses. Of their styled hair and the makeup on their eyes and mouth. I glance down at my scuffed ballet shoes and once again feel that fullness—the ache.

"Uncle," I whisper, not wanting to interrupt the boy on stage. I shift on my feet, fingers pressing between my legs. "I need to go—"

My eyes snap open, bladder screaming, swollen and achy from the urgent need to urinate. I move to toss my legs over the edge of the bed, to stand, but my knees slam into hard metal and my head crashes above. "Ow," I yelp, slowly becoming aware that I'm still in the cage. Also aware that I need to pee–really fucking bad.

"Let me out." I rattle the cage. "I need to go to the bathroom."

"Quiet," Hunter mumbles. Ares has moved his nose next to an opening in the iron, giving me a long sniff.

"Quiet, Arianette, be a good girl."

That night is burned into my psyche, the excitement of finally getting to perform. The hope that I'd win approval, show that I'm worthy. Useful.

I shudder at the memory, which doesn't help the urge forcing me to clench my legs together. I whine, "I need to go to the bathroom. For real."

"You're in there until the King says otherwise," Damon says, feet coming into view as they hit the floor and he stands up. "Fuck, that bed is comfortable."

"Can't say the same about the chair," Hunter grumbles. A moment later he also stands, and I watch their bare feet just outside my cage. "Ares, *komm.*"

"Where are you taking him?" Damon asks, standing. I crane my neck, trying to get a better view, but all I see is him shoving his hands down the front of his shorts to scratch his balls.

"Outside."

"You're taking the dog outside to pee, but you won't let me?" I shout, rubbing my hand down my back. It aches from sleeping on the floor, just like the rest of my body.

"Ares didn't sneak into the King's room and steal his shit," he throws out, before heading out the door with the dog.

Damon squats, making himself eye level with me.

"Please," I beg him. "I'll come right back in."

"Sorry, Baroness. I already fucked up by covering for you once. I'm not doing it a second time."

"I'll do whatever you want." I squirm, twisting. I think of the things I know he likes. "You can pierce me. I'll touch you. Lick you." My mind scrambles. "You can do it in public."

"Is it that big of a deal if you piss on yourself?" His eyes narrow, watching me. "You're literally locked up in a cage. Like an animal. Well, *worse* than an animal." He snorts, obviously thinking about Ares, who slept comfortably at his owner's feet. "You fucked around and found out, sister, now you reap the consequences."

He rises and moves out of view. It *is* a big deal. Good girls don't make messes. They're quiet. They're unseen. I've broken every one of those rules since I've been here and like Damon said, I fucked up.

I killed Armand because he was a traitor, but no one knows that.

"Let me out!" I scream, slipping my fingers through the grate. I jerk and shake the stiff, cold metal, but it doesn't budge. Breathing hard, I freeze when I hear the hard flow of water–no, not water–it's the steady *stream* of Damon relieving himself in my bathroom. The sound triggers my bladder, a spasm running down my body.

Squeezing my eyes, I use every ounce of will to hold it in, but I know the second before it happens that I've lost control.

A moment later, warm liquid floods out. "No," I sob, the urine spreading. "No." It seeps out from under the iron onto the floor. *"No, no, no, no…"* The wail is both foreign and familiar. Humiliating and raging. I'm angry with myself. Angry for being so weak and stupid and *bad*. I kick the end of the bed, busting my toe. "Ahh! Fuck!"

The toilet flushes and he returns, making a show about not stepping in the mess. "Gross," he says, his face out of range. "Filthy."

"Fuck you!" I shout, hating him. Hating myself. With a disgusted noise, he leaves, and I let the shame wash over me. Neither Damon nor Hunter are going to release me. The King will find out. They'll all know. I'm dirty and bad.

Just like my uncle always said.

I'VE JUST FOUND a dry spot at the top corner of the bed when the pad of soft footsteps enters the room. A series of snorts and sniffs follow, the dog's black nose edging around the wet pool, although never stepping into it. Even he doesn't want to get soiled.

"Get." I tell him when he sniffs close to where I've curled up. *"Go."*

Despite Hunter saying Ares isn't mean, dogs make me nervous. I'd grown up with them, thick and muscled, patrolling the grounds of the Manor–one more thing, I realize, to keep the inhabitants isolated from the outside world.

"Did you get sent in here to watch me?" I ask him. We feel even in this moment, nose to nose. His dark pupils ringed in a soulful yellow-brown.

The wing has fallen quiet, and I know they've left for class without me. Another failure. The brindled dog steps back and circles a few feet away, circling three times before dropping to the floor with a content sigh, on top of my dirty shirt, like he's just here to keep me company.

If I sleep, this time there are no dreams.

"Oh, my."

I blink out the cage at the pair of charcoal pant legs and dark dress shoes. Graves lifts his foot with a *squick*, the sound of his sole sticking to the floor. I wrap my arms around my knees and curl into a ball.

"I made a mess," I say quietly.

"I see." He walks away, and my heart skitters, terrified he's leaving. But before I can call for him, he returns, tossing a towel over the drying pool on the floor. Then with a hard click, the gate swings open. "Can you get out on your own?"

I'd rather stay in here and hide forever. But I'm thirsty and hungry. Cold. He must sense my hesitation.

"Come out, Baroness. It's time."

It's not a request, I can hear it in his voice. My muscles are stiff. I thrust out a leg and it slides through the cold urine, slicking up my calf. "Ugh," I mutter, disgusted with myself, but I manage to get on my hands and knees and crawl out the way I came in.

My back screams as I straighten up, face level with his pelvis. A tremor runs through me, realizing that my release must come with conditions.

"What do you want me to do?" I ask, ready to get it over with. "I can give you a blow job but I'm not sure I'm very good at it."

"What?" Graves gawks at me. "God, no."

He's repulsed. Rightfully so. I realize then he has a second towel in his hand and he quickly helps me off the floor and wraps it around my body.

He moves past me into the bathroom, turning on the shower.

"Go ahead," he gestures to the rushing water, "get yourself cleaned up."

I clutch the towel to my chest, fighting the chill that has set into my bones. "You shouldn't have to deal with this."

He chuckles, but there's a lack of meanness behind it. "Baroness, I've worked alongside the King for many years and have managed this house as well as the hundreds of frat boys that have come through." He nods toward the other room. The mess. "This is nothing."

I'm not sure this is as reassuring as he thinks it is, but I drop the towel and step inside, submerging myself under the steaming water. I soap up my body, washing off the urine and any lingering cum from Hunter the night before. I let the water soak into my hair and then massage the shampoo into my scalp. I feel like I'm taking too long, but Graves doesn't rush me.

The water is lukewarm when I turn the knobs. Two fresh towels are on the hooks right outside the door. I use one on my hair, wrapping it tightly. And the other on my body. When I step out, an outfit is on the dressing table. At first, I think Graves is gone, but I see his shadow in the thin strip under the door.

I hold up the black velvet dress. The material is body-hugging, with a heart-shaped top. The sleeves are made of lace, drapey and bell shaped, cinching at the wrist. A gentle lace fringe accentuates the edge of the skirt and along the bust. I slip it on and open the bathroom door.

"Much better," Graves says, standing a few feet away holding a pair of patent leather lace-up boots with thick heels. "These should work."

"Why are you being so nice to me?" I ask, a sense of uneasiness building in my gut.

To my surprise he says, "I'm not your enemy, Arianette. None of us are."

I glance over to the cage and the towel soaked in urine. "That's not what it seems like."

He nods toward the red velvet armchair, the one Hunter slept in last night. Smoothing out my skirt, I sit. Graves pulls a small stool from the other side of the fireplace, perches on the edge and begins unlacing the boot.

I comply when he gestures for my foot. His touch is surprisingly gentle, and as he eases it in the boot, he begins to speak.

"I'm here to make sure that the King is successful while ruling his territory." His fingers loop into the laces, tugging them snug against my foot. "You are an important part of that success, which means you're my priority."

I eye the quickness of his fingers. "And you're not just saying this so you can come on my face?"

He laughs, grinning down at my feet. "I assure you that the only face I want to come on belongs to my husband."

"Oh." A husband. "I didn't know."

"My personal life isn't common knowledge, but I've been around here long enough to understand why you'd worry about it." He tightens the laces up my calf, the leather molding around my legs. Just under my knee, he ties it off, then moves to the other foot. "The arrangement between the King and Dean Hexley is all part of a bigger plan. One you are integral to. One I am sure will succeed." He starts in on the laces. "But our King hasn't had a woman around long term in many, many years. Especially one with so much..." he searches for a word, landing on, "*spirit.*"

"He hates me."

"No." But I hear the lack of conviction.

"He ordered me in that cage," I look away from the cage, "and if he finds out about the mess–"

"He won't." He works faster this time, already tying the laces at the top of the boot. "I'll take care of it, and he'll never know."

"Why?" I ask again.

"I already told you, Arianette. You are important to Beta Rho, to the House of Night, and most of all, to our King's plans." He lowers my foot to the floor. "Now, are you ready?"

"For school?"

He shakes his head. "For the King."

19

T imothy

THERE IS NO MORE sacred place in the House of Night than the sanctuary.

Even after all these years, I feel the same powerful emotions as I did when I first stepped foot in the hallowed space and accepted my oath of fealty as a member of BRN. Later I took on the role of Baron, participating in the Hunt and Claiming. Over the years, the magnitude of that power has shifted, between highs and lows, settling on my shoulders now with the weight of my sins and the heavy curse that came with them.

Consequences.

They come for us all.

I walk the distance from the narthex to the front of the room, toward the throne. I have my own rituals to attend to, ones built over time. I pass the rows of empty pews, each step holding a memory. This is a place of ceremony, for celebration of marriages and births.

The anointing of Shadows as they pass through BRN, beginning to end. I pause just before the throne, looking back down the aisle. The memory of Amber standing at the other end flickers in my mind. She was gorgeous. *Mine.* Or so I thought.

My gaze shifts next to the throne, to the pedestal holding the bronze ceremonial bowl. Amber and I stood over it, not once, but twice, mixing our blood and promising ourselves to one another, and then later affirming to raise our child–our legacy–to the will of the King.

Bitterness rises in the back of my throat, and I turn away, hating how what once was joyous is now nothing short of sharp, continuous pain. I take the short walk to the transept, a shallow alcove jutting out from the chapel. It's decorated with the symbology of our people–our past. It's the one place I allow the festering truth to reveal itself.

Approaching, I kneel and remove my mask, prepared to face the demons of my past. There's a grainy, framed photograph of Clive Kayes, the man the majority of Forsyth believes me to be. He's frozen in time, looking as he did the last time anyone in public saw his face, just before his son, Benji, took his life. Back then I thought Clive Kayes was an old man. Ironically, I'm now the same age that he was when he was killed.

Reaching for a long match, I strike it against the rough paper. The sulfur tip sizzles and I light a black candle in honor of the fallen King.

There is no image of my cousin Benji in this place of sanctuary. No trinkets that carry his spirit. There's no candle to light. Not because he murdered his father. A son killing his father in Forsyth is as common as rain in the spring. No, it's because this is not the place for blasphemers, adulterers, or worse, those who plan to use their power to harm the innocent.

Consequences.

They came for Benji at my own hands after he led my wife, Amber, down a path of uncharted wickedness, seeding her fragile mind with dangerous ruminations. They bore a child together, which was betrayal enough, but when I found out what they wanted to do with the bastard... I swallow, striking the second match. I stare at the tip of flickering flame a moment, saying an oath of protection for the child, now a man, Whitaker Ashby.

Memento Mori is our motto, but I embraced another one that day. *In morte vita est.* In death there is life.

Before I killed Benji I didn't fully understand the truth of those words. To secure Whitaker's life, I had to extinguish my cousin's. I had the Shadows bury my uncle in the Kayes crypt, and my cousin deep under another set of bones in the catacombs, put on the mask, and stepped into the role of King.

I could have killed her, too. I had every right, and no one in Forsyth would have blinked an eye, but...

Consequences.

She was also the mother of *my* child, Remington.

Removing the gold ring from my pocket, I place it on the altar. The rage I felt when I realized it was missing–that the girl stole it–was all-consuming. Too consuming for this many years later. The hold Amber has on me is perilous. Humiliating. A risk to everything I've worked to accomplish and my plans moving forward. All the work I had done to become a better man faltered in that one moment.

With that in mind, I strike the third match and light two candles with the flame, one for Amber, one for my son. Those seeds Benji had sown in Amber, they'd worked their way from mother to son, his mind as restless as hers. At times, I fear, as dangerous.

My hopes of healing him–saving him–were lost long ago. He's entrenched with those who pander to his weaknesses. He loathes me, which is fair, I'd participated in my own manipulations, all with good intentions. He doesn't understand all of this was for him–for *us*–and now I am trapped fulfilling the obligations of a different path, one he was chosen to take. The girl I'd hoped would tie us together, in a few days, will be *my* bride, not his. She was to be his salvation, instead, now it's just another consequence.

Taking a deep breath, I reach for my mask, eyes falling to the stack of candles. Impulsively, I grab the candle and strike the final match, lighting the wick.

I swallow and speak to the powers that rule us, light and dark, the only words that suffice, "Give her the strength for what is coming. There will be no mercy."

"COME FORWARD," I say when I hear her footsteps falter near the side door. I feel soothed, the emotions I felt before no longer have me in a chokehold. I'd left them, along with the ring, at the altar.

She approaches the throne dressed in velvet and lace. It doesn't do much to take away from the dark circles of exhaustion under her eyes, or the timid way she walks–her muscles aching after sleeping on the hard floor in a confined space.

I didn't consider her state when I barged through the door the night before. Didn't fucking care. But I didn't expect to find her in the bed, naked, those full round breasts tipped in silver. Damon's work, I assume.

That's the image that flashes over her as she moves closer. The flat belly under the swell of her perky breasts, the dark thatch of soft hair covering her pussy. I stared down at her on her hands and knees, at the soft flesh of her cheeks. I call her a girl, she acts like it, but there's no doubt that she has a woman's body. It's made of a woman's curves, the kind you hold onto and plunder. It was the second time I'd seen her exposed. The first, writhing on the altar. The second, scared and confused. *Obedient.*

Both times brought the same feeling in my chest: disgust.

The woman in front of me lifts the hem of her skirt by the lace and curtsies. "Your Majesty."

I fight an eye roll, and plan to kick Graves' ass later for putting her up to this nauseating display.

"That's enough," I mutter. "Stand straight."

Our eyes hold for a long moment, until she blurts, "Please don't send me back. I won't do it again. I'll sleep in the cage. I'll do whatever you–"

"*Quiet.*" Her mouth clamps shut, although it seems to take a herculean effort. "As much as I'd love to send you back to your uncle, that is not possible." I look down at her. "As was my hope that you would adapt to your role as Baroness by attending class and your Barons with no complications."

Her jaw loosens and she starts, "I'm–"

"Shut. Up." Emotions flicker across her face. She struggles to control them–which is a problem. She struggles to control *herself.* Even more of an issue. "This is my home, Baroness. A home I open to a chosen few in Forsyth each year. I provide one worthy female a room, nourishment, safety, and protection. In exchange you are at the will and command of my Barons, who are at the will and command of their King." I pause, letting her comprehend the information before I continue, "And are currently restraining themselves at my request."

She shifts her feet, the patent leather soles scuffing softly. I have no doubt she's thinking of the carving on her chest and the bars I saw threaded through the peaks of her nipples. I can only assume she's experienced more under their hands since the Hunt, damages I can't see.

Back in the day, I would have torn her to shreds.

"The situation between us is unprecedented, which may make things confusing for you, so let me be clear: you are not to wander the House of Night without approval. You are not to touch anything that doesn't belong to you. You are *never* to go in any room that isn't explicitly approved, especially mine, ever again."

She nods, and I note that for once she's keeping her mouth shut. Good, maybe she's trainable after all.

"In less than two weeks the wedding will take place on Samhain." I gesture to the sanctuary. "Here, actually, in this room."

She looks around, taking in the space for the first time, absorbing the arched stained-glass windows, the leaded glass filled with BRN symbology. The large pentagram on the back wall behind the throne is omnipresent, a reminder of who and what we are. Her eyes skitter over to the altar, where the candles still flicker with light.

"Your uncle assured me that you were prepared to handle all of this, but it's clear I've been misled." I tap my ring against the arm of the throne. "I'll notify Graves that we need to consult a professional."

"A professional what?" she asks, then slams her mouth shut again.

"In weddings. Etiquette. Appropriate behavior. And..." I clear my throat. "Expectations."

Her brown eyes lock with mine. Her innocence oozes off of her in waves, but those eyes... they swim with something deeper. More mature. More emotion than I feel comfortable sitting with. I lift my chin. "You're dismissed."

"Thank you," she says, dropping into that curtsey again. "I won't disappoint you again."

I watch her walk away, the hem of her black skirt swishing against her thighs. She may mean what she says, but it's a promise set to fail.

DESPITE THE STUCCO walls and clay terracotta tiles tidily lined up on the roof, there's no mistaking that this is a hospital. No matter how much synthetic lavender they pump through the vents there's always the unmistakable scent of antiseptic and bleach. The halls are too bright, too polished. It's always this way, clean enough to pretend the sickness isn't rotting the bones of this place.

It hits me the moment I step through the automatic glass doors. I nod once at the young woman at the front desk. She's new. She doesn't know me by sight yet, but it won't take long. The Maddox name still means something here–money, power, an unspoken warning not to ask questions.

For years I had Amber secured abroad. I wanted her as far away from Remington as possible. *Away* from all children. But now he's a man, as is Whitaker, and it felt wrong to have her so far away. Here, at least, I can visit, keep a closer eye on her therapies, and most of all, ensure she's secure even if the views are less pleasing than those in Europe.

Not that it isn't nice here. Saint Mary's Solarium Conservatory for

Wellbeing is a top-notch facility. I donated extensively when Remy was admitted, ensuring that the program is equipped with highly trained staff and comfortable, humane residential care.

I move down the long corridor, my shoes making no sound on the thick carpet. Through the wide windows I can see the gardens -- neatly trimmed hedges, a white fountain spraying water that glitters in the late afternoon sun. I spot her immediately, sitting under a shaded canopy, her chair turned slightly toward the light. A book rests open in her lap, though her eyes are vacant, staring somewhere beyond the horizon.

She's still beautiful. Her hair, once wild gold, is paler now, and her skin, nearly translucent, looks paper-thin. A silk robe that I sent her hangs loose over her frame. She looks breakable.

I hate how soft my heart still goes when I first see her.

A nurse spots me and murmurs something into a radio, unlocking the French doors. I step outside and take a deep breath of fresh cut grass and roses. The river is in the distance, cutting its course through Forsyth like a snake. It's said that fresh air and water are good for the soul. I can only hope.

Amber blinks slowly when she hears my approach on the stone path and I brace myself, wondering who I'll be visiting with today: the sweet, fun girl I married all those years ago? The doting mother? The cheating wife? Or the delusioned lunatic, willing to throw it all away?

"Timothy," she says, voice thick, syrupy from the medication. She tries to smile. "You came."

"I always come," I answer, seating myself in the wrought iron chair across from her. I lean forward, elbows on my knees. "New book?"

Her fingers twitch over the spine. From here I can read the cover: *Modern Masters*. Amber had a way with just about any medium: oils, acrylics, pastels, clay... Remy inherited her artistic skills, among other, less desirable, traits.

Today, though, I can tell the book is nothing but a prop. She's too far under today. Too medicated to be dangerous.

"I have something to tell you."

I don't know if she hears me, but it doesn't matter. I need to say it. For me.

Her chin tilts, and from this angle she looks so much like Remy, but even more... Whitaker. That gives me a sense of resolution.

"There's going to be a wedding" I tell her, voice flat. "A Black Wedding."

For a moment, something flashes behind her eyes–something slippery and sharp.

The old Amber. The one who knew the weight of those words.

"You may remember the Hexleys." The family goes way back in Forsyth history. Early settlers and founders of the university. Their focus has always been on academics and philanthropy. Owen isn't the first dean in the Hexley family, and their name is associated with many programs, but they've always been disconnected from the Royals. The difference is that Owen Hexley has aspirations. He's not content to simply wear the title of Dean, he wants power that reaches farther than the boundaries of the campus. "Owen was in school when we were there. He's the Dean of Students now and he has a niece, Arianette."

If Amber remembers any of this it doesn't show on her expression. I continue, "Years ago... after the scandal. He came to me with a proposition: a joining of our families. Remington would marry Arianette in a Black Wedding, binding our families together."

Her eyes shift, connecting with mine. "And in return?"

Ah, she *is* listening. I continue, "There's no dowry, just the opportunity for two families, one marked by tragedy, the other untarnished by suspicion and shame, but lacking connections." The tight feeling in my chest appears, the one that accompanies any talk about what she did to us. "The goal was to have Remy and Arianette marry, for him to be linked to a reputable family and her, and therefore her family, to finally gain Royal status."

"Remy is getting married?"

"No," I stretch my neck, feeling the tight coil of muscle. "Unfortunately, our son has decided to take another path, leaving his obligations to me."

Her eyes narrow. "What path?"

I laugh, knowing the truth will hurt, wanting it to hurt her as much as it's hurt me. "He's a Duke, Amber. Through and through. First hand to the King."

From an outsider's perspective, they would think I'd just struck the woman in front of me. Her jaw drops and her hand moves protectively in front of her face. "How?" she asks. "How could you let this happen?"

I shake my head. "Don't you dare act surprised that this has happened. It's the result of your treachery and deceit. And now I will continue to carry the mantle of the Barons, sacrificing once again for your failures."

Her teeth bare, the first sign of true life I've seen in her for years. "Don't blame me for your weakness, Timothy. You're the one that doesn't believe in the old ways. The truth. You poisoned the ground the Barons walk on for eternity. *I* was the one willing to make the sacrifice." She leans forward, the book sliding off her lap with a thud. "*I* was the one who took the legacy's seed, bore him a son, and prepared him for the altar. You destroyed us with your lack of faith, and now we're all paying the consequences."

It's the most I've heard her speak in years. The most I've allowed. I let her tirade sink in, the realization that she's still the same. Nothing has changed her. Not the medication, the therapies, nor the time alone.

She's sick, delusional, and there's nothing that can help her.

"So you'll marry her then? And what? Breed her? Create another heir? One that you don't push away?"

"If I plan to create with my bride, it is none of your concern." I stand and look down at her. "The wedding will take place on Samhain. It's a spiritual wedding, not a legal one. As much as I would like to sever ties with you, I will remain your spouse legally so that I can ensure that you never set foot outside these doors again."

I don't wait for a response. There's no point. My wife was lost to me long ago, lost to her delusions and narcissism. I will not allow that madness into my house again, not with Amber or with Arianette.

This wedding, as much as it's an obligation, is also a fresh start. I have a new future awaiting me, a new bride, and I have no choice but to embrace them and finally move forward with my life.

20

D amon

THERE'S an energy about Friday Night Fury that's contagious. The fights, the booze, the Scratch being passed hand to hand. Everyone is high on something, including adrenaline. It's probably something about establishing the pecking order among the Royals.

"You've been to fights before?" Hunter asks as I muscle my way through the crowd standing outside the gym to get to the door.

"I got in my first fight when I was sixteen." I'd tried earlier, but never got past the DKS bouncer parked by the entrance. Later, when I rushed DKS, I went to a few fights with the guys but I don't mention it–another lifetime and all of that. "Paid the bouncer off with a quarter ounce of weed. You?"

"Nah." Hunter grabs Arianette's bicep, pulling her around two cutsluts dry humping against a car. He pauses. "Fuck, she's beautiful."

I eye the girls. "If you're into gutter-trash, sure."

"Not the girls, dipshit, the car. Mint-condition 1976 Trans Am." He nods appreciatively at the matte-black muscle car. "That's what I was doing at sixteen. Modifying the engine on my car with upgraded fuel injectors. I would've loved to have gotten my hands on this one."

Arianette's quiet, but listening, eyes wide as she takes in the car, the crowd, and everything else. "What about you, Baroness? This your first Fury?"

"My uncle never would have let me go somewhere like this." I haven't even tried to hide the boner I've been sporting since she walked out of her room tonight. It's not just the short-shorts with criss-crossing ties that reveal a thin strip of flesh down her hips, or the cropped, black tank with a square neckline, or the fishnet stockings. It's the fact I can see those hard little bars pressing against the tight fabric, a secret reminder of who she belongs to. "*Ever.*"

The bouncer, a thick-necked DKS named Dillon, is manning the line. On a whim, I grab Arianette, pulling her body close to mine. Jutting my hips into hers so she can feel me. In her ear, I explain, "This is our first time going in as Royals, which means everyone will be watching." I dip my face towards hers, planting my mouth against the hot, salty skin under her ear. I drag the hard ball of the piercing along her jaw, and look up to find Hunter watching us through lidded eyes. Little perv. "You remember the rules, Doll Baby?"

"Stick close," she says, fingers touching her lips. "Don't talk to anyone, men or women."

"That's right." I grab her by the ass and squeeze. Jesus, I'd give up my best piercing kit just to fuck her once, hard and quick. Get it over with so I could think about something else.

"DK!" Dillon's voice carries over the crowd. He waves me over, and we skirt in front of the growing line. "It's been a while. Heard you're a crypt keeper now."

From anyone else, that comment may have put me on edge, but Dillion's an okay guy, and more importantly, a customer. I'd had the dude's dick in my hand when I pierced his foreskin about six months ago.

"I may have declared."

One of his bushy eyebrows lifts. "Huh. I thought you were solidly independent."

"Things change," I reply nonchalantly, then add, "How's the work? Healed up?"

"Yep. No complaints." He makes a show of gripping his belt buckle, then nods to the entrance. "Go ahead. Fights are already starting."

"Royal treatment," I joke, bumping fists with him as we cut the line. "I could get used to this."

Inside, there are more people in line for beer than watching the early fight going on in the ring. It's LDZ in gold vs PNZ in purple, younger guys–probably freshman. "Tucker, get your fucking shit together!" I hear shouted from above. The three of us look up, and I see the Lords sitting in the upper level, Dimitri Rathbone leaning over the railing. "If you lose this match, you'll get two beatings tonight!"

A dark-haired woman steps next to Rathbone, and he slides an arm around her waist.

"Who's that?" Arianette asks, head tilted up. Her fingers are curled around my belt loop, sticking close.

"Dimitri Rathbone," Hunter says.

She shakes her head. "No, the girl."

"That's Story Austin." Apparently, Hunter is a Royal search engine. "His Lady. He's best friends with the King, Killian Payne."

"Majestic, like a lion," Arianette murmurs, "rawr."

Hunter stares at her, probably trying to decipher her nonsense.

"He may have the power, but his other best friend, Tristian Mercer, is from one of the wealthiest families in town."

"Oh," Arianette's expression brightens, "his name is on the concert hall on campus."

"How, and why, do you know all of this?" I ask. Sure, I know who Killian Payne is, and the guy over in the next box, is Simon Perilini, but these were the entitled, rich fuckers I loathed in high school. I did my best to forget all of them, but here I am, *one* of them.

Christ.

I can't help but notice that the Prince's box is empty—not a surprise given the fact Verity Sinclaire just had her baby. The Counts... well, no one knows if that box will ever be occupied again—at least by Royalty. There's one left—the Barons—and there's no sign of the King.

He shrugs. "First, I already knew who they all were, but once Nick Bruin accosted us on campus I decided to do a little more research."

Of course he did.

Over the ring, I see a sign listing tonight's fights. Up next is a DKS matched up to another LDZ. Then the final, and main fight will be Porterfield, one of the current Dukes, against Alvarez–Mateo.

I feel a little shitty sending him in for the first fight of the year, but neither Hunter nor I are ready for a matchup. I can hold my own, but these fucking Dukes crawled out of the womb with gloves on. I search the crowd. "Do you see Mateo?"

"Maybe he's already in the locker room getting ready," Hunter suggests. He reaches into the inside pocket of his jacket and pulls out a flask. He unscrews the top and takes a drag, then offers it to me.

"Fuck yes. Thanks, man." On the first swallow the whiskey burns going down my throat. The second goes a little smoother. I feel those brown eyes on me as Arianette watches.

"Want some?" I tilt the flask toward her.

She shakes her head.

"Hmm." I tilt the flask back and take another sip, this time holding it in my mouth. I grab Arianette and press my lips against hers, forcing her lips apart. The whiskey releases slowly, from my tongue to hers. Her tongue laps against mine, the alcohol strong.

She coughs. "It tastes like medicine."

Hunter nods across the room as I hand him back the flask. "Over there."

A group from BRN is huddled by the wall. Frat brothers we went through initiation with, along with a few familiar crypt chasers, who assess the Baroness with their heavily made up eyes. I don't usually get into girl-shit, but there's definitely a territorial vibe between the chasers and Arianette.

"You made it." A junior named Rob steps forward. "Want a beer?"

I shake my head. "Is Mateo getting ready?"

He glances around. "I saw him earlier..."

The fight bell clangs, ending the LDZ/PNZ fight. The Prince is being carried off the mat by two of his frat brothers, blood dripping from his mouth. At least Rathbone will be happy.

"I guess we can grab some seats–"

Carson pushes through the group and looks between me and Hunter. "We've got a problem."

"What kind of problem?"

His jaw clenches and he jerks his head. "Follow me."

"*HOOAARRK.*"

The smell hits the moment the door of the locker room swings open.

"Jesus Christ, what is that?" Hunter says, pushing in behind me. Arianette, like she promised, sticks to our side like glue.

Whatever it is, it takes over the basic locker room scent of sweat and balls, and seems to come from a crumpled mass on the floor. There's a chaser bent over him, her dark hair straight as a sheet. I've met her before–fooled around with her actually, at some of the parties during rush. If I remember right, her name is Bronwyn. She shifts and that's when I see it. *Him.* Fucking Mateo.

"Nnuughh," he moans, completely naked with the side of his face pressed against the tile floor. Carson tosses a wad of paper towels over the offending smell–vomit.

"What the hell happened to him?" Hunter asks, looking down at his writhing form. He gags, dry heaving at this point.

"I don't know," Bronwyn says, standing up. Her halter top is mesh and lace, cleverly placed black velvet flowers cover her nipples. The rest is see-through, giving more of a hint of her round tits. Her skin is so pale I wouldn't be surprised to learn she is a vampire. "We were in here getting ready for the match when he just started getting sick."

"Oohhwwnnn." Mateo's arms wrap around his body as a shiver of chills set in. "I think I'm dying."

Arianette pushes past me. "His tongue is black. Eyes possessed, dilated." She bends, pressing her black painted fingertips to his sweaty forehead. "He swallowed a demon."

Bronwyn lifts a dark eyebrow at the Baroness.

"For fuck's sake, sister, not now," Hunter grunts, but Mateo looks up at her and sure as fuck, his pupils are blown wide.

"Did you eat something?" I ask.

"No," he promises vehemently. "Well…"

A spasm rocks him, shuddering down his limbs like he's been electrocuted.

"Well what?" Hunter asks.

"Yes," he flips his answer. "Yes, I did eat something. Kind of."

"Jesus, Mateo," Carson rolls his eyes. "What the hell does that mean?"

"I took some 'shrooms a couple hours ago." He flops on his back, flaccid dick rolling against his inner thigh. "I wanted clarity going into the fight."

"Dude, you're not dying," Rob snorts, "you're trippin' balls."

"The demon," Arianette whispers, eyes fixed on Mateo, "it's trying to come out."

"Baroness!" Mateo lifts his chin and squints at Arianette. "Looking sexy in those shorts." He licks his bottom lip. "Wanna let me tug on one of those strings?"

"Okay, that's enough," Hunter declares, stepping between Arianette and Mateo's wandering eyes. Me? Well, I'm about to fucking snap.

"You're fucking with us, right?" I ask, looking at my new frat brothers. "Is this some kind of initiation prank? A first Fury punking?"

Their silence tells me everything I need to know. We're screwed.

"Who gave them to you?" Carson asks.

"This chick down on the Avenue."

"You took drugs from a random chick? Are you a fucking moron?"

I ask. Again, I'm met with the quiet that confirms, yes, Mateo is a moron. "Well, it's obvious he can't go in the ring like that."

All eyes shift to me and Hunter.

"Why are you looking at us like that?" Hunter asks, crossing his arms over his chest.

"We know this is new for you, and we were trying to give you a little time before you dove right into intra-frat activities, but one of you is going to have to go in," Carson says. "Otherwise, you'll look like a bunch of gaping pussies."

"Fuuuck," I thrust my hand in my hair.

Hunter exhales and says, "Look, I'll do it if you want. I can hold my own, but do you know the cognitive damage a concussion can cause? Memory loss, concentration issues, processing speed." He lists them off like they're written on his hand–which they're not because he's avoided concussions and doesn't need to. "Not to mention the physical effects like dizziness, headaches, sleep disturbances–"

"I'll do it," I snap. "Save your brain. It's not like I'm going to win a Nobel Prize in physics or whatever."

"You sure?" Hunter asks. "Because we can forfe–"

"No!" The group of guys all shout at once, and I'm pretty sure if I don't step in there will be a revolt in our first week as Barons.

"No forfeiting." I may start throwing punches sooner than later if everyone doesn't chill. Thankfully, they believe me, and I can save my knuckles for the main event. "It'll be fine. Rob, clean up Mateo and get his ass out of here so he can ride this out somewhere safe. Carson, find me some shorts and whatever else I need to get ready for tonight." I look over at Hunter. "Go let that mean older lady in the leopard print know there's been a change in fighters."

"I'll help you get ready," Bronwyn says. In the black heels she's almost as tall as I am, her long legs hidden beneath a long skirt that matches the top. Her hand rests on my chest and her black painted lips are dangerously close. I've tasted them before, even though I was high as fuck at the time. "Every fighter needs a woman in their pregame ritual."

"Isn't that the Baroness' job?" Carson asks.

"Any other year and I would have been the Baroness," she snaps, gaze flitting over to Arianette. "I put in the work over the last three years, I have the bloodline and legacy. I know exactly how to take a pregame edge off and then walk you out to the ring so that everyone is both jealous *and* fears you."

The locker room is quiet, waiting on my response. And to be fair, my brain is running through the scenarios of exactly how she'd help me with my nerves because they are on a rampage right now. But she lost me the second she mentioned bloodlines and legacy.

Because fuck her.

"Bronwyn is right. She put in the time and has the history." I look over at Arianette who has her teeth bared at the other girl. "But Arianette has something you don't." I reach out and tug her top down, revealing the bandage. Ripping it off, I say, "*Our mark.* So you may want to back the fuck off now because you won't have to deal with me, you'll have to deal with her."

And Arianette Hexley is a stone cold killer.

Bronwyn rolls her eyes and mutters, "Whatever," before striding out of the locker room. That gets everyone else moving. Rob and a few other guys manage to get Mateo on his feet and help him toward the door. As Mateo passes by, he grins over at Arianette and says, "You like waffles? Maybe we can go get waffles."

"Keep moving, dumbass," Hunter says, ushering the group to the door. He follows them out and Carson returns, dumping a duffle bag on a nearby bench.

"This is all of his stuff." He unzips the top and rummages inside. "Shorts, a pair of gloves, a cup to protect your junk, rolls of wrap and tape." He sets a pair of slides on the bench and holds up a small case. "I think this is a mouth guard..."

"Okay, Carson," I cut him off, "thanks."

He looks up, a small crease of worry between his eyes. "You need anything else? A shot? Some weed? I could try to find some Scratch, but you know the Dukes are zero tolerance on that shit."

"I'm fine."

"Awesome." He stops just short of the door. "Porterfield is a good fighter, but he tends to fall into patterns. Pay attention and you'll find an opening. He also is impatient and goes for the first hit. You can either take it and go from there or beat him to it."

I nod, trying to follow all the little details. "Thanks, man. I appreciate it."

He exits and it's just me and Arianette. I ignore her, grabbing the shiny red shorts out of the bag. A little flashy, but maybe it'll hide the blood better. I undress, kicking off my shoes before I remove my shirt and pants.

I'm pushing my feet through a pair of black compression shorts when I look up. Arianette's staring at me. "Jesus, Baroness, I'd tell you to take a picture but you're welcome to stare at me naked any day of the week."

She doesn't shift her gaze, but says, "Death found you, too."

I pull the shorts up and adjust my dick and balls. "Excuse me?"

Her finger runs across the throat. "Death. It came for you."

"No shit," I mutter, grabbing the red shorts to pull over the top.

"Was it wearing a mask?" she asks, head tilted.

"No." Sometimes I wonder what it's like in that little head of hers. "He had pimples and a chip on his shoulder."

She frowns, and I sit on the bench, pulling out the rolls of hand wraps and tape. I take a deep breath, trying to settle my heartbeat. How the fuck did I end up here again? I'm used to group home scuffles and prison brawls. Not organized fights in front of the entire Greek system.

I pick up a roll of wrap and study it, unsure of where to even begin.

"I can do that," she says, pointing to the rolls. "I wrap my feet and ankles for dance."

"No shit?"

"Sometimes I even wrap the other girls." She slides the cup and mouthguard out of the way and straddles the bench next to me. "Hold out your hand."

I mimic her position, so that we're face to face, knee to knee. I lift my hand between us and she grabs the white tape, quickly looping it around two fingers, eyes focused on my knuckles. Her hands are small but sure. Every wrap pulls just tight. She doesn't ask what I need. She already knows. Drawing in my thumb, she hooks it into place, securing the tape. Those tiny hands are firm. Confident.

"Are you scared?"

"No."

"Oh, it's just that you haven't taken a breath since I started."

Refusing to prove her point, I hold onto my breath a moment longer before taking a short inhale and releasing it. The wrist wrap comes next–crossing over the back of my hand like armor, looping tight, reinforcing the same bones I'll be throwing at Porterfield's face in under thirty minutes. But her touch isn't clinical. It's respectful. Ritualistic.

Reminds me of how I set up my tools before a piercing.

"I was seventeen at a 'last chance' wilderness program," I blurt. "It was a lot of bullshit, but better than group homes or detention. That's where I learned archery and how to use the crossbow, how to gut a fish, and build a fire." She turns my wrist around, smoothing out the tape, then gestures for my other hand. "It was a group of non-violent offenders, prime for rehabilitation." I roll my eyes. "We hiked all day and at night we'd set up camp, build a fire and cook dinner. It can always be a little tense when you have eight oppositionally-defiant, adrenaline and hormone-fueled teenagers in one place. Tempers flare over stupid shit all the time, but one night everyone was just tired and on edge..." The memory of that night is still raw, even after all this time. One second, everything had been normal, the next... "...we were just sitting there, eating our cowboy dinner–"

"What's a cowboy dinner?"

"It's a little packet you make with foil to cook meat and vegetables and potatoes and shit over the fire."

"Oh." *Riiiiiip.* She tears off a small piece of tape with her teeth. "Then what?"

"Everything was fine, until our leader, Jake, decided he wanted to get to the bottom of why everyone was so tense. Pot stirring, really. He made us go around and talk about our feelings. It's mostly a lot of petty grievances. Someone took too many potatoes, or didn't do their fair share of firewood collection. This one kid, Brad, he never wanted to talk, even though we all knew counseling is a requirement for being in the program. A lot of times, Jake would let shit slide, but that night he didn't. He wasn't going to let us go until Brad engaged." It was a fucking stand-off, and he was getting more and more pissed. "I was tired from hiking all day, had a blister on my foot, and was over the drama. I stood up to leave and Brad just snapped. He jumped me. He was a big guy, had fifty pounds and five inches on me. He flung his arm around my chest and grabbed one of the knives left out from prepping dinner." Arianette stopped taping. Stopped moving entirely. I look up and meet her wide brown eyes. "I barely felt it. Just a pinprick at first. But then the blood started to spill. Honestly, I don't remember much." I know they managed to radio a helicopter and get me life-flighted to Forsyth General. "The cut itself wasn't that deep, but the loss of blood was substantial." I shrug. "So yeah, death wasn't wearing a mask. He was a dumbass kid with an attitude problem."

The second I finish speaking, I instantly regret revealing all of that. I hate talking about it. Hate the feelings it brings back. Arianette's eyes are fixed on the scar, then she blinks to refocus on my hand. Quietly, she finishes the last loop and tears the tape with her teeth again. "There. That should hold."

"Huh." I stretch them both out, testing the support. "That's pretty good."

"You probably need to take out the piercings."

"Right." I start with my eyebrow, pushing each one free from the skin, then nose and lip.

"I'll keep them safe." She offers her hand, and I place each one in the center of her palm. Her eyes flit to my chest, to the hoops in each nipple. I'd shown them to her once before, and my cock thickens thinking of that night, how well she took my needle.

"You want to take them out?" I ask, lifting an eyebrow. "See how it's done?"

She pushes her hand into her pocket, secreting away the jewelry she's already collected. My eyes are drawn to the ties on the sides of her shorts. It's obvious she's not wearing panties and Mateo was right. It would only take one quick yank.

Those quick, small fingers that just skillfully wrapped my hands, graze my chest, moving to the ring on the left side. The pad of her finger touches the bead, pulling gently on my skin. I hiss, the sensation sending a jolt through me. Swallowing, I explain, "There's a dimple in the bead. You'll just need to pop it out."

She's hesitant, much more so than a few moments ago with the tape. Probably because her own piercings are so sensitive. "You don't have to be so gentle," I tell her, using my finger to flick the ball. "I can take it."

That loosens her up a little, but she still uses a soft touch, one that actually makes this moment more sensual than I wanted. Slowly, she pops the ring out of the ball, then takes her time easing the stainless steel wire out. My cock throbs between my legs, thickening under the compression shorts, solid against my thigh. I look at her chest and see the bars pressing into her top, she's turned on too.

The blood drains from my head, straight down to my dick. It would be so easy to tell her to get on her knees. To do what Bronwyn promised and suck me off before the fight starts.

"It's time." Carson bursts through the door, and the wild energy of the crowd follows him. "You ready?"

"Yeah." I reach for the hoop on the right side, and tell her, "I've got it," because the last thing I need is her touching me more. I give her the final ring, and she tucks it away with the others.

"What now?" she asks, standing up when I do.

I twist my neck, cracking it on both sides. "I guess it's time for me to go kick some Bruin ass."

rianette

THE ATMOSPHERE outside the locker room is jarring, especially after the quiet moment Damon and I just shared. I need air, even if it's the sweaty scent of hundreds of people packed into the gym. Being close to Damon like that was unnerving. He'd defended me to Bronwyn, asked me to stay and assist him. I felt useful for once, using my experience from dance to wrap his hands. But the story he told me about how his throat was slashed–that had been unexpected.

Death reveals itself in mysterious ways.

Tucking my fingers into my pocket, I feel the hard metal of his jewelry, and search for the hoop from his nipple. The hard ball is larger than the others, still warm from being so close to his body.

"Everyone to your seats!" A voice announces over the loudspeaker. Above the ring is a timer counting down to the final fight. The energy flowing through the gym is unlike anything I've experienced. My dance performances were always in front of crowds dressed in evening gowns and tuxedos. Patrons of the arts, not beer-drinking frat boys and girls barely wearing any clothes.

The music is loud, and I use my hands to cover my ears. I fight the crowd that funnels like a river, everyone looking for seats. Everyone seeming to know where to go. Beer sloshes, splashing on my legs.

"Keep up," Damon says, glancing back at me.

I push through, invisible to this crowd, maybe looking just like another Crypt Chaser. I'm forced to duck out of the way when a shirtless man, holding an ice pack under his bleeding eye, is ushered past me into a different locker room.

When I look up, Damon and the other guys are gone.

"You look lost."

The voice is familiar, and although I know I'm not supposed to talk to anyone, I'm relieved to see the blue hair and moth tattoo belonging to Lavinia Lucia.

"I got separated from Damon." I push up on my toes. I can't see him, but Hunter's fair hair is visible closer to the ring. "I think I'm supposed to be with them."

"Fuck yeah you are," Lavinia says. "You're his Baroness. He needs you by his side during the fight."

"To what?" I'd already done the one thing I could by wrapping his hands. "I don't know anything about fighting."

"I doubt that," she says, hand moving to her hip. "In Forsyth, a Royal is only as strong as the woman by his side. Your job is to support him simply by being there." Her eyes skim down my body. "Well, and maybe by showing a little skin and making everyone jealous as fuck you belong to him."

"That's what Bronwyn said when she tried to replace me."

"Bronwyn?" she repeats, grabbing my wrist and heading through the crowd. "Bronwyn Lee?"

"I guess so. She said in any other year, she would have been the Baroness."

Lavinia rolls her eyes. "Look, there's always some girl who thinks she's going to be the new House Girl. In my year it was Verity Sinclaire." She pushes a guy in a DKS shirt out of the way. "She thought that she had the position locked-up, and she probably would have made a great Duchess if things were different, but you know who she is now?"

I shake my head.

"She's the mother-fucking-Princess and rightful heir of West End. She's got a baby and three men groveling at her feet." She stops suddenly and spins. "Nothing in Forsyth is guaranteed, especially not with the Royals, so Bronwyn Lee can go fuck herself, got it?"

I nod. "Got it."

She moves behind me and pushes me toward an area just behind the ring, where Damon, Hunter, and a few other BRN guys are waiting. "I don't know if you like that guy or not," she looks at Damon. "He could be the biggest tool ever, but tonight you need to do whatever he needs to get through that fight, because the house odds are solidly on Porterfield and he's going to need whatever extra boost you can give him."

She places her hands on my back and pushes me forward. I stumble toward the guys and when I look back, all I see is her blue hair disappearing into the crowd.

"Jesus, Arianette, where were you?" Hunter asks, more annoyed than worried. "You're not supposed to wander off alone."

"I didn't," I reply, irritated. "I got separated."

"Do it again and I'll get one of Ares' collars and put you on a leash."

The serious glint in his eye tells me he's not joking, and I push past him toward Damon, who is fussing with the edge of a piece of tape. I take his hand and re-secure it under the wrap just as the speakers crackle to life. "Are you ready for the main event?!" A voice blasts from all four corners of the gym. "Representing the Dukes, we have Sean Porterfield, undefeated in his last three fights."

Music blares and I watch a big guy, thick with muscles, climb into the ring. His hair is flaming red and freckles scatter across his nose. He lifts his arms in the air and the crowd explodes into a cheer. A girl waits for him in his corner, in tight cut-offs and a glittery bikini top.

When he gets to her she jumps into his arms, wraps her legs around his waist, and shoves her tongue down his throat.

The crowd in the stands right behind Porterfield gets even louder, cheering them on. The couple parts and Porterfield shouts into the crowd, "To the victor!"

"Go the spoils!" The crowd of DKS responds drunkenly.

Lavinia's ideas make a little more sense now.

Moving to position myself behind Damon so he can take the spotlight, I'm startled when he grabs my hip with one of those big hands and pulls me close. "I keep telling you," he says, mouth close to my ear, "stay close."

His arm drapes over my shoulders, and I place my hand on his hard stomach. I have no idea if Damon is ready for this fight, but I'm not underestimating one of the men that hunted me down. He's strong and fast, and that scar tells me one thing: he's a survivor.

The speakers crackle again and the same booming voice announces, "Representing Beta Rho, and making his debut to the Fury is, Deeeeeeekaaaaaayyyyyy Kemp."

I feel Damon tense, his body stiffening against mine.

Music blasts, and he takes the first step forward, keeping me by his side.

At some point the crowd fades away, and it's just me and Damon making the walk. Carson rushes ahead, lifting the ropes for Damon to go through. Once he's up on the mat, the block of seating behind the ring erupts into cheers, while the other sides fall into a deep, jeering boo. Strong hands cinch around my waist and I look back. Hunter's lifting me up to the mat, into Damon's outstretched hands.

"Fuck that bastard up, brother."

They bump fists, and I'm yanked into Damon's hard body. The move, the mat, the blinding lights, all reminds me of being on stage, and I'm struck by the truth that this is nothing more than a dance between two partners–a *performance*.

That I understand. Curling my fingers into the waistband of his shorts, I tilt my head, feeling his hands, rough with tape, pressed against my lower back. Hooking my leg around his thigh, I push up on the tips of my toes, arching my back as he holds me. He looks surprised when I sweep into a dramatic arch, smiling at the Shadows behind us, who are drunk on beer and itching for the fight. My crotch grinds into him, and he pushes back–a reminder of how good this man can make me feel, and how fast he likes to take it away.

Goosebumps skitter across my flesh when he presses a hot kiss on the healing cuts.

"There she is," he says, lips quirked into a grin. "That's the girl who knows how to use a knife."

The statement is bold, but true. His lips meet mine, blisteringly hot, tongue controlling. It's a kiss that I feel deep between my legs, and when I grind into him, it's not just for show. I let him take possession of me, showing everyone in the gym exactly who I belong to.

"Good luck," I tell him when our mouths part. I like the taste of him, the lingering tang of whiskey. Maybe it's not so bad after all.

He grins and stretches out his hand, tweaking the bar running through my nipple. Pain shoots through me, and a scream climbs the back of my throat. It doesn't matter if I let it loose, no one would hear it–not over the stomping of feet and cheers from the crowd.

A second later, he glances upward, toward the balcony. Lifting my hand to fight the glare I see that the Lords and Dukes are still in their seats. Lavinia is leaning toward Story Austin, hand covering her mouth. Movement from across the balcony catches my eye.

The Baron King. He's here, his mask a dark ebony, the horns tipped in gold. A chill runs down my spine, knowing that we're not just under the scrutiny of the other frats, but from the King as well. After the last week, the time in the cage, the upset I caused him, I need something to go right.

A short bell chimes and the referee moves to the middle of the mat. Hunter grabs me, pulling me back on the other side of the mat. We take an empty spot just behind the railing and to my surprise, he settles me onto his lap, keeping his strong arms caged around me, like he's afraid I'll wander off again. My heart skips when the referee speaks to them, I assume going over the rules. The crowd around us grows impatient. They're not the only ones. Damon's already bouncing on the balls of his feet, chin tucked, eyes locked in. His dark hair's a sweaty mess. He's not the favorite. Not even close. He's got that rough-edged kind of fight to him–no polish, no choreography.

Across from him, Porterfield looks like he was raised in the gym. Big, confident stance, pale skin dotted with freckles, and that red hair slicked back from where his cutslut ran her hands through it. He's clean, but dangerous in the kind of way that's practiced, perfected.

That's the difference, I realize. Damon's volatile like a loose wire. You don't touch him wrong unless you want to get shocked. The tingling in the tit he pinched is an ever present reminder.

The bell rings.

And I swear, the world narrows down to fists and footwork.

Porterfield starts sharp–jab, cross, step out. Carson's warning rings true. *'He also is impatient and goes for the first hit. You can either take it and go from there or beat him to it.'*

Damon eats the first one, head barely snapping back. He grins. I know that grin. I saw it in the dark forest when he stumbled on Armand's dead body and the bloody knife in my hand.

Leverage.

That's all he needs.

Slam!

Porterfield lands an uppercut, knocking Damon further off balance. He's got his own rhythm, dancing just out of reach like he's showing off. Every time Damon reacts, the grip I have on the railing tightens, knuckles turning white. He's swinging wild, looping hooks and knees from awkward angles, but nothing's clean. Not yet.

"One, two, three, four..." I chant as they circle one another. "One, two, three, four..."

The bell chimes, ending the first round. He returns to the corner, bleeding from his eyebrow. Rob and Carson are ready, tossing a towel at him to wipe his sweaty face and squirting water in his mouth. I lurch up, but Hunter's arms tighten, holding me back.

I twist to look at him. "I need to talk to him."

"Let the guys do their job."

"No, I need to tell him something." I fight against him, and finally he relents, letting me loose. I climb over the railing, lunging for the ring. I wobble, but keep upright, shuffling over.

"Baroness," Rob says, when he sees me. "It's not safe up here."

I ignore him. "Damon, look at me."

Blood oozes from his eyebrow. I grab the towel and press it against the wound.

"*One, two, three, four...*"

"What the fuck are you talking about?" he mumbles.

"All dances have beats," I explain. "Rhythms. One, two, three, four... this fight? You and that guy are in a dance. To win, you just need to find your rhythm."

I wait for him to tell me to shut up, that I'm stupid and crazy and to go back to my seat, but he just takes a step back, nodding slowly.

When the bell rings for round two, I'm back in Hunter's lap and Damon is back on the mat, circling Porterfield. That's the thing I'm learning about him–he doesn't break. He bends. He absorbs. He adapts.

And then, somewhere in that mess of punches, he finds the rhythm.

It's not pretty.

But it works.

He starts cutting angles, forcing Porterfield toward the ropes. Dirty boxing, clinch knees, short elbows. He's fighting ugly–and after the mess before, ugly is beautiful.

"Yes!" Hunter shouts, when he lands a right hook that stuns the redhead. On the mat, Porterfield stumbles. Just a blink. But Damon sees it and pounces, the darkness in him releasing in a fury of hard-hitting fists. He follows it with a knee to the body. Porterfield grunts, shifting to defense. He takes another hook that sends him staggering back before he drops, hard and shattered.

The ref points to Damon and the roar of the crowd hits me like thunder in my bones.

My Baron just stands there, chest heaving, blood smeared across his cheek. His eyes find us across the ropes and he gives Hunter and I a smug grin.

The ref comes over and lifts his arm. Every Beta Rho in our section jumps to their feet, including Hunter, who lifts me in his arms.

"*Memento Mori!*" Damon shouts, lifting his other fist. His eye, already swelling, catches mine. I smile, caught up in the sheer enthusiasm of the night–of how great he did out there. Standing over Porterfield, who seems to be grimacing in both pain and humiliation, he can't seem to help but add, "There's only one victor in the house tonight, and it's a goddamn Baron."

IF I THOUGHT the gym was chaotic before the match, after it's close to a riot. Damon hopped down from the ring only to get instantly swarmed by fans and haters, both shocked at his win. But like all winners, everyone seems to want a piece of him–to bloody him a little more or to lavish praise. The members of DKS huddle around menacingly, outraged at the loss, but they're not actually aggressive. There's an unspoken tension in the air, like they're just waiting for someone to screw up and give them an excuse.

It's a different kind of ferocity that comes from the females. Damon's name is a screeching cry on their red-painted lips, clawing out with cat-like nails. They don't want a piece of him, they want his attention. His power, no matter how sweaty and bruised.

A blonde in a sequined tube top pushes her way through the Shadows, clinging into his side. "Can I get your autograph?" she asks, thrusting a pen in his hand.

He looks up, eyes a little glazed from the fight. "Yeah, sure?"

"You can sign right here," she says, pulling down her top to expose her tits. They're small, but perky, and he scribbles his initials across her flesh. "Thank you!" She slowly drags her top back up. "I'm Audrey, by the way, let me know if you want a private celebration. I can make that happen."

Her eyes flit past me when Carson drags her off, the grin on her face telling me that our little pre-fight show did nothing to assert my claim. Did it seem fake? Superficial? Could they all tell that Damon doesn't care for me? That the King finds me disloyal. I'm a murderer. A liability. The list goes on and on. That truth nags at me as we reach the back hall, an area blocked off to the main crowd.

"Kemp," a voice calls, "hold up a minute."

I turn and am instantly struck off balance at the man walking toward us, a crescent haloed around his head. He gets closer, his long legs wrapped in leather, his shirt unbuttoned down to his waist. Pale skin covered with ink. His shoulders are broad, but he's lean and I'm certain he's an angel, but there are no wings. A demon then? No, not that, a nephilim, I decide, both.

"Maddox," Damon says, pulling at the bloody tape on his hand, "come to finish the job?"

"Nah, fair is fair," he says, although he doesn't look like it. I stare at his eyes, the bottle-glass green. "At least you didn't bring a knife, like some other pricks we know."

"Ashby, right?" Hunter asks, shaking his head. "I heard about that."

"Absolute punk move," Maddox—whoever he is, lifts his shirt to reveal a jagged scar. "Whatever, just makes legit wins even better. Anyway, since Porterfield lost, I figured I'd offer you his winner's tattoo, just to rub it in a little."

"Yeah?" Damon says. "Yeah, I won't say no to a free tat."

"Good, I've been wanting you to come down to the shop anyway. See the setup. Talk about maybe working together."

Damon nods. "Yeah, sure."

"Not tonight though." The nephilim runs his hand through his white-blond hair. "I need to let Porterfield know he's not welcome in the tower tonight."

"That sucks."

"Yeah, well that's the punishment for being a loser," Maddox mutters. "Ask me how I know."

A bulky figure with warm brown skin emerges behind him,

rolling his eyes. "Dude, Lav went with you and played nursemaid for three days. I think you survived." He shifts his attention to the Barons and thrusts out his hand. "You're the new Barons, I'm Sy Perilini."

"You're the King," Hunter says, shaking his hand. "Hunter Sorrin."

"Damon Kemp." He holds up his bloody hand and they both agree not to shake.

So far none of them have acknowledged me at all, but I sense eyes on me: the nephilim.

"You must be Arianette Hexley. Current Baroness and future bride. How does that work?" His eyes assess me before darting over to Hunter and Damon. "The three of you share? Or does the King get dibs?" He scratches his chin dramatically with one of those long, inked fingers. "Or does he have your cunt on lockdown so he can make sure he's the one that knocks you up so he can have the perfect, obedient heir?"

"What the fuck did you just say?" Hunter asks, pushing me to the side.

"Chill. Ignore him." Sy grabs his friend by the shoulder, his voice firm, "Come on, Rem, let's go deal with Porterfield."

Down the hall, a figure enters the doorway, instantly consuming any remaining air. "Christ," Maddox mutters when he sees the Baron King, adding even lower, "as if meeting mommy dearest and losing tonight wasn't enough, now this bullshit."

"Simon," the Baron King says as he approaches, "Remington."

Remy grunts, but Sy steps forward. "Nice match tonight. Your Baron did well."

The tension between the men is obvious, permeating like a bad smell. I press against Hunter, who stiffens at the closeness, and I watch the meeting of Kings.

"Better than well," the King says, assessing Damon. "You were solid out there. A little sloppy at times, but you held your own against a trained hooligan."

"Okay," Remy says, ramming past Sy and pushing his sleeves up. "How about you get in the ring with me and see who wins." He grins, cheeky and handsome. "You'll have to take that mask off, though. House rules."

There's a flicker of heat between the two men, a battle that seems to cross time and space, a battle that I don't understand. "Settle down, Remington, I came down here to congratulate my Baron on his win, nothing more, nothing less."

Even I don't believe that.

"Well, we've got a party to cancel," Sy says, pushing Remy back the other way. "Congratulations, Kemp." I think we all breathe a little easier once the Dukes are gone.

"I've sent Graves a message to set up the crypt for a celebration—truly, beating a Duke isn't easy. Especially without bringing a weapon into the fight." The King reaches into his cloak and pulls out a small silver box that he hands to Damon. "For tonight."

"Thanks."

"Will you be there?" I blurt, immediately regretting drawing his attention to me. At this point it's too late and I add, "At the celebration."

"No. Not tonight." He steps back. "Once you return, stay on the grounds." He nods at me. "And *always* keep an eye on her, even on our property."

It's a directive, one that doesn't require a response.

The King starts to walk off, but I see a grimace on Damon's face. He calls out, "Wait."

He turns slowly. "Yes?"

"I shouldn't have done it. I got caught up in the moment and–"

"Don't apologize," the King says. "In war, the best weapon is the one you have." Then he adds. "But now that the battle is over, I expect you to not succumb again."

A moment later he's gone.

"Jesus, that was stressful," Hunter says, slumping into the wall. "Right?"

"Yeah, I don't even want to know what kind of bullshit the King has with the Dukes. I just want a shower and to relax." Damon pushes open the locker room door and steps inside.

Hunter holds the door open for me and I say, "Are you okay if I go to the women's room? I know the rules. No talking to people–not even women."

"I'll wait outside," he says, "just make it quick."

One step into the small room and I wish I'd just gone to the men's room to pee. The sink area is occupied with crypt chasers. I'm scanning the room when someone says, "If you're looking for Bronwyn you're safe." I look at a girl replenishing her black lipstick at the mirror. "She left."

"I wasn't looking for her." I *totally* was.

"I heard she was a petty bitch to you before the match. Tried to take your spot." The person that says this has two knotted buns at the top of her head. "I know they call all of us crypt chasers, but most of us are content with the guys in the frat. Everyone knows the Barons belong to the Baroness." She lifts her skirt, revealing a hole in her tights. "Fuck! I can't believe Kirk ripped these. It's the third pair."

I duck into the toilet, listening to them talk.

"Maybe you should just stop wearing tights in public if you know he's going to be there," lipstick says. "That's a better bet than him keeping his dick in his pants."

Bunhead sighs. "True."

"Whatever. You'll never tell him no."

I hear a snort. "Like you tell Rob no when he asks for a blow job in the car every morning on the way to school."

"He thinks better when he's just had an orgasm."

I flush the toilet, as much as a warning as anything else, hoping that when I come back out they'll stop talking about their sex lives.

As I approach the sink, the girl with the buns makes eye contact in the mirror. "I'm Jane, by the way." Her head tilts to lipstick. "That's Gloria."

"Arianette," I say, even though I'm sure they know.

"I love those shorts," Gloria says. "You've got the perfect ass for them."

"Uh, thanks." I turn on the faucet, letting the hot water run over my hands.

"Fuck." Jane stares at the wound on my chest. "That must have hurt."

"It did."

"I can't imagine," Gloria adds. "I'd never survive the Hunt."

"Which one did it?" Her perfectly groomed eyebrow lifts. "It was DK wasn't it?"

"Hunter, actually." I think back to that night when he was bent over me, the knife in his hand. Just like every other time we're together, he went out of his way not to touch me directly. "DK... he Claimed me later."

Both girls' eyes get wide and for some reason I just show them. Tugging down my top, I reveal my tit and piercing. "Holy shit." Jane looks thoroughly impressed. "I knew he was a piercer, but fuck. That's sexy."

"I wasn't sure about you," Gloria admits. I straighten my top. "Any of you, really, but maybe you're all more Baron material than I realized."

"So," I ask, working up the nerve to ask the question that's bothered me all night, "do I need to worry about anyone other than Bronwyn?"

Jane shrugs. "Not if you stake your claim."

"Claim?"

"Show everyone that they belong to you–especially DK. He's going to be hot after taking down a Duke."

The guys Claimed me with a knife and needles. Isn't that enough?

"I'll give you a hint, Baroness, since it's your first Fury, first victory and first post-win party," Gloria teases, moving close like she's sharing a forbidden secret. "When the Barons win their matches they always get a little gift from their Baroness." She winks. "Usually in front of the whole party."

I'm inexperienced, but I understand the implication. "Everyone?"

Jane takes one last look in the mirror and says, "Yep."

"Don't worry," Gloria adds, putting her lipstick back in the black purse slung across her chest. "It's a Crypt party. You won't be the only one." She grins. "See you there."

I'm still standing by the sink when Hunter sticks his head in a few seconds later.

"You ready?"

I really don't think I am.

22

H^{unter}

THE DRIVER, one of the younger guys in BRN, pulls the SUV onto a dirt road. It's pitch black outside, the only visibility coming from the car headlights. The three of us sit in the backseat, Arianette squeezed in the middle. As much as I'm not a fan of physical touch, I'm getting used to the Baroness by my side. She'd spent half the match perched on my lap, and the rest up under me, like she was seeking protection.

"You feel good enough to go in there?" I've kept a close eye on DK since he got out of the ring. He took a few solid hits and a concussion isn't out of the question. His eyes aren't dilated, and he doesn't seem sleepy. If anything, there's a crackle of energy rolling off his body.

"I feel good." His hand slides down Arianette's thigh, toying with the little string that laces up the sides of those shorts. "Better than good."

I'm not always good at identifying people's emotions, which is why I definitely can't tell what the Baroness is feeling right now.

She'd been into the fight, seeming to understand what DK was going through better than he did. I heard her counting under her breath, then saying it was like a dance. Maybe so. Martial arts tends to move at a choreographed pace. It may have been the crowd following the match, or even the exchange between the Dukes and the Baron King. Whatever it is, something has her tense and on edge, and DK touching her leg probably isn't making it any better.

For her at least. I can't take my eyes off of them.

The car rolls to a stop, gravel crunching underneath the tires. Before we get out, DK turns on the overhead light, the glow catching the silver and black of his piercings, each one carefully back in place once the fight was over. He opens the silver box the King gave him. Nestled inside the black velvet are three red pills with a gold pentagram stamped on the side.

"What are those?" Arianette asks.

"Phantom Bliss," I tell her. DK and I both experienced the drug during recruitment. It's all natural, made from a compound created by the King himself.

"Something that is going to make the night really fun," DK says, handing me one pill, and taking the other. "Give me your tongue, Baroness." Her mouth opens, tongue unfurling and flattening to receive the pill. He drops it on and says, "Good girl."

I swallow my own pill, remembering how the first time I tried it, I felt too out of my body. I hated how I felt out of control, but I gave it another shot on the final night of recruitment, which was just a big, gluttonous, party. For once in my life, I was able to embrace the way I felt in my skin. Not awkward or strange, but warm and loose.

Our driver leads us to the ivy-covered door that groans at the hinges. Straight ahead is the black opening of a stairwell curling down into the earth. I feel the bass before I hear it—distant, pulsing, like the heartbeat of some slumbering god. The air changes. Heavier. Wetter. Scented with something floral and decaying at the same time. Perfume and rot. Ahead of me, Arianette is already descending, her fingers grazing the stone wall like she's tasting the place through her skin. Each step takes us deeper, passing the sconces flickering along the walls, flames catching in iron cages. The stone underfoot is worn smooth from years of footsteps wearing them down. I'm constantly surprised at the various entry and exit points of the Barons' tunnels–seemingly spread underneath all of Forsyth–but the room the stairwell leads to is something entirely different.

The chamber is massive. Vaulted ceilings arch like the ribs of a giant beast. Everything is stone–walls, floors, even the bar in the far corner, carved right into the foundation like it grew there. The light is low and golden, flickering from the sconces and the braziers scattered around like ceremonial offerings.

And everywhere is what we've been promised as part of the sacred society: decadence.

It's different from Noir Sanctum, mostly in that these aren't masked people I don't know. I know the bodies draped over cushions, sprawled in threes and fours, sipping from goblets or licking red dust from their fingertips. Familiar with the group sitting on floor cushions, passing rolled-up cigarettes from mouth to mouth. Across the room, a girl from my engineering class is feeding Mateo–half-naked and lounging on a sofa with three crypt chasers–like a pagan god. A couple makes out in the corner, his head bent, sucking on her tit. Laughter bubbles up from a corner, the too-loud, too-loose kind that only comes from being absolutely fucked up.

And at the far end–the thrones.

There are two, and I have to assume one has been removed–disappeared the same way Armand vanished from our lives. Iron, brutal and regal. Their spines curve like twisted vines, barbs at the tips. Red velvet cushions drip over the metal waiting for us to arrive.

My skin is starting to buzz, my brain getting that heady, happy feeling brought on by the adrenaline of the night and the dose of Phantom Bliss running through my bloodstream. My cock is hard, throbbing against my thigh.

"This is…" I say, but I don't finish it.

There's no word for it. Not really.

Arianette turns back to me, pupils wide, lips parted like she's breathing the place in through her mouth.

"Magical," she says, spinning around. "Can you feel it?"

I can, and just like that, I'm not on the edge anymore. I'm in it. Stepping into the pulse of the underworld, where gods are drunk and sinners reign. This is the place of shadows, where debauchery doesn't have to hide.

This is the place I don't have to hide and finally feel at home.

The room shifts when they see us.

Cheers ripple through the crypt, rising up like smoke. Hands reach out, clap DK's shoulders, offer him drinks, pills, smokes wrapped in black paper and dusted in shimmer. Someone drapes a garland of thorns and dark red dahlias over his neck like he's some kind of king. Maybe he is, tonight.

He's still breathing like the fight's in his blood. His grin is crooked and wide, teeth glinting under firelight. People chant his name, toast to him with mouths full of smoke and wine and praise. Even with the Bliss, his shoulders tense, the experience is as unfamiliar to him as it is to me. We've been outsiders but with this one single act, kicking Sean Porterfield's ass, he brought us into the circle with every hit, every dodge, every drop of blood.

"There he is!" Mateo shouts, bringing himself to an upright position. He crosses the room, arms wide. "You not only saved my ass but the frat's reputation, too."

"I'm just glad I didn't fuck it up."

"Nah, man," Rob approaches, and they slap hands, "you took down a major DKS contender. There's no victor in the tower tonight!"

He turns to me and laughs–*a real one,* not the cocky bravado I've seen before. His eyes are wild. Not just from the high, but from winning. From surviving.

Arianette sticks close to his side. She's smiling, but I can see it in the way her fingers twitch: *nervous.* Excited, too. Drawn in, like the rest of us.

She looks at DK like he's the fire, and she's the moth that hasn't decided if it wants to burn or dance. He catches her waist and leads her toward the thrones, and the crowd parts for him like the air does for thunder. DK drops onto the iron throne like he was born there.

One leg slung wide and with the dahlias draped over his shoulders, he looks over the room like it's his, like he fought for it and won.

He did.

Not just in the ring, but in the initiation, in the Hunt. Arianette hesitates at his side. She looks back at me, like she wants permission, or maybe just doesn't want to fall into this alone.

I nod, slow, and say, "Celebrate him."

She bites her lip, then crosses to the thrones and without pause, climbs onto his lap.

The room howls in approval.

"You know, there's a seat for you, too," Rob says, gesturing to the other throne.

"Let him have this one," I say. "He earned it."

It's an excuse to continue to hang back, to observe. In validation of the ease of the group, or possibly the power I hold, no one questions my decision. Someone presses a cut glass filled with green liquid into my hand. I take a sip–sweet, sharp, like licorice. A warm fog starts to settle behind my eyes, softening the edges of everything. I stay standing, leaning against one of the stone pillars as DK's hands begin to wander over her body.

Caught in the shadows, the front of my pants tightens even more than before as I watch the two of them explore one another. The stone at my back is cool, grounding me while the rest of the crypt hums like a live wire. The music has dipped into something darker, the strings low and dragging.

I only see them.

My brother and sister.

They're half-lit by the sconce behind the throne, gold firelight turning her bare arms a warm shade of bronze. She's perched sideways on his lap, legs over one of the velvet arms, her back arched just enough that he can rest his hand on her thigh.

He hasn't kissed her yet. Hasn't rushed. Always pushing her to the edge. Her chest rises and falls a little too fast, the thrill of being the center of everything.

His fingers trace the ties at the side of her shorts–little leather laces, snug against her hip. One by one, he pulls them loose. Slowly. Leisurely. Like it's not clothing, but ribbon on a gift. She shivers when his raw, red, knuckles brush her brown skin. And then, without a word, he reaches to his boot and slides something out.

A blade.

The dagger is small, curved, with a black handle wrapped in worn leather. I've seen it before–under his pillow, kept there just in case–the same way Ares sleeps at the foot of my bed. The edge catches the firelight. He holds it up, just for her.

Her eyes dart back to me, the two of us are already bonded by the tip of a blade. I don't think DK wants to hurt her, but I know she'll let him if he wants. I lift my chin. *Let him.*

"Be still, sister," he tells her, and then he slices the strip of fabric covering her pussy clean through–*slowly,* deliberately. My mind wanders, thinking that one jerk of his hand, one flinch, and the tip of the blade would slice into the sweet flesh of her sex. Blood spilling where he could lap it up, tasting the very essence of her. I exhale and shake the thought away, the throbbing in my cock painful.

Everyone else in the room stills, but no one gasps. No one reacts. But they're watching. *Everyone's watching* as he saws away that final thread, her pussy unharmed, and beneath?

Lush dark curls, wild, just like she is.

Arianette doesn't move to cover herself, her hand lifting to his mouth to toy with the ring in his lip. She doesn't close her legs, the Phantom Bliss erasing any modesty. I feel the same, running my palm over the hard line of my erection as she lets the ruined fabric fall open like petals, breath hitching. It's not from fear, but from knowing this is hers now–this attention, this moment, this throne.

DK drops the blade beside them on the velvet, lazy and smug. He looks out over the room, all arrogance and heat, then right at me.

He holds my gaze.

It's not a challenge. Not a threat.

An ask for permission?

No. An invitation.

I stay where I am, letting the hard stone cut into my shoulder blades. Allowing the Bliss to settle in my blood like a quiet song. I don't move.

I watch.

And it feels like power, just to be here. Just to witness my brother and our Baroness, caught in a moment of pure intimacy. No fear or threats. Nothing but the primal urgency of lust. My eyes are focused just past the way her shorts hang open, ruined, but she doesn't flinch. Unlike the girl we chased in the forest, this woman doesn't hide. She spreads her legs a little wider over his thigh like she knows–this isn't just for him. It's for all of us.

DK shifts beneath her, slow and deliberate. One hand knots in her hair, yanks her head back–not brutally, but not gently either. It's a show of possession, raw and real. Her throat arches. Her lips part. His other hand slides down her stomach, fingers splaying wide like he's laying claim. The crowd's fallen quiet. All eyes on the throne. On them.

He doesn't undress her the rest of the way. Doesn't bother with softness or pretense. He keeps her straddled on one thigh and just pulls himself free, the sound of his zipper loud in the hush. My jaw tightens at the sight of him, blistering red, the silver piercings glinting against the darkness of her thighs.

I should look away. I don't.

Arianette gasps when Damon yanks her hips hard against his thigh–not slow, definitely not tentative. Her body jolts, grinding down on the thick muscle of him, and the sound she makes isn't soft. It's wrecked. Wild. High and breathless like her lungs forgot how to hold air.

And Damon–

Damon looks like a victorious god in the taking.

He can't fuck her. That rule is non-negotiable, but the scene in front of us doesn't feel one bit less of a claiming.

One arm crushes her to him, the other tangles in her hair, dragging her head back so the whole crypt can see her neck bared, mouth parted. He doesn't kiss her, instead dragging his teeth down the column of her throat. He gives her that thing he loves to hold just out of reach, that teasing release that she begged for that night in her room. DK reaches between them, toying with her clit. He watches her come undone, face set like stone, like every twitch of her hips is a desperate chase.

It's not sweet. It's not love.

He doesn't thrust. He commands. Drives her over and over onto the hard press of their thighs like she's some holy instrument meant to be played until she breaks. Her hands claw at his chest, gripping the edge of his open shirt then sliding lower–under the fabric, then lower still, until her hand finds him at the place where they meet.

He growls. Low, guttural, possessive.

Not in pain. In power.

The throne creaks with the motion of her grinding down and him growing harder beneath her touch. Her pace picks up, one of her legs twitching, her whole body flushed and shining in the firelight. He watches her fall apart while stroking himself in her hand–slow, brutal.

The sound of her panting matches the distant bass. And when she cries out, sharp and raw, the crowd doesn't cheer–they go silent–any and all questions of Damon and Arianette being worthy of their titles vanishing into the thick, smoky air.

And me? All I can do is watch, hands balled at my side, clenched. My body is heat and tension, a scream behind my ribs I don't let out. There's a part of me, dark and familiar, that drinks this in. That doesn't want to touch. Only witness.

That's always been my place, hasn't it?

On the edge of the fire. Never stepping in.

But always watching it burn.

DK's got one hand on her throat now, tilting her head back so she can't hide the expressions on her face–so we can all see them. Her eyes flutter, her mouth is slack, her body riding every brutal thrust. For the first time he lets her go all the way, allowing her to come.

And fuck if it isn't beautiful. Grotesque. Holy. Different from the gritty anonymity of Noir Sanctum.

This was a ritual made of flesh and sound by two people bound by something bigger than all of us.

I stand there in my darkened corner, still as the stone behind me, pulse hammering, every nerve lit up as I try to control the throbbing want, wondering, for the thousandth time, If watching this closely is the same as being touched.

Taking a deep breath, I barely register as Arianette rises from DK's lap, her breath still ragged, legs unsteady. Her shorts are nothing now, just tattered fabric clinging to her thighs, pretending to be the last remnants of modesty.

She doesn't adjust them, doesn't fix her hair.

There's no need.

The crowd watches her like she's untouchable, as she walks toward me. Straight across the crypt, bare thighs lit in the firelight, Damon's seed glistening on them. My breath stills in my chest. I don't move. I can't.

She stops in front of me, looking up through dark lashes, lips still parted from the sounds she made from his hands.

"Can I touch you?" she asks.

Not breathy. Not shy. Just honest. Ritualistic.

Like she knows what this is. Like she understands what I've been doing from the shadows.

Watching.

Waiting.

And I should say no.

But I don't. Not this time. Not with the Bliss running through my bloodstream, or the erection rock solid against my inner thigh. Not with the opportunity to be part of it, instead of just passively sitting by the side. DK won them over tonight in the ring, but we're brothers–in this together– they need to see my power as well.

I nod and she kneels.

Obeys.

Her breath is still uneven, her lips slightly swollen from where she'd been biting down on them, and the fabric of her ruined shorts brushes her thighs as she lowers herself between mine. Her fingers are sure, reverent, as they undo me, belt, button, zipper, all while holding my gaze.

I'm already hard, a fucking hair-trigger away from blowing like a rocket. It takes everything in me not to go off at that first touch.

Jesus Christ.

She wraps her fingers around me, her touch confident, slow. The warmth of her hand is nothing compared to the heat that pours off her. She strokes me once, then again, a lazy drag from base to tip that makes my breath hitch. My thighs tense, unaccustomed to the sensation of a woman's hands.

Then her lips part.

She lowers her head, tongue flat as she licks the underside of my cock from base to tip–slow, deliberate, not missing a thing. Like she's mapping me with her mouth. I bite the inside of my cheek to stay still, to keep my grip tight on the edge of the stone and not her.

And then she takes me in.

It's not her first time sucking a man's cock. Damon claimed that too, but this time it isn't about leverage and betrayal. There's no blood on her hands, not tonight. There's no teasing. No fear. Just deliberate rhythm, like she instructed Damon during the fight. Her lips stretch around the head, then down further, warm and slick and obscene. Her mouth is wet heat, the pressure perfect. She doesn't stop until I hit the back of her throat, and then she pulls back, dragging her tongue along the underside with that same steady rhythm that Damon set in her earlier.

Every movement is deliberate. Ritualistic.

She uses both hands now, twisting slightly at the base while she sucks, her eyes half-lidded, watching me. My hips twitch, but I stay rooted. Watching her. Feeling everything. Letting her do this for me.

To me.

She moans low around me and I feel it, the vibration up the shaft, down to the base, into my spine. It's too much. It's not enough. She sinks deeper again, choking a little this time, but she doesn't stop. She wants it messy. Wants it raw.

I wonder how often she thinks about that night in her room,

when my cum was coating her pussy, thick and sticky. How I left her drenched. Saliva drips down the sides of her mouth, catching in the hollow of her collarbone. She moves faster now, one hand pumping, the other pressed to my thigh to anchor herself.

I don't say a word.

My jaw is tight, legs trembling. It builds, hard and sharp, right behind my eyes. I feel it coiling, violent and inevitable. And still, she doesn't let up. I grip the wall harder. Try not to shake. Try not to lose it too soon.

But she knows. We both do.

She pulls me deeper one last time, and when I come, it's like a detonation, my body going rigid, everything unraveling in heat and pressure with a groan I can't hold back. She takes it all. Doesn't flinch. Stays right there, lips sealed, eyes locked on me as I fall apart in her mouth.

And when she pulls back, slow and filthy, wiping her mouth with the back of her hand...

I can barely breathe.

She smiles—soft, secret—and rises without a word. And all I can do is lean against the wall, chest rising and falling, cock limp and twitching. Undone.

Still the watcher.

But now, watched back.

23

I WAKE IN MY BEDROOM, face smashed in my pillow. My mouth is dry. My head is fogged, but not empty.

The fight. The crypt. The hard pill of Phantom Bliss, turning soft and melting on my tongue. All of those are just embers and echoes. Real but also wisps of a dream. I can still smell the smoke, sweat, and wine. Feel it in the way my body aches, not painfully, not like when I woke up in the cage. This is different, a whispered reminder that I didn't just survive another night with the Barons. I actually *lived* last night with them.

Reaching down, I find that my shorts are still ruined. One side barely clinging on, the crotch in shreds. There's a velvet cloak draped over me. If I had to guess which Baron made the effort, I can't pick. Maybe neither. Maybe someone took pity on me, not wanting to look at me in the raw morning like this.

My thighs are sticky. The rush is gone, but the memories are sharp in places–Damon on the throne. His hands. The husky sound of his voice. The pressure of his thigh between mine, the hard slickness of his cock thrusting into me and for once, not denying me pleasure. The way he made me feel like I was a thing worth claiming–not just used.

And then...

Hunter.

Still. Silent. Always watching.

I can still feel the weight of eyes on me as he watched Damon bring me to the brink, my body melting under his touch. The heaviness of his erection in my hand. The salty taste of him in my mouth. I'd taken him all, choking back the thick spurts of cum. It was worth it for the way he never looked away–not once. Not even when he broke.

I should be ashamed. My uncle would be disgusted. The other girls from the Manor, horrified. What I'd done was not how I was raised. It was not how good girls behaved.

But the biggest question: what would the King think?

I'd come in with a vague plan to make the crypt chasers know the Barons belonged to me, but something different transpired–something dark and feral. I don't know if it was the drugs, or the girl that gave her tits to Damon to sign, or Bronwyn and the presumption I wasn't up to the task of taking care of my men. Whatever it was, I walked down that dark staircase one way and woke up this morning someone else.

Someone who was *seen*.

For the first time since they stumbled on me standing over Armand with the bloody knife in my hand, Damon saw me. And Hunter?

He let *me* see *him*.

And me? I said yes to all of it. I gave myself over. To the ritual, the heat, the performance, the power. I liked it. Fuck yeah, I liked it.

I push myself upright, and the velvet slips from my shoulders. The cold of the room hits my skin, and my temples throb. I need water and food. But what I want, what curls somewhere low and lingering, is to go back to the heat. To the throne. To the place where I wasn't thinking, just *feeling*.

A knock at the door breaks through my thoughts.

"Come in," I croak, voice dry as bone.

The door opens softly, and Graves steps inside, precise and unbothered as ever, carrying a silver tray. Food. Water. Juice. A few capsules in a small dish: supplements. Recovery. The morning-after ritual of someone in power. It's like I summoned him with my mind.

He places the tray on the side table with the same ease he always has, then turns to me.

"Good morning, Arianette."

I sit up slowly, clutching the cloak to my chest.

"Morning." My voice is raspy. "Do you know how I got back here?"

Graves doesn't pause. Doesn't blink. "The Shadows always look after the Baroness," he says simply. "You were carried back. I believe you slept through most of it."

"And the boys?" I ask before I can stop myself. "Damon?"

"Still sleeping, I believe." He hands me the glass of water. "As is Hunter."

Of course they are.

Men sleep well after conquest.

Tipping back the glass, I drink until my throat no longer feels like sandpaper.

Graves watches me. I've started to suspect that everything I do or say, he takes back to the King. "Make sure you eat. You need the nourishment after last night." He gestures to the pills. "Those too. Everything is organic, picked out by the King to ensure you're at your best for the appointment today."

I blink at him over the rim of the glass. "Appointment?"

"To begin planning your wedding." His eyebrow arches. "Unless you're not up to it."

No matter how I *felt* last night–wild, claimed, unbound–this is the story I was born into. The role written for me long before Damon and Hunter entered my orbit. My true destiny is to marry the Baron King, to support him. It's finally happening.

"I'll be ready," I tell him, throwing my legs over the bed as I grab a piece of toast.

His eyes dart down my body. To the shredded shorts and the cum dried on my legs. "Perhaps a shower first."

"Right." Heat rises in my cheeks. "Of course."

"Arianette." The gravity in his voice gains all of my attention. "You did good last night. You all did. Made the King proud."

"Really?" After so many fumbles and mistakes and humiliating moments, the words mean more than he can imagine.

He smiles, it's small but genuine. "Yes, really."

SOMETHING ISN'T RIGHT.

Everything is pink and gold. Delicate with tiny flowers and little blue birds. I frown at the vase of blush-colored roses, perky and bright. A complete contrast to the black lace dress, the top tied up in the back like a corset, and the black Mary Janes on my feet.

"Are we in the right place?" I whisper to Graves. With every second that passes I feel more and more like an intruder.

"Yes."

I'd closed my eyes once he drove away from the House of Night, my head throbbing and stomach rolling with the threat of nausea–lingering effects of the excess I'd taken part in the night before. I sat in the backseat praying that what happened in the crypt, stayed in the crypt, because if anyone outside Beta Rho found out–someone like my uncle? I'd melt into the floor.

It wasn't until we were across town at this little bungalow nestled in East End territory that I opened my eyes again. He'd dutifully wiped his feet on the doormat and placed a silver revolver with a mother of pearl handle into a basket just inside the door.

"Are you sure?" I ask again, but his attention shifts to a woman walking down the hall. She's tall with dark shiny hair, her skin like porcelain, gleaming and smooth, much like the pearls around her neck. "Adeline, it's like you never age."

"Hello, Gibson, *always* the charmer."

I watch as they press a kiss against each other's cheeks. I'm used to pretension and social niceties. I was raised on them at the Manor. In fact, we had classes. Boring and tedious, but I understand the language these two are speaking: polite but not friendly.

Her cool blue eyes land on me. "You must be Arianette."

"Yes, ma'am." Like a worn pair of ballet shoes, the lessons slip back on easily.

"Gorgeous," she says, eyes sweeping over me. "There's no doubt you'll make the King a beautiful bride."

The compliment hits me square in the chest, unfurling the hope I have just a little bit more.

"Arianette, Adeline runs the Gilded Rose, the most premier salon and spa in East End–"

"In Forsyth," Adeline gently nudges. "Otherwise, why would you be here?"

His cheeks suck in, like he's controlling himself. "Under normal circumstances, a Baron wedding would be a simple affair, but nothing about our circumstances is normal. The Black Wedding is unique, even for the Barons, and it requires the kind of attention to detail that only one person in Forsyth is known to have when it comes to traditions and ceremonies."

"So you acknowledge it." Her chin lifts. "Am I hearing that correctly?"

"Yes, Adeline," he barely contains a sigh, "you are that person, and we are eternally grateful for your assistance."

I can't follow the subtext between these two.

"Thank you," she says, as if that's all she wanted to hear. "Now, shoo," she waves Graves off, "we've got work to do."

"You're leaving?"

"Only women are allowed past the foyer," he explains, then nods to a floral love seat in the next room. "I'll be out here. Call if you need anything."

Adeline turns her back on Graves and links her arm with mine. "Now, let me get you settled and I'll grab you a cup of tea, then we'll go back to my office to get started working on your special day."

I shoot Graves a final look, but he seems entirely at ease as she leads me down a hallway. Framed photos fill the walls, woman after woman, dressed in white. The earlier ones are in black and white, but they change to color photographs as we get farther down the hall. She ushers me into her office, all-white furniture and pristine decor, a strange contrast to the world I come from. The black lace of my dress is stark as I sink into one of the tufted chairs. I keep my knees together, hands folded, pretending not to notice the way my skin looks. Too brown, too loud in this bright space.

She returns with a delicate china cup balanced on a matching saucer. "Special blend," she says with a smile. "Perfect for perking up a Royal post-celebration."

I take it cautiously. The tea is fragrant, sharp with citrus and something deeper beneath it, an herbal undertone I can't quite place. I glance up at her, one brow lifting.

"The King likes me to have organic and natural foods," I say carefully, as if reciting a script.

"I'm well aware of the Baron King's ways." Her voice is calm, clipped. "I would never give you anything that violated his policies."

I sip, tasting the warm concoction. It's smooth on my tongue, and whatever was coiled in my chest begins to unravel–not entirely, but enough.

"Now," she says, moving to the corner of the room, "let's get started." She enters a code into a discreet panel in the wall. With a quiet click, a sleek white drawer opens, and she lifts a heavy, leather-bound book from within.

I blink; not what I expected from a wedding planner.

Adeline places the book between us with reverence, smoothing one hand over the embossed pentagram on the cover. It gleams under the soft light, dark leather, nearly black, with age-worn edges and red thread peeking out from the spine.

"Graves was right about one thing," she says, voice low. "I do tend to be the keeper of East End traditions, and quite a few secrets, many just coming into the light. But many years ago, your King brought this to me. An effort to preserve the rites and rituals of the Black Wedding. For the future."

I trail my fingers along the edges of the cover. It feels like touching history. Heavy, sacred, laced with things best left unnamed.

"Why didn't he keep it at the House of Night?" I ask, voice quieter now.

Her lips curl, not unkindly. "Sometimes the safest places are in enemy territory."

She opens the book and I brace myself–I survived the Hunt after all, I know what the ceremonies of the Barons look like, but still, I'm not prepared.

The first page is a photograph: a bride standing in a circle of salt and bone, arms bound in crimson silk, her head bowed. No veil, no bouquet. Only the black crown balanced on her forehead like a curse. Beside her, the groom: bare-chested, with blood smeared down his arms in sacred patterns.

"The King took the liberty of sending invitations during your recovery," she says as I stare, "but there are other things we need to talk about. Like flowers–dahlias, of course. Decorations. Your dress."

Her fingers turn the pages slowly. Each one more surreal than the last, black altar cloths stitched with intricate designs, symbols in a language I don't understand. My hand flits to my chest at the next photo, an image of the ceremonial dagger I know intimately, and the chalice that held the blood Damon and Hunter painted over my skin.

Then photos of brides in shadowy gowns with veils that sweep the floor like mist. Grooms in robes or leather, their faces obscured, some masked, some painted.

"Black Weddings were more common in the past–before the current King. Arrangements made between members of Forsyth's society, securing a woman's fate to a powerful man. But there have been no ceremonies like this in the last three decades. Yours will be the first," she looks at me with bold admiration, "quite a feat for your uncle."

I hear the question behind the words. Why me? Why was I

chosen? This awkward, confused girl for a man as powerful as the King. Her guess would probably be better than mine.

"You're expected to choose the elements that speak to your bond," she explains. "The Black Wedding is not just a celebration. It's an initiation. A blood rite. A claiming. What you wear, what you say, what you offer–it all speaks volumes."

There's a pressure building in my chest again. I swallow.

"Do they all... bleed?" I ask, eyes catching on a photo of a bride pressing a blade to her palm before offering it to her groom's mouth. It's no less animalistic than what we've been through already, but I know that what I give to this man must be more important than what I gave to the Barons.

"They all give something," she says softly. "And they all take something in return."

I stare at the photos, my stomach fluttering with fear, anticipation... maybe even a touch of awe, but deep in my chest I know the one thing that the King will require of me, the one thing that Damon and Hunter haven't been allowed to take.

That purity the men in Forsyth hold so dear, that is what I will give the King on the night of our wedding. I just hope that it will be enough to finally win his approval, but even more, enough to make me his wife.

24

T imothy

I'VE INHERITED many things over the years. My mother's eyes and my father's allergy to pollen. The title of Baron in college, and later the role of King, when I murdered my cousin. But the most valuable thing I've inherited was land. My parents both died tragically, young, their lives extinguished in mere seconds when their vehicle was rammed off the road by an intoxicated driver. That single act changed my future. I inherited what my father thought was a burden. A useless tract of land right outside the Forsyth University campus.

A piece of land would become a building that rose into the Forsyth skyline, and ultimately, would become my true legacy. Brick and stone, anchoring the Maddox name to the city. I spared no expense, replicating the neo-Gothic architecture I'd seen in Europe. I hired the best, wanting the feel of high-arched windows and intricately carved stonework. There are two distinct towers with ornamental spires, turrets, and a steep, slate roof.

I didn't just want a place to provide rest and retreat. I wanted the kind of place that knew how to keep secrets.

I stand behind the wide pane of my office window on the top floor, looking down at the street below. The city doesn't sleep, it pulses, especially when the sun sets.

The door opens without a knock. Only one man walks into the King's office like he owns the floor beneath his feet.

Another King. Simon.

My son's best friend.

"You're late."

"And you're paranoid."

"Shouldn't I be?" I ask. "Two girls taken from the south. One from the East. Another from yours, and of course, the Baroness. It's not paranoia. It's a pattern."

Sy makes a noise low in his throat and settles into the leather chair across from my desk, those long legs that move with alarming quickness in the ring stretching out. "A pattern the police seem to think has stopped now that Ballsack has been arrested."

He makes an imposing figure, with the tattoos and thick muscles. He's not just strong, he's smart.

Like his father.

I walk to the bar and pull out two glasses. I'm not one for drinking, but this topic is easier to swallow with a bit of fuel. "Or whoever is snatching those girls got spooked when Arianette escaped, and Knight got a hard-on for West End punk." I pour a splash of whiskey into Sy's glass and club soda into mine.

"A hard-on encouraged by a whore at the Velvet Hideaway," he mutters.

"Yes, Augustine seems to have sway with Agent Knight." There's a connection between the Madam and the FBI agent. A client? A lover? Maybe just a friend? Whatever it is, she's got his ear.

"Well, he locked up the wrong man. Ballsack is innocent."

I hand him the drink and glance around the room, weighing whether I'm ready for this conversation. Simon's practically family. But if there's one thing I know, it's that family doesn't always mean you're on the same side. Especially when there's so much on the line.

"I'm inclined to agree," I tell him, walking around the desk. "Warren is nothing but a scapegoat."

Unlike the outside of the hotel, my office is black-walled, like a tomb. There are no family photos. Just a single painting above the fireplace–a crowned stag pierced through the heart with three blades.

"You're serious." Sy's surprise at my revelation quickly turns to anger. "Then why the hell aren't you doing anything to get Ballsack out?!"

I take a deep breath. I'm still not used to dealing with the hot-headed tempers of the new Kings. They're fueled by testosterone and lust. Drunk on newfound power. They don't understand the precarious balance of being in this position. The nuance. Not fully.

"As you know, I come from a long line of hunters," I say, settling into the chair across from the younger man. "I know the woods–the terrain, the subtle signs most people overlook. A snapped twig. A strand of hair. Scuffed bark. But whoever's hunting these girls... they're making themselves damn near impossible to track." I take another sip. "Hexley installed a device in Arianette the day she turned eighteen. It was removed while she was missing."

Sy's expression doesn't change, other than the deepening of the line in his forehead. "I knew this," he admits. "Ashby procured a video of the girl in the hospital. She's..." as he searches for a word, my hackles start to rise, "...unreliable."

Unreliable. Well, that's one way to say it.

I open up the desk drawer and pull out a file. Unmarked. Inside: photographs. Satellite printouts. Medical records. Implant schematics. Pushing them over to Sy, I wait until he flips through them. "As you can see, we can trace her movements from the exact moment she went missing on that street corner after dance class, to a spot out in the forest."

He studies a map carefully. "That looks very close to your land."

"It is, but that area is vast, undeveloped, with rocky terrain. I'm not even sure how they would get out there. As you can see, the nearest road is miles away."

"On foot?"

"Or..." I'm uneasy about revealing secrets, but Killian has ties to the Feds, and I need time.

"Or what, old man?" He shakes his head. "Spit it out."

"Underground."

The word hangs between us, the implications loaded. Only two active fraternities are aware of the depths of the tunnels that traverse under Forsyth. The Dukes and the Barons.

"Lavinia blew those up."

"She blew *some* of them up. The ones Lionel had access to." Lionel Lucia had been the leader of the Counts and the Duchess' father. He'd planted bombs underneath various points in the city–a threat used to keep all of us in line. Lavinia, in an act of revenge, triggered the one beneath her father's compound in North Side, eliminating him for good. "I've had my Shadows securing entry and exit points, but the tunnels are far-reaching and not even I have access to all of them."

Particularly those running beneath the university or that stretch up in the forest.

"Have you told Knight that?"

I shake my head. "Not yet."

"What the hell are you waiting for? Ballsack could be home right now."

"I need time, Simon. I need the authorities to think they have their man, while I do my own search." A search I'm starting to suspect will lead to something bigger than a few missing girls. "But to do that I need you and the Princes, the two loudest about Warren's innocence, on board."

Sy leans forward, his elbows propped on his knees. The position makes his biceps strain at his black T-shirt, forcing the sleeves to rise. I take in the intricate artwork on his arm, the bruin, teeth bared. My son's skillmanship. "What's in this for you?"

"I want to find out who's taking the girls. Before they find a way into my house again. Before another one of ours shows up gutted on a riverbank, or anyone else goes missing or worse, shows up dead." I swallow, adding, "But most of all, Simon, Death is my territory and someone is encroaching. Your girl, Laura, showing up dead like that... it shouldn't happen. Not on my watch."

Sy is quiet for a moment. Then he nods. "Alright. I'll talk to Nick and Remy. Get their cooperation. I don't think the Princes will have any issue. They've already been sniffing around Lex."

"Because of his father."

This isn't the first round of missing and murdered women in Forsyth. Lex Ashby's biological father earned the moniker, 'The Forsyth Carver,' for the terror he caused. Then there are the Princesses that were never heard or seen from again.

"Remind him of that when you tell them that I want access to Pace's extensive feeds."

"Fine."

"Also, notify all three parties that there will be no more excluding me from your little meetings." He has the decency to look guilty for that. "I want your cooperation with Knight's requests. I want to know *everything* about Stella, and Laura, and every goddamn girl that's gone missing."

Sy stands, placing his empty glass on the desk. Then he softly asks, "The girl...the wedding... she's part of this, isn't she?"

"That's a business arrangement, one I made for my son a long time ago." I shrug. "I'm merely fulfilling an obligation."

Remington has been released to live his life with the Dukes and Simon Perilini is able to give him what I never could–a real family. Arianette... she's a means to an end.

Sy's expression indicates he doesn't believe me, but that was a battle I lost long ago. It's not until he's at the door that he stops and issues a warning, "Be careful, Maddox. You dig deep enough in Forsyth, you might not like what you find."

I don't relax until he shuts the door.

He has no fucking idea.

THE FIRE'S already lit when I enter the library. We're almost to Samhain, meaning the days are getting shorter, ushering in cooler temperatures.

This is my favorite room in the House of Night. Probably my favorite room in all of the properties I hold. The stained glass throws reds and greens across the floor and the leather chairs are buttery soft with age. My desk, the same one every other Baron King has sat behind, stands near the far wall, a heavy black curtain draped behind it, hiding the details of my obsession.

Pushing back the curtain, I reveal the wall.

It's covered in newspaper clippings, documents, and printed forms. All copies–the originals are stored safely elsewhere–but I prefer to see the crimes laid out like this, the threads of each story exposed. People call these setups "murder boards," and now that one girl's confirmed dead, the term finally fits.

I pause at Laura's photo. She looks like any of the thousands of girls who've passed through Forsyth. So painfully ordinary no one suspected foul play when she disappeared. Even her friends thought maybe she'd just taken off in search of something better. But why her? What made her stand out? What did they see in her? Why was she the first to die?

And is that even true? Was she the first... or just the first we've found?

Next to her is Stella–straight black hair, bright eyes. She's smiling in every photo. I run my finger along the space between their pictures, stopping at the name that connects them: Eugene Warren. Ballsack.

I understand why the police are circling him. I don't believe in coincidences either. But this? This feels too neat. Too obvious.

Like I told Sy earlier today: death is my business. And someone is out there meddling.

I don't involve myself in the small-time greed of the gun trade, or the vulgarity of human trafficking. Lionel Lucia's obsession with drowning Forsyth in narcotics never interested me, until he created Scratch and started stacking our morgues with bodies. That crossed a line, and thankfully his daughter had the guts to deal with him.

I believe in free will. At Noir Sanctum, there's no price on desire. In the shadows, there's no judgment on a deserved death. We tend to the dead. We shepherd their remains from one realm to the next.

But this? This isn't justice. Whoever's taking these girls–*hurting them*–has no reverence for death. And when they took Arianette Hexley, they made it my problem.

I don't need a picture of Arianette to recall her features. They're etched into my mind. Her dark eyes, wide with fear up on the altar. Hands bloodied from killing her Baron. But there's more. She's soft in all the ways men like women soft. In the mouth and hips. She's pliable, eager to please, but there's steel under it. A defiance I suspect she has no idea how to control. That's why she ended up in the cage. A lesson in self-control.

I have no doubt that defiance is what carried her to the river-bank–what saved her life.

There are moments I wonder if it would've been better had she stayed dead on that sandy riverbank. It would have spared her every-thing that's coming. Not just the Black Wedding. Not just becoming my bride. But the invasion of her mind I'm going to have to carry out. The ways I'll have to dismantle her, piece by piece, to get to the truth.

She's the best lead I've got. The only one.

Noise in the hallway alerts me to their arrival. I drag the curtain over the wall, keeping my activities under wraps.

Hunter arrives first, the faint scent of cigarette smoke trailing in after him. Damon follows, darker, quieter, eyes always scanning. He's still carrying that low-level burn from the Fury. I can see it in the way he stands, coiled and ready.

"DK," I say, stepping forward, "your win at the Fury was impressive."

His jaw tics, but he nods.

"You two," I glance between them, "seem to be working well

together. That's not nothing. It can be hard taking over leadership in a group without prior connections."

Hunter nods. "It's been a challenge getting our footing. The win and the party at the crypt seem to have helped."

I've heard about the gluttony that took place in the crypt on Friday night, reported by my Shadows. They'd followed my rules, no fornication, while still enjoying the passion of the night. It's important. Necessary.

"Connections can be our greatest weapon. Or the very thing that gets us all killed. I'm pleased you've been able to create a bond." I move behind the desk, rest my palms on the wood. "I have two projects. Quiet, specific, and critical to the integrity of this House–and to the city itself."

They both nod, posture shifting subtly. Men who've witnessed death–experienced it–and will again.

I look at DK first. "You're taking her to the river." His brow lifts. "To the place she was found," I clarify. "The spot where Arianette crawled out of the water half-dead. I want you to walk her through it. Not as a protector, she has too many of those already, but as a student of the terrain. Maybe something jogs her memory. A sound, a scent, the way the wind hits the trees."

"You want her to remember," DK says.

"No," I say, cold and even. "I want her to *see*. Remembering comes after."

Hunter leans back, arms crossed. "And what about me?"

I tilt my chin toward him. "You're already doing it. That late-night voice of yours–people listen. Not just the college kids, but the insomniacs, the drunks, the ones who know things and don't realize it. I want you to start asking the right kinds of questions."

He quirks a brow. "On air?"

"Veiled. Slanted. A riddle, a metaphor, a game." I wave my hand, not interested in the specifics. "I don't care how you spin it, but spin it. Find the thread. Pull it until something snaps."

"And if it doesn't?" Hunter asks.

"It will."

The fire crackles across the room. I step back, letting the weight of the room press down around us. "People think women vanish because they're weak," I say finally, voice low. "Because they're careless. Sluts and whores. Expendables. That's a lie. The girls in Forsyth vanish because someone out there is trying to tear down what we have by taking the people that belong to us. I want to know who that someone is."

DK's nod is barely perceptible. Hunter seems to already be deep in thought.

"If that's settled, I want to remind you the Black Wedding is in five days. Per tradition, you'll be at my side, witness to the ceremony. Graves will prepare you."

Having no interest in explaining further, that's the last thing I say before turning my back to them. They'll take the hint. The meeting is over.

Behind me, the leather of the chairs groans as they stand. Damon's boots are always heavier than Hunter's, he drags a little more weight, carries a little more anger. I don't turn around. I listen instead, to the way the old hinges sigh as the library doors close behind them. That pause. The one where they hesitate, like they want to ask more questions–get more clarity on my commands.

Unfortunately, I don't have the answers.

In five days, I marry a woman barely of age. I'll make her mine, give her a title, fulfill my duty, and reap my reward.

I walk to the fire and lean one hand against the mantle, the heat crawling up my wrist like a warning.

The men are loyal. The House is quiet. The dead are buried.

For now.

But I can feel something moving beneath it all.

And it may destroy us all when I drag it into the light.

Damon

EVEN WITH GPS COORDINATES, the trailhead is nearly invisible. I pass by it twice, cruising at less than five miles an hour, until I realize that the rotten stump on the side of the road is the marker.

Pulling off, the tires crunch over the fallen leaves. I park the SUV on the edge of the road. I know the river twists nearby, we'd already passed over it once on a bridge.

Arianette sits beside me in the truck, curled up like some Victorian doll left in the attic too long. Her dress is too delicate for the forest–lace cuffs, soft gray wool, ballet flats that won't survive the mud–but she insisted on wearing it. Said it made her feel "more like herself."

Whatever that means.

I haven't been alone with her since the night in the crypt. She'd spent Saturday prepping for the wedding while Hunter and I slept off the effects of the party. Fuck, it had been amazing. Pure gluttony and excess. Sex and drugs. Orgasms and victory. Overwhelming lust and the ability to claim it–her–as mine in front of the whole goddamn frat and crypt chasers.

Being confined in the small space of the vehicle is almost like having her in my lap again, pussy bared, wet and slick for me. It'd be so easy to drag her across the seat, to push up that dress, and do it again.

But that's not why we're here.

She hums low under her breath, fingers twitching in her lap like she's a cat playing with an invisible string. I don't ask about it. I've learned not to ask her much unless I want a riddle for an answer. She does seem to notice I've stopped the car. "Are we here?"

"You tell me," I prompt, killing the engine. "Look familiar?"

She peers out the window and shakes her head. The leaves are turning, changing from green to yellow and orange. She'd been found in the late summer. It would've looked different.

"I don't remember anything." This is something she insists, but there's a faraway look in those brown eyes that makes me think that isn't true. The King obviously doesn't believe her either.

"Well, let's see what happens if we go out there."

I climb out, sling my pack over one shoulder, and grab my compound bow out of the back seat. When I open her door, she moves slowly, different from the other times I've been around her, like she's unsure her bones will hold. There's no sign of the dancer. Of the killer I met in those woods. I offer my hand, but she doesn't take it, hopping out on her own.

It's colder than I expected for early fall, the damp kind that clings to the back of my neck. I lift my collar up, shielding my skin, and step into the woods. We move in silence, Arianette sticking close enough that her shoulder brushes my arm with every step. The forest smells like rot and water. The river isn't far, I can hear it rushing ahead, aggressive and alive.

She stops suddenly, her head cocked like she's listening to something I can't hear.

"What? Do you remember something?"

I glance around. Broken branches. A patch of disturbed soil. Maybe a boot print half-swallowed by time. It's old, too old to tell much, but it's something. I crouch and run my hand through the dirt.

"There were others," she whispers behind me. "Crying. Screaming, sometimes. I think... I think one of them had a necklace. I could hear it clink when she moved."

"Here?" I ask, having a hard time thinking there was a crowd in here.

"Not here." She shakes her head like she's trying to remove cobwebs. "There."

There. I try to sort through the riddle. Maybe Hunter would have been the better one to come on this little journey of futility.

"You mean the other girls–the ones missing?"

She says nothing, just tilts her head toward the sky and stares up.

"Do you remember anything about who took you?" I ask, still crouched.

Her voice drops to a murmur. "A mask. Like a beast. I thought it was him at first. I thought it was *him*."

I look up. "The King?"

She doesn't answer. Just turns in a slow circle, then takes the trek toward the river, her movements dreamlike, disconnected. I stand slowly and watch her as she stands at the edge of the riverbank, arms folded tight around herself.

"I've been here," she says, frowning. "Right?"

I unfold the map in my pocket, the one Graves gave me before we left. There's a spot circled, coordinates at the bottom, a photo paper-clipped to the top.

"This is where they found you." I clear my throat. "The two kids that were fishing."

One had given her CPR while the other ran out to the street to flag down help. She was covered in bruises and had ties still bound around her wrist. I lift her hand now and push back the sleeve, rubbing my thumb over the ridge of scar tissue wrapped around her wrist like a bracelet.

"They said I was gone for at least three minutes." She looks at my hand. Her wrist. "Do you know what three minutes feels like when you're not in your body?"

"Yes." I'm still able to feel the heat of the blood spilling in my hands. Her eyes flick to the scar. To the story I'd told her in the locker room. I can't tell if the feeling in my chest is because I'm pissed that I'd let that slip in a moment of vulnerability or glad that it's out of the way and I don't have to tell it again.

"Then you know that it's everything. It's nothing. It's..." Her mouth twists. "It's what I had to do to get away. Risk it all. Embrace the ether. It was a decision, I could end my life on my terms or the beast could take it on theirs."

"Are you saying you jumped in the river? To escape?"

From the notes I've read, the police report, they weren't sure if it was intentional or not.

"It was the way."

I notice she's wary to label the beast as male or female. I step closer, close enough that she can lean against me if she wants. Use me to dig into that place of darkness she's clearly afraid to go. She doesn't, but I feel the way her breathing slows, like my presence alone is enough.

"I'm going to find out who did this to you," I say. "No matter what it takes."

She blinks slowly, turning to look up at me. "That's why he sent you. You're not afraid to get your hands dirty."

"I've been dirty since birth," I say. "Might as well make it useful."

The wind picks up, whipping the ends of her dress around her legs. The memory of them wrapped around me in the crypt barrels into me. Her skin was so soft and supple. My cock gets hard in an instant. I glance out over the water, where the river churns, white and frothy, pure after going over the rocks.

I don't think I understood why the King chose me until this very moment.

Arianette may have died here, but now, she's *his*. The King's.
Ours. Me and Hunter.
And it's my job to make sure she stays that way.

THE TRAIL NARROWS as we climb, the dirt soft beneath my boots. The river hisses below, seeming to grow louder the higher we go. Arianette walks ahead of me, her steps light but unsteady, hands trailing along branches and mossy trunks like she's blindfolded and feeling her way through a dream. Predictably, her shoes aren't up to the task and more than once, I place my hands on her hips to leverage her out of the muck.

"There," she says finally, pointing toward a flat patch of stone overlooking the bend in the river. "That's where I jumped."

I nod. It's just a slab of stone and dead leaves now, nothing remarkable, nothing that screams of a girl willing to throw herself to her death. It's not the landscape I'm trying to read, it's her.

She lowers herself slowly to the rock, skirt pooling around her dirty feet, eyes scanning the treeline as if something might flicker back to life there. I crouch nearby, resting my bow against a tree.

Arianette starts to hum again, soft and tuneless. "I used to count the windows," she says after a minute. "To make sure none of them were open. Just in case one of the little ones thought about flying."

I freeze. Little ones?

"There was a girl," she continues, eyes glassy, like the world has peeled away and left her in memory's hollow shell. "Red. That was her color." She lifts a hand to her face and flinches like someone's just hit her, even though there's only wind. "At night they'd take her, after the music and dancing. After the *entertainment*."

I swallow and ask in an even voice. "Did she have a name?"

She thinks, head tilted. "Em? Emily? Emma?" Her eyes flick to the dirt. "It was a long time ago."

I've seen the transcript of Arianette's conversation at the hospital after she was found. That FBI agent and police officer probing her for details. Much of it had been gibberish, and the toxicology reports did come back saying she'd had drugs in her system. It makes her story even more unreliable and hard to understand. There are times when she seems to confuse the present with the past. Or maybe they're the same thing. There's no real way to find out.

"I was there to dance," she says. "But sometimes, that's not all they wanted."

"What did they want?" I ask, playing along.

She looks at me then, something sharp and unspoken in her eyes. "They made me *watch*, Damon. I had to *watch*. That was the rule."

My throat tightens. I sit beside her now.

"The hallway outside the blue room always smelled like sweat and old flowers. Expensive, oily perfume. They'd leave the door open just a crack. Just wide enough. I could hear the crying. Other times laughing. One of them still had their baby teeth."

She wraps her arms around her knees, rocking slightly.

"There's a kind of sickness you get from seeing too much and doing nothing. I still have it. It lives under my tongue, behind my ribs. I carry all their screams in a glass jar inside me. Sometimes it rattles. Sometimes it breaks."

I put a hand on her shoulder, gently. She leans into it without looking at me. "Who, Arianette? *Who* are you talking about?"

She looks over her shoulder, like we're in the middle of the student center and not deep in the forest. "It's not a who. It's a them. A beast. Maybe more than one." She presses a hand to her chest. "When they took me I thought it was to finish what they started. But it wasn't. It wasn't *them*. It was worse."

"Why was it worse?"

"Because the beast doesn't care about altars and blood. It only cares about locking the past in a teeny-tiny box." Her hands clamp together, snapping shut. "Forever."

Silence stretches between us, thick and sour, despite the wind and rushing water. Arianette may be confused, and hell, more than a little crazy, but there's truth here, something that was freed in this damp forest.

Something, I have a feeling, that is worth killing over.

The sun dips behind the treetops, cutting the light into golden slashes across our skin. Arianette is quiet now, but it's not the shut-down kind of quiet. It's the quiet that comes after a release. A terrible truth settling over us like dust.

I stand, brushing the dirt from my palms, and grab my bow from where I'd leaned it against the tree. She watches me, eyes still glassy but clearer now, the way she looked after she came on my fingertips at the party.

"You always bring weapons when you're alone with a girl?" she asks, voice light, teasing.

"I bring weapons when I go into the woods with someone who survived death and still hears ghosts in the trees," I answer.

"Damon," she says, my name soft on her lips. No one really calls me Damon, other than judges and probation officers. I don't hate the sound of it from her.

"Yeah?"

"Teach me," she says suddenly. "To hunt."

I raise an eyebrow and ask, "To kill?"

Not sure the King would approve. Plus, we already know she's capable.

"To know," she replies, stepping close, her voice a breath now. "What it feels like. To be the hunter instead of the prey."

"I think you have some idea," I tell her, noting the hunger in her eyes. I saw it the night of the Hunt when Armand was dying at her feet. But I get it. I brought her out here and picked at her wounds, dragging her through the muck and mud, to hear her story. She feels vulnerable and wants a little of that power back.

Slowly, I hand her the bow. She stumbles a little, laughing, "It's heavy," but steadies herself fast. She's small, but all tension and wire underneath. Wound tight, like one of those little ballerinas in a jewelry box.

"Let me show you," I say, stepping behind her. My hand wraps around her wrist, guiding her fingers over the grip, the curve of the string. The first time I picked up the bow, it felt as familiar as my own cock. I just understood how it worked. "You keep your body square, like this. Elbows high. Shoulders relaxed."

She shifts, and her back presses flush against my chest. I don't step back. I could. But I don't.

Her breath comes shallow. I feel it where my hand still rests on her ribcage, just beneath the swell of her tit. Her skin is warm. Damp with sweat after the hike. She doesn't pull away.

"Now," I murmur, voice in her ear, "focus. See everything and nothing. Don't just look–feel it."

Her exhale shivers across my skin. Moving her arms slowly, I pull the string back with her, guiding her through the motion. Her body arches slightly, and I catch her hips against mine to keep her steady.

"You feel that?" I whisper, lips brushing the curve of her neck. I'm hard, strung as tight as the bow. In a blink I could drop it, shove up that skirt, and have my cock slick between her thighs.

"Yes."

"Good. Let the tension build. Don't rush it. That's how you miss."

She adjusts her stance, and the movement grinds her against me. Not accidental. I'm desperate, and she feels it. For the first time since I met the Baroness I feel the push-pull of flirtation, the tease of something more. For once, we're not in a fight, we're in this moment together.

My fingers trail down the side of her tit, running over the hard metal bars. She keeps her grip firm. "Now."

She releases the string, and it sings as it cuts through the air. The arrow thunks into a nearby tree with a satisfying, violent thud.

Her breath catches in her throat. That sound–she liked it.

"Good girl."

"Did I hit something?" she asks, twisting to look up at me.

"Not the target," I murmur. "But definitely something."

We're nose to nose now. I should pull away. Tell her this is over. That she's spoken for, and every time we're together it's one step closer to me breaking the King's trust. I won't be the one to break the rules, even if way out here in the woods, no one would know.

He'd know, I remind myself. And he'd have me fucking castrated.

But she leans in first. Her lips hover at my jawline, not quite touching, her breath fanning across the heat of my skin.

"Teach me more," she whispers.

I don't answer right away. Just watch her lips part as the words slip out, sticky-sweet and soft, and I feel her pulse flutter under my hand. She's still holding the bow, but it's slack in her grip now. My other hand slides down the curve of her thigh, slowly. Testing. Asking without asking. She doesn't stop me.

"Say it again," I murmur, my lips brushing her temple.

"Teach me," she breathes, voice trembling now. "Please."

That is within the rules. *Firmly* inside the boundaries the King gave us. The word lights something primal in my chest. I grip her hips and turn her, backing her against a moss-slick tree. Her mouth falls open as I slide a thigh between hers and press. Her skirt hikes up.

Fuck.

"Show me your tits," I say, and she obeys like a child, pulling her dress up and over her head. Her bra and panties are black lace, a tiny bow at the front of each. That depraved combination, silly little schoolgirl wrapped in lace. It shouldn't be as hot as it is, but...

Fuck. Jesus Christ, my cock approves.

Too impatient to take off the bra, I yank down the cups, exposing those pretty brown tits that I think about every time I touch myself, getting my eyes on the piercings.

The bars gleam in the low autumn light, short and snug, little metal knobs catching on the curve of her healing nipples. There's a faint bruise around one, and the skin is still a little tender. My mark. My doing.

I trace the underside of one breast with my knuckle, then tap the bar lightly. She flinches, just a bit, but doesn't pull away.

My cock twitches beneath my jeans.

"They're healing perfectly," I murmur. "Tight. Clean. Pretty."

She swallows hard, watching me with wide, wet eyes.

"Hurt?"

She nods and admits, "Hunter gave me some salve to help."

My tongue darts out, running over the hoop in my lip, thinking about Hunter checking on her. How I feel about it. "Good," I decide for the both of us, but still ask, "did he touch them?"

She shakes her head, and yeah, that's even better. I want to be the first to play with them once they're healed, when I can wrap my teeth around them and pull. I'm going to dress them up in different charms, link them together with chains. Most of all, I want to hear her scream.

But for now, I just press a gentle kiss against each one and listen to her soft gasp as I slide my hand between her legs, over her underwear–the black lace already soaked through. I press my thumb there, hard, watching her writhe against the bark. Her nose wrinkles in pain, like it hurts to be touched but hurts more not to be.

"Please," she moans, twisting, trying to grind against my hand, but I pin her thigh with my knee.

"No, sister," I growl. "You don't get to take. You *earn*."

I want so badly to slip my fingers past the lace, to touch hot slickness. I hold back, circle her clit once over the fabric, twice, then pull away. She nearly cries out.

"Damon–"

"You want it?" I ask. "Say it."

"I want it," she gasps. "Please, please–"

"Want *what*, sister?" My voice is a snarl now. I tease her entrance, the restraint it takes not to plunge in driving me insane. She clamps her thighs together, breath caught in her throat.

"This," she whispers, dazed. "You. Anything."

Any sense of control and restraint shatters and I warn, "Remember you said that."

I reach for my quiver and slide out an arrow, the black shaft catching the faint light of the fading sun. She watches with wide, dazed eyes, lips parted, panting. I crouch low, the predator in me prowling now–careful, patient, hungry.

"Stay still," I murmur, voice thick with gravel.

I trace the feathered fletching along the inside of her thigh, slow and deliberate. She trembles like a leaf in a storm. The feathers whisper against her skin, teasing up, closer, until they drag over the lace clinging to her soaked center.

She whimpers, knees buckling, breath catching.

I brush the fletching over her clit through the lace, again and again, light as smoke. She shudders, trying not to grind down on it. Trying to obey. Trying to please.

"You're so good when you want to be," I murmur, leaning in to bite her shoulder. "So desperate to prove you're still that good little girl."

She gasps, hips jerking. "I have to…"

"Not yet."

I flip the arrow in my hand. The sharpened tip slides down the crotch of her panties. I pierce the lace and jerk down, shredding it into pieces.

"You really should just stop wearing these when I'm around."

I drop the ruined lace on the forest floor. Pussy bared before me, I hover the sharp tip just above her slit. Not touching. Just threatening.

Her pupils blow wide.

I press it gently, just the edge of the tip, against her clit. Not enough to break skin, although, God, I want to. No, it's just enough to feel dangerous. Electric. Her back arches like she's been shocked. She lets out a strangled moan.

"Damon–"

"Shhh." I tap it, stroke it. Just barely. Her belly trembles. "You're so close. And I haven't even *touched* you."

She's panting, shaking now, every nerve lit and burning. Her hands grip the bark behind her, trying not to fall apart, trying not to come before I say she can.

But I want it. I *need* it.

I press the arrow down, feathering her clit in slow, deadly circles with the metal tip, until she's writhing, every muscle coiled.

"I'm going to let you come this time," I growl, needing this to be over before I do something stupid. Something so fucking stupid. "But do it now, before I change my mind."

Mercifully, she does–with a cry that's part sob, part scream, part prayer. Her body seizes and melts all at once, legs giving out. I catch her before she collapses.

The arrow drops to the ground.

"One day," I tell her quietly, "I'm going to have you the way I want to, and you're not going to be able to escape the sharp tip of my blade, but first the King gets your purity." I breathe into her skin. "But the rest of you? *This*?" My palm presses between her legs, feeling the aftershocks of her orgasm, sticky and warm. "This is *mine*."

"Thank you," she says and I have no doubt she means it. I hold her against my chest, breathing hard, heart still pounding from the feel of her breaking open under me like that. Marked without a mark. Claimed without a claim.

For now.

26

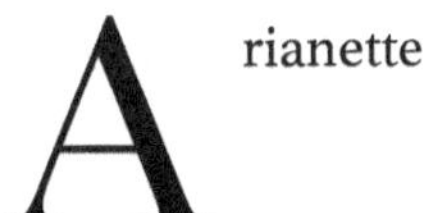

rianette

THE FOREST IS BEHIND US, but I can still feel it. Still taste the moss on my tongue, still smell the river, the air. In the backseat, sitting next to the compound bow, are our shoes, dirty and covered with mud. Much like my dress that Damon picked up off the ground and lowered over my head. While he disappeared behind a tree, I tried to brush off the green streak of moss on my dress, and the little pieces of dried leaves. It wasn't until I heard a heavy grunt and saw him zipping up his pants that I realized what he was doing.

"I could have done that," I told him, feeling guilty.

"It's getting dark," he said, then flashed me a smile. "When your mouth is on me, sister, I don't want to rush."

The walk back to the car seemed shorter than the way up, and now that we're in the car I'm too tired to think straight. Orgasm-sore. Mind-wrecked. That trembling kind of raw where my body doesn't feel like it belongs to me anymore. Except it does, because he reminded me. Claimed me again in the trees. I ache in the best, weirdest, way.

By the time Damon gets behind the wheel of the car and cranks the engine, I'm shivering, the cool night air settling in my bones.

"Here," he says, shrugging out of his jacket, and then hoodie. The sweatshirt is warm, and when I pull it over my dirty dress I press the sleeve to my nose, inhaling his scent. Pulling off the side of the road, he drives with one hand on the wheel, the other messing with the GPS. We don't talk and the silence stretches into something uncomfortable. That's the hardest part of all of this: being thrust into the role of Baroness, being owned by men you don't know. The silence. I was raised to know how to make small talk, but with a man like Damon...I don't think he'd want to talk about the weather or gardening tips.

Thankfully, he flicks the radio on just as we hit the main road. Static fuzz, then Hunter, smooth, slow, serpent-soft.

"...and if you're out there, listening, and you've seen anything—anything at all—you call me. You don't wait for the cops. You don't wait for your conscience to kick in. Forsyth doesn't have time for silence."

My chest tightens.

Damon takes a left at a four-way stop, in the direction of a town called Northridge. We're still miles away from Forsyth. He drives cautiously, keeping an eye out for deer, their glassy eyes reflecting in the headlights, a reminder that we're never alone.

The sound of deep inhalation persists through the speakers. I sniff, like I can smell the lingering smoke on Hunter's clothes. I've never seen him smoke before, but I've smelled it.

"And now we're taking callers. You've got something to say? Speak up, Forsyth. We're listening."

There's a click of a line connecting, then a woman's voice crackling in.

"I... I don't know if it's anything, but a girl used to live next door to me. College-age. Real quiet. I thought she moved out, but... I still see her car parked sometimes. Same place, same angle, like it hasn't moved in weeks. Something's not right."

Hunter hums. *"Did you report it?"*

"No," she admits, voice cracking. *"Didn't seem like my business."*

Damon exhales through his nose. Disgusted. I don't blame him.

Hunter must be too, because he puts on a song, moody music that seems to fit all of our moods. Up ahead are lights focused on a large brick sign angled toward the highway. Gold letters shine back, "Preston Preparatory School," I read aloud, wondering what kind of students go there. I crane my neck as we zip by, and I think I catch the pointed peak of a bell tower.

"Those guys are the worst," Damon says, as if I asked the question out loud. "I came to a few parties up here during high school. They were fun, I guess, but I learned pretty fast that each and every one of them is a fuckboy suckling at the rich teat of generational wealth. At least in Forsyth the guys get their hands dirty." He shoots me a look and a wink. "Well, maybe not the Princes."

There are so many places I haven't been–haven't seen. Missed out on parties, traditions, rites of passage. I have questions, more than I know how to even articulate. Too many years holed up in the Manor. *Watching,* but not living.

The SUV slows as we enter a small town, and without a word he pulls into the drive-thru of some place glowing with neon pink and blue. I blink at both the sudden color and the fact that the parking lot is surprisingly full of both cars and teenagers.

"Sugar," he says, without preamble. "You need something sweet. Ice cream?"

I nod, because I do. I need something soft. Safe. Warm. Something that's not the dark behind my eyes when I close them.

"What flavor?" he asks, once it's our turn at the window.

"Chocolate."

He gets me a single, pressing the cone in my hands. He gets two scoops, a mix of chocolate and vanilla. I hold the cone with both hands, licking slowly. Creamy and cold, trying to shock the ache away with a new sensation.

Hunter's voice floats through the speakers again, talking about the girl found down by the river. About how the town needs to wake the fuck up.

I press the cone into the napkin and let it melt.

My mouth is cold. I want heat again, any way that I can get it.

Shifting, I reach for him, like I've done this a hundred times before. Maybe I have in my head. Damon doesn't flinch. Just spreads his legs a little wider.

"You okay?" he asks, voice low.

I nod, but it's a lie.

I unzip his pants slowly, reverently, and his hips rise, allowing me to take him out. He's already hard, warm and heavy in my hand. I don't say anything as I bend forward, my head between his abdomen and the steering wheel. I lower my mouth onto him—not to suck or excite, just to *hold*. To keep. To soothe.

He hisses between his teeth but lets me take him. One hand tangled in my hair, the other on the steering wheel, already directing us back on our path.

"This what you need, sister?" he murmurs. "Just to hold me like this?"

I can't speak. My mouth is too full, which may be the entire point. If I can't talk, I can keep the pain and secrets buried inside, where it's safe.

With the soft vibration of the car around us, Hunter's voice threads through my ribs like a lullaby instead of a horror story. Resting my cheek against Damon's thigh, his thumb runs along my neck, slow and steady, occasionally trailing down to my lip. I keep my mouth around him, not moving, just wrapped around him. Warmth radiates up through my belly, grounding me in ways nothing else can.

On the radio, Hunter's voice reaches us.

"And now we're taking another call. You've got something to say? Speak up, Forsyth. We're listening."

"Love your show," the guy says. *"I listen right when I get home from work. I make a cup of ramen, pack a bowl, and settle in."*

"I appreciate that," Hunter says, tone slightly impatient. *"Do you have anything relevant to add?"*

"Yeah, right. F–(beep)." The word is censored out. *"There's this stretch of woods behind the freeway–near where that girl was found. Cops searched once, but not deep enough. I hunt out there. There's shit in the trees. Scorch marks. Bone piles. Someone's doing something out there."*

I jolt, drawing up and down. Damon tugs at my hair, hard.

"Don't tease if you're not gonna finish," he warns.

I swallow and still, listening for Hunter's voice again–quieter this time.

"If you're out there... if you've seen something... if you know something... don't let silence be your sin."

BY THE TIME we pull into the parking lot behind the station, I feel... emptier. Not in a bad way. Like something tight inside me finally uncoiled and slithered off into the night.

I wipe my mouth with the sleeve of Damon's hoodie and unlatch from him, slow, quiet. My jaw aches, but it's better than what I felt before. I spoke too much, allowing the secrets to spill from my tongue. Thankfully, now, we don't say anything. Not about what I did to make myself feel better. Not about how he let me. Not about how he went along with it, like he knew it wasn't about him at all.

It's a relief, honestly. I don't think I could take being looked at too closely right now. I'm barely stitched together.

Hunter's voice hums through the air like a phantom as we walk in. I follow Damon down a narrow hallway. The walls are covered in posters, imagery of old bands, protest flyers, schedules written in Sharpie and held up with peeling tape. We're in a room outside the studio, a glass window and door separating us. Hunter's leaned back in his chair, the fingers of one hand stroking Ares' ears, a slim cigarette in the other.

Damon knocks, and Hunter looks up. Large headphones cover his ears, and his eyes dart between us. I pull the zipper up higher, as if the hoodie can hide the grime and truth of the forest. He rolls his chair over, opening the door with his finger pressed over his lips. We step inside. I take it all in. It's warm. Smoky. Cluttered. Lived-in.

Ares pads up to me with his ears perked and his head low. He sniffs at my legs, then higher. I freeze, heart stammering, wondering if he can smell the secrets I can't remember. But he just licks ice cream off my fingers and moves from me to Damon, where he takes a long, satisfied sniff of his crotch.

Oh God. He knows. He can smell what we did in the woods.

"Nose down, big guy," Damon whispers, pushing him away. The dog obeys, pulling back.

"I'm fine," I murmur to no one. Maybe myself. Either way it's a lie.

The station feels like a church in a junkyard. Books and knobs and glowing equipment everywhere. There's a red light blinking above the door.

It's funny to hear Hunter's radio voice in person, without the distance through a speaker. "We're not asking you to name names. Just tell the truth. You've seen something, haven't you? Say it out loud. Even if your voice shakes."

Someone breathes into the phone. Then, *"I heard screaming. A house out by the east orchard. Thought it was nothing. Just college kids screwing around. But it didn't sound... right."*

My stomach knots. The orchard's not far from the dance studio. Too close.

"Another night comes to a close for me at WXFU. A special thanks for everyone who had the courage to call, for the DM's in my box, and whispered secrets around Forsyth tonight. We may just be one step closer to finding the person who did this, and even better, the missing. Remember, you're not forgotten." The strains of a new song build under his voice and he pauses to take a long, final drag of the cigarette. "As always and forever, wake up, Forsyth. Wake up, and smell that sweet decay..."

Once the song is playing, Hunter takes off the headphones and gestures for us to follow him to the outer room. Another DJ has just shown up, a female.

She coughs and waves her hand around. "I see you're still smoking."

"I see you're still a ray of sunshine," Hunter says, then makes quick introductions. "Everly, this is DK and Arianette."

She takes Damon in first, soaking in the dirty boots and wet jacket. The drop of ice cream on his jacket. "The other Baron and," her eyes flick to mine, "the Baroness."

"We got ice cream," I blurt, immediately feeling dumb. She's poised and polished, the kind of girl any guy would want to be with. The kind without piles of trauma, and a mouth that speaks too much, and a husband-to-be that hates her. She looks smart too, and not like she just spent the day crawling around the mud chasing ghosts.

I'm not sure she notices because she's already turned back to Hunter. "That show was different from your usual moody intro- spectives."

He shrugs. "Just using my platform to spread awareness and offer discourse on an important subject."

Her eyebrow arches. "By encouraging people *not* to go to the police."

"Fuck the police," Damon mutters, face twisting up. "They've had time and have done jack shit with it."

I have a feeling she would love to argue a little bit more, but the song is winding down and her shift is starting. She steps inside without another word and shuts the door behind her, sealing us out.

"Any leads worth following?" Damon asks as he sinks into a chair, legs sprawled like he owns the place.

I perch on the arm next to him, still trying to ground myself.

"There was that one call about bones in the woods. That felt," he searches for the word, "real."

Damon leans back, rubbing a hand over his face. "We'll check it. First thing tomorrow."

"It's already tomorrow," Hunter grins, "you know that, right?"

Ares curls at his feet like a guardian. I stay still. Quiet. My skin still tingles from the woods, from the ice cream, from the warmth of Damon's body in the car. I feel haunted. Hungry.

Hunter loops his bag over his shoulder, nodding toward us. "What about you two? Make any progress out at the river?" His eyes roam up and down my body, at Damon's hoodie, at what I'm sure is disheveled, messy hair. "Other than falling in?"

I go still. Waiting. Bracing. Ready for Damon to tell him everything–how I cried in the woods, how I begged him without words and he made me forget everything with the tip of an arrow. Why my lips still ache. I know what I must look like.

Damon's eyes flick to mine, unreadable. He shrugs. "Nothing we didn't already know."

That's all.

Just that.

And somehow, that answer makes my chest hurt more than the truth ever could.

27

H unter

I'M WALKING out of statistics, sun glaring hard off the concrete, when I see her again.

Sofia Martinez.

She's a graduate student and TA for my electrical engineering class. Smart, and serious in an 'I'm busy and important' way. She's tough with grading and a stickler for not wasting her time in tutorial. I've never spoken to her outside of class, but the past few days I've caught her looking at me more than once.

This time she doesn't look away.

"Hey," she says, falling into step beside me. "You're Hunter Sorrin, right?"

Before my initiation, I roamed the campus incognito, no one realizing the guy next to them in class was on the radio at night. But after becoming a Baron, that gift of anonymity is no more. "I am." I frown. "Is there something wrong with my project?"

"No." She tightens her grip on the tablet tucked to her chest. "This isn't about stats." She tucks a piece of dark hair behind her ear and glances over her shoulder. "Can we talk somewhere quiet?"

"Sure. Lead the way."

She takes me around the back of the building, where there's a cement bench half-eaten by ivy and the hum of generators in the walls.

She taps the edge of her tablet. "You host the radio show on WXFU."

So this really isn't about statistics. "Yep."

"I listen sometimes, when I'm working in the lab. There are times coffee isn't enough."

"I hope it helps."

She laughs, showing her white, straight teeth. "Well, your taste in music is shit, but there are other things I find interesting." Again, she looks nervous. "You know, some of the chatter in between."

I talk a lot during my show–probably more there than I do at any other time of the day. I bullshit and bluster, gossip and report, but I have a feeling she's talking about something else. Something more recent. "You mean the part where I call out the fact that girls keep disappearing and nobody seems to give a damn?"

She nods, but those shoulders don't loosen. "Do you believe in patterns?"

I angle toward her. "I'm an engineering major. Of course."

She swallows. "Three weeks ago, someone followed me home from a bar."

I go still.

"Some guy I didn't know bought me a drink. I didn't touch it. Something felt off. I went outside to call a rideshare. He came out five minutes later. No jacket. No phone. Just followed me down the street like he was out for a walk."

"Did you get a good look at him?"

She shakes her head. "Baseball cap. Average face. Could have been any frat boy on campus."

"What happened next?"

"I found two girls waiting on a car and asked them if I could join in. No one asked why." A shiver runs up her spine. "Everyone on campus is taking extra precautions right now. So yeah, I got home safe, but after that I started getting DMs."

She pulls out her phone and shows me.

Anonymous accounts. Blank profile pictures. Messages like:

"You looked beautiful in blue."

"I like how your hair smells."

"Working late again tonight, Sofia?"

I clench my jaw. "You report this?"

She scoffs. "Campus security said to walk with a friend and change my password. Cops told me unless he touched me, their hands were tied."

"Fuck." I rub my temples. "That's scary. I get it. But I'm not sure it's enough to make the connection. We haven't heard of any evidence of repeated stalking or harassment."

Her jaw tightens. "So you don't believe me. You think I'm lying? Looking for attention or something?" She rises. "I knew this was a bad idea."

"Shit," I say quickly, grabbing her forearm and dragging her back down. "I believe you have some creepy fucker watching you and sending you messages. It's not that."

"Then what?" she asks, glaring. Hurt.

"You asked about patterns. I'm not sure that's a pattern. If anything, it feels really different. Like maybe you've really got a stalker following you around. Someone interested in you, specifically."

"But there is a pattern," she argues, looking both stressed and annoyed. "The women going missing, they all have ties to the Royals, right?"

"Yes, so far that seems to be a pretty consistent connection."

She tugs at the sleeve of her sweater. "There's something most people don't know about me."

I watch as she rolls the edge of her sleeve up, revealing a tattoo.

It's black and green, an image of a coiled snake, posed ready to strike. The letters for KNT, underneath.

"The Counts," I state, staring at the tattoo. The location and precision. It may as well be a brand. "A former Countess?"

She shakes her head. "My half-brother was a Count. An important one."

"I assume he's dead?" Like almost everyone else in North Side.

"He's dead," she affirms. "But not from the explosion and I do my best to keep my relationship with him a secret. No one needs to know, and until all of this, I didn't think anyone did know. It's not good for my aspirations of becoming a professor. And we're half-siblings. Different fathers. Different lives that only intertwined when we both landed here."

"Then why the snake tattoo?"

"His idea." The dark way she laughs makes me think it wasn't just his idea but forced. "To 'keep me safe.'"

"Any particular reason why?"

She shrugs. "He had a lot of enemies, and in Forsyth it isn't uncommon to go after family."

That's a little hard for me to understand as an only child. Sure, I call DK and the other Shadows my brothers now, but even after the oath and bloodletting it's still ceremonial. Having that bond with someone is unfamiliar.

"So what you're telling me is that your connection to a Royal is probably what made you a target."

She nods.

"Fuck." I sink back and thrust my hands in my hair. "Okay, I see what you mean, but I will point out that the texts are different."

Unless maybe they aren't? Has anyone checked phone records? Deleted messages?

"I know. And I'm willing to admit this could be something else. But you put the call out for *any* information." There's a beat of silence. "I don't know why I came to you, but the way you talk on the radio–like you're not afraid to piss people off. I figured you might actually believe me."

"Thanks for trusting me," I say, even though it feels weird. It's not like I'm a good guy here. If anything, the King is looking to protect the Barons' reputation and shut down whoever is fucking things up. She's not exactly full nobility, which is exactly why I add, "I'm going to need to know."

"Don't." Her voice is soft–small compared to the voice of the brillant woman I've seen instruct an entire class. The softness betrays the truth: she's terrified. "Don't make me say it."

"Sofia, who exactly is your half-brother?"

The conflict that flits over her face ranges from fear to anger to what I think is a touch of humiliation. She sucks in a breath and says, "Perez. Bruno Perez."

THE DINER on Sixteenth isn't technically located in neutral territory. The shiny aluminum building is situated on the edge of West End, but it's only a half a block to the East End line. The greasy fried foods, hot coffee, and homemade pie make us willing to enter enemy territory, but the intimidating presence of the owner, Clarence, makes it a safe place to eat as well as a location for off-the-record discussions.

DK and I push through the door just as the bell overhead lets out a tired jingle and note the sign over the counter: *No Weapons. No Smoke. No Drama. Just Eggs.*

Sy's in the back booth, taking up more than his share of space. He's massive–thick-shouldered, blue-eyed, and built like the kind of guy who's more weapon than man. Lavinia's curled beside him, all blue hair and a mesh top that does nothing to hide the pink bra underneath.

There's a mountain of pancakes in front of Sy. Lavinia's plate isn't far behind. It's filled with bacon, eggs, and hash browns covered in what looks like every leftover in the kitchen.

I slide into the booth across from them. DK sits beside me, eyes sharp, scanning everything like he always does before we get down to business.

"Nice scratch," DK says, tipping his chin at Sy's face.

Sy wipes a hand across the small cut on his cheek. "Damn cat. I keep saying we should declaw him."

"Absolutely not," the Duchess says. "That's inhumane."

"Seriously," DK says, sounding truly offended.

I raise my brows at the King. "You got a cat?"

"She has a cat," Sy's thumb jerks at his Duchess, but his tone softens just a notch.

"I've got a dog," I offer. My mother always said to offer something about yourself if you want to get something in return. With that settled, I lean forward. "We've got a problem."

Lavinia's fork pauses halfway to her mouth. Sy keeps chewing.

"It's a North Side thing," I continue, "which is why we asked the Duchess to be here."

DK picks up a menu and scans it. "You left a lot of people behind when you decided to blow daddy dearest off the map."

Sy grunts like he's already over it. "Not our problem."

Lavinia wipes her fingers on a napkin. "There was collateral damage. I feel terrible about it, but the alternative would have taken out a lot more people."

"This one is probably adjacent to collateral," I tell her. "Sofia Martinez."

"Who?" Sy asks, forehead creased. "Never heard of her."

"Hold up," DK says, waving over the waitress. She walks up, smacking gum between her overly red lips.

"You boys ready to order?" Her oval name tag says, 'Gert.'

"I'll take the breakfast plate. Scrambled, no toast, extra pancakes," he peruses the back, "and a juice."

He offers me the menu, but I wave it off. "I'll have the same, but make my eggs over easy."

"How about you, hon? Need another coffee?"

Sy gives her a tight smile. "Please."

"Be back quick as a jiff," Gert says, heading off.

"Who the fuck is Sofia Martinez and why should we care?" Sy asks, clearly growing impatient.

"She's Bruno Perez's half-sister."

That gets Lavinia's attention. She sets her fork down and brushes a lock of blue behind her ear.

"She kept it quiet. She *is* quiet, and she's trying to stay that way. But someone's following her. Sending her messages. DMs. She got marked and now she's being hunted."

Sy shrugs. "Still not our problem."

"I thought you wanted to find who was picking off girls in Forsyth?" DK snaps. "Girls with connections to Royalty. Does it not matter if she's related to someone you hate?"

I glance at Lavinia. Her lips are pressed tight, but there's something in her expression that wasn't there before. It seethes under the surface.

"Let me tell you one thing," she starts, "if I didn't know for a fact that Bruno Perez was dead, as in, I didn't see his decapitated head at my feet, he'd be my number one suspect. He was a pig with zero respect toward women, or anyone else, unless it got him ahead. His frat, his family, no matter how distant, is not our problem."

"We're new to all of this," I admit. "I asked around with the guys in Beta Rho, it's well known that Perez had beef with everyone in Forsyth. He'd kidnapped the Lady at one point and word has it Nick Bruin killed him for simply looking at you."

Lavinia blinks, but Sy simply pushes his clean plate in front of him and props those massive arms on the table. "What's your point?"

"Story Austin had her Lords to save her from Perez when she needed it. If Bruin hadn't gotten to him, I suspect one of your other Dukes would have." My gaze flicks from the King to Lavinia. "Not only does Sofia Martinez have no one looking out for her, she may be a way for us to catch whoever is doing this."

She doesn't say anything for a moment. Then, "Where is she now?"

"I can take you to her."

"We'll see what we can do," Lavinia says softly.

Sy's jaw tightens. "We're not babysitters."

"No," she says, glancing at Sy. "But I'm not losing another North Side sister if I can help it."

The look they share is a full conversation, complex, and frankly something I don't think I'll ever experience with another person myself. Gert chooses that moment to return, placing plates in front of me and DK and pouring a fresh cup of coffee for Sy.

The moment she walks off, he sighs, pushing his hand into his curly dark hair.

"Fine," he relents, "but I want something in return."

"Sure," DK says, cutting into his pancakes. "Name it."

An uneasy feeling stirs in my gut at the casual way he sips his coffee before stating, "The Baroness."

"What the fuck?" DK growls. "Are you insane?"

"He doesn't *want*, want her," Lavinia cuts in, shaking her head. "Jesus."

"Then what?" I ask, feeling the rage vibrate off of DK.

"I want to talk to her about what she went through."

"Good luck," I tell him. "She doesn't remember much."

DK snorts. "And what she does remember sounds like it's been scrambled with these eggs."

"Yeah, well that's where I come in," he continues. "I can talk to her, or I can do something that may be even more effective, if I have your approval."

"If you think you can figure out what's going on in that crazy little head, be my guest."

Sy doesn't look at me. Doesn't look at anyone, really. Just stares down into his coffee.

"I want to try hypnotism," he says, quiet but sharp enough to slice through the air.

The table goes dead still.

DK stops chewing. I just blink at him.

"Hypnotism?" I repeat, like maybe I misheard.

Sy lifts his eyes, steady, unreadable. "I've been studying it in my graduate program. It's not like the crazy mumbo-jumbo you think. It's just about getting a person to a relaxed, safe state where they're able

to process things easier. If there's something buried in her head–
something she saw, something she *knows*–we need it. I can get it."

DK shoves his chair back, the legs screeching against the tile.
"You're not screwing with her brain."

"I wouldn't hurt her," Sy says, voice firm. "But if you want to catch
whoever took her, then we need answers. Fast."

My pulse kicks. DK told me what happened when he took her to
the riverbank. Arianette's mind is as fragile as an antique clock. One
wrong twist and the whole thing malfunctions. And now this guy
wants to open her up and poke around?

DK looks like he wants to throw his plate at the wall, but he
doesn't. He just breathes hard through his nose and mutters something that sounds a lot like *fuck all of this.*

"The King will say no," he says definitively.

Sy shrugs. "Then we don't tell him."

An airless beat covers the table.

"For what it's worth," Lavinia says slowly, "I think it's a good idea,
but," she rests her hand on Sy's, "I think we should wait until after the
wedding."

"A few more days won't hurt." Sy picks up his cup again and
drinks, like we just agreed on the weather and not treason for me and
DK and a potential war for him and his Dukes.

And me? I sit there, watching him over the rim of my cup, trying
to ignore the voice in my head that says this is a very, *very* bad idea.

28

T imothy

THE HOUSE OF NIGHT feels colder than usual, though the heat roars and the candles have all been lit. Every shadow stretches long and dramatic, flickering over the hand-painted mural on the wall, bringing it to life. We sit around the long, ebony dining table–five bodies that seem to be sitting vigil, rather than celebrating impending nuptials.

This dinner is a traditional meal between families to celebrate tomorrow's ceremony. If I could have come up with a viable excuse, I would have. Graves shot that down immediately.

Arianette is seated to my right. She hasn't spoken since she took her seat, not even to greet her uncle. Graves informed me she'd spent the afternoon holed up in her room, with a team of stylists preparing for tonight–*for tomorrow*–and the results are stunning. It's not a girl sitting next to me, but a woman. Her eyes are painted with a smoky shadow, gold glitter shimmers with every flutter of her eyelashes. Her hair is pulled back in tight braids, the rows precise as they gather into a cluster at the back of her head, before cascading in a soft ponytail.

Her dress is exquisite, the bodice a deep, rich purple satin. It's structured like a corset, with satin buttons running down the front. The top edge is trimmed with delicate ruffles, adding a touch of femininity to the otherwise severe design.

The skirt is a voluminous cascade of layered black tulle. It's full and dramatic, evoking a sense of dark elegance. A gothic ballerina. The candlelight bounces off the warm mahogany sheen of her exposed shoulders, and any sense of rebellion that I've seen in her has vanished. In place is a delicate yet deliberate posture. The change is dramatic. Curious. Who is she dressed for? Behaving for?

Even with our unsettling interactions, I suspect it's not me.

Hunter sits across from her, trying not to stare. DK beside him, tight-jawed, arms crossed, his fork untouched. Dean Hexley holds court at the head of the table like a man who's just signed a million-dollar deal.

A plate of venison is set before me, garnished with blood orange reduction and some pretentious sprig. I chew methodically, aware of how quiet the room has gone. Only the scrape of silverware, the crackle of fire, the dull drip of wine from Hunter's glass.

"So," the Dean says at last, dabbing his mouth with a cloth napkin, "tomorrow is a momentous day."

No one replies.

He continues, "When the Hexleys and the Barons finally merge into one."

Arianette keeps her gaze down. DK watches her, not me.

I nod once. "A necessary alliance."

The Dean chuckles, low and wolfish. "Don't sound so thrilled."

"I'm overjoyed," I lie. "I've waited a long time for this to happen."

Hunter coughs into his wine. For all his social awkwardness, the young man seems very aware of the mood and tone in this room. The Dean ignores him, as he seems to do with anything that doesn't suit him.

"Arianette's entire childhood and adolescence have been in anticipation of this moment." The Dean smiles wider, but continues, like he's auctioning a lamb at the market. "Raised in seclusion. Prepared for society. Taught discipline. The Baroness title won't be wasted on her."

"You know she's in the room," DK smirks. "She can hear you."

The Dean says, raising a brow, "Her silence is a virtue. Isn't that right, my dear?"

Arianette nods slowly. Her hands are folded in her lap like she's praying. There's only one god in this room, and unfortunately, I'm not here to save her.

Hexley gestures to Graves, who has been standing attentively in the corner. I'm annoyed at the command, Graves isn't a fucking lackey. I open my mouth, but Graves clears his throat as he steps forward, presenting a long velvet box and a smaller one, both placed delicately on the table in front of me.

"A wedding gift," the Dean says, eyes brightening.

"You shouldn't have," I say, prepared for a cheap bauble or a tacky commemoration of the impending nuptials. The moment I lift the lid, I realize I've misjudged him.

I open the smaller box first. Inside, a collar. It's made of a blood-red leather with brushed brass details, worn but well-kept. An old inscription in Latin is carved into the buckle: *Obedientia ante omnia*. Obedience before all.

"It belonged to her grandmother," Dean says softly. "Wore it every day of her marriage. The Hexley women wear it until they earn the privilege not to."

Hunter and DK share an unreadable look.

Arianette, to her credit, doesn't move.

I shut the box slowly. "And the other?"

He gestures for me to open it.

Inside the longer velvet case lies something strange, beautiful and awful. A ceremonial rod–black polished wood, thin and light, with carved designs spiraling down to a velvet-wrapped handle. At first, I think it's ornamental, but one glance at Arianette and the tension in her jaw tells me otherwise.

"The Switch of Silence," the Dean says reverently. "Passed down through the Hexley women for generations for use at the Manor. Not a tool of cruelty, but of correction." He leans forward slightly. "She knows what it means."

DK fidgets with the piercing in his eyebrow, a tell for his growing impatience. He doesn't like another man speaking so intimately about the Baroness. Good. He's learning.

"You'll find you won't have to raise your voice, or your hand," he continues. "Just hang it where she can see it."

That patience snaps, and DK jumps to his feet.

I hold up my hand. "Sit down."

His jaw clenches, but he obeys.

Hunter, on the other hand, doesn't take his eyes off the rod until I replace the lid.

The Dean smiles again, wider now. "She's still a Hexley. No matter whose house she sleeps in, isn't that right, sweetheart?"

Arianette finally speaks. Two words, soft as dust. "Yes, Uncle."

I meet her eyes. They're wide, brown, and brimming with something I can't place. Pushing the boxes aside, I say, "A thoughtful gift in honor of the union."

The Dean lifts his wine. "To Forsyth."

"Memento Mori," I reply, only meeting his eyes.

The glasses clink, and the room is thick with wax, secrets, and the weight of what it takes to protect my people.

THE LAST OF the plates have been cleared and the decanter of wine is empty. Arianette is silent beside me, her hands folded tightly in her lap, knuckles pale against the swell of her dark skirts. She's desperate to leave the table, we all are, but the night isn't over.

Across from me, Dean Hexley lifts his napkin, dabs at the corner of his mouth, and folds it back onto the table with all the slow precision of a guillotine blade being readied.

His eyes shift to me. Cold. Businesslike. "When I agreed to let

Arianette move in before the wedding and fulfill the role of Baroness," he says, "I was told her virtue would remain intact."

Hunter and DK have spent most of the meal quiet, only speaking when forced into the conversation. They're both uncomfortable with this formality, but they have the smarts to just keep their mouths busy eating, and their thoughts to themselves.

The mark of a good Shadow.

But I don't miss the way DK's chair creaks as he shifts. Guilt? A little, but I don't believe he's crossed my established boundaries. I asked them to break her in. To prepare her for what's to come. I need her compliant–at the very least aware of what's coming.

"We adhered to the traditions," I assure him.

Hexley leans forward slightly. "I require proof, as you know, that your men have kept their word."

"I can assure you that she's pristine," I say, already regretting this entire performance. But this isn't a negotiation. It's theater. Ritual. Something archaic and vile.

Hexley doesn't blink. "I'd still like proof."

Arianette turns to me, brow furrowed. "What are you talking about?"

She hasn't been told. Of course she hasn't. There's no good way to prepare a girl for this part.

"Hunter. Damon," I say quietly. "You're dismissed."

DK looks like he's about to lunge over the table. "You're not seriously–"

"Out."

Hunter touches his sleeve, grounding him. DK glares, then shoves back from the table.

His chair screeches against the stone, but thankfully, they leave without another word.

Arianette watches them go, confusion bleeding into unease. She knows something's wrong. That instinct she has, sharp, animalistic, raw–it's starting to stir.

I rise from my seat. Graves is already there, silent and waiting by the arched doorway to the adjacent den. Hexley stands, motions to her. "Come now, girl."

She hesitates, looking to me again.

"It's alright," I lie. "Just follow us."

The den is dim, old, lined with wood panels and shelves of untouched books. A faint fire burns in the grate. There's a chaise lounge in the center, dark leather and velvet, like something stolen from a Victorian parlor.

"Remove your bottoms," Hexley instructs. "Then lay down."

Arianette stiffens. "What?"

"Don't make this harder than it has to be," he sighs. "It's not a request."

She looks at me, panicking now. My jaw is clenched so tight I feel the bones creak. I don't appreciate another man–a non-Baron and even worse, non-Royal, acting as if he's the one with power.

Graves turns his back out of some misguided sense of decency. Hexley doesn't.

Her hands shake as she reaches behind her to unclasp the skirt. Layers of tulle and silk whisper down her legs. Her corset stays on, tight and unforgiving, but now the lower half of her is covered in silk panties. She's trembling.

"Those too," he says gruffly, gesturing to the panties. Slowly, she pushes them down, bending forward as she does. Her breasts spill from her top, both tantalizing and obscene. Once she's bare, he points to the chaise. "Arrange yourself."

She lies back slowly, covering herself with one hand until Hexley barks, "Move it."

I step forward, placing a hand on his meaty forearm.

"Enough," I say, voice low but sharp. "If anyone checks her, it'll be me."

"And why should I allow that? You could be covering for your men."

"Because she's your niece," I snap. "And although the Royals are lax on many things, I'd think you'd like a little decorum."

Hexley pauses. His expression is unreadable for a beat. Then, he gives a grunt and steps back.

I kneel beside her. Her eyes are wet now, lashes spiked with tears she hasn't let fall. "I don't understand. Did I do something wrong?"

"It's customary," I explain. "It'll be quick. Just... breathe."

I watch her chest rise and fall with a quick inhalation. My fingers touch her thighs, smooth and supple with a vitality I haven't known in years. She flinches, her legs pressing together involuntarily.

"Spread them," I say, trying to make my voice softer than what this moment deserves.

She obeys, just barely. Her skin is so soft it makes me furious. A child. Not in age, no, but in experience. Groomed to be bred like livestock.

I use two fingers to push aside the soft hair thatched above her sex, noticing the slick pink just underneath. Without warning, I press two fingers inside.

She cries out, jerking under my hand. Her back arches. It's instinct, not desire. She trembles violently. God, she's tight. Not just inexperience, but untouched. Utterly. No one else has been here. There's no denying it.

"Pretty little thing, isn't she?"

The urge to beat Hexley to a pulp flashes through my mind, but I'm consumed by other wicked thoughts. My pulse hammers in my throat. Something hot and shameful stirs in my belly as I think about how hard she'll fight the invasion when it comes. How she'll clench, wrapping that sweet pussy around my–*fuck.*

I shove it down. Pulling away roughly, cool air meets the slick heat still coating my fingers. I leave her there, breathing hard. I nod to Graves and he quickly steps in, handing her the panties and skirt.

Her lip trembles but she won't meet my eye.

"She's a virgin," I say, rising to my feet. "Satisfied?"

Hexley exhales like he's just completed a trade deal. "Good. Then everything proceeds as planned."

Behind me, Graves helps her sit up. "Get her dressed," I tell Graves.

He nods, moving quietly to her side.

Hexley claps a hand on my shoulder as he turns to leave. "She's your responsibility now, King. Don't let her forget who gave her to you."

I doubt she will.

And neither will I.

"It's time."

I'm starting to think this day will never end.

Graves stands in the doorway of my bathroom, holding a clean, black linen shirt. I'd just stepped out of the shower–a futile attempt to remove the stench of the evening spent with the Dean. With a towel wrapped around my hips, I wipe the steam off the bathroom mirror, revealing my face, and scrape the blade of the razor along my jaw.

"We could skip this, you know," I suggest. "No one would ever be the wiser."

"You would know." The sympathy on my oldest friend's face tries to be kind, but I see the truth: pity. "It's tonight. Everything is prepared."

Ignoring him, I dip the razor into the water, rinsing off the blade.

Unfortunately, Graves still wants to talk. "The dinner was…"

"Exhausting? Disturbing? A prequel to a five person murder-suicide?" By the time dinner was over, I was one second from wrapping my hands around the other man's throat and putting us all out of our misery. In my life I've never met such a pretentious, tone-deaf buffoon. And I knew Rufus Ashby. But our deal isn't complete until after the wedding, so I need him alive. For now at least. And there has been a purpose to this arrangement all along, that's the one thing keeping me going.

I almost gave it up after watching him hover over his niece's exposed body, his meaty fingers preparing to touch her. Whatever happened at the Manor is their business, but once the girl took the oath and survived the hunt, she didn't just become the Baroness, she became *mine*.

With or without a wedding.

"Adeline says everything is ready for tomorrow," Graves' voice interrupts my thoughts, in a clear attempt to change the topic. "The flowers are ordered and the sacraments ironed. She'll pick up Arianette's dress in the morning, which, by the way, I'm told is exquisite."

A flash of black tulle bunched on the floor, along with the feel of soft pink lips buried under the dark nest of curls, slams into me. The blade flinches, nicking my throat.

"Dammit," I mutter, splashing water on the cut and making it sting.

"Careful."

"For the record, Adeline thinks everything she touches is exquisite." I roll my eyes at him in the mirror. "That includes you. Did she try to get in your pants again?"

"No," he makes a face. "She seems to have finally accepted that she's not my type."

"It is your fault, you know." I laugh, thinking how a tryst twenty years ago, during a historic hurricane, is still the cause of poor Adeline's heartbreak. "You fucked her."

"Timothy!" Graves hisses, looking over his shoulder as if someone could hear me. "That was a mistake during a night of a million, even more unforgivable, mistakes."

Yes, what happened to Liberty Sinclaire that night is a black mark even for the Royals. Although, ironically, the result of such treachery resulted in Ashby's eventual downfall. Delicious revenge, the kind usually reserved for macabre fairy tales, but I learned a long time ago that anything is possible in Forsyth.

Finished shaving, I wipe my face and chest with a towel, soaking up any excess water. The cut is small, a thin line, and it seems to have stopped bleeding. I take the shirt from Graves' outstretched hand and pull it on over my head, then drop the towel and slip on the matching pants, knowing they won't stay on long.

Running my hand through my hair, I meet Graves at the bookcase. "It's going to be okay."

Here we go.

"I never said it wouldn't be."

"I like her," he admits. "She's quirky and strong-willed. Eccentric, yes. But she wants to do this."

This. What a resounding vote for marriage.

"She's a child," I remind him, reaching for the book, *The Hexalogion: A Study of Forbidden Rites,* giving the spine a sharp tug. "Who has no fucking clue what 'this' entails."

The tight sensation of her pussy told that story alone. I probably should have had either DK or Hunter pop that, and then lie to her Uncle. Whatever, and however, they prepared her, it's not going to be enough.

The hidden door springs open, revealing a staircase that leads to the underground.

"Regardless, the wedding takes place tomorrow, and this is part of the process." His smile is sad. "It doesn't have to be terrible, you know."

So says a man without the blood of his family on his hands, or come tomorrow, a virgin's blood on his dick.

"Goodnight, Graves. I'll see you on the other side."

My friend closes the door, and I start down the narrow stairwell alone, aware that with each step I'm moving that much closer to reality–to my future. Even before I've descended fully into the ritual chamber beneath the House of Night, my skin prickles with a heat that makes the shower pointless. I'm sweating, nauseated by the cloying scent of incense filling the air–crushed dahlias.

It's claustrophobic, intentionally.

Each step is part of the ritual. Each breath, a letting go. Above, the House of Night slumbers behind its fortress walls. But here, beneath the surface, something stirs.

The chamber has been prepared: low-lit by red and violet candles, the scent of melted wax thick in the air. Shadows dance across the carved symbols on the walls–old language, older meaning.

The altar is obsidian, oval with smooth edges. Around it: five women, kneeling in a half-circle like offerings. Faces painted, bodies slick with oil.

My stomach turns at the sight. Not from disgust, although I've done my best throughout the years to maintain my vows to my wife. No, from the familiar weight of bitterness crawling up my throat. Like so many things about being the King to these people, this isn't about want. It's about tradition. About loyalty to a set of rules older than logic and far crueler.

Lore says that before the Black Wedding, the King must be cleansed of his past. That his sins must be scattered among the veiled, his soul stripped bare, scrubbed down with oil and lust and ancient ceremony.

So here I am.

Participating. Pretending.

Wishing I could drown myself in booze and drugs until none of it matters.

The altar waits. Cold stone like a funeral slab. I glance at the circle of women, each chosen, each disguised, each representing what I'm meant to leave behind.

Lust. Betrayal. Grief. Power. Silence.

Named for the sins I've committed, the pieces of myself I want to leave in the past.

Amber would've laughed at this.

No, she would've watched from the shadows. Lips pursed. That dangerous, quiet sort of disdain in her eyes. I'd always seen the fire in her–the difference. I felt it in her body when we made love. In her words when we fought. I didn't know about her demons, not really. I loved her, and I thought that love was enough.

She gave me Remy. And then... well, then she lost her mind.

"Cleanse me," I whisper, not as a plea, but an invocation.

Lust rises, and she rids me of my clothes, pulling off the shirt and pants. With hands, with tongue, with heat and submission. My sins rise like steam off skin when she strokes me, working my cock into a hard weapon. The ritual demands I break apart and with their help come back together again. Ironic. Breaking is what I do best when it comes to women, to family.

I'm weak to her touch, thrusting hard into her hand. Crumbling in the same way I broke the vow to my first wife. I close my eyes and see Amber's back instead–her walking out the door, Remy screaming behind her.

Grief joins in, touching my spine, warm and deliberate. Her tits are firm against my back, her hips a cradle. I don't turn to face her. She whispers a name against my neck–my name, only different. *Timothy*, the way Amber used to say it when she was drunk or angry or wet. "*Let go.*"

I jerk away like her voice burns me.

The third–*Betrayal*–slides between my knees and licks the salt from my skin like she's a penance. I don't stop her. I don't move, feeling the warmth of her mouth engulf me, shuddering between her red, soft lips. Rage simmers under my ribs. Not at her. *At all of it.* At how this isn't sex. It's theater. It's legacy. It's me selling myself piece by piece just to keep the Barons' name in blood and bone.

She brings me to the edge, they all do, drawing out something in me I'd long kept buried. But *Betrayal* isn't the one to tip me over, that belongs to her.

Power.

She sits on the edge of the altar and spreads her legs wide. She looks straight at me. Daring. Unafraid.

She is not Amber.

She is not Arianette either.

She is every choice I made that led me here.

And when I take her–lining my cock up to her wet, slippery entrance, it's hard and brutal, without ceremony, her nails clawing at my back. It isn't about dominance.

It's about *defeat.*

The last, *Silence*, stands. She doesn't touch me. Doesn't speak. Just kneels beside me when it's over, when I'm sweating and stained and hollowed out. Her fingers find mine and interlace.

"Are you clean now?" she whispers.

I almost laugh. But there's nothing funny in my chest.

"No," I breathe. "But I'm ready."

Because it doesn't matter how I feel.

Tomorrow I marry a girl whose eyes are too wide, whose skin is too warm and soft, whose spirit is lost in a web of trauma. She should belong to my son. She deserves better than this ritual. Better than me.

But she'll get a king.

And kings do what's necessary.

Even if it threatens to tear my soul apart.

29

rianette

I HAVEN'T MOVED since the door clicked shut, the King and my uncle leaving me here. I don't let myself take a full breath, because I'm unsure if they'll come back and if they do, what they'll want.

I only need enough air to feel something move in my lungs besides shame.

I'm still in the den, smoothing the mesh tulle skirt of my dress with trembling fingers. My knees are pressed tightly together, aching from the awkward bend on the chaise. The sharp scent of my uncle's cologne lingers in the room. I can still feel their eyes. His hands. I blink hard and try to find my place.

"You're in a field, right? Sun beating down. Warm breeze. Flowers everywhere."

It doesn't work. Not in this claustrophobic room. Not with his cologne in my nostrils. It's not appropriate anymore. I can't keep running away. Physically or mentally. I'm the Baroness now, after all.

Tomorrow I'll be his wife.

The fireplace crackles, casting shadows across the room. My skin feels hot. Or maybe that's just the humiliation. I thought that when I left the Manor, I'd be out of his reach, but tonight proved otherwise. I'll never be free of that man. Not even a king can protect me, especially one that looks at me with such contempt.

I hear the creak of the door.

Startled, I turn, catching Damon as he steps inside. He's still dressed in black, dinner jacket undone, tie removed, with his sleeves rolled up his forearm showing the tattoo on his wrist. His eyes flick to mine, then down to my disheveled dress, then back up again.

Somehow he knows.

"I saw your uncle leave." He stands in the doorway like he might change his mind and leave again, but he doesn't. Just looks at me with that strange, unreadable face of his. His lip is curled at the edge, the piercing glinting, like he's half-disgusted with something. I don't think it's me, not entirely. But maybe. "For what it's worth, Hunter was also leaving, on his way to the station. Ares chased the Dean's fat ass all the way to his car."

I laugh, but it feels hollow. Somehow, I'll get blamed.

"You just going to sit here the rest of the night?"

"I don't know." My voice is too soft, too weak. I clear my throat and try again. "They just left. No one told me where to go."

There's a pause. Then Damon exhales sharply through his nose and steps into the room. "Something happened. After we left."

My stomach twists.

He looks down at me, voice flat. "Did he touch you?"

My eyes flick to the fire. "Why would you care?"

"Don't start with me, doll baby."

"Don't call me that." It's too close to how I feel. Like a plaything for men to manipulate, arms and legs and...

He kneels in front of the chaise and stares at me, all sharp cheekbones and harsh judgment. "Answer me. Did he?"

I hold his gaze. My mouth opens but no words come out.

His jaw tightens. "Hunter said Graves stayed behind, too. So whatever it was, it was official."

I swallow hard. "They had to check," I whisper. "To make sure I was still…"

Damon's face twists. "You're kidding."

"No."

"So they don't trust us either," he says, because if anyone would have broken the rules it would have been him. He could have done it easily, so many times. During the hunt. At the party in the crypt. By the riverbank. "And he just stood there and let it happen?"

Damon doesn't give me time to answer, just standing abruptly and pacing to the far end of the room. He runs a hand through his dark hair. This bothers him, although I'm not sure why.

"He stopped the Dean," I say, softly. "The King… he stepped in."

"Yeah?" Damon snaps. "And did it himself, is that supposed to be better?"

I know he's thinking about trust. How the King put his faith in the Barons, but for me it's just another violation on top of all the others.

"I don't know," I admit. "I think it was. I think… it may have been worse." I look up at Damon. "That's not how he was supposed to touch me for the first time. It should have been on our wedding night. It should have been as man and wife, not some…"

"Perfunctory act." He assesses me, teeth tugging at that lip ring, like he's trying to make a decision. Finally he asks, "Do you want to get out of here for a bit?"

I blink. "What?"

He shrugs, trying to sound casual but failing. "An errand. Something small. You look like you need air. And I need a pair of hands."

I hesitate. "It's the night before the wedding."

"All the more reason, doll."

"Won't we get in trouble?" My heart flutters under my ribs, like wings in a cage.

He smirks. "Only if you're planning to run off and fuck me behind the courthouse."

I wince while my body rushes with heat. "Don't joke."

He sighs. "I'm not. But I am serious about the errand. You coming or not?"

I nod. "Okay. Let me change."

His eyes skim over the gown. "You look fine."

"I don't feel fine."

"Yeah, well I know one way to fix that," he says, and walks out.

OUTSIDE, the air is sharp and damp, fall rushing toward winter. We walk in silence past the gravel drive and down the side path of the estate. Damon has his hands in his pockets, head ducked, eyes scanning everything but me. I have no idea where we're going. I don't ask. It feels better not to know.

We reach the garage. Hunter took his truck, but the SUV is parked behind the side of the carriage house, tires still caked with mud from the trip to the river. He unlocks it with a grunt and opens the passenger side for me. The skirt of my dress is ridiculous, unwieldy.

"Jesus. Fucking. Christ," he mutters. "This thing is like fighting a fucking tiger."

His hands cinch around my waist and with a hard lift, he chucks me in.

"*Oof.*" I flail across the seat, struggling to keep myself upright. The corset top threatens to slip down, and I tug at it to keep it over my tits, while he continues his battle with the tulle, ultimately using both hands to shove it in and quickly slam the door.

I've composed myself by the time he gets in the driver's seat. He starts the engine, pulling away from the House of Night with a little more force than necessary. Something metal rattles in the back.

After a long silence, I ask, "Why did you ask me to come with you?"

He flips the turn signal and heads toward town. "I told you. I need an extra set of hands."

I turn my face to the window and watch the trees blur past while he flips on the radio to WXFU, but instead of Hunter's voice an annoying commercial sings a jingle about air conditioners.

"Did it hurt?" he asks suddenly.

I know what he's asking. I wish I didn't.

"Yes," I whisper. "It hurt."

He looks at me for a long moment until there's a flash in the corner of my eye. "Damon! Watch out!" He slams his foot on the brake and the SUV skids erratically. The white tail of a deer bobs into the trees.

"Sorry," he mutters, gripping the wheel. "I'm just–*fuck*."

My hands are flat on the dash, holding myself upright, my heart pounding against my chest. "It's done. It's over."

He snorts. "Until tomorrow night, yeah."

It takes me a second to understand what he's referring to, and that same humiliated burn ripples across my skin. I'm nothing but meat to these people. Flesh to be owned. I don't think for a minute Damon cares for me. He's just pissed he didn't get his piece first.

Hunter's smooth voice drifts out of the speakers.

"It's just past midnight, on October thirty-first, and if you're still with me, congratulations. You've made it to the edge of the veil... it's sacred here, maybe cursed."

Damon turns up the volume.

"Tomorrow, the city wakes up to a ceremony that isn't printed in your church bulletins or listed on campus calendars. A wedding, but not the kind with lace and doves. This one's soaked in bloodlines and old money, secrets whispered through oak-paneled rooms. The girl's barely grown. The man? We can only guess the man behind the Baron King's mask."

There's a long pause, one marked only by the flash of passing headlights.

"They're calling it the Black Wedding. I don't know if it's a merger or a sacrifice, but either way, Forsyth will change."

The mic catches the sound of a match catching fire, the long inhale of him smoking one of those hand-wrapped cigarettes.

"Stay tuned, Forsyth. The monsters are getting dressed for a wedding."

Damon snorts, leaning back in the driver's seat as Hunter's voice fades into some moody guitar riff. "Jesus. You'd think he was narrating the end of the world, not a goddamn wedding. Somebody get that boy a therapist and a hug."

I lean forward, my breath fogging the passenger window of the SUV. Hunter's right, the monsters will be out tomorrow night, dressed in silk and lace, in masks.

The Beast.

"That wasn't just a broadcast," I whisper. "That was a premonition."

Damon snorts. "He's not a prophet, Ari. He's just high on grief and late-night melodrama."

But I don't laugh with him. I can't.

"I already died once," I say, more to myself than to Damon. "Right on that riverbank. Maybe this isn't a wedding. What if it's my funeral?"

I glance at Damon, waiting for him to mock me again, to tell me I'm being foolish, but he just watches me out of the corner of his eye, jaw clenched. He turns down a dark road, the crunch of gravel replacing the pavement. It's pitch black other than his headlights. When we finally stop, I look into the dark.

"Where are we?"

He opens the door and I hear it, the sound of water lapping against a shore. Ahead, just outside the beam of light, I see a half-collapsed boathouse, its walls tagged with angry, spray-painted graffiti including a faded devil face with a pitchfork for a tail. The area around it is littered with trash and rusted cans. Damon cuts the engine, then reaches behind the seat to grab a dented metal box and a brown paper bag.

"What are we doing out here?" I ask, scrambling out of the car. Maybe it's all been a scam. A ruse to lull me into complacency, to trust the men that are my enemies. My pulse thrums, wondering if this is it. This is the night I'm sacrificed to the gods and demons of this hellmouth.

He slams the door shut with his hip. "Feeding cats."

I stare. "Excuse me?"

"You heard me." He starts walking toward the building. "We're feeding cats."

Sure enough, it smells like mildew and piss. Something floral, too, probably from the crushed body of some cheap air freshener tossed among the junk. Damon crouches near a broken pallet by the side of the warehouse and shakes the bag.

A high, ragged chorus of mews and rustling answers him.

"There's like six of 'em. Mostly kittens," he mutters. "Little monsters. I didn't mean to get involved, it just kind of... happened."

I stand a few feet back, arms crossed, watching as shadows slink from the corners with their small bodies and suspicious eyes. The cats emerge slowly: a few scrawny kittens, a male with a torn ear, and then, finally, the sleek, narrow shape of a black female who stops just out of reach, tail twitching.

Damon reaches into the brown bag and comes out with a handful of dried kibble. He tosses it down, but the black cat watches with suspicion, waiting until the others dive in before creeping closer.

He points to her. "That bitch. That's the one I want."

"She's beautiful," I murmur, looking at her shiny black fur. She's got a white patch on one foot.

"She's a menace." He opens the box, and I realize it's an animal trap. He hooks the mechanism, and drops a little kibble inside. "I've been trying to catch her for a week. The others'll let me handle them now. But her?" He shakes his head. "Smarter than me, apparently."

I kneel a few feet from him, still in my gown, now grimy at the hem with dirt and dust. I don't care, it was ruined the minute my uncle told me to take it off, when it just became another obstacle to his violation.

Out here, in the smelly boathouse, I'm breathing easier. Something about the cold and the stray cats and Damon's quiet fury calms the noise in my head.

"She reminds me of myself," I say.

Damon snorts. "Yeah? You think you're a sleek little alley cat with trust issues?"

"I think maybe I have nine lives."

He glances sideways. Doesn't smile. "Well. That makes two of us."

The comment makes me look at his throat. At the story he told me about how he got it. We sit in silence, waiting, the trap between. One kitten hobbles over, its paw crooked, and I gently extend a finger. It sniffs me, then bats my hand, bold and rude.

I laugh before I can stop myself. Damon raises an eyebrow.

"Oh, she laughs," he mutters. "Didn't think we'd get that out of you tonight."

I shrug. "I think my nervous system short-circuited two hours ago."

"That tracks."

The black cat edges closer to the trap. Damon freezes. His fingers tighten on the bag of food.

"C'mon, sweetheart. Just step inside," he murmurs. "Just a little farther..."

The cat sniffs the metal lip. Pauses. And then, with perfect contempt, she walks *around* the trap and grabs a piece of kibble from the side.

"*Fucking slut,*" Damon hisses.

I burst into laughter. I can't help it. It comes out sharp and high and unhinged, but it's real.

Damon watches me for a second, then shakes his head, grumbling. "You two deserve each other."

"I think she likes you," I tease.

"She's got a funny way of showing it."

My laughter fades, and the silence after feels too big. Too real. I look at him, this man I barely know–hardly trust–yet we're thrust together.

"Damon," I say quietly as the cat snags another piece of food.

He glances at me.

"Thank you. For bringing me."

He grunts. "Don't thank me. I didn't do it for you."

"You didn't have to do it at all."

He opens his mouth. Shuts it. Stands up and wipes his hands on his pants.

"You ready to go?"

I nod and push up to my feet, trying not to step on my dress. I know that once this night is over everything in my life changes. Probably for both of us.

"Do you ever wonder if people see us like that?" I ask, glancing back at the cats swarming the piles of food he left scattered about.

Damon frowns. "Like what?"

"Feral. Uncatchable. Just... surviving."

He stands in the bright light of the car beams and says, "No." His fingers reach out and trail down the curve of my cheek, not soft, not tender, just anchoring us together. "People like us? They don't look close enough to see anything other than what they can take..." His voice roughens. "They don't want the mess. They don't want the noise inside our heads. They want the shape of us, the story of us, broken things dressed up pretty, pliant, fuckable."

He drops his hand, turns his back to me. His shoulders rise and fall like he's trying not to say more. The problem is that Damon thinks he understands the darkness in Forsyth, but he has no idea what I know–*what* I've witnessed.

The pain I felt today? That's nothing compared to the pain I saw in the Manor.

The humiliation? That's just penance for the secrets I've kept buried for so long.

If I need to be pretty, pliant, and fuckable just to survive?

I've done what I've needed to before and there's no reason I can't do it again.

30

———

D^{amon}

SHE'S quiet the whole time we're walking back to the SUV, her dress rustling with every step, dragging in the dirt. The hem's a mess, but she doesn't seem to care. I'm sure she doesn't plan on keeping it anyway, not after everything that happened tonight.

The crazy thing is that the wilder she looks, the rattier that dress gets, the more I feel like I can see the real Baroness. The true Arianette Hexley. A woman made of bone and flesh, trauma and memory, who can charm a feral cat with her presence.

Tossing the empty trap in the back, I slam the door harder than necessary. She flinches.

Great.

I'm not used to bringing people out here. Hell, I'm not used to bringing people anywhere. I've been operating on my own for a long time. But I knew I needed out of that house, and I figured she did too.

I guess I felt like maybe showing her something alive and small and innocent might make her feel less alone. I don't know.

Christ. It's been a long day, and tomorrow is going to be worse.

I start the engine, the lights skimming over the river as I turn and shift us back onto the road. She sits with her hands in her lap, eyes glassy and distant. The kind of look I used to see on guys after bad phone calls in prison—when the outside world slipped through the cracks and reminded them they were still inside and not getting out any time soon.

The SUV rumbles over gravel, then pavement, then we start over the long, dark stretch of Forsyth backroads. She hasn't looked at me once.

"You're thinking too loud," I say finally.

She blinks. Turns toward me, like she forgot I was here. "Sorry."

"Didn't say it was a bad thing. Just loud."

Silence again, and then she shifts in her seat, pulling at the seatbelt and then the neckline of her dress like it's suffocating her. Her tits look incredible in that dress, all round and swollen, and I feel a sense of pride knowing my little barbells tweak against the fabric here and there.

"You good?" I ask, glancing at her as the headlights sweep through another empty bend in the road.

"I don't know," she whispers. "Everything's too tight."

Her voice breaks, a fray at the edges. I exhale through my nose and roll down the windows an inch. Cold air fills the cabin.

"Better?"

She nods, but it's not the cold she's fighting.

"I hate this dress," she blurts. "It's like... a costume. Like my body's not even mine in it."

"You want me to rip it off right now, doll baby? I can make a real scene for whoever drives past."

She gives a half laugh, but it dies fast. Her fingers twist, her nerves rising as we get closer to home.

"I've always felt like that," she says. "Like my body belonged to everyone but me. My nannies and teachers: they were the ones picking out my clothes and commenting on my posture. The dance instructors wanting more from my body than I could actually give." She swallows. "Everything with my uncle today felt both awful and familiar."

I grip the wheel tighter. My knuckles pop. It's the kind of thing you want to fix by breaking something. Or someone.

"I keep thinking, this wedding, this marriage..." Her breath shakes. "Is it just more of the same? Just another cage?"

I don't say anything. Not right away. Because what the fuck am I supposed to say to that? We *do* own her. Me and Hunter. The King. She belongs to us, those are the rules in this city, but I also understand, because I've been in that place where my body wasn't my own. The prison guards, the warden, they all had dibs. I understand the lack of autonomy and how it starts to chip away at who you really are.

The first stoplight we hit flashes yellow then red. I roll to a stop and look around, tense. We're too exposed here. The kind of place someone could see us, or worse, recognize the SUV.

She shifts uncomfortably beside me. I can feel her body wound tight.

"Fuck this," I mutter and roll through the red, checking the side streets. Nothing. No one. Just dark storefronts and flickering lights. We drive on.

I glance at her again, the way she's practically folding in on herself. Like she's shrinking. Like she wants to disappear.

And it hits me. Not just the weight of what she said, but what she *didn't* say. That she's still trying to hold it together. That her nervous system really *did* fry hours ago, and she's just floating now, barely tethered. We've been here once before, and there was one thing that brought her back to the ground.

"I mean..." I exhale and rake a hand through my hair. "You don't always have to be used, you know, you can do the using."

She blinks. "What?"

I don't look at her. I just keep driving. "Remember when we got ice cream?"

Her head turns slowly. "Yeah."

"I know what it's like. Feeling like you have no control. Like people take and take and take. But if you need to, if it helps–" My throat's dry. I cough once. "If it helps to suck my cock like you did on the way home from the river, you can."

She stares at me. Those brown eyes wide. Lips parted.

I smirk, but it's weak. A front. "I mean, I'm not gonna pretend it won't be hard for me, having that warm little mouth around me. I'm walking around with a loaded gun in my pants half the time you're near me. But this..." I shrug. "This wouldn't be about that. You wanna feel like you've got a choice, I'll give you one. No strings. No pressure. No demands. Just you taking what you need, like you did last time."

"No strings," she repeats. Even in the dark, I can see the embarrassment on her face, but in her voice I hear the interest.

"If that's what you need, I'm giving it to you."

The silence after is thick. Her breathing getting shallow, faster.

"You're serious."

"As a fucking heart attack."

And then she shifts. Slowly. Like she's testing gravity. Like she can't believe I'm real.

Her hand slips over the console. Rests lightly on my thigh.

"Okay," she says. "I want to."

I exhale, long and slow, adjusting my grip on the wheel as she leans over and unbuckles her belt. She's hesitant at first, still unsure, and I almost help her, but then her hand presses to my zipper. Her fingers tremble a little as she pulls it down, pulls me out. I'm hard, just talking about this got me thick, but I don't apologize. This is about her. She needs it, in a way that I don't really understand.

Her head lowers into my lap, and I keep my eyes on the long, dark road, with nothing but pines and shadows ahead. I adjust my seat back an inch, giving her room while keeping one hand on the wheel, and the other braced against the door, jaw clenched like a vise.

She touches me with careful hands, like she's holding something delicate, which makes it worse. I bite back a groan when her lips part and the warm, wet heat of her mouth surrounds me.

Fuck.

This is a bad idea.

I use every ounce of strength to keep my hips on the seat. She takes me in slowly, inch by inch, lip catching on the piercings I have threaded on the underside. Her eyes flutter closed like it soothes her, like *this* is the only thing in the world that makes sense. Her hands curl around the base, steadying herself. I can feel her breath in sync with mine. The hum of her contentment melts into the rhythm of tires on the blacktop.

I keep my eyes on the road, but it's getting harder to focus. My thighs tense. Every nerve in me lights up like a match. Still, I don't move. I don't thrust. I *don't take*. This isn't about that.

She's still, barely moving, holding me in her mouth, slick and warm. Her cheeks hollow as she suckles gently. I run my hand down her head, smoothing her hair in the same slow rhythm that she holds me between her lips.

"Good girl," I manage through clenched teeth. My voice is tight, rough. "Take what you need."

She hums at the praise, and the wheel jerks. I nearly slam into a telephone pole. I grip the wheel harder. Veins popping in my forearms. I breathe through my nose, steady and low, while her tongue flattens along the piercings, pulling a hiss from my throat.

I could come in seconds. But I don't.

I won't.

This is a test, I tell myself. I've edged her more than once, drawing her as close as possible before taking it away. She liked it, and fuck, I think I like this too–the closeness without chasing something bigger. The soothing feel of her warm mouth around me. It's calm and gentle. Her hand squeezes around the base, like she wants me closer.

We drive like that for miles–her body relaxing, the tension melting off of her, while I white-knuckle restraint. Although, after a while, I settle into the rhythm of it, the soothing nature. I'm less on a hair trigger and just enjoying the sensation.

She's so quiet, so still, that I think she may have fallen asleep. It's not until the trees thin and the lights of Forsyth appear on the horizon that she shifts, like she senses that we're back in the real world. She pulls back slowly, giving me one suckle of the tip. There's a tug on the final piercing that I feel deep in my spine. Finished, she rises up, lips slick, eyes glazed, tucking and zipping me back into my pants.

When I glance over again, she's got her hands folded in her lap, but they're no longer tense and twisting. No, she sits there in that ruined dress, lips a little puffy, like nothing happened.

I exhale, aware that my heart pounds like I ran a race. My cock aches, twitching behind wool. But I don't complain, knowing she looks calmer. More *here*. Her back is straighter, chin higher. Her lips are swollen, and she's breathing steady again.

We don't talk the rest of the way back. There's no need. She used me, and I let her, and somehow, that *fixed* something for her. Gave her control in a world that keeps taking it.

When I park outside the House of Night, it's quiet, no sign of what's going to happen in the next twenty-four hours. I hop out, walk around and help her out of the passenger seat. The light over the back door illuminates our way, and we enter the house together.

It's not until we're inside standing in front of her bedroom door that I turn to her, brush a stray curl from her cheek, and speak. "Feel better?"

Arms wrapped around her upper body, she nods. "Thank you for letting me do that."

"We're in this together," I tell her, "our fates sealed during the Hunt. There are going to be times we need to rely on one another."

She looks a little apprehensive, like I'm going to demand to come inside and get repaid for being nice. I'd meant what I said, no strings. Not tonight.

"Good luck tomorrow," I tell her, straightening up, even though the words feel strange in my mouth. Like I'm sending her off to war, or into something holy, which I guess I probably am.

She nods, clutching her arms a little tighter. I could offer to stay, I could force it, but that's not who we are tonight.

I brush a final glance over her, messy, that tattered dress hanging off her small frame.

Tomorrow she'll belong to the King.

But after that?

After that, the rules change.

I head back to my room with that thought burning low in my gut–like a promise I've waited too long to keep. Soon I'll claim Arianette. Not just with my needles and fingertips, but deeper and more lasting. I'll make her mine.

rianette

THE DOOR SHUTS and I wait a moment, listening as Damon walks down the hall toward the room he shares with Hunter. He didn't ask, or demand, to come in, which surprised me a little. I want to learn to trust him, especially after how he was tonight.

I know it's not really a sacrifice to have my mouth on him like that. But the act goes beyond the sexual. It's calming in a way I don't fully understand. The first time had been purely on impulse, but tonight... that had been intentional and it shifts things into new territory. I'm not sure why, but I understand that it does.

I shiver, noticing that the bedroom is cold, like someone opened a window and forgot to close it. But there's no breeze. Just still air and the light scent of flowers curling in through the curtains.

Ready for the night to be over, I strip off the wrinkled dress, the hem damp and dirty from walking near the boat ramp. It'd been interesting seeing that side of Forsyth–that side of Damon. No less crass and rough than the other parts of the city, or of the man, but less polished. We were on the quiet outskirts, where it felt a little more real. More authentic.

I'm too tired to shower, only taking the time to wash my hands and face. I avoid my reflection, turning to slip a cotton nightgown over my head, not wanting to look at the girl who is about to become a woman. *A wife.* I'm ready to put the past behind me, both the memories and the scars. I pull the silk bonnet over my head and flipping off the bathroom light. I'm halfway to the bed when I see it: a glass jar nestled against my pillowcase.

I pause, breath caught in my chest, and look around the room. It's quiet and still. Nothing else out of place. Stepping closer, I see that there's a ribbon the color of burnt orange wrapped around the lip, with a small rectangular tag attached. It's squat and sealed, like a canning jar used for jam. But inside, I see slips of paper. Folded carefully, each one identical, packed into the small space.

I don't move for a moment. My spine itches. I think of the gifts my uncle gave the King for our wedding, the rod and collar. Is this just another one of his humiliations, another attempt to pour salt in my wounds, to remind me of who I belong to? Did he sneak in here after Ares chased him to his car and leave me one last piece of him?

No. That doesn't feel right. Owen Hexley likes to see the discomfort on the face of his victims. He likes an audience, and this is too private, too intimate. There's no malice in the air.

I sit. The mattress gives under me and the jar rolls toward me. I pick it up and lift the tag. Scrawled in script it says: *The Chrysalis Notes.*

The words mean nothing to me, and I unscrew the lid. The scent hits me first, parchment and ink. I sniff the contents and catch the slightest hint of rose.

I take the first slip out and before I unfold it, look around again, making sure I'm truly alone.

The King protects what's his. So mark him. Claw his back. Leave lipstick on his cock. Let the others see you own him, too.

I blink. My lips part, surprised, but no sound comes out. It's written in cursive–swooping, fast, confident. A woman's hand. I read it again. It doesn't change.

I reach for another.

Don't be fooled by the silence afterward. That's not shame, it's worship. He's just realizing you unmade him and he liked it.

The words are uncomfortably intimate, like I'm reading someone's journal. That doesn't stop me from unfolding the next and devouring the words.

After a bad day, feed him something salty, sit on his face while he recovers, then stroke him until he feels whole again.

My cheeks heat at the overt boldness. The sexiness. Addicted now, I dip my fingers in and reach for another slip of paper, this one folded twice, bigger than the others.

He's going to be angry. Desperate. Challenged by forces outside of his control. It'll make him hard. Maybe even cruel. He'll take it out on you because you're the only one close enough he can fully trust. Let him. Show him you can take it. Take him. That you're the one thing in his life strong enough to break and still come back wanting more. That's how you win a king.

I read it again, absorbing the words, mind racing trying to figure out who left this. Adeline? Regina? My mind shifts to the woman in the photo on the King's dresser. His former wife?

I pull another note.

They need softness like they need air. Just don't let them know you know.

That one hits hard. Different, and I let the short passage roll around in my head for a moment, inhaling the words of advice and support.

There will be a night when he breaks. Don't panic. Stroke his hair. Swallow his tears. Ride him anyway.

Then: *If he collapses after, don't panic. That's normal. You've just emptied a man who spends all day being God.*

A few are sharp, dagger-pointed, and some oddly kind.

You are not a girl anymore. You are the thing he kneels for in private.

And then the ones I feel in my bones.

It's frightening, isn't it? To be the thing a powerful man loves most. Because love like his doesn't end. It devours. He'll carve your name into his future, and there will be no exit after that. But if you can stand it, if you don't run, you'll never be unprotected again. Or untouched. Or unloved. Not even in death.

I pause on that one. My fingers shake. For a second I think I might cry, but then the feeling skips sideways, and I just breathe through it.

I get to the last one.

He needs them as much as he needs you. Your job is to tie them together: body, mind, and soul. Use your mouth, your words, and yeah, your pussy, to make them stronger. Let them watch. Let them play. Let them fill you with all the anger, rage, love, and devotion they have. It's the only way any of you can survive and ultimately, thrive.

Finished, I lay them out across the bed like little bones, pale and precise, reading them over and over again. It's then that I notice some of the handwriting is different. One flows like poetry. Another is full of capital letters, rushed and chaotic. One is printed in blocky lowercase, no flourishes at all. I have no idea who wrote them, but it feels like they know me and what I'm about to go through.

I lay back on the bed, the notes spread beside me, jar clutched to my chest.

Tomorrow I will be the King's bride.

Tonight, I am something else entirely.

A girl spoken to by women who understand. Or the ones who lived to tell the tale.

Whoever they are, I'm taking their words to heart.

It's early in the morning when Regina shows up at my room. It feels like I've barely slept, Damon and I sneaking in a few hours before dawn. I'm stunned to see her, elegant and regal, standing in the middle of my room.

"What are you doing here?" I ask, rubbing my eyes.

"I came to help you prepare for the ceremony." A thin eyebrow raises as her gaze sweeps past the gown tossed over the chair by the fireplace, the hem torn and dirty. She steps into the bathroom and comes back out with a robe in her hands. "Put this on."

A few minutes later we're exiting the back door and heading down a stone path that leads away from the house toward a cottage nestled at the edge of the forest.

"What is that?" I ask, trying to keep up. Everything in the past few days seems to be moving fast.

"A bathhouse," she replies. "Used by the monks before the Barons took over. Historically, it's common for women to have a place of their own, particularly when surrounded by so many men. The King made this for the Baronesses as a way to have rest and rejuvenation."

The air is cold enough to sting my ankles as we walk, dew gathering on my skin. The robe brushes my thighs, and I clutch it tighter around me, trying not to shiver. Regina doesn't look back once. She walks with her shoulders back, her heels sharp on the stone and her presence even sharper.

No wonder the King admires her. I bet he never had to lock her in the cage.

Inside the cottage, the heat hits me—humid, floral. I don't recognize any of the faces in the room. The women are of varying ages, too old to be crypt chasers, but still aging gracefully. There's a maturity I can't comprehend, not after growing up in a house full of children. There's a sureness and they seem to understand their roles more than I understand mine.

They're quiet as they whisper to one another and arrange small bowls and silver trays across a long wooden table. A woman smiles when she sees me and beckons me toward a bench near the center of the room. Her critical eye skims down to my dirty feet.

"Sit, honey. We've got a lot to do."

Regina nods at them once and then disappears through a door at the back, leaving me alone. I lower myself onto the bench as two of the girls begin loosening the robe from my shoulders. The room spins in rose-petal steam and perfume. I feel like I've been dropped into a different world—one without feral cats, locked cages, and dark secrets. Like the Gilded Rose, this is a hush-hush place just for women.

"Arms up," one of the women says softly.

They strip me slowly and even though I try not to flinch, I do. It's not that I'm shy–it's that I still feel sore. Inside and out. Last night is a raw edge in my brain, the sound of my uncle's voice, the King's hands, the soft tremble of my thighs as they were forced apart. I remind myself that this isn't a violation. It's a celebration, and because of that I don't resist. I let them undress me. This is part of it.

They draw me toward a sunken marble tub steaming with milky water. Rose petals float at the surface. I step in carefully, and the heat burns at my skin.

They pile my hair into a bonnet, my braids still neat from the day before. The stylist had taken hours, but I'd asked for them, wanting the same, sleek look Regina had when she stood by the king. With them safely out of the way, the women bathe me, scrubbing away the old Arianette and transforming her into something new.

Dried off and smelling of flowers, they stretch me on a table, and wax me top to bottom, murmuring small apologies when I wince. I stare at the ceiling beams and try not to cry.

Good girls don't cry.

It isn't pain that gets to me, anyway. It's the fact that I feel removed from everything, like I've already left my body and someone else is preparing this one in my place.

For once in my life, I don't want to lose myself. I want to remember this.

"I know it's painful, but it's important that you be ready for him," one of the women says, assessing her work. "Even under the circumstances, the King deserves a proper bride."

Another pipes up, "Not just proper. Obedient."

"Soft."

"Good," I say before I can stop myself. I've never been any of those things with the King. I killed his Baron. I stole from his room. I fought against his punishment. I'm not good and he knows it.

"You're the Baroness, so I'm sure you know your way around a man's body," my cheeks heat at her knowing look, "but a man like the King will be different. You're there to meet his needs, however wicked they may seem."

Wicked.

The word rolls about my brain. That sounds much more like me than 'good.' I'm still tasting the word on my tongue, their firm fingertips slathering me with lotion, when Regina returns. Her eyes rest on my nipples, at the healing silver bars that have started to feel better instead of worse.

"Those are new."

"Damon gave them to me," I explain, happily accepting a clean robe.

"As part of his Claiming?"

"Later," I say, sitting in a chair that swivels, "after the ceremony."

If she has any opinion, she keeps it to herself, coming up behind me with a silver tin. She removes the bonnet, letting my hair fall, and begins working jojoba oil into my scalp. She's careful, methodical, part caretaker and part priestess.

At my feet, a woman crouches, painting my toes with a glossy black polish.

"You're going to be sore after," she says, handing me a tiny glass vial of white crystals. Salt. "Bathe in this if you bleed too much. It helps."

One of the women who gave me my bath leans in, more daring, and adds, "If he lets you ride him, rock forward on your knees. Don't just lie there like a corpse."

My mouth goes dry. "What...what if I don't know how?"

They all pause.

"You'll figure it out fast," the woman at my feet says. "Or he'll teach you."

"Or punish you," Regina mutters from behind me. She runs a brush through the ponytail, making the hair shiny and curl at the end, then sprays a light oil over the top.

"He already has," I admit, catching her dark eyes with mine. "He put me in the cage."

She pauses. "The one under the bed?"

"Yes." My heart hammers, not out of fear, but possible camaraderie. "Did he lock you in there too?"

"Not the King. It was one of my Barons," she says. "He got jealous once that I was flirting with someone else. Thought it would teach me a lesson."

"Did it?"

"Yes and no. I was committed to my Barons so that was pointless, but I realized that he was projecting his betrayal and disloyalty on me. He was the one cheating–"

"With another woman?" I blurt.

"God, no. With another *king*. He was working for Ashby behind the Baron King's back. Caused a lot of trouble and ultimately cost him his life." She shakes her head. "I saw the signs, I just couldn't place them. He was paranoid, accusatory. He'd flip everything back on me or the other Barons, act like we were the ones at fault."

"I killed Armand," I admit. It's the first time I've said it out loud. "He caught me in the Hunt and despite the King's strict directions he tried to rape me."

Her lips twist, impressed. "Seems like you have better instincts than I do."

I shrug. "Maybe. He wasn't trying to hide it..."

'You never should have run and once you did, you never should have stopped.'

His words slam back into me, the threats he made right before I slit his throat. It was like he knew me. Or knew *of* me.

"The King rewards loyalty," Regina says, drawing me out of that dark place. "You did him a favor."

She lifts up a piece of black netting–a veil, held together with a shiny black bow.

"Isn't that a little childish?" I ask, thinking of how offended the Barons were at my schoolgirl outfit.

"He'll like it," she assures me, pinning the oversized black satin into place at the back of my head. It's huge, sticking out from both sides of my head. "It makes you look young."

"I am young," I note.

She meets my eyes in the mirror. "Exactly."

Daddy, she had called him the night of the Hunt. She's his true Daughter of Darkness. I'm his burden.

I want to ask her how to make him like me, to accept me, but I remember the advice given to me in the glass jar and decide not to. I already know. Regardless, she's already moved on, and I'm directed into another room where I see it: the dress.

It's spread across the table like a shroud. Black satin, boned corset, lace sleeves so tight they feel like a second skin. Carefully, I touch the soft satin, fingering the tag sewn into the back.

Jaded Society

"Did Adeline pick this out?" I'd half expected the dress to be a glaring white, maybe with tiny roses around the edge.

"Actually," Regina says, reaching into a nearby box, "there's a card I'm supposed to give you." The envelope is black and one of the women hands me a nail file to loosen the wax seal. Inside is a small card, I flip it open and read the smooth penmanship.

Arianette—

You'll walk into the chapel a girl.

You'll walk out a queen.

Do not disappoint me.

—Your King

A chill runs down my spine, and I hold the letter close to my chest, not letting the others see. "The King gave this to me."

Regina lifts the dress and holds it out. "It looks exactly like what I'd expect him to pick."

I quell my shaking as she and the others help lace me into it, pulling the strings until my ribs feel like they might crack. I gasp and lean forward, trying to suck in enough air to stay conscious.

"Don't faint," the woman that painted my toes says, patting my cheek. "At least not until after the vows."

When the dress is fully on, I hardly recognize myself. The bodice is sculpted to my body, the corset pressing my breasts high and full–seductive. The skirt sweeps back into a long train trimmed in velvet and subtle embroidery. My arms are bare from the elbows down, pale and trembling.

This is the woman he expects to see walking down the aisle, apart from one thing.

The collar.

Our eyes meet as she carries it to me, like she's well aware of what this is–what it *means*. Slim red leather, buttery soft, with an interior that looks worn. I think of how he said my grandmother wore it. My mother too? I never knew her, but I suppose she did, maybe until she died, pushing me into the world. It fastens at the back of my neck with a delicate silver clasp, but the ring at the front is what catches my eye. Ornamental, yes–but also practical. Like something could be hooked into it.

I remember the box my uncle brought it in. Lined in black velvet. I remember how his hands looked holding it, offering it as a reminder that as long as I wear it around my neck, I still belong to him.

Regina buckles it around my throat. Her fingers linger a moment too long.

I swallow. It tightens.

They stand back and admire their work. I look like a little ghost bride, trussed and ribboned, the scent of roses and sugar clinging to my skin. My reflection blinks at me like she's about to cry. Or scream.

Regina steps beside me and pulls the veil down over my face. "You're ready."

Ready.

For the ceremony.

For the King.

For the final claiming.

After tonight, I won't belong to my uncle anymore, or the secrets in the Manor. I won't belong to anyone but him.

32

D^{amon}

WHAT THE *FUCK* have I gotten into?

That's all I can think as I take in the hundreds of candles burning from every crevice. There are sconces and candelabras and tall stands flanking the altar. Bowls of firelight flickering at the end of each pew. Shadows dance across stone and gold, licking up toward the arched ceiling like something sentient. It's dark, on purpose. The kind of dark that swallows sound, expectation, and doubt.

I've never felt so out of place.

There's no color here, not in the vases of flowers around the room. The petals, like everything else in the room, are ash white, drained of color entirely, or dyed black. Whoever put this together, and I assume it's goblins that live underground, did their work quietly, turning a dusty old sanctuary into all this.

The chapel is ready, and I assume, somewhere nearby, so are the King and Baroness.

Hunter stands beside me, silent, his cloak pulled up around his neck, hands jammed into the deep folds of velvet. He doesn't look at me, but I can feel the energy coming off him in waves. He's tightly wound, and it coils in his shoulders, his jaw. We're both dressed like acolytes to something ancient and unspoken.

We're not groomsmen. We are watchmen.

Witnesses, the King said.

We're here to make sure the King gets what he wants.

"Is this normal?" Hunter asks me, eyes focused on the Shadows moving at the back of the chapel as they begin to usher in the guests. "I've never been to a wedding before."

"Nothing in this godforsaken town is normal," I mutter.

The Shadows play into all of it, emerging like wisps of smoke from the outer doors they move deliberately, their faces obscured, escorting the soft rustle of silk and wool down the main aisle. Black formalwear only–rules established by the King himself.

Forsyth's upper echelon walks in–a blend of old money, young ambition, and quiet curiosity. Many are alumni–identifiable by the rings on their fingers or pentagrams pinned to their lapels. They look comfortably at home. The others? Well, it's obvious they've never been invited inside the stone walls of the House of Night. They gape as they walk in, filling the creaky wooden pews, excluding the three that remain empty at the front, the ends draped with rope, reserved.

"Who are those for?" I ask.

"The Royals," Hunter says, nodding at the back of the room. Sure enough, once the normies are seated, they start down the aisle.

Killian Payne is impossible to miss. He's a wall of a man, all former football bulk dressed in custom wool. He looks the most at ease, probably because he was the only one raised for his position. His stepsister, Story, walks beside him–small, soft and graceful, the kind of woman who could slit your throat and smile doing it. Together, they look a perfect match, a king and queen on the chess-board. They nod once to me and Hunter as they turn into the pews.

Flanking them are Killian's inner circle–Tristian Mercer, all blond hair and cocky smirk, a champagne-drunk gleam in his eyes. He looks like he's already bored and thinking of ways to get in the Lady's skirt during the reception. Next to him, Dimitri Rathbone, quieter, darker, and suspicious of everything.

As he should be.

"We had someone check for weapons at the door, right?" I ask Hunter quietly as they settle into the first row.

He nods. "Carson and Rob."

"Good."

Killian's barely wedged his body in the narrow pew when movement near the narthex draws our attention. The Dukes come in next.

Sy enters like a bear in a china shop, like he's stepping into the ring during the Fury. His skin glows warm against the candlelight, his dark curls tucked back in a polished fade, and those eerie blue eyes scanning the room with measured calm. Lavinia trails slightly behind. Her blue hair is three shades darker than it was at the Fury, and her dress is slinky, the black making her pale skin nearly translucent. Her hand remains on her King's arm, but it's clear she doesn't belong to just him.

Nick Bruin walks in next–wild-eyed and mercenary. No one in the chapel is fooled by the suit. The inked numbers under his eye are a signal declaring what lies underneath: Mayhem. Halfway to his seat a middle-aged woman in the pews catches his eye. A silent conversation flits between them, and his shoulders relax–slightly.

Interesting.

And then... Remy.

Christ. My old roommate strolls in less like a Duke and more like a God. This is *his* house, his bloodline direct to the Barons' legacy. His coat is expensive, possibly custom design, his shirt strategically crumpled. The knot on his tie is loose, matching the casual smirk tugging at his lips. His white-blond hair is tousled in a way that lets you know he just fingerbanged his Duchess on the car ride over. He saunters down the aisle like the son of the devil–which, arguably, he is–and then stops halfway to the pew.

"Can't believe we're all dressed up to watch a girl get sacrificed," he mutters under his breath, loud enough for a few people nearby to hear.

Sy doesn't turn, but Lavinia snaps her head in his direction. Remy just shrugs and slouches into his seat, throwing his long arm behind Sy's shoulders to stroke the Duchess' neck. The row tightens with tension, like a wire pulled taut.

I look through the crowd for his father, Timothy Maddox, to see his response to his son's outward defiance, but he isn't here. I met him once–the day we moved into the dorm. He was polished and intimidating, in a suit when everyone else was dressed to haul in suitcases and boxes.

I couldn't judge. My parents didn't bother to come.

I realize that no one else in the chapel is looking for him, because every other eye is on the back of the room.

"Is that the Princess?" I ask, seeing the redhead at the arched doorway.

Hunter, the search engine of Royals, nods. "Yep, according to Everly at the station, this is the first time she's been seen in public since having Justice."

With hair the color of fire, she walks down the aisle in a black velvet gown, tits about to spill out of the neckline. Her hips are rounded, and there's a subtle curve to her belly. It strikes me hard and fast: motherhood is sexy.

Whitaker Kayes Ashby walks just behind her. Blonde, blue-eyed, more comfortable in his suit than I ever could be in jeans. His last name tells the story. Kayes is the name connected to Clive Kayes, the man everyone assumes is behind the Baron King's mask. His grandfather.

Both Wicker and Remy have more of a right to be in this cloak than either Hunter or I do, yet both have abdicated their legacy. It's confusing, but also further proof the bloodlines in Forysth twist and turn like a vine strangling its own roots.

To Verity's right is Pace Ashby. Of everyone in the room I probably have more in common with him than anyone else. We met in lockup and were released on the same day. He looks intimidating, buff from hours of playing hockey, but nothing is as scary as his mind. He's the most alert person in the room–the most paranoid–scanning every corner like he expects an enemy to strike from the shadows. Every few seconds, his hand brushes the Princess' lower back, grounding her. Our eyes meet as he eases into the pew, and he lifts his chin in recognition.

"You know him?" Hunter whispers.

"As much as you can know someone in a ten-by-ten cinderblock room."

His eyebrow lifts, but the Princes' procession wraps up with Lex Ashby taking his seat. The long hair gives him a sense of serenity that balances the others. He takes Verity's hand and kisses her knuckles. Together, they are a wall. A unit. Protective to the edge of paranoia.

Hunter shifts beside me. I don't look at him, but I know we're both thinking the same thing: the ceremony has barely started and it's already weird as hell.

33

H^{unter}

I HATE THIS.

The chapel's too quiet now, which is saying something with all these bodies stuffed into the pews, shoulder to shoulder, like the bones down in the catacombs. If that's not enough, the heat of the candles feels suffocating, the hundreds of flickering flames sucking up all the oxygen.

Under my cloak, I tug at my collar. Our outfits were laid out in a room off the narthex. Black suits with crisp button-down shirts and a silk tie. The cloaks are ceremonial, different from the ones we've worn before–nicer.

Heavier.

DK hasn't said a word since the Princes walked in and he told me he knew Pace Ashby. He's more connected than I realized, although it doesn't seem to matter. His independence is palpable, the weight of the cloak seems even heavier on his shoulders than on my own.

His jaw is now locked in place, like he's bracing himself, and I follow his gaze to the back of the sanctuary, understanding why. The Dean has arrived, all bluster and bravado, like a champion taking a victory lap. He strides down the aisle, smiling and greeting guests, making this day about him. His suit is black, but his tie is red, glaring like a bloodstain.

When he reaches the reserved seating area, he attempts to engage the Royals. Killian gives the man a stare that would shatter souls. And Lucia looks like she knows exactly what kind of man he is. The Princes disregard him, his status too low on the food chain to even acknowledge.

There's a lesson here on how to handle men like Hexley. One I'd like to learn, because I'd spent every moment since last night's dinner with my gut twisted in knots.

The Dean's voice keeps replaying in my skull, clipped and clinical: *"I require proof."*

And the King's cool, oily response: *"I can assure you that she's pristine."*

All through dinner she'd been dutiful and quiet, the total opposite of how she is with us. There was no fight. No passion. No glimmer of the blood-splattered girl standing over a dead man. Not a trace of the sexy-mouthed vixen kneeling before me, taking me hard in between her lips.

She was soft and demure. Compliant. Snapped back to some version of herself that her uncle expected.

Once Graves shut the door, sealing her off, I only had my imagination to think of what happened next. How she was stripped and forced to spread her legs? How she was *touched*?

It took everything in me not to follow his shiny silver sedan off the property. To call Ares to the truck, grab my knife out from under the seat, and go on a *real* hunt. I'd love to see how the Dean fared under pressure, with a collar on *his* neck. Even now, in the cool air of the chapel, my blood starts to simmer. She doesn't belong to *him*. She belongs to *us*.

The Baroness is *ours*. That happened the night of the Claiming. He doesn't seem to understand that.

When I got on campus, the sedan continued on to the Manor and I let him slither away. I drove on to the station where I completed my shift, prophesied, and smoked my two cigarettes down to ash. When I left, I took the long way home.

The hotel stands quietly on the edge of campus and around back, the lure of the non-descript door that led to the Sanctum. I sat in the truck with Ares, thinking about how easy it would be to go inside and work off some of this anger. To go back to that place where I felt comfortable–as a viewer not a participant.

An outsider, simply watching.

In the few weeks I've lived in the King's house, shared a room with DK, experienced life with Arianette... I'm no longer sure observing is enough. Especially after last night.

I came back to the House of Night.

The music shifts and people start to stand, just slightly, shoulders turning, necks craning. Even the candles seem to hush, like they're holding their breath at the event we're about to behold.

She's here.

The doors open at the far end of the aisle, and everything slows.

Arianette Hexley.

Not the girl I chased through the forest or the waif with bloody hands and a thousand-yard stare.

This version of her?

She's unrecognizable.

The side door creaks open, barely audible over the hum of the organ. He enters like the boldest of shadows–our King. Face covered in an ebony mask with horns tipped in gold. He sweeps into the chapel in a long black cloak. His presence is calculated, quiet author-ity, while not taking away from his bride's entrance. The pentagram ring glints on his finger. He doesn't glance at the crowd, or over at Graves, who is standing next to the altar prepared to officiate the ceremony. His eyes are locked on *her*.

Made of black satin, the dress clings to her body like a second skin, her waist cinched so tight in a corset it might as well be armor. A large bow sits at the back of her head, and I'm taken right back to the first day we went to campus and she was dressed like a schoolgirl.

Now, I get it. It suits her. That twisted mix of innocence and the taboo. It comes off her in waves, like the way her skirt flows behind her, lace trailing over the stone floor. Her hair is done up, coiled into an elegant silhouette with curls twisted in place, the bow mounted at the top of her ponytail, childlike and chilling all at once. A doll in a funeral dress.

Her face is covered by black mesh–a veil protecting her from this world. It's impossible to see her face, her features hazy like a mirage, something intangible. I know Arianette is real. I've seen her run. Dance. Writhe in ecstasy. I don't need to see her face to know the woman underneath.

She walks slowly. The music low as a whisper.

I'm an engineer. I deal in facts and figures. Calculations and hard truths. I don't believe in religion. I don't believe in fate, or curses, or whatever it is that makes men create agreements over a woman's body, much less her soul.

But standing in that chapel, watching the shadows stretch long across the altar, it doesn't feel like pageantry. It feels real. Ancient. Like the ground is shifting beneath us, ready to swallow us into the catacombs that run beneath the city.

Something bigger than us is about to happen.

I glance toward DK. His face is unreadable, but I think he feels the shift too. That somehow we went from outsiders to insiders, although she doesn't look at anyone. Not me. Not Damon. Not the crowd of women whispering behind their hands.

Arianette doesn't smile or flinch.

She just *walks* toward the King, a sacrificial lamb who already made peace with the knife.

34

T imothy

I STAND AT THE ALTAR, shadowed beneath the flickering chandelier of candles, my cloak heavy across my shoulders, the mask pressed firmly to my face. Every eye in the room, from the city's elite, to the snakes in elegant clothing, to the young Royals in the front rows–including my son–have their eyes on the bride as she walks toward me.

We aren't the only ones in the room. There are ghosts dead and alive that seem to linger just beyond the candlelight, sitting in judgment, waiting for me to fail.

Again.

The chapel is cold stone and smoke, the scent of incense clinging to the air like blood to silk. My gloves are black leather. My vows memorized, twisted and old.

And then, she appears.

Arianette. Walking slowly, almost tentative, down the center aisle.

Black satin clings to the curves of her body, making her look both hard and soft. Her veil floats over her shoulders, grazing the swell of her breasts.

Then that bow. It's bigger than the width of her head. Sexy, yet innocent.

Daughter of Darkness. The Barons' Sinister Sister. Our Baroness. *My bride.*

Despite everything I know–her fragility, her madness, the violence threaded through her blood–I'm struck by how she carries herself, those flaws and deviances tucked away.

The difference between a Black Wedding and my first, conventional one, is that this is a binding between two parties where something is gained and lost by both sides. It can be legal, financial, or proprietary: Land. Money. People.

Or in some cases, secrets.

This arrangement is a little of all three, and I feel a wicked heat lick my spine as I drag my eyes down Arianette's body, stilling them over the gentle sway of her hips. One thing that is always required: a virgin sacrifice. A trembling creature made to be claimed, to be torn apart by a man with unlimited power.

By night's end, she'll hate me, and I'll hate myself more.

Pulling my gaze from her, I look to the pews, where my eyes find Remington's cool, bored glare. His bottom lip twitches and just next to his half-brother's ear, I see his middle finger flip in the air.

Fuck you.

For all the regret I have over losing him to the Dukes, I see the sharp clarity in his eyes. He's healthy in a way I never could give him. Stable, without losing his personality to a medicinal haze. Remington loathes me. All the Royals do. I represent everything they detest. I'm old and unfeeling, traditional. I'm the enemy and none of them will rest until I'm deep in the ground like the kings they have already toppled.

I should be standing here with him, a proud father and best man.

Instead, I'm waiting for the young woman–the innocent pawn–walking toward me.

The music slows as she reaches the altar and I snap back to the moment. I owe her that.

The veil trembles slightly over her lips. I wonder if it's from nerves or fear–or both.

With gloved fingers, I reach forward and gather the delicate edge of her veil. The mesh is fine, soft as breath, and for a brief moment I hesitate, aware that this act, this unveiling, is more than ceremonial. It's a claiming. A stripping away of what's left of her girlhood.

The mesh lifts, I draw it back, and then I see her.

Excitement.

That is what the trembling is from. I see it now as she fights to still herself, head slightly bowed, but I feel the heat of her gaze before I meet it. She is a vision, made for this altar. Skin rich and flawless, glowing against the black satin of her gown. Her lips, painted plum-dark, quiver just enough to betray her nerves. And those eyes, deep brown, wide and unblinking, search mine with something between fear and devotion, as if trying to read the shape of her fate in the man about to bind her.

She's beautiful in a way that unnerves me. Too soft for this life. Too fragile for what's ahead. And yet, strong enough to endure this madness.

My fingers twitch. I want to remove the gloves. I want to feel her skin, the curve of her cheekbone, the tremble in her jaw. I want to see if she flinches.

I don't.

Instead, I let my eyes drop to the collar wrapped around her throat. Crimson leather. Ornamental to most, but not to me, or the witnesses surrounding the altar. We're all aware that it's less of a gift and more of a warning. A reminder of who she belongs to–first to her uncle, and now, to me.

It gleams beneath her veil like blood at the base of a blade, an opening to the swath of smooth skin that gleams in the hollow of her collarbone and her shoulder blades, a temptation that leads to the swell of her breasts, buoyed by youth, marked by temptation. The top arch of the carving is present–her first mark by the House of Night. A reminder that she's worthy of standing next to me. Strong enough.

Graves stands before the altar, dressed in ceremonial black, the bronze medallion of the Barons glinting at his throat. He's the officiant. The witness. The keeper of our old rites.

"Brothers and Sisters," his voice carries through the chapel, smooth and commanding. "We are gathered here, in this place of sanctuary, to bear witness to a union forged on the steps of Samhain, a holiest of days, when our world opens to the next. A wedding of souls spanning between life and death. Not of softness, but of strength."

The crowd shifts, a hush broken by the rustle of breath and fabric. Some lean in, fascinated. Others look away. The discomfort is palpable. Good. It should be.

Graves' voice cuts through it all. Measured. Unforgiving. "Arianette Hexley. You stand here in the presence of the King of Barons, having offered your body and your blood to bind yourself to this house. Do you give yourself to this union?"

She lifts her chin. There's a tremble in her breath, but her voice is steady, like a girl who's already seen hell and decided she'd rather walk straight into the fire than go back.

"I give myself to the King and promise to follow him down the path. A daughter of darkness. A wife of wickedness."

My gaze never leaves her. Not her painted mouth, parted slightly. Not the way her lashes lower as she avoids my eyes, like the sight of me might be too much–too real, too dangerous. She's trembling, but not with fear alone. There's something else beneath it. Anticipation. Submission. Hunger she hasn't even learned how to name.

Graves turns to me. "And you, the Keeper of Death, the King and ruler of this territory and the caverns and crypts beneath, do you accept this woman as your bride? To own and to protect. To command and to punish. To keep until death claims you both."

I step closer.

The scent of her hits me–flowers and incense, something faintly medicinal from the bathhouse and beneath it all, the electric trace of her fear. Her desire. It clings to her skin like perfume.

That collar. Red leather at her throat, trembling as she breathes, waiting for my hand. She's offering herself–body and blood. And I can see it in the way her hands twitch at her sides, how her pulse hammers just beneath the surface. She wants the fairytale–wants the very thing I can't give her.

Still, I lean in, my voice pitched for her alone, though the whole chapel hears it.

"I do."

Her breath hitches, just once, causing her breasts to rise and fall.

And with that, she is mine.

Not just in name. Not just by blood.

But in every broken, burning way that matters.

The guests remain seated, their breath caught in their throats, when Graves raises one hand. "The King and his Bride will now enter the Rite of Flesh and Flame."

The Shadows move as one.

Hooded figures line the edge of the chapel, arms raised, forming a dark perimeter that ripples with quiet, pulsing magic. A barrier of shadow rises–soft and undulating like smoke, but thick enough to obscure the altar from the prying eyes of the crowd. Hunter and DK step forward, silent and solemn. They lift Arianette in her black gown–one at her back, one beneath her knees–and place her upon the cold, candlelit altar in offering.

She watches me with wide, glassy eyes.

I step to the edge of the altar. Remove my gloves. The oil waits in its dish, thick and fragrant with dahlia and myrrh. I begin the rite by pushing the satin up her thighs. Slow. Reverent. Then removing the lace between her legs. I dip my fingers into the oil, gliding my fingers across her skin, leaving oil-slick markings in my wake, symbols only the oldest Barons would recognize. Her body is a map. And I'm rewriting the borders.

She's trembling, but she does not speak, not even when Graves appears beside me, bearing an ancient reliquary–dark wood and bone, carved with a pentagram. Within it, nestled on white satin, is a ceremonial piece: delicate, wicked, pointed at the end. It's older than the crypts.

It's meant for one purpose.

"Blood on the altar," Graves intones. "Blood to bind. Blood to break. Let the sanctity of innocence give way to submission."

I kneel between her thighs, the world narrowing until it is only this, this soft, holy violence. I part her gently, reverently, softer than I did last night when giving proof to her uncle. Because of that I know how tight she is. How punishing the walls of her pussy can be. I move with swift assurance, pressing the tip of the object forward, breaking her seal.

She gasps and DK's hand comes down over her mouth, snuffing out any sound. Her hips flinch, but she doesn't close her legs. Not to me.

The barrier shivers with energy as the moment passes. A thin line of blood wells, red on white satin. A sacrifice given freely. I lower my mouth. Not lust. Not hunger.

A rite.

I press my tongue against her, tasting her–the salt and iron of new blood, sweetened by submission. I lap her once, then again, the heat of her soft lips sending a jolt through my body. She lets out a sound, breathy and broken, and her hand moves to touch my hair before she catches herself.

I catch myself.

This isn't about pleasure.

This is about ownership.

About claiming something untouched, untainted, and stamping it with the seal of something dark and eternal.

"It is done," I whisper against her skin.

I rise, nodding at Graves, then at DK and Hunter, suddenly aware of the loyalty they've shown to me over the past few weeks. The girl is a temptation, one that requires insurmountable strength.

I chose them well.

Arianette's body stays sprawled upon the altar, her gown rucked up, the hoop on the collar gleaming, a single tear gliding down her cheek. But her eyes? Her eyes are locked on mine, wide and full of something too complicated to name.

Not love.

But something sacred, and for the briefest moment I see something else: a future.

rianette

"I DO."

The words echo in my chest as I stand at the edge of the reception.

It's held in the garden behind the House of Night. Strings of amber lights flicker along the cobbled paths, creating something magical. Samhain night settles heavy over Forsyth and there's only a few hours left before the veil slips away for another year. There's fire in the air–actual bonfires, crackling at the far corners of the lawn–casting a glow of yellow light over the tables of food and drink. It's a feast I hadn't even realized was being prepared: roasted meat, figs stuffed with blue cheese, candied apples, all topped off with spiced red wine that stains the lips of the wealthy like communion.

The flowers out here burst with color. Reds, yellows, and orange, nestled in vases that look like skulls. It's the opposite of inside the chapel. Out here under the stars and moonlight is a celebration, a party. I'm just too nervous to enjoy it.

I'd gotten separated from the King when I went to the bathroom to clean up, and now I'm stuck wandering alone, barefoot, my shoes kicked off the instant I stepped into the grass. People gather in little clutches, coats draped over black-tie finery, drinks in hand. The guests are still buzzing about the ceremony.

"That was *wild*," a girl in a sequined shawl gushes to a date in a velvet tux. "I mean–did you see the altar? What do you think happened back there?"

Her date sips from a blood-red glass. "It was a lot. I was here for a wedding three years ago for one of the brothers, but it was much more tame."

"The King's always been a bit dramatic," someone else chimes in. "It wouldn't be a Baron wedding without a little blood."

I drift through the garden, the hem of my satin gown brushing fallen leaves, trying to ignore the ache between my legs. Last night the sensation of the King's fingers had been a painful intrusion, but what happened on that altar was much more. An invasion between my hips.

Now I walk as though nothing happened. Like I can't feel the blood soaked into my panties, or remember what the object he'd inserted in me looked like after the King showed it to my uncle. He'd grinned down at the white satin, now stained red, and shook the King's hand.

The deal, whatever it had been for, was secured.

Most people at the party seem oblivious, but a few have a knowing look in their eyes. The Lords' King and Lady–Killian and Story–offer a small smile and raised glasses. Tristian walks up with a plate piled high with fruit and other delectables from the buffet table.

"Eat," he offers the plate to Story. "I know you're starving."

"I'm saving room for cake," she tells him, nodding over to the dessert table. "There are two, and I want a piece of each."

"Sweetheart, I know you've got a sugar addiction, but it's not like you're Verity and eating for two."

"She's not eating for two, dipshit," the dark-haired Lord–Dimitri Rathbone–says, fingers wrapped loosely around a bottle of beer. "She's already had the baby."

Tristian rolls his eyes. "She's nursing the baby. How do you think she gets the extra calories to feed him too?"

"Are you saying that if I get pregnant I can have extra cake?" Story asks, tapping her chin thoughtfully.

"Jesus," Killian mutters. "Tris, stop monitoring Story's food. We're at a party for God's sake. Rath, seriously, don't be a dipshit, and Story..." His hand flattens on her belly, "as much as I want to see your belly filled up with our baby–"

"And some super big tits. Have you seen Verity's tits?" Tristian whistles. "No wonder they left the party early."

Story pinches him in the side. "Gross. They left early so she could get home to her *son*."

Killian sighs. "Like I said, as much as I want to see your belly filled up with our baby, we are in no way prepared to handle that right now, even though there may be perks for all of us."

I slink away, feeling like I just heard way too much about the Lords, Verity's tits, and their conception plans. I move quickly and stumble straight into Remy Maddox and Lavinia, who are speaking with a couple of older guests, cloaked in black and silver. Remy's hand grips Lavinia's hip, his thumb making tiny circles. Their voices hush when I approach.

"Arianette," a woman says, stepping out from the little group. "You look lovely."

"Thank you."

"I'm Sarah, and these are my husbands, Manny and Davis." She gestures to the two handsome men with her. "We wish you all the best."

They offer their congratulations, and I can't help but note that her tone is soft, *genuine*, like she means it, unlike many of the other people here. But I also see the small crease at the corner of her eye. Worry? It makes me uncomfortable, and I shift my gaze to Lavinia. She gives me a small smile.

"Your dress is gorgeous," she says. "Looks like one of Jade's, don't you think, Rem?"

Those startling green eyes skim down my body and then he shrugs. "Could be."

"It is," I grin, "Jaded Society? Do you know her?"

"We're friends," he allows, eyes listing to the side. I notice his thumb is still on her hip, but no longer moving. "Your choice?"

I shake my head. "No, the King gave it to me as a gift."

"Black," he mutters, rolling his eyes. "As if."

There's an awkward moment, mostly because I'm trying to decipher his words, but Sarah breaks it saying, "It's nice to know the King is supporting small creatives in Forsyth."

"Rem," the husband with the darker complexion says, "let's go get some food."

"Grab me something too," Lav calls after the men as they walk off.

I exhale, and look around. "I should probably find..." I feel my eyes widen, "my husband. How weird is that to say?"

"Super weird," Lavinia says. Sarah shoots her a stern look. "You know, just because it's new and stuff."

I nod and step back, meeting something hard. Hands steady my hips, just for a moment. "Careful, Baroness."

I don't have to look to know it's Hunter, but I turn, grateful for a reason to escape.

"Have you seen the King?" I ask, searching through the sea of black suits and gowns.

"He sent me to find you. Said you shouldn't be wandering around on your own." His chin lifts, and I follow the direction he indicates to see The King near a dais. It's the first time I've noticed it.

As we cross the yard, we pass a table of women near one of the bonfires.

They're young. Pretty in the polished, practiced way of royalty. They're not crypt chasers, at least not current ones. It's not their looks that get my attention, but their conversation.

"I couldn't sleep with a man I've never seen," the one in a faux-fur stole says, taking a bite of a honey-drenched tart. "I don't care how rich he is."

"Do you think he takes the mask off during sex?" Her friend giggles. "Or does he make her close her eyes?"

A third girl, blonde and bored-looking, pops a pomegranate seed between her teeth. "He's *old*. No one even knows how old. I bet he can't even get it up."

"Oh my god," the girl in fur says, laughing. "His sperms are probably like the dinosaurs. Dusty and extinct."

The group dissolves into sharp little giggles, their laughter shattering the air like glass.

I freeze, the taste of wine thick on my tongue. My skin prickles.

"Ignore them," Hunter says, continuing to walk. He touches me more often now, but it's still rare, brief gestures as he's herding me in one direction or the other. "They have no fucking idea what you've been through."

He's right. They didn't feel the altar's cold stone against their back. They didn't see the look in his eyes behind the mask when he took what I offered–not just my body, but my blood, my breath, my fear.

They didn't hear me cry when the object pushed inside, breaking me, or when Damon stifled the sound with the palm of his hand.

They didn't feel the way the King's mouth–hot, intimate and reverent–*sealed* me to him.

The girls keep laughing, oblivious. I take a step back, breath catching in my throat.

"They can talk all they want," he continues, his hand tensing at my elbow, adding, "but you're the one he claimed."

He delivers me to the base of the dais where the Baron King waits.

His black mask shimmers in the bonfire, sleek and gleaming, the surface broken only by the curling gold tips of the horns rising from his crown. My fingers itch to pull it off–to see the face of the man I just married–not just the tease that is only enough to imagine more. The line of his jaw is unmistakable. Sharp, rugged. Masculine in a way that confirms he has long been a man, and the thought makes something flutter low in my belly.

He watches me approach with a calm I realize he projects in public, not the deep intensity he showed me when he ordered me into the cage. When I reach the steps, he rises. Doesn't offer a hand. Just turns and ascends, expecting me to follow.

I do.

The throne is different from the others, because there are two seats on the red tufted cushion. Next to that are two smaller thrones, one for each Baron.

Just in case anyone forgets, I'm still the Baroness for the House of Night. Damon and Hunter claim their seats and the music dims as cloaked servers approach the dais, offering me a silver chalice embedded with jewels. The King takes another, its bronze finish matching his ring.

Once everyone has their own drink, Graves steps forward, his cloak rustling behind him like wings.

"On this sacred night of Samhain," he begins, his voice rich with gravitas, "when the veil thins and the dead draw near, we bear witness to a union that will mark this house for decades to come."

He raises the glass higher.

"To the Baron King and his Bride. Let this binding stand against the rot of the modern world. Let it remind us that power is not taken, but *offered*, and blood is never given freely, but with sacrifice."

I feel the King shift beside me, pleased.

"May the old gods bless this night. May the dead take note of what was promised. And may *we*," he pauses for effect, voice low and reverent, "never forget who we are."

The crowd remains still, as if waiting for the final note.

"Memento Mori," he finishes, and drinks.

All around us, glasses lift. Some high in the air, others hesitant, wary of our ways. But no one can argue the truth.

Memento Mori.

Remember you must die.

I glance up at the King.

He takes a small sip, but his eyes are on our guests, his expression unreadable behind the mask. Then, slowly, he turns his head toward me. "The reception will be over soon." He sets down his glass. "And I have something for you."

From somewhere within his cloak, he draws something between his fingers–a small black tablet, no bigger than a button.

"Natural aphrodisiacs are part of the Barons' custom. We're one with the elements. One with the earth and air. Fire and water. Everything combined. It sharpens instinct. Softens resistance. Makes the body remember what the mind tries to forget. Tonight, you don't need to overthink the past few days–only feel what's to come."

He holds it out, and I react without direction, opening my mouth, letting him press it to my tongue. His gloved fingers graze my bottom lip.

"You'll like this one," he promises, his voice pitched low enough that only I can hear it. "It's clean and won't mess with your head. Warm. Erotic. You'll feel it start in your spine then melt between your thighs. Let go. Let the night have you. Let *me* have you."

I swallow: the pill and the promise.

He leans back on his throne. "Once they leave the *real* Baron Samhain will begin."

I sit beside my *husband*, the pill already melting down into my bloodstream. Below us, the other Royals start their retreat, the party is ending for them, and soon it will just be the Barons embracing who and what we are.

For once, I feel part of something–not on the outside looking in. Or worse, looking over my shoulder to see who is chasing me.

THE PARTY DISSOLVES like a dying spell–embers and smoldering wood. The guests vanish, slipping into cars or disappearing through the estate gates, their duty done. The Shadows don't follow them. They stay here.

With *us*.

The party shifts, like the path of the moon, stretching farther into the sky. The energy changes. Cooler. Hungrier. Someone lights smaller bonfires. Another uncorks a bottle and pours fizzy champagne into crystal glasses. The Baron King's throne has been moved beneath the arching limbs of the forest canopy, now surrounded by low couches and cushions, silk and velvet tossed like offerings across the earth.

How did we get here? I wonder, not remembering. My skin prickles. The Shadows close in. Not oppressive–but possessive. They want to watch.

The King, *my husband*, leads me there with a gloved hand resting on the small of my back, and I follow without question. The drug is a hum now, coursing warm and heady through my blood. Every sound tastes like sugar. Every movement flutters against my skin like a kiss.

He sits and watches me.

I remain standing, that innate anxiety tripping up my spine. I'm not good enough for him. I'm nothing but a pawn. I'm damaged.

I turn, trying to escape his gaze, coming face to face with Damon. He's shirtless now–lean muscle and tattoos in the firelight, that scar at his throat catching a glint of orange. He's lounging on the cushions with Hunter beside him, the two of them vibrating with the same lazy energy. But their eyes... they're sharp. Hungry.

The drug the King gave me hums across my skin. He promised that I'd feel it, but I didn't know it would pulse in every heartbeat, rise in every touch. The sensation between my legs is no longer an ache of pain, but a deep, throbbing want.

I glance over my shoulder and my eyes meet the King's. He doesn't speak. Doesn't move. But I feel his permission. So I walk–barefoot across the soft, damp grass, my black dress trailing behind. Damon catches my wrist and pulls me into his lap, his hands already pushing aside fabric. "You did a good job up there," he tells me, fingers stroking against my thigh. "You were brave and strong, even when he pierced you."

That's what it was. A piercing. The sharpest pain I'd felt other than the needles Damon pushed though my nipples. I see a streak in his blue eyes, and ask, "Are you jealous it wasn't you?"

"Doll baby," he says, pushing my hair over my shoulder, "everyone at that wedding wishes they were the one that had you sprawled out on that altar and fucking tonight."

My skin warms, hot from the idea. Of the rich entitled men and women jealous of *me*. The idea makes me laugh, a giggle bubbling up from the inside. I feel bold. Magical.

Like a queen.

I glance over my shoulder, back at the King, and meet his eyes. Nothing in them tells me to come back over. To stop what I'm doing.

Hunter murmurs from next to me, "Do you like knowing he's watching?"

I do.

But...

The flicker of doubt must show on my face.

"He gave us rules, you know?" Hunter speaks into the shell of my ear, not quite touching me, low enough no one else can hear. "We were told to get you ready for tonight. He needed you to be pure, but prepared."

"We could do whatever we wanted to you–*except* that." His jaw tenses. "And fuck that pissed me off."

I close my eyes thinking of all the ways they showed me how to be with a man. The salty taste of their cum, the way it felt, slick and hot covering my pussy. Their thickness in my hand, in my mouth. The feel of the tip of an arrow, the threat of pain, bringing me to orgasm. The mix of good and bad, and dirty and taboo all combined.

"Sometimes I think he doesn't want me," I admit. "That this is all for show."

Hunter laughs and hooks his finger into the loop of my collar, tugging me close. "Oh, he wants you." Damon's fingers trace down my collarbone and over the swell of my breast. They dip just below the boning in the corset, finding the hard metal bar in my nipple. It's less painful now, and more sensitive, pebbling into tight, desperate peaks. "He may not have touched you since the party started, but that mask of his, it doesn't hide the hunger. It's the way his jaw tenses. The way he grips the armrest like it's your throat."

"How do you know?" I ask.

Damon bites my shoulder, just hard enough to make me twitch.

Hunter shifts next to me, fingers curled into the cushion. "It's the look of a predator who is ready to pounce."

"Are you ready for him?" Damon asks. "Because I think if I checked, your pussy would be sloppy wet."

I shiver and nod.

"Good girl," he whispers. "Then go to him."

I rise, missing the heat of Damon's touch and the reassuring words from Hunter's mouth.

To my surprise, the King meets me halfway, the Shadows clearing as he gets closer.

He directs me deeper into the woods until we pass through an iron gate, into the darker edge of the forest and to a small clearing. In the center of the space is a solitary fire pit resting on top of a patio made of smooth, stone pavers. A single chair sits to the side. I look around and see that just a few feet away, tucked into the trees, is a small cabin.

I'm learning the House of Night, and the sprawling estate surrounding it, is endless and filled with many secret spots.

He stops beside the couch and turns to me. "Dance for me."

Not a question. Not a request. A command from my husband.

I blink up at him. "Here?"

His mask tips downward, and the corner of his mouth moves, just enough to let me see the edge of a smirk. "You're a dancer, aren't you?"

I nod, but I haven't danced for anyone since I left the Manor. Since they found me by the river and I came back from the dark place with bruises on my thighs and scars on my wrists.

Still, I step onto the stone.

The satin of the gown clings to my legs. I lift the damp hem, knotting it at my hip. He watches from the edge of the torchlight, silent, hooded, shadowed. I can feel his gaze like teeth on my skin.

I close my eyes and count.

One, two, three, four...

It starts slow. A lift of the arms, a turn of the head. I rise onto the balls of my feet, arching my spine. My hands paint lines in the air as I twist, a slow *pas de chat* that melts into a broken arabesque. My hair spills down my back as I pivot again, this time with more violence.

The steps get faster, sharper. Not ballet anymore–something rawer, more feral. Like I'm becoming part of this night, twirling in the veil itself. Neither here nor there for once in my life, but everywhere. I want him to see this side of me, the one where I'm confident in my arms and legs. Where I'm *stable*.

Breathing quickly, I leap and land in a crouch, then look up at him through my lashes. Baring my teeth, I let out a final hiss. I understand innately that this is the moment. The place before and after, more than the wedding itself or all the rites and rituals that led up to it.

He's still watching, his gloved fingers curled around the armrest of the couch.

He knows it too.

I stand slowly, one leg stretched behind me, arms open like an offering.

A long beat stretches between us. I could keep going, or...

"Is this what you wanted?" I whisper. The real question buried underneath: *Am I?*

His voice answers, low and hungry, a tone I haven't heard from him before: "Almost."

36

Timothy

The cabin door clicks behind us.

The day has been a blessing and a curse. Ceremonies like the Black Wedding bind more than man to wife. They bind the Barons, new and old, back to our ancestors. To our creators.

To death.

It's a reminder about sacrifice, about arrangements for the betterment of our organization. It's about obligation.

An obligation that now stands uncertain in the center of the small room. Exquisite in that shimmery black dress–a vision any man should want. I'm not any man, which is why I gave her the drug at the reception. I can almost see it pulsing through her bloodstream, doing its job to loosen her up, to shake away the tedious procedures of the last few days. But as we stand in this confined space, away from the party and her protective Barons, it isn't enough to take away her nerves.

Good.

She should be nervous.

She gave herself to me at the altar, and the sooner she accepts what that means, the better.

I strip off my gloves as I approach, dropping them to the table by the door. Then my mask–*the outer one*–not the soft felt one underneath. This one covers my eyes and nose, leaving my mouth free. It's a relief to get it off and I fantasize about removing it entirely.

Not tonight.

A fire burns in the stone fireplace and candles flicker on the mantle. A small suitcase sits against the wall. I assume it's filled with lace and silk, sexy little things packed to thrill a new husband. It's been years since I've been with a woman outside ceremonial duties, including my wife. The idea of this fresh little thing should have me begging.

A king doesn't beg.

She stiffens when I reach her, but she doesn't move away. Brave. With a hand beneath her chin I tilt her face up, forcing her eyes to meet mine. The collar shifts as she swallows.

"I made your Barons save two things for me," I look into her eyes. It's not fear I see–I'm not convinced this girl knows fear. Wildness is more accurate. Wild, defiant, feral. Who else could escape from her captors? Who else could so easily kill one of my chosen men? "Your mouth and your pussy."

I crush my lips against hers, swallowing her gasp. No soft coaxing. No gentle invitation. I dominate her mouth, demanding she open for me. When she hesitates, I bite her lower lip, just enough to sting, to draw blood. Her lips part instinctively, and I deepen the kiss, rough and possessive.

When I finally pull back she's breathless, dazed.

I press two fingers to her swollen mouth, smearing her red blood across them.

"Lick," I command.

Shaking, she obeys, her tongue flicking warm against my skin.

Ah, there's that good girl hidden under the wild-eyed gaze.

I grab her by the arms and turn her roughly, tugging at the laces of her corset. Each pull is deliberate, stripping away her armor. When the final lace gives, I let the dress fall, until she stands in body-hugging, *virginal*, white lace. Her breasts pushed together, her waist thin. That fucking collar around her neck.

Trembling. Vulnerable.

I lick my bottom lip and sit on the cushioned bench at the end of the bed.

"Undress for me," I order, wanting to see her–wanting *her* to show herself to *me*.

She hesitates, then reaches behind her back to unclasp the bra. It falls and I take a long, deliberate look at her, at her dark flesh, scarred here and there with the story of her life. Her full breasts, perky with youth, bedazzled with hard little bars DK pierced into her. They glint in the firelight. *Teasing.*

My mouth waters, and my cock swells tight and throbbing against my thigh.

"Come," I tell her, spreading my legs. Once she's close enough I reach out, grabbing her by the hips, pulling her between my knees. I hook my fingers into the thin lace strap of her panties, pulling them down. Her pussy is nearly bare, the thatch of hair I'd seen the night before waxed clean. In the crotch of her panties the spot of blood has dried, a signal of our arrangement, as valid–as binding–as a signature on a contract. I could get away without all of this. Spare the girl the violation, but I'm not that strong.

I *earned* Arianette, my wretched Daughter of Darkness, and I'm going to take her.

But first.

"Kneel."

Slowly, she lowers herself to her knees. I have no doubt she's been in this position before, my Barons would have had her there, filling her mouth with their greedy little cocks. Wide-eyed, she licks her lips, readying herself for me, but I reach for the slim column of her throat, thumb grazing over that leather strap.

"Tonight is between us." I unbuckle the collar and set it on the bench. "Your uncle and the ghosts of your family aren't invited."

I touch her, feel her body tremble under my fingertips. Feel her pussy quiver. My fingers come back slick, likely from DK and Hunter's attention outside. I'd enjoyed watching them, pleased that my little family is finding unity. She'll need them once this is done.

Standing, I lift her body off the ground and carry her to the bed, throwing her across the mattress. There's no gentleness when I spread her thighs with my hands, wanting to see the woman I've claimed. The first time I touched her was too quick, too exposed with her uncle leering over my shoulder. The second was too sacred, a moment less about me and more about ceremony.

But now... I can take my time. I kneel between her thighs, breathing in her scent. There's copper mingled with oily florals. There's something deeper, a musk that belongs only to her. I inhale and run my nose along the smooth skin of her inner thigh. Her legs tremble, and her hips shift.

When I finally taste her, I don't go slow, devouring her, licking, sucking, punishing her with pleasure. She squirms and whimpers under my mouth, grabbing at her sides, desperate and overwhelmed.

"*More*," she whispers.

I lower my mouth to her again, dragging my tongue up the seam of her sex, slow and filthy. I don't stop at her clit. I tease every part of her: the soaked folds, the tight, sensitive entrance that's been forced open by my mouth, the little fluttering pulse just above her slit.

She gasps my name–*no, not my name*, I correct, *my title*–a whisper of something else torn from her lips like a prayer. Then...

"*Daddy.*"

It makes me both furious and aroused, my cock throbs painfully against the tight press of my pants. It stills me, because that is not who I am. I am her husband. Her *King*, but it also ignites something in me that electrifies me from limb to limb. I hear myself murmur against her soaked cunt, "That's it. *Beg* for me."

I seal my mouth over her clit and suck hard.

Not tender, not gentle.

Relentless.

Her whole body arches up off the bed, her fingers digging into the covers like she's trying to anchor herself to the earth. She's never been touched like this before, never been undone by a man who knows exactly how to *wreck* a woman.

I flick my tongue over her swollen clit, again and again, punishing her with pleasure until her legs quake and her cries turn desperate. I *feel* the moment she shatters for me: her thighs clamp around my head, her hips buck against my mouth, and she sobs out a broken, shivering moan that ends in a whimper.

Her orgasm floods my mouth, hot, sweet and utterly innocent.

I lap it up, groaning into her pussy like a starving man given a feast. When she finally slumps back against the bed, spent and wrecked, I lift my head. My mouth is slick with her juices, my face wet from the force of her climax.

I lick my lips, savoring every drop of her.

She blinks up at me through heavy lashes, stunned and dazed.

I wipe my mouth with the back of my hand and smile darkly at her slick thighs, still spread open, her chest heaving, those little bars winking back.

She watches as I undress, peeling layer after layer, until I stand over her, hard and muscled. Her eyes drop down to my fisted cock. I feel like a teenager, like one of the young men over in the dorms. Like I could pop off in two seconds, humiliating myself and leaving her unsatisfied.

Fortunately for the both of us, restraint is something I know well. She's still panting, wrecked and shining with sweat, when I rise up over her.

For a moment, I just stare at the swollen flush of her cunt, glistening with her pleasure and the faint trace of blood. At the way her parted lips tremble. At the dazed, blown apart look in her wide brown eyes.

My cock twitches.

Whatever sweet little fantasy she thought she was stepping into–a wedding night of gentle kisses and tender promises–she's about to learn the truth about who I am and what I'm made of, but I'll wait until I'm buried inside her and feel the tight grip of her innocence around me.

"The ceremony, the bloodletting, the oaths and toasts... *that* is between me and the men of Forsyth. Chess pieces on the board between kings and their pawns. *This...*" I reach between our bodies, finding that shiny metal bar and tweaking it hard. "*This* is the truth between the two of us. The spoils of all of those arrangements. The reward for hard work and perseverance. For sacrifice. What I just gave you is a gift, one that I hope makes what comes next a little more bearable." I exhale. "Do you understand?"

She nods, too fast, too eager to please.

I grab her jaw, forcing her to look at me, pressing my thumb against her lower lip until she parts her mouth.

"I asked," I drag the head of my cock against the soaked seam of her pussy, "do you understand?"

Her breath hitches.

Goosebumps rush down her throat, her chest, to the tips of those pretty little nipples.

"Y-Yes," she whispers, voice shaking. "I understand."

"Good girl."

Without warning, I thrust forward, slow at first, cruelly slow, forcing the thick head of my cock past the tight resistance of her body. She gasps, tries to move, but I've got her hips pinned.

Nowhere to go.

Nowhere to hide.

She's *so fucking tight* around me. My vision blacks out for a moment, the sensation is so overwhelming. Hot. Wet. Virgin-soft. I drive deeper, watching the way her eyes widen, the way her nails scrape at my arms in helpless, useless protest. Every inch I sink inside her feels like I'm burying myself into her bones.

And she *is* mine.

By the end of this, there will be no part of her that will be untouched by my hands, my mouth, my cock. That I know for sure.

When I'm seated fully inside her, I pause, trembling with the effort it takes not to just rut into her like an animal. I give her time to stretch, those warm walls holding onto me. She's so fucking small compared to me. So fragile.

But this is what she was promised for.

What she was given for.

And I will *take*.

I drag my mouth along her throat, biting down just hard enough to make her whimper. Then I start to move, punching in long, deep strokes that force cries from her lips.

She clutches at me, overwhelmed, eyes shut like she's blocking everything out. She can try, but I know she feels me from the inside out. Whatever innocence she had left, whatever fantasy she tried to cling to... I shatter it with every punishing thrust.

Every filthy, perfect drag of my cock inside her virgin body brings out another sob that I swallow on my tongue. It only makes me fuck her harder.

"That's it, my wicked little thing," I snarl into her ear, "cry for your Daddy."

And she does.

She cries and writhes and clutches at me like I'm the only thing tethering her to her body, until she's shaking beneath me, legs splayed open, pinned helpless to the mattress by the weight of my body and the force of my thrusts.

Tears leak from the corners of her eyes, and I catch one with my thumb, smearing it across her cheek. "Perfect," I mutter, voice breaking into a growl. "Fucking *perfect*."

The cabin fills with the brutal sounds of our bodies colliding–flesh on flesh, her sweet whimpers, my ragged breathing, the creaking of the bed under my relentless rhythm. Her pussy clenches around me, hot and greedy, sucking me deeper with every stroke.

Taking me.

Accepting me.

Unlike the ghosts of my past.

Her cries pitch higher as I angle my hips, grinding against a spot deep inside her that makes her scream, arch her back, and clutch at me with desperate little hands.

She's coming again, without permission, her whole body convulsing around my cock.

"That's it," I snarl against her mouth. "I want to feel you clench around me." I don't slow down. I fuck her through it, through her shaking climax, while chasing my own release. I'm losing control. The thin thread of restraint I've held all night is fraying, snapping. I sink my teeth into her throat without warning, biting down hard where the leather collar once was, marking her with a final, bleeding claim.

Mine, not theirs. Not Hexley.

Maddox.

Her blood fills my mouth, hot and coppery and *ours.*

She moans, raw and broken and beautiful.

And that's when I break too.

I drive into her one final time, burying myself to the hilt, grinding against her as my cock jerks and spills inside her, claiming her in the oldest, darkest way a man can claim his wife. Holding her there, trembling, panting, our mouths locked together in a brutal, bloody kiss.

When I finally lift my head, her lashes flutter.

She's ruined.

Beautifully, completely ruined by me.

For a long moment, there is nothing but breath and the crackling of the fire. The aftermath of something I can never undo and will never risk again, which is why I stay buried deep inside her, her thighs trembling against my hips, feeling the way she clenches and spasms even now, and I brace for it, the tears. Silence. Maybe regret.

Instead, she laughs. A strange, fragile sound, curling out of her throat.

Arianette shifts underneath me, her soft, ruined body writhing as though she's chasing more pain, more pleasure. She cups the back of my neck with shaking hands, pulling me down until our foreheads touch.

"It hurt."

She hums, soft, dreamy. Her nails scratch lightly at my scalp.

"It's common," I say, wary of her lilting voice.

"I wanted it to," she whispers, and the words are a kiss against my skin. "Hurting means you're *real*."

I rear back enough to see her face.

Her eyes are wide, glassy, filled with stars and madness. A saint kneeling at an altar, high on holy visions. A doll cracked open.

I've been here before and just like last time, I'm drawn like a moth to a flame. Except the spark isn't bright. It never is, it's dark and twisted, demented and damaged, and I can't say no.

Why can't I say no?

"You took me apart," she says, almost wonderingly. "You made me yours. Now the world can't touch me."

A low growl escapes my throat. Possessive. I cup her jaw roughly, tilting her face up to mine, forcing her to meet my gaze. "You don't belong to the world," I tell her. "You belong to me."

Arianette shudders, a rapture passing through her thin frame. Her hands fist in my hair, desperate, greedy. "I *was waiting*," she says, voice distant, as if remembering a dream. "All this time. I was waiting for someone to come for me. To *claim* me."

Her head falls back, baring the throat I marked, the throat I own, offering herself again without hesitation. I run my teeth lightly across the tender skin there, feeling the frantic flutter of her pulse. I murmur against her flesh, "My broken little wicked thing."

Her laugh bubbles up again–sharp, stuttering–but this time it's a sound of relief. Of recognition. As if being shattered was the only thing she ever truly wanted.

That, I can do.

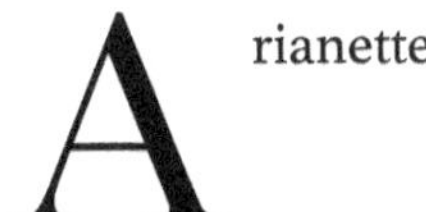

rianette

I FEEL HIM EVERYWHERE.

Inside. Outside.

Under my skin, inside my ribs, between my trembling thighs.

The cabin is dark but my body glows–flushed and raw and aching, slick with sweat and his seed. And I know, deep in that shattered little part of me, that something important has happened.

I'm not alone anymore.

I'm his. The Baron King's wife.

I blink up at the dark wood planks that make the ceiling, dizzy, my legs still spread wide across the ruined bed. The air smells like sex and smoke and *bliss.* He watches me from behind that mask, his body on the edge of the mattress, breathing hard, his fists clenched like he's afraid of what he'll do if I ask for more.

As if he doesn't already know.

I shift, feeling the sweet throb between my legs, and I whimper—soft and broken —*deliberate*. His head jerks toward me like a predator catching the scent of blood. I don't wait. I can't. Now that I've had him I want more. I crawl up over him, my hair wild and damp with sweat, sticking to my flushed cheeks.

Straddling his thighs, I feel the heat of him, the sheer *size* of him, and it makes something deep and reckless unfurl inside me.

"Tell me what you thought the first time you saw me," I purr, trailing my fingers lightly over the hard lines of his stomach, the dark trail of hair leading down. There's also a scattering of gray, reminding me that this isn't a boy I'm playing with. His body is incredible, masculine, with hard, defined muscles. I touch them, exploring him with my fingertips, stopping only to bend my head and lick his skin.

Marking.

Tasting.

My nails scrape lower, feather-light, just enough to make him suck in a breath.

"You were half-dead," he says, cradling my face. "With the shine of someone who'd seen the other side."

"A daughter of darkness," I whisper, leaning down so my lips just barely brush his ear. "Daddy."

He growls—a low, warning sound—but his hands stay fisted at his sides, liking the heat of my pussy against him. "You shouldn't call me that."

"Why not?" I pout.

"Because I'm not a good father," he says, reaching out to flick one of the bars. Pain shoots through me, startling right down to my cunt where the muscles squeeze. His tongue darts out, but I'm only thinking of the little blond boy in the photograph on his dresser. The one that doesn't live here anymore.

"Were you a good husband?" I ask, knowing I'm teetering on something dangerous.

He snorts. "Apparently not."

"I don't believe that." I slide down his body, pressing open-mouthed kisses to his chest, his ribs, his hips. I hear the sharp hiss of his breath when my tongue flicks against the sensitive skin just above his cock, teasing, taunting, refusing to give him what he wants.

He's hard for me.

Because of me.

I glance up at him through my lashes–and I see the murder in his eyes, the pure, feral need to rip control away from me and take.

"Let me be both," I say, just before dragging my tongue along the length of him, slow and cruel, savoring the salty taste of his skin. I wrap my hand around the base, squeezing just enough to make his hips jerk. "I can be both, a wife, a daughter, anything, whatever you want. We'll build a life together. A home. A place where you can feel safe with me, and I'll feel safe with you."

I almost ask him to remove the mask, to let me see his face, but he snarls something low and filthy under his breath, words I don't quite catch. His hands snap up, burying in my hair, forcing me closer. I hollow my cheeks and take him into my mouth, inch by inch, keeping my eyes locked on his. He groans–a broken, brutal sound–and I feel the bed shudder under us, the whole world narrowing down to the desperate push and pull between my lips and his body.

I'm relentless.

Wicked.

Devoted.

And when he finally loses that last shred of control, when he curses and thrusts into my mouth, fucking my throat with bruising need, I moan around him, the vibration pulling another vicious sound from his chest. When he comes, it's violent, and I take it all, greedy and grateful, swallowing him down like the wicked little thing he wants.

I pull back, wiping my mouth with the back of my hand, and I grin up at him, sweet and victorious.

"I can be good," I promise, voice hoarse and wrecked. We've been in this bed for hours. I've transformed into something he wants–something he can't live without: daughter, Baroness, wife. I don't care which.

As long as we walk this wicked path together.

~

THE FIRST THING I feel is *soreness.*

A deep, throbbing ache between my thighs, across my hips, in the tender, bruised places where his hands left fingerprints on my skin. He'd taken me again just after daybreak, flipping me on my stomach and settling me on all fours. He slid in and out of me like an animal, hips rutting against my backside. Panting and empty, he'd fallen against me, muscles taut, skin sweaty.

Insatiable.

The second thing I feel is *cold.*

The next, *silence.* It presses down over the cabin, thick and final. I reach blindly for him–the King, *my* King–but my hand meets only rumpled sheets.

The bed is empty.

How long has he been gone? A pit opens up in my stomach. Slow and widening.

"Hello?" My voice is a scratch. Weak. Dry from using it to lick and suck. I listen carefully.

No answer.

I sit up, looking around the room. His shoes are gone, as are his clothes. Only my crumpled wedding dress where he tossed it after stripping it from me. Panic blooms sharp and bright behind my ribs.

No.

No, no, no.

Not after last night–not after what he *took* from me. What I *gave.*

I stumble out of bed, dragging the tangled sheet around my naked body. My legs tremble. I make it three steps before the door to the bathroom opens.

Steam curls out, warm and damp, and he steps into the room–

Fully dressed.

Buttoned into a black shirt, slacks, polished shoes. His regular mask is back over his face, hiding him from me. No mussed hair. No feverish hands. No kiss-bruised mouth. The man who destroyed me last night is gone. This is the King now. Impenetrable. Remote. I stop, blinking up at him like a fool. Am I? Am I a fool?

My heart flutters, desperate, a trapped thing against my ribs.

"You're here," I breathe, almost laughing with relief.

He doesn't answer.

Just looks at me–cool, assessing. I shuffle closer, the sheet slipping lower on my shoulders. "I thought we would spend the morning together. Ask Graves to send up some breakfast, then we could pick up where we left off?"

I want his hands on me again. His cock inside, driving into me with insatiable want. I want that feeling of being *owned*... not the cold spot currently building in my belly.

"The honeymoon is over, Arianette." He steps past me. "I have work to do."

"Oh." I try not to show my upset. It's obvious he doesn't like that. "Well, then let me help you. I can–I can make you something to eat," I say quickly, my words tumbling over each other. "Or tea. I'm good at tea. I can... I can be good for you." I don't know why I'm babbling. I just can't seem to stop. "I'm your wife now," I remind him. "I can take care of you. I can do wifely things. Take over for whatever it is Graves does for you. Laundry, sewing, cleaning, cooking..." the words just keep coming. "I learned all of these at the Manor."

I hover there, trembling, half-naked and clinging to the threadbare sheet, searching his unreadable mask for a crack, a sign, anything–

"I'm not hungry," he says, voice void of any of the emotion we'd shared overnight, "and I have a busy day ahead." He tugs at his cuffs, pushing the tiny buttons into place.

"We can do other things," I offer. "Back in the bed. Or out of the bed." I reach for his hand, but he jerks away, as if he's been burned.

"I had Graves bring you some breakfast, water, tea, and some supplements." He walks calmly over to a tray I didn't notice in my panic. A dome sits neatly over a plate of food. He lifts a glass of water and carries over the capsules. I blink once, then take the glass from him, and he holds out that smooth hand, the one that made me cry out over and over last night. The one that made me beg. "These will help with the dehydration and any side effects of the revelry last night." He drops them into my still, open hand. One, two, three...

I look at the pills. One is filled with brown powder. The other white. Then there's a tablet, hard and pressed. Different from the supplements I've been taking. There's a nagging at the back of my skull.

"What is this?" I ask, staring at it. "It looks different."

"It is," he says, looking into a mirror and brushing a loose strand of dark hair into his waves. "It's an emergency contraceptive. Your uncle was so insistent about your virtue, we didn't think to plan ahead."

"Contraceptive?" My eyes flick to his. "To keep me from having a baby."

"Yes."

"You don't want to have my baby?" I ask, an unexpected emotion crashing into me.

"Last night was a mistake. A loss of judgment after the stress and strain of the ceremony. I allowed myself to get caught up in the celebration, in Samhain, and frankly," his eyes dart down to where I clutch the sheet, "in you." A hollow pounding echoes in my ears, and I try to keep upright. He sighs, taking the pill from me and holding it up. "You are a child, Arianette, and neither of us are in a position to bring another one into this world." He lifts his chin. "Now, be a good girl and take the pill."

My jaw drops open, and he pops it on my tongue. A moment later I'm swallowing the water and the bitter, chalky pill.

He watches to make sure I swallow, then steps back, dusting his hands as if he's brushing off something unpleasant.

"What is happening?" I ask, trying to make sense of it. "Daddy?"

He winces, then says, "I gave you what I could. Made it good for you in a way that I don't think your Barons would have."

My lips part. Words scrape against the back of my throat but I can't force them out.

"This is what being my wife looks like," he says. "A beautiful woman who sits by my side when I need her. A fixture for celebrations and ceremonies. Nothing more, nothing less." The floor seems to tilt under me. "Get dressed. Go to class. Take your dance lesson. See to your Barons. Fulfill your oaths."

I clutch the sheet tighter, feeling it slip against my sweating palms.

"And what if I don't?" I ask, voice splintering like glass.

He turns slowly, his shoulders stiff, his mask glinting dully in the gray light. Stern. Displeased. "I don't think you'll like the result."

Whatever hold I have on myself slips, and what emerges is something unfamiliar but true.

"*Fuck. You.*" I seethe.

"Excuse me?" His head tilts, like he truly didn't hear.

"I should tell him," I threaten, grasping at straws. "Go back and let him know that you reneged on the deal. That it was pig's blood at the wedding. That you left me here, alone, instead of taking me like a man."

He crosses the room, each step deliberate, each footfall sinking into my bones like hammer blows. He picks up the red leather collar from the bench at the end of the bed. Faster than I can blink, his hands are around my throat.

I cry out, his fingers pinching. "Let go."

"You seem confused, Arianette. You don't have the power here, I do. Your uncle doesn't give a shit about you as long as the association to my title gives him the prestige he so desperately wants." His face is close to mine as he buckles the strap tightly around my throat. I flinch, the metal ring at the front burning cold against my skin. His finger loops inside it and pulls *hard*. "I warned you about disobeying," he murmurs. "Your uncle warned me too."

"I should have let Armand fuck me during the Hunt," I grind out, sucking in air. "Let him fuck me and kill me then. It would have been better than this."

He growls through a clenched jaw, and releases the loop. I bend over, drawing in a full breath, as he walks to the dresser and opens the top drawer.

From within, he pulls out a black velvet box and before he even opens it, I feel the tremor snake down my spine. Inside lies the punishment rod, gleaming in the low light, waiting. He lifts it out carefully, reverently, like a priest with a holy relic. "I didn't want to use this," he says softly. "But I will."

Something inside me cracks. Fractures into jagged, splintering pieces. I stumble back, clutching the sheet tighter around myself. My heart slams against my ribs, a frantic bird desperate to escape. The words tumble out of me–shrill, childish, furious.

"You're nothing but a monster hiding behind a stupid mask!" Tears blur my vision, hot and stinging. I shove my fists against my eyes but it doesn't stop. It won't stop. "You live here alone pretending like you have a family. That your Shadows are more than stupid frat boys playing dress up and hand-picking Barons to do little more than clean up the messes in Forsyth."

His eyes narrow, his fingers tight around the rod. "I'd watch your mouth."

"What happened to your wife?" I ask, going straight over the edge, because that's the place that feels best to me. "What happened to your son? Did you fuck her and turn her away the next day? Did you lock him in a cage? Play manipulative games? Treat him like dirt under your boots?"

The air goes razor sharp. "Don't you speak about my wife and son. *Ever.*"

"*I'm* your wife!" I scream. "*I'm* the one you married in front of a church full of people!" I take a stumbling step toward him, trembling so hard the sheet slips dangerously low. "Where are they?" My words are poison now, wild and reckless. "Why do they hate you?" I sob. "Why are you all alone?"

Something *snaps* across the room. It's not the rod. It's him.

In two long strides, he's on me. All power and muscle in full control. He rips the sheet from my body, yanking it so hard it burns across my skin. I stumble, naked, gasping, hands grabbing at air. He fists a hand in my hair and *shoves* me down onto the floor. Forces me onto my hands and knees.

"Since you want to behave like a brat," he growls, "you'll be treated like one."

The first strike of the rod lashes across my backside: searing, sudden, cruel. I yelp, the sound punching out of me without warning. Another blow falls. And another. Each one driving me deeper across the floor, my fingers clawing at the rug.

"You will learn," he snarls above me, punctuating each word with another brutal strike, "that my life–my past–is none of your goddamn business."

The rod snaps across my thighs, my hips and ass. Heat blooms under my skin, welt after welt, forcing out a wail.

"You are *nothing* more than a business arrangement," he spits, voice low and venomous. "A means to an end. Your uncle had something I wanted. Something worth shackling my family to a foolish, deranged girl."

Another blow.

Then another.

I flinch and brace myself for the next blow. Knowing it's useless to tell him to stop; I don't think he can even hear me, not anymore.

"You exist to serve a purpose, you stupid, deranged girl. To obey. To behave." The rod slashes down hard. My vision whites out at the edges. "To be a vessel for my Barons to pour their lust and rage into. I need them sharp and focused, not frequenting bars or clubs. They get their fill at home, and then work for me. That's how being a Royal works."

He tosses the rod on the floor, and I feel his fingers curl around the leather collar, knocking a cry out of me as he jerks me back. His breath is on my ear, hot and dangerous. "It's a bold threat to pretend you'll run back to the Manor, but you and I both know you'd rather die first." His fingers twist, cutting my air off. "So look at it this way, if you don't want to be sent back to your uncle's house in disgrace, you will learn to submit, my sweet, sweet, Daughter of Darkness, you will learn to never cross me."

My body collapses fully onto the floor, trembling uncontrollably. I hear his footsteps on the floor, the door slam as he leaves.

I don't move. Not an inch, staying on the floor humiliated, shattered. The room grows still. An eerie, disturbing silence, one that widens and gives space in my chest to the truth of it all:

This is exactly what I deserve.

38

D^{amon}

I WAKE at the click of the bedroom door. I'm used to it by now–Hunter taking Ares out for his morning ritual. Still, this morning it yanks me half out of a dead sleep, my head pounding, mouth dry as cotton. I'm not even sure how we got back to the house.

I shove my face into the pillow and groan. The sun is already too bright, too full, spilling through the parted drapes. It feels *wrong* to be awake in a world that still looks normal when everything under my skin feels shredded.

The hangover isn't just from the booze, the pills, or the endless bottles of champagne, but from the whole event itself. It was from rituals, the blood, the goddamn sight of her–broken open for us all to see. I push myself up, scratching at my chest. Outside the window, I hear Hunter whistling, calling out in German.

I swing my legs over the side of the bed, shove on a pair of jeans, and head down the hall to the door that leads outside, blinking into the light. The cold fall air hits my bare chest, waking me up like a splash of water.

"Hey, man," I say, walking over to where he leans against his truck. Ares sniffs around the treeline. Hunter's hair is wild from sleep and he's in a rumpled white T-shirt and jeans. His tattoos creep above the collar, and cigarette smoke curls from between his fingertips. He looks like he went through hell and back last night. Maybe we did. I nod at the cigarette. "Thought those were only for the radio show."

"Yeah." He looks a little guilty. "I needed something to wake me up after last night."

He offers me a hit. Pinching the cigarette between two fingers, I take a long, much-needed drag. The buzz is light, but hits the mark. I inhale a second time, deeper, before slowly blowing out.

Handing it back, I say, "I've gotta piss," and walk around the other side of the garage. I've got my dick in my hand when I see it, the flash of slick black paint through the trees. The King's Jaguar, coming down the drive.

Hurrying, I shake off, zip up, and turn just as the car slows, finally stopping right at us. The window whirs down. Cold air leaks out, carrying the sharp scent of leather and something darker underneath—copper. Blood? One of the Shadows, a junior named Kendrick who seems to be made up entirely of muscles, sits at the wheel. The King is in the back, one leg crossed over the other with today's newspaper in his lap, his mask glinting in the morning sun, as if the night before never happened.

Hunter tosses the cigarette and straightens up.

"I'm heading into town," the King says. His voice is sharp, brisk. Like we hadn't just all experienced the ceremony together the night before. "Business."

Hunter shoots me a look. I shrug.

"Honeymoon's over already?" I ask, smirking.

The King's gaze shifts to me, impassive behind the mask.

"Samhain is over," he says. "As are the festivities."

There's a beat of silence. He folds the paper in half before adding,

"The Baroness is at the cabin. She's yours now. All restrictions are lifted."

Hunter blinks, like he's trying to translate it. But I get it immediately. The words hit like a jolt of adrenaline straight to my gut. *All restrictions.*

Finally.

My cock twitches, thinking about how sweet it's going to be to bury myself in that tight little cunt. The King says nothing else, which is good because the blood is already thudding in my ears as it makes the swift retreat to my crotch. The window hums back up, sealing him away, and Kendrick eases the car back into motion, dust curling in their wake.

I rub my hands together, grinning. It's a shit-eating grin. I don't even try to hide it.

Hunter raises a brow at me. "You look like you're about to do something illegal."

"Maybe in some states," I say.

I'm half-hard already just thinking about it–thinking about *her*. The way she looked at the altar, the way she moved at the reception, all soft and shiny and perfect and broken in all the best ways.

Hunter is quiet, but those wheels are turning in that big, fat brain of his. He wants the Baroness as much as I do, just... differently. I get that about him, I sense it, which is why I ask, "You wanna watch?"

WE HEAD TO THE CABIN, shoes crunching over the dead leaves. The scent of bonfire lingers in the air, slightly damp from the morning dew. The building is isolated, perfect for privacy, to get away from prying ears.

To get loud.

I've been waiting for this. Since the moment I took the oath. The restrictions were necessary, I get that. She had to remain a virgin for the arrangement to go through, but he's done with her.

She's ours.

"Jesus, DK, wait up," Hunter mutters as he tries to catch up to me, but I barely hear him. My heart's pounding, and my dick's hard against my thigh. I run through the options as I climb the porch steps. Missionary? Doggy? Cowgirl? Fuck, the thought of her riding me, those pretty little pierced nipples bouncing in my face–

"Where is she?" Hunter asks, stepping in the room first.

I snap out of my fantasy, taking in the room. The bed is torn apart, sheets slung over the edge like a discarded skin. The wedding gown is heaped on the floor like she crawled out of it, her lace bra and panties pushed under the bed. The rod–the one her uncle gave the King–is lying just beside the rug.

The sight of it makes me uneasy. No one at that dinner table had been impressed by the Dean's methods of control. It'd been creepy, territorial, and the Baroness looked like she'd seen a ghost the moment it appeared.

Hunter bends, picking it up, feeling the weight in his hand. He inspects the end. "There's blood on here."

Whatever happened here was thorough. Brutal. The King hadn't just taken her virginity, he'd broken her down.

Jealousy pricks the back of my neck, but it's tempered by the knowledge that I'll be next.

"Hey," Hunter says quietly, chin lifting toward the back of the room. The bathroom door's ajar, and a single line of golden morning light cuts across the wood floor. I step forward, pushing the door open slowly, and see her. She's bending over the sink. Naked except for the red leather collar buckled around her throat. Her lower back and ass are a mess of dark bruises and rising welts–some angry and still forming, others already purpled. One curves all the way across the swell of her hip. The faucet's running, water spilling over her fingers like she doesn't even feel it.

She stares at herself in the mirror. Wide, vacant, red eyes. Hair messy and hanging down her back, her lips are dry and cracked. She looks like something wild and hunted. Like something that's already halfway gone.

Our eyes meet in the mirror.

Leaning around her, I turn off the tap. Her hands shake and I press mine over them. Cold. Damp. So small.

Hunter lingers behind me, silent. Watching.

"What happened?" I ask, brushing my fingers up her spine. Her back arches, jutting that pretty little ass out. I trace one of the welts, and she flinches. "He punished you?"

She nods, tiny and pathetic. Hunter grabs the wet washcloth in the sink and squeezes out the water. Carefully, he dabs the cloth over each welt, making her hiss with each press.

"What did you do?" I ask, trying to imagine what incited such rage. "Did you refuse him?"

This time it's a shake of the head and she says softly, "Everything was good. Better than good. We had an amazing night. He made me feel so amazing, and I made him feel amazing, too. I know I did."

"Then what?" Hunter asks, turning on the faucet again and rinsing off the cloth.

"Then came this morning," her voice trembles. "He told me he didn't want me. That he would never want me."

"And that's why he punished you?" I glance at Hunter's creased forehead in the mirror.

"He punished me to control me, like every other man in my life." She sways, just slightly, like the weight of everything is too much. "Even you."

I catch her hips, pulling her back against me. I press my palm to her belly, my other hand cupping her breast. Her skin is so warm. I feel her breath catch. "Being controlled by a man in Forsyth is how you stay safe," I tell her. "And what did you think? That the King would suddenly decide he was in love with you? Just because he wet his dick?"

My hand slides up, fingers reaching for the silver bars. I give them a tug and watch the pain cross her face. She's gorgeous like this, hurt and bruised. The shattered, fragile mess he left behind. My cock thickens behind my zipper, pressed hard against her ass.

She doesn't move away. Doesn't push me off. Just keeps looking at herself in the mirror like she doesn't know who that girl is anymore.

Fair. The girl we dragged out of those woods, who laid on the altar last night, is no longer the same. Which is why I let her know, "He may not want you, but he gave you to us," I say, breath hot against her neck. "He's not the only one that can make you feel good, doll baby."

I slide my hand lower, between her thighs. She's warm. Wet, even. Whether it's for me or just leftovers from him doesn't matter. I can pretend. Her breath catches. She grabs the edge of the counter like she might collapse, but still–no protest. Her thighs clench, but not to close me out. She's trembling, not resisting.

"I've been waiting for him to give the word," I whisper. "For him to tell us that we can have you the way we want." My fingers are already working between her folds, slow and rough.

She gasps. It's soft.

Hunter doesn't move. Doesn't say a word. He's behind us, leaning against the frame, arms crossed. Watching. I know what she's hoping. That he'll say something. Step in. But he won't. He's here for the show.

I wedge a knee between her thighs, spreading her apart, then hook a finger inside her, pushing in deep. The gasp that rushes from her is desperate and panicked, making my cock twitch.

"How tight is she?" he asks, moving closer. He bends, getting an eyeful of her pussy.

"Tight as that collar around her throat." The tension in her walls is still there; she'll stay that way for a while. More reason to fuck her good while she's like this. Her knees buckle and I catch her, hold her steady, letting her weight fall back against me. "Don't fade out on me yet, doll baby."

"Damon," she begs, "I can't–"

"You can and will." I press a kiss to her temple, then drag my tongue across the edge of her ear. "I've protected you, haven't I? I've waited. I've played nice for the King. For you. Not anymore."

I unzip my jeans, pull myself out, hard and angry in my fist. Pre-cum builds at the tip and I rub it with my thumb. I grind against her, sliding along her slickness without pushing in. "Look at us," I growl, staring into the mirror. "You, bent over like this. Me, finally getting what I earned. What should have been mine that night in the woods."

A small noise escapes her throat. She doesn't answer.

I don't need her to.

I grip her hips and thrust inside.

Finally.

I exhale as she tenses, body jerking. The move makes her tits bounce and fuck, I slam into her again to see them rise and fall. A cry rips from her mouth, and I almost come right then. She's too tight, too raw, *too fucking good.* I hiss through my teeth and grip the edge of the counter, steadying myself.

"Shhh," I whisper, rocking into her again. "I know. I know. You can take it."

Her fingers go white around the sink edge. Her eyes are locked on the mirror, locked on *me.* I don't look away. I want her to see me while I'm inside of her.

Hunter shifts, standing up straight. His jaw's tight, hands in his pockets. I fist her hair and yank her head back just enough to whisper against her neck, "You were made for this, weren't you? To be used."

"No," she sobs, "I was made for him."

"But he doesn't want you." Each thrust sends her forward, bumping into the porcelain. The welts across her ass slam into my pelvis. I brush my fingers over them again and she whimpers.

"You like the pain." Hunter licks his bottom lip. "Don't lie."

She shakes her head. It's barely a motion. Almost pitiful. But her body's giving her away. Tight and soaking, clenching around me like she doesn't want to let me go. Her legs keep buckling, but I don't let her fall. I just keep using her the way she's meant to be used. Over and over, whenever I want.

"Tell him the truth."

"I like it," she grinds out. "I deserve it."

"Why's that?" he asks, moving as close to her as he can without touching her. "Why do you deserve it, Baroness?"

"Because I'm bad. Wicked." She winces when her hips hit the counter, and I hold her pinned there, trying to control myself.

"Because I'm broken. No one ever wanted me at the Manor. Not my mother or my uncle or the people who came for the other children."

Her breath hitches, sharp and uneven, fogging the mirror in front of her. She doesn't look away from her reflection, she doesn't dare. I see the shame flicker in her eyes, but something else too. That little seed of hunger. The part of her that wants to be broken open and filled again.

Hunter leans in close to her ear, voice smooth. "What does it feel like to have DK in you?"

"He's big," she falls forward on her elbows. "It hurts."

Unable to hold back any longer, he shoves his hand down his pants and grips his cock. She whimpers, biting her bottom lip hard enough to leave a mark. My hand grips her hip, fingers digging into the bruises already starting to bloom. I shouldn't care how fragile she is, how wrecked. But I do. I care because it makes her mine in a way no wedding contract ever could.

I drag my fingers down her spine, feeling her shiver all the way to her knees. "You belong here," I remind her. "Right here, caught between pain and pleasure. Right between your Barons. That's where you're the most honest."

Hunter finally touches her, just the edge of her jaw, tilting her head slightly so she has no choice but to see the both of us in the mirror. His gaze is unreadable–dark and unreadable, but his presence is grounding, a tether between where she's been and where she's going.

I slide my hand between her thighs, feeling the heat of her, the slickness. "Still pretending you don't want this?" I ask, even though we both know the answer. Her body's betrayed her a dozen times over. And even if it didn't, I wouldn't stop.

She shakes her head again, this time slower. No more lies. No more pretending.

"Good girl," I whisper, and watch the words strike her like a match. She closes her eyes, lips parting, breath catching again.

I hold her there in that stillness, not moving, not speaking, just breathing her in. Her pussy trembles around me, the telltale sign she's ready for release. "You want it don't you?" I stroke my hand down her hair, then around her body to the metal bar. I pull sharply and feel her pussy squeeze in return. "You want to come on my cock, release all this pent up dirtiness you're carrying inside." I glance at Hunter, who looks as frustrated as I think she feels, his cock is in his hand now, and he strokes slowly up and down his shaft. "If it was just me and you, I'd let you suffer, but it's not. It's your lucky day, doll baby. Let's give your Baron what he wants."

I pull back, almost fully out, before punching back in, this time faster, picking up the pace. Her breath breaks–sharp, shallow. She shakes her head, but her body tells the truth. I feel it tightening around me, pulsing. Her knuckles bend, nails digging into the porcelain as if it could hold her together. But nothing will. Not after this.

"That's it," I whisper against her throat, gripping tighter. "Give in. Be good for me, just once."

And she does. Her body jerks, surrendering with a strangled cry that she tries to muffle against her shoulder. I don't let her. I want Hunter to hear every sound. Every broken gasp.

She tenses around me, that hot little pussy strangling me with tight little clenches. I'm loud when I come, a groan rumbling deep in my chest. It's like I'm releasing everything I've been holding onto for weeks.

We're both hot, sticky with sweat, our bodies both tight and loose. I pull out, wet and slippery, and grab a towel off a hook on the wall.

Hunter's still got his cock in his hand, stroking slowly. I lift an eyebrow. "You going next?"

He shakes his head, and Arianette's holding herself up by draping her body over the counter. Their eyes meet, and he just says, "Turn around." She moves slowly, but follows his order, her chest rising and falling. "Get on the counter."

"I can't," she says, looking half dead. She winces as she moves, the pain from the welts probably worse than before.

"You can, and you will," Hunter tells her, and even though I don't think she has what it takes to leverage herself I watch as she lifts herself up, those pretty little tits swaying with every move.

I'm going to fuck them next.

For now, I step back, letting Hunter move close in front of her. "Spread apart," he says, eyes hazy, but zeroed in on her pussy. Her fingers slip through the sticky wetness, the cum I left behind. Their eyes hold as he jerks off, hand moving along his shaft, his thumb rolling over the tip, spreading fluid with every pass.

He never touches her. It's just the sight of her like this turning him on. The red-rimmed eyes. The messy hair. The welts imprinted in her flesh. She's a terror, but she's *our* terror, and that's what makes this so incredibly hot.

It's on those slick lips that he comes, thick and ropey, dripping all over her pussy. My dick twitches, wanting to be a part of it, wanting to go at her again. Wanting to take everything we can. It's a compulsion. An all-consuming need.

But I let them have their moment, this time the observer, and watch this ruined girl slump back on the counter. We've broken her with both our bodies and words, shattering her with every thrust until there's only one thing left for us to do.

Pick up the pieces, and do it again.

39

H unter

WE DON'T SAY much on the walk back to the house. Ares trots ahead of us, although he's looked back at the cabin more than once. I could tell he didn't want to leave her, sprawled across the sheets, marked and used.

Next to me, DK seems lighter, shoulders loose after getting some release. I'm the opposite. My stomach's tight. I'm not sure how I feel.

"She'll get used to it," he says, suddenly, shoving his hands in his pockets. As if the statement absolves us of our actions.

"Yeah, maybe." I pick up a stick and whistle at Ares. He perks up, tongue lolling, excited. I throw the stick, and he darts after it.

I sense DK's eyes on me. "What?"

"You having regrets?" There's an accusation in his tone.

I close my eyes and exhale through my nose. Not because I disagree–but because I remember it too well. The way her back arched. The way her eyes begged even as her lips said *no*. And the way I didn't touch her. Not the way I wanted.

"It's not that."

"Then what?" He stops in the middle of the yard. "Because we're in this together, and I need to know where your head is at."

"I can't just fuck her," I blurt. "Not like you do." It's getting harder. Harder not to touch. I wish I was more like DK, able to take what I want, able to do it without going too far. She looked at me. Right before. Right after. Eyes wide, glassy, begging for something I didn't give her. And I could've. That's the worst part. I could've fucked her good. Felt her clench around me, but I didn't.

"Yeah, I figured. Some kind of kink, right?" He eyes me. "You like watching."

"I..." The lump in my throat makes it painful to swallow. "I can't help it. And it's safer this way. For all of us."

Every step we take toward the house requires enormous strength not to turn around and go back to the cabin to take what belongs to me. To leave her with a mark inside, not just out.

"She's made for it," he goes on, low now, confident. "You know that. For the pain and the pleasure. You saw it when she came apart. That wasn't fear. That was surrender. Real, dirty surrender."

My jaw tightens. That's what's eating me. Not that it happened– but that I *want* it again. That I want her crying, wrecked, my name in her throat. That I'm fucking mad I held back. I clench my hands.

"She's not going anywhere," he reminds me. "Plenty of time."

"Ares! *Komm!*" I shout as we reach the house, its colored-glass windows and peaked roof looming ahead.

Graves meets us at the doorway. "The King asked me to bring some information to your quarters. He said, and I quote, 'Now that the wedding is over, it's time to stop fucking around and get to work.'" His lips quirk. "Everything is on the table in the den."

After Graves walks off, DK says, "Damn, I guess the King was right. Samhain is over."

Inside, Ares picks up his bone and jumps up on the cracked leather couch. On the game table is the stack of paperwork Graves left us, and it only takes a moment to realize it's information on the missing girls.

"I've been working on something." I walk into our bedroom and grab the folded-up map out of my backpack. "I took all the information I got from my radio show and started tracking it." Spreading the map out on the table, I point out the key. "The red dots are for hard evidence," he says. "The blue circles are for suspicious activity that we need to follow up on. The Xs mark every place a girl was last seen alive."

DK flips through a file. "These have all the details on the missing girls, including things like name, date, age, class schedule, and medical records. I don't even want to know how he got those."

The more we study it, the more obvious it becomes that everything circles back to the same thing the Kings, the police and Feds have had all along: nothing.

"Does this look like a sort of straight line to you?" DK asks, tracing a line down the map with his finger between two of the dots. "Stella was last seen here." He points to one spot. "And Arianette was seen here."

I lean over and study the map. "Close enough. Except the university is in the middle."

Something pings in my mind, and I flip through the papers, pulling out a hand-drawn schematic of the tunnel system. It's crudely drawn and the King implied that not all of it is on official maps. "We've got the crypts, an underground rail, emergency systems and campus facilities. Some seem to connect and others don't."

DK sits back and runs his hand through his hair. "Nothing indicates that these are linked in any way either."

"Since when do the powers that be cooperate in Forsyth?"

"Any word on Sofia?" he asks, toying with his eyebrow piercing.

"Last I heard the Dukes had her in a safe spot in the West End and someone goes with her back and forth to campus." I drop a file on the table and sigh. "I can check in on her at my next class, see if anything suspicious has come up."

DK grunts. "At the reception Sy asked me again about the hypno-tism shit. I promised we'd bring her by sometime soon."

Hunter gives me a skeptical look. "You think she's ready?"

"No," he grins, "but since when does the Baroness get to decide when she's ready?"

"Now?" I ask, partially because I want to get back to the cabin. There's an itch under my skin, the urge to see her and maybe finish what I didn't earlier.

"Eh, let's give her a bit to rest and clean up," he says, slinking back in his chair. "But after that, it's like the King said, it's back to business."

ARES TROTS beside me as we head back through the trees. Sun's starting to dip, slicing orange through the thinning canopy. The path is quiet. Too quiet. Even DK notices.

"Fuck, it's kind of creepy out here." He glances over his shoulders. "I've heard that bobcats live in this area."

"You ever see one?" I ask.

"No, but I came upon a mother black bear and her cubs when I was in the wilderness program." He zips up his jacket. "Just about shit myself."

I laugh, thinking about him in a state of panic. He's always so even-tempered, and fearless. But I've seen the scar on his throat. That shit will change a person.

"I just hope she's cleaned up and ready to go."

"She was barely moving," I say, but something feels wrong. My stomach's a knot. Not guilt–just instinct.

We climb the porch and I push open the door. The bed is stripped. Her wedding dress is gone. The air is heavy, warm and humid with sweat and sex and blood.

"Jesus Christ."

I turn and see DK staring at the wall. Well, not just the wall.

There's writing–*everywhere.*

Smeared and dripping. Thin, frenzied strokes, off the tip of a finger.

Horns and hooves. He breathes inside my head.

Monsters. Blue eyed. Devil's hair. Shiny silver.

Shhhh. He'll hear you.

I'm not her. I'm not her. I'm not her.

The Beast is hungry. He'll eat the pretty girls first.

"What the fuck..." DK steps forward, turning in a slow circle. A piece of a broken teapot sits on the dresser, the sharp tip coated in red.

The letters are smeared in places like she tried to scrub them out–or clawed at them. Some of the prints are small and bloody. Her hands must have been shaking. There's a streak leading to the door. A trail.

I step forward and swing the door shut. The back is covered, in one word, repeated over and over.

RUNRUNRUNRUNRUNRUNRUNRUNRUNRUNRUNRUNRUn
   runrunrunrunRUNrunrunrunRUnrunrunrunrunRUN
   RunrunrunRUnRunrunrunrunrUnRunrunruNrunrUn

AND AT THE BOTTOM, in bold.

BURN. IT. DOWN.

"SHE'S FUCKING LOST IT," he says, jaw tight. "She's gonna hurt herself. Or someone else."

"No," I say, already thinking, moving. "At least not yet."

She's done it twice before. Once by the river. Then in the Hunt. When Arianette feels trapped the first thing she does is figure out a way to run away. I turn, eyes searching, then kneel beside the bed and reach under, grabbing the scrap of lace I'd seen earlier in the day–her panties. The bloodstain from the night before is dry, but it'll do.

Ares perks up as I hold them out.

"*Such,*" I whisper, pressing them to his nose.

He sniffs, wanders around the room, then bolts for the door.

"She'll head for cover," I say, following fast. "Somewhere we don't know about."

"We should have put her back in the cage." DK jogs to keep up. "The King is going to fucking flip."

After seeing the rod and the wounds on Arianette's back, I'm not eager to see what punishment he would dole out on us for running her off. Which is why I mutter, mostly to myself, "Not if we find her first."

40

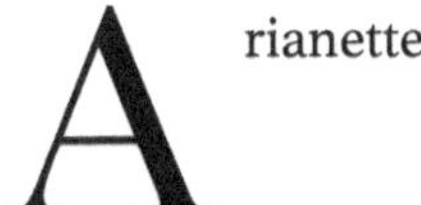rianette

THE FOREST SWALLOWS SOUND.

It's just me and dead leaves underfoot, the slap of my bare soles against dirt and moss. The wedding dress drags behind me, heavy with dew, mud, and blood. Underneath, the welts sting, burning with every step. I should take it off. Burn it. Bury it. But I can't. It's mine. It's proof something happened. Proof I mattered–even if just for one night.

The bonfire smoke is long gone now, replaced with the sting of pine and rot and sweat. My knees keep buckling. My thighs are slick. I can still feel all of them. The King taking my body: the hard swell of his cock, the warm feel of his semen. I hear Damon's voice as he stood behind me, hands angry and rough, whispering all those teases and taunts. I feel Hunter's eyes. Taste his silence. The bite of the counter under my ribs. The bruise of the rod before that.

"You were made for this."

I laugh. It comes out like a hiccup, sharp and cracked. It sounds like someone else. Not the girl that married a king. I sound like *her.* The girl from before all of this. The girl that survived and escaped and ran. The Barons think I belong to them now. That because he handed me over like a discarded toy I'm theirs to break. They don't know what they've done. They don't understand what I am.

I was supposed to be *safe.*

The hem of the dress catches again, snagging on a root, and I stumble forward, catching myself on my hands. I stay there for a second, letting my breath even out, but I can feel it building–rising inside me. I rewrap the bandage on my arm, covering the fresh wound, then scrawl something in the dirt with a stick. A spell. Something to ward myself in the dark forest. A protection for the crying girls still behind the walls.

The cabin is far behind me now, too far to go back. Damon and Hunter probably think I'll just lie there in the bed like a good little Baroness, waiting for them to come use me again.

I thought about ending it all there, in that little cabin where I lived those perfect moments. Where I felt the snapping teeth of hell. I didn't need to look in the mirror, I'd done that while Damon forced himself in me. I knew what I'd become. I found a piece of china, sharp and pointed, and sliced it down my arm. Blood spilled, hot and slippery. I walked to the fields.

Periwinkle.

I knew then I had to go home.

Pushing back to my feet, I continue, ignoring how my legs ache and my back burns. The welts criss-crossing my skin throb with every movement. I keep walking, through the branches that claw at my arms and chest. The collar at my throat pulls tighter with every step. I want to rip it off, but I don't. It's a reminder of who I am, for now and forever.

Rotting from the inside out.

I laugh again, just a puff of air, but it gets caught in my throat and turns into a sob. I clamp my hand over my mouth and fall against a tree, breathing hard. My skin is slick with sweat. I'm dizzy. Hungry. My body is begging me to stop.

But I can't stop. Not now. Not until I *fix* it.

I don't know where the thought comes from, but once it's there, it anchors me.

Fix it.

Go back. Start again. Be better.

Tears stream down my cheeks, mixing with the dirt and blood. I wipe my face with the back of my hand and smear it worse. I don't even look human anymore. A flash of movement draws my eye— between the trees. I freeze.

There.

A shadow. Huge. Masked. Watching.

My breath stutters.

No. No, that's not real. That's not him. That's the forest playing tricks on me.

I bolt. Dress ripping, feet pounding the earth. I don't care where I'm going, I just need to move. I fall once, scrape my palms. Keep going. I find a ridge and slide down the embankment on my hip, nearly tumbling into the creek at the bottom. My ankle twists hard, but I crawl to the other side and claw my way up the slope like an animal.

Fix it. Fix it. Fix it.

It comes like a mantra. A light burning bright.

If I get back to the Manor... if I get to my uncle, to the place where I *started*... to where I *began*, maybe I can undo it. Undo the threads that keep the cycle going, that fuel the beasts snatching girls off the streets. Undo the pain and chaos and madness and decay.

And when it's all undone, when there's nothing left?

I'll be free.

～

IT TAKES hours before I hit the road, the black asphalt stretching toward town. It's then that I almost stop. Give up and wait for them to find me. What was I thinking? The House of Night is too remote, too far outside Forsyth. It's almost like it's planned. Another way to keep me isolated, keep me in their cage.

I'm walking the shoulder of the main road when headlights slice through the dark. I don't even flinch when the sedan slows. It purrs to a stop beside me, hazard lights blinking orange in the trees.

The passenger window hums down.

It's a woman. Late thirties maybe. Blonde, tired, kind-looking in a hard sort of way. The kind of face that's seen shit and doesn't bother pretending otherwise.

She leans over the seat and squints. "Sweetheart... do you need help?"

The dome light makes her eyes look soft, that's why I don't run back into the forest. This is not the Beast. Not the King or a Baron or my uncle.

I nod.

"I'm trying to get home."

She unlocks the door. I slide into the seat, trembling, trying not to wince when the soft upholstery touches my legs. I'm filthy, inside and out, and now I'm getting that filth on this woman's seat. She glances at me again. Closer now. Really sees me. The bruises. The dirt. The roll of tissue wrapped around my forearm. The blood dried under my fingernails. I wait for her to ask what happened. She doesn't.

"You sure you're okay?" she says instead, gently.

I nod again. "Just... just take me to the Hexley estate. Just off Forsyth campus."

That gets a flicker from her. A glance. Not shocked. Not confused. Just something wary and knowing in the corners of her mouth. She pulls back onto the road.

The car smells like vanilla and the radio plays something soft and instrumental–a song that sounds familiar, like I've heard it before. The heater hums. I wrap my arms around myself and close my eyes for a second, letting the warmth bake into my aching skin.

"Are you a student at the college?" she asks.

"Yes." I watch the trees become thinner the closer we get to town.

I look down at the water bottle in the holder between the seats. "Take it," she says, "you must be thirsty."

I grab the bottle and unscrew the cap, gulping down the water. I remember the last time I had something to drink was when the King forced me to take the pill.

"I went to Forsyth once," she says. "A long time ago. Left after my junior year." Her fingers tighten on the steering wheel. "Things were dangerous when I was there. A killer was on the loose. They called him the Forsyth Carver. One of the girls in my dorm was a victim."

I watch her profile, take in the curve of her cheekbones.

"They caught the guy. But not until he killed his wife and himself, right in front of their little boy. Everyone thought things would be different. Safer, but it never felt that way, not really." She adds, "The worst kind of people hide in plain sight and they're the type that see a pretty girl walking barefoot after dark, and think she's an invitation."

I swallow, then whisper. "I'm not."

"No," she says quietly. "You're not."

Neither of us speak after that.

She turns onto the driveway. I wonder if she's dropped someone off here before. Or if she just knows the way. The Manor looms ahead, cold and gray. Imposing. No lights but one, burning in the library.

The car stops, but she doesn't kill the engine.

"You sure you're gonna be okay?"

I reach for the door. Nod again. "Thank you. For the ride."

But before I can slip out, she puts a hand gently on my wrist. Her fingers are cool. Dry. She doesn't squeeze, just holds me there a second longer than necessary.

"You don't owe anyone anything," she says. "Especially not the men in this town."

Then she lets me go. I shut the door behind me. The car idles for a moment longer, then backs down the drive and vanishes into the dark, leaving me staring at tail lights so long that I'm not sure the car ride even happened. If that woman even existed.

The house in front of me is real, I know that, and I enter through the back door. The one the housekeeper never locks, going in and out for smoke breaks.

She's not in the kitchen, and the house is quiet, but he's exactly where I expect him to be. Seated in his favorite chair, legs crossed at the ankle, firelight flickering across his gold signet ring. Not a king's ring. He wishes, but one he had made on his own, an H stamped into the metal.

He looks as if he hasn't moved since the wedding. Still dressed in his suit, although it's rumpled now. Like the last twenty-four hours didn't happen. His glass of whiskey is half-full. I wonder how many came before that and glance over at the bar where the bottle sits on top.

His eyes drag over me in the doorway, slow and incredulous. "Christ, girl."

I can't imagine what I look like. Maybe like a corpse that's dug her way out of a grave. I feel like that, like I've already started rotting, like the decay eating away at my flesh has set in my bones. I'm streaked in dirt and dried blood. He takes in the bruises blooming along my collarbone, the blistered welts across my thighs, the bare feet.

He doesn't ask if I'm hurt. He just says, "I told him you weren't ready. He must've figured it out himself."

I blink, trying to process his words.

"You weren't good enough for him, were you?" He lifts the glass to his lips and shakes his head. "I knew you'd fall apart the second a man got a real look at you. You couldn't even hold onto him for a full day."

I don't answer. I stare at the fire. The flames crackle loudly between us. In the corner, the grandfather clock ticks. I hate this room. I hate him.

He sets the glass down. "Well?" he asks, voice cold. "Why are you here?"

I step closer. My skin tightens with heat, too much after the cold forest air. My hands twitch at my sides. The lace on the hem of the dress tears further, unraveling like I am. I lick my lips. They taste of salt and copper.

"Where are the children?"

A pause, then he sighs. "Please don't do this."

"Where are they?" I need to know. "Are they in their rooms? Or did you send them somewhere? Where are they?"

His answer is swift. Concise. "There *are* no other children, Arianette, you know that."

The lie slips off his tongue as easily as rainwater down the drain. That same tense panic crawls up my spine. "Don't lie to me. I know they're here. Downstairs? In the attic?"

"Girl, I've told you time and time again, there are no children." His expression softens, as if he's as tired as I feel. "You are the *only* child, you were *always* the only child. The others were a figment of your creative, but fragile mind."

I sway on my feet, breath catching. Mind spinning. "That's not true," I blink fast, "we shared a room. Classes from Mrs. Whipple. I heard them crying. I comforted them."

My throat tightens as those memories shift and fade. Each child, each interaction, their smiles, their tears, their laughter... they vanish into smoke. I fold to my knees in front of the fire. The heat scalds my face. I don't care. I've never felt so cold, inside and out.

He finally turns his head and there's no mistaking his disgust. "You're not worth anything to me like this," he says, his tone flat. "The only quality you had was your pristine cunt, and now that's wasted."

I flinch, but I don't cry. I deserve it. I let Hunter carve my flesh. Damon pierce my skin. The King steal the one thing of value. I let them ruin me.

"I can still be useful," I whisper. "I'll listen. I won't run again. I'll make it right."

His jaw works. Then a sneer. "None of this would've happened if Armand had done his job."

"Armand..." I lift my head, dizzy with dread. "What did you say?"

"You never should've made it out of those woods." The fire crackles. "Not alive at least."

"You wanted me dead?" I stare at him, confused but not. "But what about the arrangement? The wedding?"

He exhales like I'm stupid, taking up his precious time. "I thought maybe over the years you'd snap out of your delusions. That you'd mature and let your mind grow along with your body. But you've always been weak. Prone to fantasies and make-believe." He rises slowly from the chair, adjusting the cuffs of his shirt. Calm. Bored. "I had no choice but to fulfill the obligation with the Barons. A deal's a deal, and in this town my reputation is all that I had–at least until I had you married off to a king. I figured that I would hand you over as planned and then tragedy would strike in the name of Armand Stein. It would be quiet. *Convenient*. And that idiot would be blamed and I'd be released from the deal."

My mind staggers. "You wanted me dead..."

"Don't take it personally." He lifts his brows. "You've always been expendable. Just like your mother. Just like these stupid girls everyone is searching for."

Something inside me rips. Slowly. Softly. Like silk splitting down the center.

"You never should have run, Arianette. And once you did, you never should have stopped." Armand's voice comes whispering back. *"It's simple really. You know too much."*

He turns his back to me and stares at the fire. It's a dismissal but it feels more like a slap in the face.

That's when I know. I understand it with a clarity that cuts through my muddled, exhausted mind. I'm going to burn everything. The Manor. Him. Myself.

The whole bloodstained history.

I rise quietly. First grabbing the small knife next to the bowl of lemons, I pick up the bottle of whiskey by the bar, still uncapped. My fingers are steady now. I'm beyond fear. Beyond hope. That left me hours ago, somewhere back in the forest, maybe on the side of the road.

The thick scent of alcohol hits me hard and I grab another bottle. Then another. I trail through the parlor, sloshing liquor over the Persian rugs, the silk-upholstered chairs, the base of the velvet drapes.

When I look back he's still facing his books, studying the spines. He doesn't look at me. Not once. Why should he? I'm trash. Used up garbage of no value to him or any other person in this godforsaken town. I light one of the long matches from the fireplace and hold it up. Watch it burn to the tip. Let it kiss the hem of the drapes.

It takes instantly.

There's a sound–*whoompf*–as the fire surges up the fabric, catches the rod, leaps to the alcohol-soaked rug like it's alive. He turns, his expression finally something other than disdain. Fear. Panic. *Terror.*

Good. Feel what we've all felt under this roof.

"What the hell do you think you're doing?"

My lips crack open in a smile. My last one and fuck, it feels glorious.

"I'm fixing it."

41

T imothy

Noir Sanctum hums like a pulse beneath the Maddox Hotel. I can feel it in my teeth when I descend the staircase–thick bass, moaning synths, muffled cries of pleasure behind velvet walls. Down here, names don't matter. Titles mean nothing. Everyone kneels the same when they're told to.

Except me.

I sit in my usual booth, the one at the back with the best view. The leather seats are worn in all the right places. The lights are low, red-gold and decadent. In this place I'm not required to wear a mask. I'm Timothy Maddox, owner of the hotel, powerful and rich. Legacy of the Barons, but spared the crown.

I tried to throw myself into work, pretending like today was any other day at the hotel. I'm an executive, busy with inventory reports, vendor delays, some bullshit about the wine cellar flooding again. I signed papers I didn't read. Spoke to workers I didn't hear. Smiled, occasionally. Nodded where I was supposed to, and did my best not to think about my wife.

The *new* one.

The one whose pussy brought me to my knees.

I grip the glass tighter, wishing it was anything other than club soda, and scour the room for distraction. *Any* distraction.

Couples writhe in half-light. A girl with a collar cries on her knees while her Dom praises her. Two men kiss like they've been starving for years. Someone thanks someone else through a choked sob. It's all beautiful, consensual, perfect.

There are two girls across from me putting on a show. They keep glancing my way, eyes full of challenge and invitation, like they're daring me to look away. I don't. I let them have me as an audience.

One of them is curled into the other's lap–lithe and smooth, body draped in soft white fabric. The other is taller, with painted fingers and red lipstick smeared from a kiss. Her hand disappears beneath the mesh fabric of the other girl's dress and the girl gasps–real, not performative. It isn't just for me.

They kiss, slow and wet, mouths open. Not sweet. Starving.

The girl in mesh moans when the other bites her bottom lip, then arches her hips against a palm I can't see. Her thighs part wider, in a show of submission, angled to give me a peek of her slick, bare cunt. Their bodies move in rhythm, grinding slowly to the beat pulsing through the Sanctum. The taller one pushes her fingers deeper under the hem and the other girl's head falls back with a breathy cry. It's beautiful. Intimate. Honest, even.

It's why I built this club–a place for people to be their true selves.

I should feel something watching them. Jealousy, maybe. Lust. Satisfaction that they come to my club, spend their money, and find pleasure. But all I feel is hollow. It's not the same tonight. And I sense the change. There's going to be a before and after.

Before the wedding.

After *her.*

I'll never be the same person I was before I took Arianette apart with my own hands and left her in the ruins. She was so small in that bed. So breakable. I'd told myself it was duty. That taking her would be necessary. Ritual. Binding. But it hadn't been. Not really.

It had been *better*.

Better than I thought it could be. Samhain clouded my judgment, luring me in with the drumbeat of celebration, with the promise of sacrifice. She was beautiful. Soft. *Innocent*. Dancing under the moonlight like a garden sprite. She'd been a vision, her skin slick with revelry, her eyes filled with desire. She hadn't fought me when it was time to claim her.

No.

The way she cried under me–it wasn't from fear. Not really. It was trust. She gave herself to me, and I took her like a starving animal. I didn't stop when she asked me to slow down. I didn't *want* to.

For a heartbeat I allowed it. Allowed this fleeting thought to float through my mind. A new beginning. A new family. Someone soft and sexy and warm to crawl into bed with at night.

But then the truth set in while she slept, warm and satiated, cradled against my side. She hadn't even seen my face. She'd married a phantom. A demon cloaked in black and gold. A monster who destroyed families. Escorted death.

Filled crypts.

And now, sitting down in a room of flesh and pleasure, all I can think about is that look in her eyes when I rejected her, clasping the collar around her throat, and pulled out the rod. The quiet betrayal. I'd done what I do best. Made her pay for getting too close–for believing that there was more to me than just obligation.

She brought out the monster. Which is ironic, considering how long I've worn the title.

"Someone looks haunted," a voice purrs. "Want some company?"

I glance up. A woman slides into the booth across from me, uninvited. Early thirties. Sheer black dress, no bra, nothing underneath. Her confidence is louder than the music. The exact opposite of the little doll I left broken on the cabin floor.

"I don't bite," she says. "Unless you ask nicely."

I don't smile or react to her unsubtle flirting, but I don't send her away either.

She plucks my glass from the table, takes a sip of the soda. "Club only? That's dangerous. Means you're really feeling it."

My fingers curl against the table. I decide to play. "What do you think I'm feeling?"

"Regret." Her gaze sharpens. "Or guilt. Same flavor, different vintage." I lift an eyebrow, which only seems to embolden her. "You're Timothy Maddox," she states, leaning forward until her breast touches my arm. "Your name is on the building."

"I am, and it is."

"What's got a man with your power sitting down here all alone instead of up there, looking over the city like a god?"

I let the silence hang before I answer. "I lost control. Allowed myself to feel things I shouldn't."

She doesn't mock me for it. She just tips her head. "You're allowed to feel, especially the good stuff. Even men like you."

I laugh once, sharp and humorless. "Nice try, sweetheart, but no, even when we experience it, we don't get to keep it."

She licks her too plump lips, altered, just like her tits. "How about you let me show you? Right here in front of everyone. Maybe that'll make it better."

Her hand stretches across my thigh, her razor-sharp fingernails grazing over the top of my pants. I let it happen, just for a second. Just long enough to imagine what it would be like to let go again. To forget. To drag someone into the dark and lose control.

And for that second, I *do* want to. I want to prove that it's just a woman I needed. Any woman with a warm, wet pussy to release into. That's all. But the second passes, and I pull my hand back like she burned me.

"No," I say. Cold. Final. Something shifts behind her eyes. Disappointment, maybe fear. I lean in, low and quiet. "You don't want what's under the surface, sweetheart. You think you do. You don't."

She sits back.

I catch my reflection in the black lacquered table... Jaw clenched. Eyes rimmed with exhaustion.

That's not Maddox. That's the *King*.

I leave the same way I came, alone, climbing the stairs out of Noir Sanctum. I feel the mask sealing back on, piece by piece. Cold and silent. The weight of the crown returning to my spine.

Time to go home.

Time to clean up my mess.

Time to deal with the girl I never should've touched.

KENDRICK'S already waiting by the curb when I emerge from the Sanctum, engine humming like a beast half-awake. He'd shown an affinity for driving, for expensive cars, and for the patience it takes waiting on a man like myself. I'd plucked him from the Shadows and given him the assignment. The black Jaguar is spotless, as always. He keeps it that way–like it proves something.

I slide into the backseat without a word. He nods, eyes on the road, and pulls away from the curb.

I stare out the window, watching the city blur. The neon halos and smeared streetlights. The tallest, of course, is the hotel, the backlit 'M' watching as we head home. We've just entered the forest when the car jerks to a sudden stop. Kendrick slams the brakes, nearly fishtailing on the curve. The seatbelt locks across my chest, snapping me into place. "What the hell?"

Two figures stand off the shoulder, half-shrouded... one of them lifts a hand. The other crouches next to a familiar shape. Eyes reflect off the headlights. Ares.

I push the door open before Kendrick even puts the car in park. "DK? Hunter?" I stop a few feet away. "What the fuck are you doing out here?"

DK straightens slowly, and I notice the compound bow on his back and how the soles of his boots are covered in mud. Ares lets out a low whine, pacing in a tight circle like he's still tracking a scent. These men are hunting, and I have a terrible feeling I know who.

Damon runs a hand through his hair, confirming my fear. "She's gone."

I step closer, voice flat. "Gone where?"

Hunter speaks this time, voice quiet. "We tracked her all the way from the forest down here to the road. Ares has lost the scent."

My pulse slows, then starts to pound. "Was she taken?" My mind spins, thinking of all the people on the grounds for the wedding and reception. I let my guard down, left her alone. "Did you find anything?"

"No," Damon says quickly. "No. It wasn't like that."

"She–" Hunter hesitates. "She snapped. Or something close to it."

I stare at them, waiting. "What do you mean, 'snapped?'"

DK shrugs once. "We went to check on her after you left. She was upset."

"I'm aware of the state of the Baroness when I left her this morning."

His teeth pull at that ring in his lip. "You said we could have her and..."

He doesn't finish.

Hunter does. "DK fucked her."

"Well you came all over her pussy," he argues.

I close my eyes for half a breath, say nothing, and let the silence stretch until they squirm. The weight of this presses behind my ribs like a knife laid flat. I don't ask what they did to her, not specifically. I don't need to. I know both of their inclinations. What they didn't know is that I'd already shattered her–mind and body–and removing their restrictions so soon after was on me.

"And then?"

"We left her to rest," Hunter says, "and to dig into the assignment you left us. We figured she'd sleep, shower, get herself together, but when we went back to get her the place was a fucking mess."

"She wrote all over the goddamn walls. Psycho shit." DK's hand rakes into his hair. "We started searching right away figuring she couldn't have gotten far, but like we said, once we got to the road her trail vanished."

"Because she got in someone's car," I say, casting a look down the deserted road.

My Barons glance at one another, both aware of the danger of any young woman in Forsyth being out alone right now, much less one that had already escaped a killer.

But I don't think that's who Arianette ran into tonight. I think she had a purpose. She told me she had one when she was begging me not to discard her. I turn back toward the car, already barking over my shoulder. "Get in. All of you. Even the damn dog."

I slide in last and slam the door shut, then punch the directions into the GPS.

"She's not just running," I say, holding on as Kendrick makes a tight turn to go back toward town. "She's going back to where it all started."

The car surges forward, tires shrieking against asphalt as we tear through the trees. The lights of the city glare as he cuts through Forsyth. The hookers on the Avenue, Scratch-heads pacing on the corners, desperate for their next hit. The DKS clocktower hovers over us, a reminder that they're watching. A reminder that my son is so close, but also so far away.

I'm not ready to lose anyone else. Not yet.

Not today.

Kendrick turns onto University Drive, and I can see the glow before we get to the gates.

"Holy shit," DK mutters. The Manor is on fire.

"Jesus Christ," Hunter echoes. Ares pants loudly, whining at the shift of energy in the car. We're all frozen, watching as the flames lick up the columns, smoke billowing out of shattered, hollow windows. There's no sign of life, inside or out.

"Stop the car," I command, this time bracing myself as Kendrick slams on the brakes. The car skids to a stop and I snap, "Call 911."

Kendrick nods and exits the car, walking toward the perimeter as he speaks into the phone. I turn on the others. "Hunter, find her."

Hunter bends before Ares, and reaches into his coat. He pulls out fabric–small and lace. Arianette's panties. I'd ripped them off myself. He holds them to the dog's nose and commands, *"Such!"*

The dog inhales quickly and instantly turns, starting toward the backside of the house. Hunter follows and a moment later, they're gone.

"What do you want me to do?"

I turn and face DK, who stands before me, rigid, like a soldier. His bow is gripped tight in his hand. "Bring her back to me. *Now*."

If he senses my desperation he doesn't show it, just nods once and takes off in the opposite direction, bow still in hand. I stand in front of the burning Hexley estate, fists curled at my sides.

I don't want to lose her.

I *can't*.

"She wrote all over the goddamn walls. Psycho shit," DK had said. Once again proving that if you come into my home, become my family, the madness comes creeping in.

Is it them? Or me?

Cause or catalyst?

There's no doubt in my mind that this fire was deliberate. She had a purpose and that was to never come back here again. Now there's nothing left, but Arianette doesn't get to decide the ending.

I do.

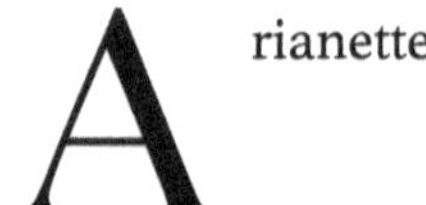

Arianette

RED.

Everything around me is red.

Smoke twists through the beams. Flames crawl up the curtains and swallow the old wood shelves, devouring history, memory, blood. *Everything* burns.

I'd spent years in this house, locked in the walls, talking to the other children. Did they really not exist? Were they all a figment? Was it real?

Is this?

The heat tells me this is happening. That I set my uncle's home on fire.

Except, he's still here, standing in the doorway–his tie loose, sweat slicking his temples. "You crazy motherfucking bitch! What are you doing?" he screams, voice rising over the roar of the fire.

"Ending it all." My hands shake, but not from fear. From fury. My fingernails are torn, knuckles bloodied. The knife from the bar still clutched in my fingers.

"I kept you alive when no one else wanted you," he coughs. "I gave you a bed, a roof over your head, meals, your stupid, pointless, dance lessons... *everything*."

"You gave me nothing!" I stalk toward him, barefoot on the warm wood, dress hanging in ribbons around my ankles. "You put a curse on me. One where I live in one circle of hell after the other. It's over. All of it."

The air tastes like the end of times and when I get close enough, he reaches for me. I swipe out, slicing the blade down his hand. He jerks back with a yelp. "You're insane. Just like your mother. Just like every other woman in this family."

"No," I whisper, my voice hollow, echoing in the way madness does. "*You* made me what I am."

He lunges. I twist, stumble, and slam into the grandfather clock, sending it to the floor with a crash. He grabs my wrist, but I bite him–*hard*–until he lets go. The blade sinks in again, this time across his chest. A scream–his, not mine–cuts through the firestorm. He falls against the burning shelves, face twisted in disbelief.

"You don't get to walk away from this," I tell him. "Not for what you did to me, or them."

Not for the children he claims don't exist. Or the arrangement to have me sold off to a monster. Not after what he did to my body. My mind. My soul.

He tries to crawl toward me. The fire eats the carpet between us. I back away, dragging myself toward the doorway, breath coming in ragged sobs. The walls are closing in on both of us, and all I want is to be alone. I want peace. A quiet mind.

I'm low on the ground, crawling away from the library when I see him.

At first, I think I'm hallucinating–smoke and memory blurring together. But then he sniffs, whines, nose to the ground. He finds me. His wet nose touches my cheek. A lick, followed by a warm sound, a real one, rumbles in his throat. He nuzzles closer.

I press my face into his fur. "Ares," I whisper. My voice is barely there. "Go. *Los.*"

He whines again. Impatient. Angry. Then he's gone, paws skidding on ash-slick floors.

My eyes flutter shut. Alone. Finally.

I lay there, wondering if any of this is real. If I'm back in the Hunt, or maybe by the river. I see something. Someone. Dark long hair, bright eyes, high voice. *"Run! Tell them I'm here!"*

Hands grab at me. Hard and strong. I fight against them, kicking and lashing out. But this time, I don't run. I can't.

Blinking up, I see the mask, feel the heat, sense the fury.

Damon.

"Stop," I beg. "Just leave. Leave me."

But he doesn't. He picks me up like I weigh nothing. I feel everything. The pain, the shame, the fucking loss of it all.

"Sorry, doll baby," he growls against my temple, his voice choked. "Death isn't coming for you today."

And just like that, he carries me out of my funeral pyre.

Alive.

But not the same.

I REMEMBER THIS BED.

The exact slope of it under my spine. The itchy, paper-thin blanket that does nothing to fight off the sterile chill of the room. The crooked hook of the IV stand looming beside me like some metal skeleton, clear fluid dripping in a steady beat. I know the lights flickering overhead–too bright, glaring twenty-four seven, washing the color out of the world.

The smell hits next. Antiseptic laced with vinegar. Bleach and blood. Disinfectant and dread. I know this. My body remembers before my mind does, like everything about this place is trying to convince me that I've gone back to the day after the river.

Everything from the too-sweet voice of a nurse telling me it was a miracle I was found at all. I can almost hear it. The low beep of monitors. The whisper of technicians behind the curtain. The sting in my skin, the ache in my lungs. The boys had found me by the riverbed and pushed on my chest until they came alive again. My lungs were full of silt, wrists raw, my neck bleeding from the dug out tracker. Back then I'd slipped under so far I didn't know what was real anymore.

It's the pain that anchors me to the present.

Fresh. Real. *Now.*

A shock tears through my throat as I try to breathe in too fast, like dragging sandpaper down the inside of my windpipe. It burns, raw and scraped from smoke and screaming. My ribs ache with every shallow breath and the edges of my skin feel tight and swollen, like I've been scorched from the inside out.

This isn't the river.

This time, I lit the match myself.

There's a sound beside me. Rhythmic. Steady. Mechanical. Someone breathing, but not naturally. A soft hiss and release. I turn my head, the movement slow and heavy like swimming through glue.

Damon.

He's right there, in the bed next to mine. Slumped in half-conscious sleep, his face slack and pale. His piercings are gone, like they had been at the fight, and for some reason it makes him look younger. The oxygen tubes plug up his nose, tape pulls at his cheeks, and his lips are cracked like desert earth. The muscles in his jaw twitch. If it weren't for the soft beep of the heart monitor behind him, I'd think he was gone. That I'd taken him with me when the fire came.

That I killed him, too.

A sick pulse of guilt curls through my stomach.

Movement on the other side of the glass draws my attention, and I see a man pacing. Tall and with a dark coat over his broad shoulders. The sharp lines cutting across his silhouette like armor. A Shadow? No. No. Not one of the King's men. This man's expression is unreadable–cold, remote. *I know him.* Even from here, I know that set of his jaw. That stiff, calculated posture.

Agent Knight.

He's from before. From the last time. After the river. The man who asked questions I didn't want to answer. Didn't know *how* to answer. The one who came with a notepad and quiet suspicion. A shiny belt buckle that looks like the devil. He was calm then, and calm now. Like all of this is normal for him. But it's the words I hear next that pull me tighter into the present.

"No," snaps Hunter, stepping into view. "Absolutely not."

He looks wrecked. His pale skin is streaked with soot, ash clinging to the edges of his jaw and threading into his tattoos. He's still wearing the same white T-shirt from this morning, from when he...

I swallow, remembering the look in his pale eyes as he watched. Participated.

The shirt is now torn and singed in places, revealing a burn on his forearm. He's furious, but he's holding it in like a grenade with the pin halfway pulled.

"She doesn't answer to you," he growls.

Agent Knight doesn't so much as blink, but his voice raises just enough for me to hear. "Mr. Sorrin, she's a key witness–"

"She's nothing to you, Agent," Hunter spits. "She's mine. She's the King's. And no one speaks to her until he gives his approval."

That word–*mine*–hits like a cuff. Hunter's voice is pure authority, razor-edged and absolute. Like he's daring anyone to question it. But I do. I question it. Am I still theirs? After everything I've done?

Agent Knight's mouth tightens, but his tone stays flat. "A man is dead. His house burned to the ground. And the same woman is tied between that and a half-dozen other mysteries in this town." His gaze cuts toward me through the glass, and I sink back into the pillow hoping to get swallowed up. "This makes twice that I've found her in that hospital bed. I don't believe in coincidences," he says. "Not in this city."

Quietly thinking, Hunter squares his shoulders before stepping toward Knight. "I don't give a shit what you believe in or not. She's not the key to anything. She's a victim. So why don't you go figure out who wanted that house burned down with Owen Hexley in it. Figure out who would target the Baroness *twice*. Once you do, I'll be happy to listen, until then, you need to leave."

There's a beat of silence so thick it's almost physical. Then I hear a muttered curse followed by a door slamming somewhere down the hall. Knight is gone. Which means now we're alone.

Hunter throws the door open and storms inside, his rage vibrating off him in waves. I smell the smoke on him, the sweat. His hair is a mess, like he's been tearing his hands through it for hours. His eyes flick to Damon–still unconscious–then land back on me.

"Ares," I croak. My voice is wrecked. "Did he–?"

"He found you," Hunter says, tight and bitter. "Led us right into the house. Just like you hoped, right?"

"No," I say, forcing the word past the shards in my throat. "I told him to go. *Los.*"

That word–his word. The command that means leave.

"He did his job," he says softly, "making sure that you were safe, making sure that *we got to you.*"

"Is he okay?" I know the answer before I ask it, but I ask anyway, because I need to know for sure.

"No, he's not fucking okay. He's at the emergency animal hospital." His voice cracks. "He spent too much time in the house looking for you and inhaled a lot of smoke. They don't know if he'll make it."

My heart shatters. "I didn't mean–"

"Don't." It hits harder than a slap. His voice, low and lethal. "Your reckless, foolish, childish actions almost killed my dog." His eyes dart to the other bed. "Damon. And yourself."

The silence that follows is vibrating. Fragile and sharp. I can't breathe without tasting smoke. It clings to my nostrils and throat. Damon shifts slightly in the bed, but doesn't wake. Still tethered to this world by wires and tape and a too-steady rhythm of machines keeping him alive.

I look between them. These two men who destroyed me. Who saved me. Who handed me the match and waited for me to strike it.

"If you hate me so much, why didn't you let me die?" My voice is thinner than the sheets. "I wanted to end it. Once and for all."

Hunter steps closer. The lights gleam against his eyes–eyes gone pitch black with fury and something worse beneath it. Possession. Grief. Madness.

"Because you don't get to decide whether you live or die," he says leaning over me. "You belong to me. And to DK. You belong to the King. And none of us are finished with you yet."

It's not a comfort. It's not a rescue. It's a verdict. A sentence. The promise of consequences that haven't even begun to unfold yet. I roll over slowly, pulling the thin blanket up like it can shield me from their world. From myself.

I didn't escape hell.

I just entered a new circle.

I FEEL it before I open my eyes, the weight of another presence, the wrongness in the air. Maybe it's the silence; the machines aren't beeping anymore.

I stir. Slow, groggy, drugged. My skin is clammy with sweat. The light is low, but it doesn't matter. I know who it is even before I see him.

I blink once. Twice. He slowly comes into view, his wide shoulders blocking the light as he stands over the bed. He's not touching me–not really–but his hands hover just above my throat, fingers curled.

He's removed the oxygen tubes from his nose, the tape hanging limp against his cheek. His gown is open at the chest, wires dangling from where he's torn them free. The scar on his throat glares down at me like a gaping, second mouth. He doesn't seem like he's in pain.

All I sense is rage.

"You almost killed me," he says, voice low and precise. Each word pronounced clean and even, like he wants to make sure I hear him. "And I'm still trying to figure out if I should return the favor."

His hands dip lower, thumbs brushing over my clavicle. A tremor ripples through my limbs, but I stay still. I know better than to flinch. Fear will just encourage him. One wrong move and he won't just hover–he'll strike. The man standing over me isn't the one who feeds stray kittens or let me tape his hands at the Fury. He's the man the King chose to be a Baron. The one who raped me against the bathroom counter. Someone with the ruthlessness to be a Royal.

To keep me in line.

"I should kill you, sister. Right here. Right now. No more second chances. No more cleaning up your messes. You're a fucking liability. A danger. Not just to yourself." His mouth twists into a cruel smirk. "Even the damn dog isn't safe around you."

I try to speak, but all that comes out is a croak.

He leans in, face close enough that I can smell the smoke still clinging to him. "You think I forgot? That I don't remember finding you in the forest and seeing you with a knife in your hand, blood-spray splattered across your face? The sight of Armand dying at your feet?" His eyes burn into mine. "That was the first sign of who you really are. I should have known then."

"I was trying to stop him," I whisper.

"No. You were out of control." His jaw clenches. "Dangerous. A fucking lunatic."

"I'm not crazy."

The word hangs between us, like the punchline of a joke.

"You pushed me," I grind out, my own anger flickering under the strain of fear and exhaustion. I think about the King, *my husband,* forcing me to my knees and brandishing the rod, and worse, the rejection that followed. "I was hurt and you made it worse."

His face stills. Then, slowly, he smiles. "Don't you fucking dare pretend like you didn't want it." A flush of shame scorches my face. I turn away, but he grabs my chin, forcing me to look at him. "You don't get to play innocent now, not with the way your pussy clenched around me, milking me for every last drop. Or how you looked at Hunter, begging him to cover you with his cum. You want it,

Arianette, because deep down you're like every other woman in this town, a filthy little slut."

"I told you to stop." It comes out hard.

"You don't have the right to tell me to stop!" He winces, breath catching from the injury to his lungs. The pain doesn't stop him from continuing. "I own you. I have a right to you, *Baroness*. And I will continue to use you any fucking way I want." He loosens his grip on my face, sliding his hand back down to my throat. "You put my life in danger. You put *everyone* in danger. I didn't claw my way out of a prison cell, didn't survive death, and take the oath to the King to be snuffed out by some broken little girl determined to bring chaos into our lives."

"I just wanted to stop my uncle! You don't know what he's capable of!" I reach for his hand. "I didn't know–"

"You *never* know," he snaps. "Because you don't think. You *feel*. You act. You destroy."

I flinch, finally, and he sees it. Enjoys it. Enjoys hurting me, the same way he thinks I hurt him. His grip softens, but only so he can draw it out.

"I carried you out of that inferno," he says, voice low and mean. "Because I'm not done with you yet. You think today was bad? You think waking up here, wrapped in bandages and consequences, is punishment?" He leans closer, lips brushing my ear. "It's going to be worse. So much worse. And I'm going to enjoy every last fucking second of it."

He releases me.

The room is still. His shadow flickers in the dim light, stretching long and monstrous across the wall. He doesn't leave. He can't. We're both trapped with one another until someone tells us we can leave.

We both may have survived death for the second time, but I don't know if we're going to survive one another.

EPILOGUE

T imothy

I FIND THEM OUTSIDE, behind the former rectory. Ares' nose is to the ground, tracking something as he heads to the trees–tail high, eyes alert. The dog came home from the vet yesterday, and I don't think Hunter's let him out of his sight since.

"Dog's looking good," I say as I approach. "What's the prognosis?"

"The vet said to have him take it easy for a while. No long runs." Hunter doesn't look convinced. His arms are crossed, his jaw tight. DK looks up first, still pale, still moving slower than a man should at his age. But he's alive and he'll heal.

"How're you holding up?" I ask him directly. "Dr. Stallworth is convinced you'll have a full recovery."

DK shrugs, then winces like the motion pulled at something deep inside. "I'm alright. Lungs are still pissed at me for going head first into that fire. But I'm okay."

In another situation they'd be replaced. Three new Barons

selected for the rest of the year, but the events of the past few days will make them stronger and even more loyal. I chose them for a reason, and now I know my instincts were right.

"Take a walk with me."

They follow without question. We walk past the dormitory, where lights glow in the windows, a sign the Shadows are at home, safe and secure.

My family is all back in one place.

"Did I ever tell you why I chose you two to wear the mask?" I ask, my hands folded behind my back, eyes fixed on the path ahead.

Neither answers. They're quiet. Listening.

"I picked you," I say slowly, "because you've both been touched by death. Real death. Not the loss of someone close, or a distant relative, but the kind where you're grazed by its fingertips and left scorched. The kind that leaves something inside you blackened."

I turn slightly. DK meets my gaze, uncertain.

"You," I nod toward him, eyes on that wicked, beautiful scar. "You held death's eyes while that other boy sliced you in two. You know what it's like to come back different."

"Yeah," he says, eyes cast to the ground, "I do."

Hunter's eyes flick to me, quick and sharp. I ask, "Death doesn't always leave scars, does it?"

He shakes his head. "No, sir."

A crease appears on DK's forehead, a tell that he's unaware of Hunter's history. It's too precious. Too raw. Humiliating. It's his story to tell. Not mine.

"When death comes for you and lets you escape, there's a reason. You've been given a third," my eyes flick to Hunter, "if not *fourth*, chance." They don't speak, but something shifts in the air between us. "People think that we're obsessed with death, but that is only part of the story. The Barons are obsessed with *life*. We understand the fragility–the gift of having a heartbeat, a pulse throbbing through our veins. You two more than anyone else."

We stop at a statue in the garden. A shrouded king cast in bronze. A crown sits on his head, a skull cradled in his hands. A pentagram hangs around his neck and at the bottom are the words *Memento Mori.*

"I want to thank you for the efforts you made to save the Baroness," I tell them both. "No matter her flaws, she is precious to this house, not only because she is my wife, but because she too, has been blessed by death, and we must respect that."

Tension shifts between the men. Ares looks between them anxiously. They don't have to speak to let me know how angry they are with her. That anger will fuel them to become better, stronger men, and it'll be their choice on how they'll process her betrayal and dole out the consequences for her actions.

I take a deep breath, prepared to take the next step.

"You've shown nothing but loyalty and respect to the BRN, the House of Night, and to me, and in response, I want to show you the same consideration."

I reach behind my head and loosen the ties that hold up my mask. Hunter and DK glance at one another, aware of the magnitude of the situation. "You risked your lives for me and my kingdom. At the very least I can show you the man behind the mask."

Slowly, I remove the mask, giving them a moment to process what—no, who—is in front of them. Silence crashes down until DK, staring with his eyes wide, says, "You're—"

"Not Clive Kayes," Hunter finishes quietly.

I shake my head. "No. Clive is dead. He's been dead for over two decades," I add. "Let the dark cradle his secrets."

DK's voice cracks on the truth as he tries again. "You're... Timothy Maddox."

The name hangs there, shuddering through the dark like a curse.

And it feels like peeling off more than a mask. Like laying myself bare. Like every secret I've buried just clawed its way to the surface. These men proved I can trust them and I want to give the same back to them.

"Yes. I'm Timothy Maddox."

Rich. Powerful. Feared. Hated.

"King of the Barons."

"HOW MUCH LONGER?"

"Five seconds." Graves checks the stopwatch and waits for a moment. The seconds pass by painfully, each one stabbing like pinpricks. "Time."

Exhaling, I rise out of the frigid water, the brisk morning air slapping against my wet skin. It's cold as fuck, but I feel invigorated. Alive.

I step out of the tub, taking the towel Graves has extended toward me, and I quickly dry off.

After days out of my routine, now that the wedding is over and everyone is back home, it's time to get back into the steady rhythm of life.

"Would you like your breakfast up here or elsewhere?" he asks, standing in the doorway that leads from the porch back to my room. "The men have already had their meal in the dining room."

"Very well," I say, glad to know they're also moving forward. "Here is fine."

I slip into my clothes, slow and methodical. Starched white shirt, black slacks. The cufflinks with the Greek insignia for BRN in gold. Graves hands me my mask, black, functional for the day, and the smoothie–greens, protein, raw egg. My supplements wait on the tray: zinc, magnesium, and activated charcoal. Discipline in all things. Routine is a comfort.

As he pours tea, I move to the small dining table by the window. The light is dull and gray through the frost-glass, just the way I like it. I sit and notice the report on the edge of the table.

"This just arrive?"

"Dr. Shepard had it sent over right away."

Curious, I pick it up and skim the details of the coroner's report. Male, age fifty. Theres's documentation of a laceration on the palm of his hand, and bruising on his back, most likely from a beam falling on him, trapping him under the weight. Cause of death: asphyxiation.

Attached to the report is a second one from the fire chief.

"Anything interesting?" Graves asks, opening the door to the armoire. His business does nothing to hide the edge of concern in his voice.

A quick look at the typed, official, sheet takes a way that worry and I read aloud. "There was no evidence of tampering or accelerant in the home. But there was some kind of fraying in the wiring."

"Old houses tend to have that problem."

"They do," I agree. "So from this report, it seems like a malfunction in the electrical system." I take a sip of tea, allowing the warmth to spread through my chest. "Remind me to send the Chief a complimentary stay at the hotel–all-inclusive."

Graves nods. "I'll add it to your planner."

Setting the report aside, I place the cloth napkin in my lap and focus on the meal Graves has placed in front of me. Scrambled egg whites, chicken sausage, avocado. Lifting my fork, I announce: "Today is Day One. You will not speak unless spoken to. You will not ask questions. You will be bathed, fed, and trained. But privileges must be earned."

A soft clink.

"In the past, I would have sent you away," I say calmly, "made you someone else's problem. But I've learned the hard way that method isn't effective, at least not in the long run. I can't rely on others to take care of what's important to me, and I accept that I'll need to take a more direct involvement in your welfare and training."

Only then do I glance across the room. The cage is tucked inside the massive wardrobe, metal bars custom-forged in the shape of thorns. She stands with her hands clenched around the bars, a thin cotton dress covering her curves. The new collar–black leather, gold pentagram gleaming at her throat like a brand. *My brand.*

Her eyes are wide. No tears. Not now. Just that trembling, suspended edge of fear and fury. Something darker she's still too proud to name.

I fold my napkin and place it neatly on the table.

"Your disobedience was a kind of madness, and madness is something I can not, and will not, abide. Not in this house. Not by my wife." I rise and continue. "But I will fix you, wicked one. We start with silence. Then stillness. Then surrender."

I walk over slowly, crouching before the cage.

"You were given to me, Arianette. I made an oath." I smile, warm, practiced, patient. All the things I wasn't with my first wife and my son. I lost them both and I will not fail again. "'*To own and to protect. To command and to punish. To keep until death claims you both.*' That was my oath, Arianette, and I want you to understand," I slide my hand through the grate and hook my finger through the loop in the collar. "I never go back on my word."

ACKNOWLEDGMENTS

Dear Monarchs & Friends,

Thank you for reading Barons of Decay. I hoped it lived up to your expectations and if not, I hope you enjoyed it anyway.

2025 was hard, many of you probably understand why. Mr. Lawson passed away in May after a long, and challenging fight with the worst disease, cancer. It sucked y'all, and as I'm writing this, I am tired. But please know that writing this book, engaging with readers, thinking about upcoming book signings and talking to my author friends helped me through each and every day.

We all deal with stress and grief differently. I'm best when I'm in my quiet little office, ice coffee next to me, with head down, typing away in my book and working. For some this seems ridiculous, but I have a feeling this is probably how I've always handled stress in my life—slipping into my imagination (or, lets be real, an episode of Dateline.) Just know that I'm grateful to everyone that comments, posts, shares and engages to keep my energy flowing.

I want to add a special thanks to a few people that have been by my side over the past few months. Lisa for taking a first look at BOD when I was still unsure about my path, Megan for talking me through a few difficult spots. Vicki and Cat for edits and proofing. My PA's Anna and Chelsey held everything together while I was either writing or handling family, health emergencies. I appreciate them so much!

I want to drop in a super special thank you to my sensitivity readers, Lo and Crystal, who helped me reframe many spots in the book. As I said in the forward, it was important to me that Arianette's character be written with authenticity, depth, and respect. Their feedback helped make her the strongest, most fully realized version of herself, while also staying true to the dark romance vision and the emerging Queen we know she'll become. I also want to thank the readers from the ROFU ARC team who graciously gave their time to do one more early read with an eye on sensitivity issues. Each of your insights were invaluable.

Finally, there is no Royals of Forsyth U without Samantha Rue, and for that collaboration, I am eternally grateful.

Angel

You can find Samantha Rue's work at samrue.com

To join an amazing community of readers, please join us at the Monarchs Facebook group.